READER'S DIGEST

CONDENSED BOOKS

FIRST EDITION

THE READER'S DIGEST ASSOCIATION LIMITED
25 Berkeley Square, London W1X 6AB

THE READER'S DIGEST ASSOCIATION SOUTH AFRICA (PTY) LTD
Nedbank Centre, Strand Street, Cape Town

Printed in Great Britain by Petty & Sons Ltd., Leeds

Original cover design by Jeffery Matthews M.S.I.A.

For information as to ownership
of copyright in the material in this book see last page

ISBN 0 340 22706 0

READER'S DIGEST
CONDENSED BOOKS

THE WHITE LIONS OF TIMBAVATI
Chris McBride

MERLIN'S KEEP
Madeleine Brent

THE HOUSE OF CHRISTINA
Ben Haas

THE MELODEON
Glendon Swarthout

COLLECTOR'S LIBRARY
EDITION

In this volume

THE WHITE LIONS OF TIMBAVATI
by Chris McBride (p. 9)

In South Africa's Timbavati Nature Reserve, an oasis in a world of disappearing and endangered species, what appears to be a new strain of lions has emerged. Chris McBride's first reports of white lion cubs immediately caused a zoological sensation; the full story of his discovery and its fascinating aftermath is now an international literary success.

MERLIN'S KEEP
by Madeleine Brent (p. 87)

The author of *Moonraker's Bride* has excelled herself. In *Merlin's Keep*, her formidable talents for weaving a tale that is both tantalizing and thrilling are more brilliantly combined than ever. It tells how young Jani, living happily with her guardian in the Himalayas, is forced to question her mysterious past when a local oracle prophesies a more mysterious—and adventurous—future.

THE HOUSE OF CHRISTINA
by Ben Haas (p. 263)

1936: Hitler threatens Austria, yet life at General Helmer's manor house in the Vienna Woods is determinedly normal. Christa, the widowed general's daughter, is an enchanting hostess. Three men fall in love with her, and in their bitterly opposed political beliefs lie the inevitable seeds of national and personal tragedy.

Ben Haas took twelve years to write *The House of Christina*. With its noble theme of love and war, the result is a powerful and timeless epic.

THE MELODEON
by Glendon Swarthout (p. 447)

This is a novel of extraordinary courage and remembrance. It is set during a particularly cold and bitter Christmas Eve, a night when, for a small boy, the midwinter birth of a lamb is perhaps the less strange of two apparently miraculous events. The other concerns his family's melodeon, a much cherished heirloom through which past, present and future suddenly seem to meet.

In this haunting story, Glendon Swarthout has merged action and poetic vision into an unforgettable tale of compelling beauty.

The White Lions of Timbavati

a condensation of the book by
Chris McBride

Published by Paddington Press

At a time when we hear so much about disappearing species of wildlife, it is heartwarming to read of a phenomenon that could mark the beginning of an entirely new strain.

Chris McBride had taken his wife and young daughter to live in the Transvaal's Timbavati Nature Reserve so that he could study the local lion population. At the time he could not guess that he would stumble upon a discovery that has recently caught the imagination of the whole animal-loving world, the discovery of the white lions of Timbavati.

Here is his own account of how he first came upon Temba and Tombi and later Phuma, each as white as a polar bear, and of how he has managed to keep track of them throughout the early and some of the most dangerous months of their development. His love and concern for them and their environment is mirrored on every page, not only in the text but also in the remarkable photographs. *The White Lions of Timbavati* is a unique record of a unique event.

CHAPTER ONE

One May morning in 1975 I was driving a battered old jeep through the North-eastern Transvaal. A low orange sun was burning through a stately wild fig tree as I pulled into a clearing down by the bed of the Machaton River. I didn't know exactly what I was looking for, but I had a feeling. With lions it's more often a feeling than anything else. And this day I felt I was in for something special.

I watched for a while and suddenly I spotted a lion coming out of the bush about twenty yards away, a superb male unconsciously enjoying his virility. I recognized him immediately as the one our family calls Agamemnon.

A few minutes later a lioness appeared. I don't like imputing human characteristics to animals, but I swear there was something coquettish in her lithe, supple movements. I recognized her too—the lioness we have named Tabby, a bit paler than the others. She stalked tautly up to Agamemnon and lifted a paw to his massive head. He stood his ground. Next she withdrew a few paces, then walked briskly past his nose, rubbing herself against his mane and leaving not the slightest doubt of her intentions.

Agamemnon got the message. He wrinkled his scarred muzzle at her, not in a snarl but in a grimace of acknowledgment.

You could say it was the beginning of a flirtation. What I didn't realize then was that its outcome would be something unique.

THE AREA WHERE this scene occurred takes its name from a river which flows through its southern part. Flows is not quite the right word because for most of the year the Timbavati, like the Machaton, is a wide expanse of soft sand. Paradoxically, though, Timbavati means "the river that never dries out"—and this is true to the extent that you can always find a few pools here and there along its length.

The Timbavati Nature Reserve was formed in 1955 when twenty-eight land-owners agreed to combine their holdings in order to preserve and foster the area's wildlife. Since there are no longer any internal fences, the animals are free to wander through two hundred and eight square miles of virgin bush which the owners once used as hunting grounds and country retreats.

Timbavati's only year-round residents are the game warden and his family, the staffs of two commercial game-viewing lodges, a few officials of the South African Department of Nature Conservation and about three hundred aborigines—Shangaans—scattered in small encampments throughout the reserve.

At the last count, the population also included 13,000 impala, 2,800 wildebeest, 1,400 zebra, 1,050 giraffe, 500 kudu, 450 buffalo, 70 elephant, 300 waterbuck, lots of warthog and duiker, vervet monkeys and baboons, and the predators—about 150 lions, 200 hyenas, 100 leopards, 80 or more cheetahs, as well as polecats, jackals, mongooses, honey badgers, eagles, vultures. And that's only the beginning of the catalogue.

This is the Lowveld, the lower of South Africa's two vast plateaux. To the newcomer, it looks flat and featureless. The trees seem stunted. Some have simply died of old age and stand there, gaunt and bleached by the scorching sun. Others have been pushed over or uprooted by elephants, who eat the leaves and roots as well as the bark.

10

With all these shattered trees, and the whitened skeletons left over from the predators' kills, there are those who say that the place looks like a World War I battlefield. But people who have learned to appreciate its vast, brooding silence return to it again and again; they are never very happy too far away from it.

Beauty is a difficult word to use because it means so many things to so many people, but to me the Lowveld—and specifically Timbavati—is unquestionably one of the most serenely beautiful places in the world.

THIRTY YEARS AGO my father and his brother bought nearly ten thousand acres along the Machaton, when the land was worth less than three dollars an acre. I was about five at the time and, having been born in the city of Johannesburg, I was intrigued by the bush. I have remained so ever since. My older sister Lan, my younger brother Ian and I spent long periods of our youth at Timbavati, where we made friends with the local African children and went out with airguns, shooting hare, francolin (a small bird rather like a pheasant) and other game. Curiously enough, many people like myself who have later become deeply involved in ecology and wild-life management first felt the lure of the bush while out hunting.

Since an early age, I have wanted to earn my living in the wild, but I didn't want to become a game warden because that involved too many chores like mending fences and not enough close contact with wild animals. In those days there were no courses in wildlife management or ecology at any of the local universities, so giving up the idea for the time, I went to Witwatersrand University in Johannesburg, where I studied English literature and the Zulu language. I continued to spend as much time as possible at Tim-bavati, walking in the bush with my father and Jack Mathebula, an expert tracker.

When I left university, I taught for a while in an African school, primarily to earn money for a trip I'd planned to the wildest part of Africa I could find. As soon as I had saved up enough, I set off for the Okavango Swamps in northern Botswana. There I found an African guide called Masaki, and for nearly eight months I lived

11

The beginning of the flirtation between Agamemnon and Tabby.... What I didn't realize at the time was that its outcome would be something unique.

with him and his family. In all that time I never saw another white man nor spoke a word of English. Masaki and I travelled in his *mokorro*, a dug-out canoe still widely used in Africa. The *mokorro* is hacked out of a single log in a way that hasn't changed significantly since the Stone Age.

The country was teeming with wildlife. Apart from a gun and a camera, all I took with me was a sack of cornmeal—or "mealie meal", as it's called locally. The Africans knew exactly which plants we could eat: the hearts of palm trees, various nuts, and roots like water lily roots. It was surprisingly good, sustaining food. We used to walk or canoe from daybreak until about eleven, then rest in the worst of the heat. In the early afternoon we'd catch a fish or two or shoot something for a meal, and leave again about three.

There were lions in the area but I didn't see much of them. The bush people have a habit of avoiding anything dangerous. They knew where the lions were, and the lions knew where they were, and by common consent they avoided each other scrupulously.

In Botswana I did a bit of tracking, and when I went back to Timbavati I began tracking lions as a hobby. With Jack Mathebula to help me, I seldom lost the spoor. The bushmen of Botswana are said to be the world's best trackers, but Jack is superior—perhaps because in his youth he was a highly successful poacher.

Eventually, I ran out of money and had to go back to work. I got an appointment at the same African school and remained there for the next five years. Meanwhile I met Charlotte. She was working in television, modelling and doing voice-overs and graphic design. We were married in her parents' house in Salisbury, Rhodesia and spent our honeymoon up the Zambesi, sleeping on the ground with elephants all round us.

Charlotte is probably the best partner in the world for me—or the worst, according to the way you look at it. She shares my passion for the bush and for living rough. Neither of us cares very much about the things that other people regard as essential—security, a comfortable home, even electricity. We both prefer candlelight.

Charlotte's parents, the Masons, were English. Her father had worked with the British Colonial Service in India, in Malaya and in

14

the Luangwa Valley, in what used to be Northern Rhodesia. He was every bit as interested in the wild as was my father, and he brought Charlotte up with a healthy respect for animals. If you are careful, he used to tell her, there is no need to be afraid. Nevertheless, as careful as she was, she had some terrifying experiences.

On one occasion her father took the whole family—Charlotte, who was then about six, her mother and her younger sister, Chloe— into the bush for a picnic. While he went off to hunt buffalo, Mrs. Mason started to spread out their lunch on the grass near an anthill. Anthills in this part of Africa are quite spectacular. Built out of the red earth of the area, they are often as high as ten feet, and have bases as thick as old oak trees. They are frequently used for shelter by wildlife a good deal bigger than ants.

The Mason's family dog, a huge Labrador, kept sniffing around the anthill. Eventually he plucked up enough courage to go into a hole in the base and investigate. A second later he came flying out again, followed by a large male lion which had been resting inside. At the unexpected sight of the humans, the lion ran off—in the direction of the buffaloes that Charlotte's father was hunting. Disturbed by the sudden appearance of a lion, the herd stampeded —straight for the picnic spot.

Used to this kind of emergency, Mrs. Mason quickly put the two girls up a tree and climbed into another herself. A few seconds later the herd came thundering through. The Mason ladies barely missed being trampled to death.

Another time Charlotte and her father were tracking a leopard that had been mauling cattle in the area. They were wading through some tall grass when they turned round and saw a couple of fully grown male lions following them. By rights, the lions should have run away as soon as they became aware of humans in the vicinity, but these didn't. They just sat down and watched.

"We'd better sit down too—very quietly—and wait," Mr. Mason whispered. It must have taken a bit of doing, to sit there silently in the long grass with two lions only a few hundred yards away, but that's exactly what Charlotte and her father did. After a while, the lions got up and wandered off into the bush.

Charlotte was also charged by elephants when she was a child, more times than she can remember. In fact, her father developed a technique for avoiding charging elephants. He would drive right at them until the last moment, then suddenly veer off and take a zig-zag course over rocks and gulleys and tree stumps until he could shake them off.

Charlotte didn't have a gentle upbringing by any means.

AFTER OUR DAUGHTER Tabitha was born, I was accepted at Humboldt State University in Arcata, California, to study ecology and wildlife management with Professor Archie Mossman. He had spent six years in Rhodesia researching game ranching on exactly the same sort of terrain as the Lowveld.

I set off for California in late 1971. Charlotte and Tabitha followed me a few weeks later, when I had established myself in a trailer caravan which Archie Mossman allowed me to park on his land. He had twelve acres of redwood country not far from the university, and that was our home for the next three years.

Charlotte found a marvellous nursery school for Tabitha, which enabled her to go out and work. She sliced salmon on the wharf, she made pizzas in a pizza parlour, she served beer in a bar, she even sold insurance door to door. Eventually she got a very good job as administrative assistant to a dentist, Joe Zamboni.

In the meantime, I was working at my studies. But it wasn't all work. Fishing is the second great passion of my life, and our trailer was parked beside a river. We would often go after salmon and steelhead (sea trout). Tabitha—more often known as Tabs—came with us. We'd just throw her into an old canvas knapsack and cart her around wherever we went. Even at that age, she knew where the best fish were to be found, far better than I did. And living in the trailer among the redwoods, she became completely accustomed to outdoor life from the time she could walk.

I finished my course work towards the end of 1974, but I still had to do a thesis based on at least six months' fieldwork. I've always been fascinated by lions, and I decided to go back to Timbavati to study one pride in depth.

CHAPTER TWO

When we arrived back in Africa in early 1975, my father lent me his camp at Timbavati as a base from which to do my research.

It is typical of the bush camps of the area. The main building, which has two bedrooms, a kitchen and bathroom, is normally reserved for guests. It is flanked by two rondavels (pronounced ron-dá-vels), circular mud and wattle structures with conical roofs thatched with reeds. One is used as a living room, dining room and study; the other is a bedroom. Finally, there's the *guma*, a circular enclosure of reeds, more than twelve feet high, which serves as a windbreak when we eat outdoors around a *braai*, or barbecue.

My sole equipment for the fieldwork was a notebook, a borrowed rifle and camera, and a jeep. I knew that I was going to have to spend a lot of my time just hanging around, watching, waiting and listening. It's the only way you can learn about lions.

I planned to observe their courting, mating and breeding habits, the frequency and nature of their kills, their use of the terrain, their routes; I was even planning to go into such details as their panting rates and their roaring patterns in order to build up a complete picture of a pride of lions in the wild.

I didn't have any particular pride in mind. I didn't even know if there *was* a resident pride near the Machaton. But I did know that there were lions. My father, after all, had been seeing them there for thirty years. So I decided to find out for myself if there was a resident pride, and if so, to get acquainted with it as rapidly as possible.

It isn't easy to identify the members of a pride initially, because they tend to break up at times into sub-groups—partly to protect

17

the cubs, and partly because a sub-group is a more efficient hunting unit. The only way it is possible to recognize members of the same pride is by the way the individual lions greet each other by rubbing cheeks, and by the absence of aggressive tendencies, unless they are on a kill.

For the first three months, I walked the territory hour after hour after hour, about a thousand miles in all, usually with Jack Mathebula. Charlotte, Tabs and I also spent a good deal of time driving around the bush in a jeep, trying to get the animals conditioned to the sound and smell and sight of the vehicle.

We did this for a very simple reason. You can find lions on foot— it's probably the best way to go after them—but if they spot you or get your scent, they move away immediately. Once they become accustomed to a vehicle, however, they behave perfectly naturally. It could be that the smells of petrol and oil and rubber are so strong that the animals can't scent the humans inside and therefore don't associate the vehicles with man. We usually walked through the bush following the spoor until we found the lions, as often as not asleep. Then we would retrace our steps, return in the jeep and watch for hours.

Within a few months, the lions became completely accustomed to the jeep and would approach within a few feet of it, provided those of us inside sat tight and talked in whispers. They'd even come and lie down within the shade of the vehicle.

Gradually we sorted out the Machaton pride from the other lions in the area, and came to know them amazingly well. Charlotte could tell the individual lions apart before I could. Her knowledge of the bush is quite uncanny. And even Tabs, scarcely four, soon became adept at spotting lion spoor. So, all in all, it was very much a family affair—both on our part and on the part of the lions we had begun to study.

OUR PRIDE is led by two magnificent males we call Agamemnon and Achilles. Between them they share half a dozen lionesses: Golden, Dimples, Scarleg, Greta, Lona, and Tabby, soon to be the mother of a very special litter. Then there were Golden's sons, the

18

Three Musketeers, and their sister Suzie Wong. These were "teenage" lions, not quite half grown.

The pride leads a highly organized life. The two male lions seem immensely proud, to the point of arrogance, and yet they are totally loyal to each other. Each of them mates with all six lionesses, and apparently without the faintest hint of jealousy. It's an arrangement that works out very much in the lions' favour.

Almost invariably, the lionesses of the pride do what might be called the "family hunting". They are better equipped for it than the males because they are lighter and much more agile. The resultant feast—be it wildebeest, impala, warthog or giraffe—is served in a very strict order, particularly in times of stress, when food is scarce: first the two big males; then the lionesses themselves; then the juniors of the pride; and finally the cubs, if any. There's no sentiment about seeing that the youngest or weakest of the brood gets a fair share.

When they're not out hunting for the pride or caring for their young, the lionesses are available for mating. Available is an understatement. According to George Schaller, author of many lion studies, a mating bout between two lions can last for as long as two days and involve as many as one hundred and fifty couplings. Lions, incidentally, have no fixed mating season because lionesses are polyoestrous—they can come into heat at any time.

In return Achilles and Agamemnon make their own special contribution to the pride. The two lions cover every part of the pride's range. In a single night I've heard them roaring from a dozen different directions. And by day I've often seen them marking out the range by squirting a special glandular secretion on trees and shrubs. In this way they are serving notice to all lions that the Machaton is occupied territory.

If they had to, Achilles and Agamemnon would fight to defend their territory, although I've never seen it happen. (I've only once seen a lion dead as a result of a territorial fight; the death rate from fighting is extremely low.) Normally if nomad lions impinge on a pride area, they get a severe warning from the pride males, and clear off without attempting to fight. Nomads are not welcomed

19

A great passion of my life has always been fishing: here I am angling for trout in Lesotho.

Our meat in the bush is mostly impala, shot by me and butchered by Charlotte.

Jack Mathebula has taught me most of what I know about the difficult art of tracking.

Tabitha strokes one of her pets, a baby warthog.

The cage built around our jeep gives us a feeling of security.

by any pride. Basically the whole social structure, the stability of the pride, depends on the dominance of its leading males.

When they are not eating or mating or worrying about the defence of the range, Achilles and Agamemnon are fully occupied conserving their energy. All lions are good at that. Most of them spend between sixteen and twenty hours a day resting.

In the Southern Hemisphere the dry season lasts from March to October. It is a good time for the lions. The pride prefers the relatively cool days of winter and the longer nights mean more time for hunting, for most lions are essentially nocturnal stalkers. The hunting itself is easier too, as the prey is drawn by thirst to the few remaining water sources in Timbavati—two dams, a marsh and a perennial spring.

The pride's range is roughly oval-shaped, about six and a half miles from tip to tip and nearly four miles across at its widest point. At the heart of the region is a five-mile stretch of the Machaton River. It is dry for about three hundred days every year but fringed with a border of thick riverine bush, which has roots long enough to reach underground water and thus always has green leaves. In the dry season the game tends to congregate along the river—in particular, the browsers, animals like giraffe and kudu that eat tree leaves.

Encircling this stretch of river are black-soil plains. In the rainy season these support a rich grass highly favoured by grazing animals such as wildebeest. During the summer the lions hunt there, extending their range by a few miles. The arrangement ensures them a year-round supply of prey.

Between the bush and the dark-soil plain is a belt of sandy alkaline plain—flat, level land with stunted trees, no grass and consequently no ticks. This is where the lions like to rest, ideally in the shade of a shingayi tree. This tree, with its wide, umbrella-like canopy of leaves, offers a maximum of shade. And because it is low —seldom taller than ten feet—the area of shade does not vary much during the day. The lions don't have to move often to stay in the shade, and that suits them well.

So it is here, on the banks of the Machaton, in the shade of a

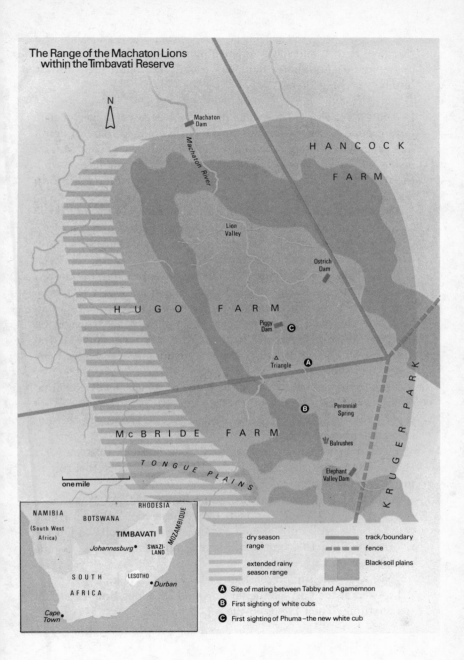

The Range of the Machaton Lions
within the Timbavati Reserve

N

Machaton Dam

Machaton River

HANCOCK FARM

Lion Valley

Ostrich Dam

HUGO FARM

Piggy Dam C

Triangle A

B

Perennial Spring

McBRIDE FARM

Bulrushes

TONGUE PLAINS

Elephant Valley Dam

KRUGER PARK

one mile

NAMIBIA (South West Africa)

BOTSWANA

RHODESIA

TIMBAVATI

MOZAMBIQUE

Johannesburg

SWAZI-LAND

SOUTH AFRICA

LESOTHO

Durban

Cape Town

dry season range

extended rainy season range

track/boundary

fence

Black-soil plains

A Site of mating between Tabby and Agamemnon

B First sighting of white cubs

C First sighting of Phuma – the new white cub

shingayi, that Achilles and Agamemnon and their pride are usually to be found. And here, too, may usually be found the McBride family, watching them.

IN ORDER TO observe the lions properly, I decided to have a cage built around the jeep—for the purpose of keeping lions out. I doubt if it would have stopped a really determined lioness, but at least inside it I felt safe. I couldn't possibly have relaxed enough to watch the lions' behaviour if I had been in an open car with a full-grown lioness only a few yards away.

There was another good reason for the cage. I didn't want to have to kill any of my lions. Looking at them through the iron bars we could accept threatening behaviour, even mock charges, without overreacting and shooting at them.

In the same way, whenever I walked on foot among the lions, I always carried a gun big enough to stop a charging lion in its tracks. If you carry a powerful gun, you probably won't ever have to use it. The gun gives you confidence, and the animals sense it. Knowing that you can stop them, you can afford to let them come at you until the very last moment. A lion is a big animal. You'd have to be a very bad shot to miss.

But carrying a small rifle can be dangerous. Sensing your feeling of insecurity, a lion may well attack and you may be tempted to shoot before you really need to. Also, if you do shoot, you may not kill the animal instantly.

When I first went tracking with Jack Mathebula thirteen years ago, I was young and rash, and we had an experience that turned my stomach to water.

Near the Machaton we found some lion tracks and drag marks. A kill had been dragged down towards the river. Perhaps there was a lioness with cubs around somewhere. In the soft sand of the riverbed we saw the drag marks again and I said to Jack, "Come on, let's go across."

"No, wait," he said urgently in Zulu. Then, "Look."

I looked at the bush on the far side, and for a long time I couldn't see anything. Then I spotted the top of one ear.

24

We decided to go back to higher ground for a better view. The previous day we'd come across twenty-five lions feeding on a giraffe and as soon as we'd appeared, they'd fled. So maybe I was feeling a bit overconfident. When we couldn't see the lioness at all from the higher position, I decided to throw a stone into the bush to see whether she was still there.

"*Haye.* No," Jack said, and shook his head.

The stone went through a shrub and hit the ground. Nothing happened.

I threw a second . . . and there was a slight movement.

Then there was a sudden explosion. The trees just burst apart and the lioness charged over the riverbed and came straight at us. Her tail was going like a whip and there was this terrifying, rumbling roar.

I had my rifle up and she was big in my sights when Jack said, "*Yima! Ungalibulali!* Stand still. Don't shoot." The lioness stopped about twenty paces away from us. A low rumbling sound was still coming from deep within her stomach.

Again Jack spoke softly but very firmly, "No. Don't shoot."

The lioness stood her ground for a few seconds. Then she backed off slowly, still growling, towards the river. Sheepishly I lowered my gun.

That lesson served me well on other occasions. One time a friend and I were out tracking, and three lionesses came at us, straight out of the riverine bush—all at once and at full speed. It was a terrifying predicament. When they stopped about twenty-five paces from us, we had our rifles trained on them. We stood our ground, and remembering Jack's advice, I held my fire. Eventually we were able to back away, reasonably confident that the lions wouldn't charge again.

Jack was equally insistent on driving home the point that if you did turn and run, you'd be dead within seconds. I've yet to try this one out, for obvious reasons.

In all the time I've been tracking lions, I've been charged six times—usually by a lioness, I might add, and probably because there were cubs around. Thanks to Jack's counsel, though, I've shot

25

only once. I'd be the last to deny that it's a completely natural reaction to fire at a charging beast, but I often wonder how many charging lions have been shot quite unnecessarily.

WITH THAT KIND of experience behind me and a cage around our jeep—plus a Westley-Richards .404 rifle—we felt safe enough to sit for hours and hours getting acquainted with the Machaton pride.

Of the two pride males, Achilles is the more alert, more the leader. When they wake up after a rest, he always moves off first. Agamemnon looks battle-weary; he has many scars and his left eye is slightly recessed, almost certainly the result of a fight with another lion. Achilles and Agamemnon are very close to each other. They are almost always together, sometimes on their own, sometimes with one or another sub-group of the pride, or sometimes with a single lioness.

My own feeling is that they grew up in a different pride. Then, when they were between two and three years old, they were thrown out by the pride and became nomads, travelling together. Probably they then came across the Machaton pride, threw out the pride male or males, and took it over. It seems likely that they are brothers, and that their period as nomads, hunting together as partners in order to survive, strengthened the bond between them.

Golden, the mother of the Three Musketeers and Suzie Wong, is very aggressive, very alert. At the time we started our observations, she was the leading lioness of the pride. I've seen the other five lionesses make submissive gestures towards her. She's large for a lioness and deeply golden in colour, hence her name.

Scarleg—obviously so called because of a scarred leg—seems to be second in the lioness hierarchy. She's also very aggressive, and has become much more so since she had a litter of her own. She's even made mock charges at the jeep.

Tabby, named after my daughter, seems to come third. She's a bit paler than the others, small, probably very young, with a slight scar on the middle of her nose. She's completely casual. Right from the beginning, she's shown no fear of us and will occasionally come up to the jeep to investigate.

26

Then there's Dimples, Tabby's great friend, who has a black mark like a dimple on one cheek. The other two lionesses are Greta and Lona (both names inspired by Greta Garbo, who always wanted to be alone). They don't appear to be an integral part of the pride, and they're both very wary.

And that was the Machaton pride as we came to know it in the early months of 1975.

IN MAY, I saw Tabby flirting with Agamemnon. A few weeks later, on June 6, 1975, I was out in the bush again, bumping along in a closed Wagoneer (another jeep-type vehicle) with Joe Zamboni, our friend the California dentist who happened to be staying with us. We saw something dart across the road a long way ahead. Thinking it might be a lion, Joe and I hopped out. We had just started to look for spoor when we heard the unmistakable mutterings of lions in the bush nearby. So in we went—I with my Westley-Richards .404, Joe with his camera right behind. But there was no sign of the lions.

Suddenly we heard a peculiar growling noise—a noise I'd never heard before in all the hours I'd spent listening to lions. We walked very quietly towards it. Then we saw a big lion—it was Agamemnon, standing in a low combretum bush. He was a long way off, and looking the other way, so we crept back to fetch the Wagoneer.

We returned to the spot in the vehicle, and there was the lion standing over a wildebeest kill. There wasn't much of the carcass left. Agamemnon had fed, and fed handsomely. Then a lioness came out of the bush—Tabby again. She walked straight up to Agamemnon and he started to trail her, nose to rear. Tabby kept flicking her tail. She was probably not much more than a teenager; she could easily have been his daughter or grand-daughter.

Eventually she lay down on her paws and he mounted her, growling the way a lion growls only at mating, and biting the nape of her neck very softly. During the next two and a half hours, they repeated the mating ritual ten times and the sequence of the actions was the same. We watched them spellbound until it was too dark to see, or photograph, any more.

27

In mid-September Charlotte saw Tabby looking extremely pregnant. Two weeks later she again spotted the lioness, looking much more slender. It seemed likely that Tabby had had her cubs, and Charlotte told us roughly where to look for them.

The weather wasn't good that day, and as I was suffering from the flu, I decided to stay in bed. My sister Lan, who was up from Johannesburg for a visit, went off in the Wagoneer with her son James, and Johnson, a Matabele, one of the older trackers in the area. They headed straight for the place that Charlotte had described.

Suddenly Lan braked and switched off the motor. "Look, James, a lioness," she whispered.

"Where?" he asked. Lions are notoriously difficult to spot, even when you are right on top of them.

Then he saw her. It was Tabby, only about twenty-five yards from the track, under a shingayi. She lay there, quite unconcerned, looking back at the jeep. Beside her was the remains of a wildebeest kill on which she'd been feeding.

In absolute silence, Lan, James and Johnson sat and waited.

Within a minute, a little head popped up behind the lioness. To Lan's amazement, it was snow-white.

Then another little head appeared—tawny.

And yet a third—snow-white again.

Lan was staggered. She'd heard of very rare albino cubs, but these cubs were not albinos. Albinos appear to be white, due to an abnormal, total lack of pigmentation, which also affects the colour of their eyes. These cubs had normal yellow eyes. They were ordinary, seemingly healthy lions. Except that they were pure white.

Lan drove back to get me—"like a maniac", as she put it. She found me still in bed, reading and unable, because of the flu, to get as excited as I should about the news.

"Are you sure they're not just pale?" I asked her.

She was furious.

"No. They're white. Pure white," she insisted.

By this time I was sufficiently interested to drag myself out of bed and grab a camera. I was only sorry that Charlotte had gone to help out in the Sohebele game-viewing lodge, too far away to be fetched in time. The news about the white lions had quickly spread around the camp and a rather impressive viewing party had assembled.

There were Lan and James, naturally, and Johnson, who couldn't wait to have another look, and Tabs, and a sixteen-year-old African named Gracie who used to look after Tabs for us, and Gracie's sister, who turned up at the last minute.

The Wagoneer was full as Lan drove back to the spot where she'd seen Tabby and the cubs. They were all there, still in the same position. The cubs stayed close to their mother, but now and then we would get a glimpse of one of them over her tawny shoulder. I worked away with the camera.

After twenty minutes the cubs grew bolder. One by one they wandered off into the bush. We now spotted Dimples, Tabby's pal, lying in the shade nearby. Tabby stood up and called softly to her brood. It was a short, sharp sound, something like the *oo* in *book*, the sound that lions make on a hunt when they want to communicate without alerting other animals.

Tabby called again, and yet again. From a thicket emerged a tiny tawny form. Then two more furry shapes—white as polar bears, but unmistakably lions.

I could see them clearly now that they were in the open. One had broad, quizzical features, suggesting an adventurous male. We came to call him Temba, the Zulu word for "hope". The other had the triangular face of a female and was much more cautious. She became simply Tombi, Zulu for "girl".

Temba and Tombi ambled over to join their brother, whom we

29

later named Vela, meaning "surprise". And there they all stood—Vela and the white lions of Timbavati—in a secure patch of Lowveld grass, listening as their mother called.

Thirty yards away, Lan started the engine and we turned discreetly for home, leaving them to the wildebeest carcass that had so fortunately pinned them to the spot.

LOOKING BACK ON it that night, I began to realize what a momentous find we had made. For centuries there have been rumours and legends of white lions in Africa. The reality of having discovered—even photographed—the first truly white lions in recorded history overwhelmed me.

Suddenly it dawned on me that these extraordinary white cubs were the result of the mating Joe Zamboni and I had witnessed in June. I tried to reconstruct the timing. The cubs were now roughly two weeks old, and since the gestation period of lions is between one hundred and six and one hundred and ten days, there wasn't much doubt of their parentage. We had plenty of documentary evidence. Joe's pictures showed Agamemnon with his recessed eye, and Tabby was equally easy to identify in the photographs with the small scar on her nose.

Even then, I felt a special responsibility for these cubs and began to wonder what we should do about them. The casualty rate among lion cubs in the wild is as high as seventy per cent. Lionesses abandon their litters or lose some of their cubs, which are immediately brought down by hyenas. Or male lions lie on the cubs, crushing them to death, or fatally injure them when driving them off a kill. There is even cannibalism, though on an extremely small scale.

(Schaller gives an evolutionary explanation for this high mortality rate. Lions live for a relatively long time, sixteen or seventeen years on average, and are so immensely strong that they have no natural enemies apart from man. Therefore, they cannot afford to raise indiscriminate numbers of young, or they would wipe out their sources of food.)

So, realistically, what chance of survival did the white cubs have?

30

Perhaps the wisest thing would be to bring them up in captivity, in a fenced-off area or even a zoo. And yet I was determined, initially at least, to let them stand up to the odds in the wild.

THE NEXT MORNING Lan found Tabby and her fabulous cubs exactly where they had been the previous day. She parked the Wagoneer under a leadwood tree and settled down to watch. Tabby gave her a few anxious moments when she got up and stalked towards the vehicle looking as if she meant business, but she was interested only in what was still left of the wildebeest, about five paces away. She took a leg in her jaws, dragged the kill a short distance and fed briefly.

Temba, Tombi and Vela sat watching with ears cocked. Tabby called to them and they came forward and fed, sucking and chewing bits of the meat.

The other lioness, Dimples, was lying in the grass nearby. Tabby went off and lay on her belly near her. She tried to rest but the cubs had other ideas. They played all over her, but the game they liked best was discovering which one could walk farthest along her back without falling off. Tabby was extremely patient and there was never a suggestion that she preferred the normal tawny cub to the two white ones.

After a while the lionesses began to doze off. But suddenly they both sprang up, their eyes fixed intently on the bush at their right. Lan saw two giraffes peering over the trees at the young lions. They were clearly intrigued by the white cubs, which stood out sharply against the surrounding foliage. One of the giraffes—rather sensibly, Lan thought—soon moved away to a safer distance. The other one seemed quite incapable of abandoning this uncanny sight.

The lionesses soon lost interest in the giraffes and flopped down to doze again. Eventually the giraffes wandered off.

Half an hour later, a vulture swooped down, aiming to perch on a dead tree near the kill. In a second Tabby was on her feet, a tawny surge of angry power, jumping and growling at the circling bird until it lolloped off.

LAN AND JAMES went back home to Johannesburg without catching another glimpse of the world's only white lions. The days stretched into a week, and then another, and nobody saw them again. Like a vision, they had vanished. We began to doubt that we had seen them at all.

But the photographs were there; they established beyond all doubt that Tabby's litter had included two snow-white cubs.

When a lioness has a litter, she temporarily withdraws from the pride, usually with one or more of the other lionesses, and forms a sub-group for the protection of the cubs. Lions can be vicious on a kill. If a cub attempts to defy the strict feeding order, it is in grave danger of being wounded by a senior member of the pride. A sub-group can also live off smaller animals, such as impala or wildebeest; a full pride would need to kill a giraffe.

During this time, I continued to track and observe the rest of the pride. About a week after we lost sight of Tabby and the cubs, I spent an afternoon watching nine of the Machaton lions slumbering on the sand. Shortly before sunset they began to yawn, stretch, walk a few paces . . . and then flop down again. Some lazily groomed themselves. The younger lions stalked one another and played at wrestling.

It was like watching an orchestra warming up, except that it was far more prolonged. Finally the leading lioness of the group, Golden, began to roar softly and repeatedly. Then she stalked off to start a hunt. One by one the others followed. Last to get up, and most reluctant, were Achilles and Agamemnon.

I often saw Golden get the pride moving like this. The only members of the pride to whom she ever gave way were the two big males. All the other lions adopted submissive postures. Golden, like Achilles and Agamemnon, was very much concerned with defending the pride's range. Only twice while watching the pride have I been threatened by a lioness—a mock charge accompanied by a deep rumbling and a thunderclap growl. And both times it was by Golden.

But no matter how much I was caught up in observing the rest of the pride, I could not get the white cubs out of my mind. Although more than two weeks had gone by, I felt confident that I would soon catch up with Temba and Tombi again. Whenever I met one of the park rangers I inquired about *amahlope*, the white ones. But the reply was always the same, "We haven't seen them."

October is the end of the dry season in the Lowveld. Here and there the stirrings of spring bring fresh leaves and blossoms, but most of the trees are still bare and the grass is as pale as straw. No rain has fallen for months and rivers have slumbered dryly through a Southern Hemisphere winter of relatively cool blue days and sharp, starry nights. When the heavy rains come in early December, rivers like the Machaton become brief torrents up to ten feet deep before they are swallowed up again by the thirsty soil.

October 19 was a scorcher—and still dry, dry, dry. I'd invited a local farmer friend, Hugh Chittenden, to help me look for the cubs that many people now suspected were a hoax. We set off in the jeep about 11:00 a.m. with a rifle and a camera, and ranged the lions' territory for a good three hours in that brutal heat.

Two o'clock in the afternoon and success at last. There they were, the white cubs, taking their siesta under a spreading shingayi. The lions were clearly feeling the heat. Tabby was panting one hundred and twenty times a minute and the breathing rate of the cubs was not much slower.

They stirred after a while, and we watched with almost reverent awe as this perfectly ordinary lioness walked nonchalantly out of the shade and straight past the jeep, trailed by two little white cubs and their tawny brother. They went down the dry riverbed and disappeared into the thick bush. Though sorry to see them go, we were relieved to know that they were still alive and well—and less vulnerable with every passing week.

THERE WERE SEVERAL other prides whose ranges fringed on the Machaton River. One of these we called the Velvet Paws pride, because of their unusually velvety paws. Another we named the Flop Ear pride, because one of the young male lions had a very

Overleaf: *Our neighbours at Timbavati include wildebeest, impala and giraffe....*

floppy ear. At the time that the white lions were born, the Flop Ear pride consisted of fifteen lions and the Velvet Paws pride of nine.

Lion prides are almost as individualistic in their behaviour as are human families. For example, the Flop Ear lions are much more aggressive than the Machaton lions. Charlotte had several unpleasant experiences with them. On one occasion, when she was making some observations for me, she and Tabs and some friends drove right into the middle of the Flop Ear pride. The lions hid behind the trees and then charged right up to the Wagoneer, which was pretty frightening for everyone inside, even though they were behind glass. Charlotte reversed a bit and waited for a few minutes before following them again. When she did so, the same thing happened. In all, they charged about six times that morning. One male even jumped up and put his paws on the side of the vehicle. He could have smashed the window with one blow and not felt a thing.

There were other differences between the prides. The Flop Ear pride seems to rest mainly on the sand of dried-up riverbeds. I've seen my pride in a riverbed only once in nearly two years. Eating preferences also differ, not only from pride to pride but also from area to area. Most of the prides in Timbavati seem to avoid buffalo. Yet in East Africa, where Schaller did his research, buffalo comprised more than half of the kills.

By following the Machaton lions on foot, I soon discovered they had a number of established routes linking the various parts of the range. As a rule they would choose the easiest path, particularly if it avoided the long grass and was relatively free of both ticks and thorns.

At first I often travelled, with the aid of a compass, by a more direct route from one point to the next. I soon discovered that it needed more energy to wade through the long grass and thick bush than to negotiate the lions' slightly longer route. In terms of time and effort, the lions' bush roads could not have been better laid out. I was able to draw up maps, marking out the lions' paths and giving names to the various places where we most often sighted them: the Plains, Lion Valley, the Bulrushes, Piggy Dam, Elephant

36

Dam, and the Triangle—a triangular area where two small dried-up riverbeds joined the main river.

We also used to track the lions by listening to them roaring at night. Machaton lions rarely, if ever, roar during the day, but at night we could hear them quite clearly from the camp. Charlotte was particularly adept at identifying our lions, and she conditioned herself to wake up every night at about three o'clock to go outside and listen. As soon as the lions started to roar, she would point her arm in their direction. Then she would bring her arm down and draw a line towards her body in the sand. In the morning I would take a compass and, with a tracker, walk along the bearing indicated by Charlotte until we came across either the lions or their spoor.

Before long we could tell from a glance at Charlotte's mark where they were most likely to be and head straight there. Lions are terrible creatures of habit; we kept finding them in the same handful of resting places.

Charlotte sometimes came out tracking the lions with me, bringing Tabs with her, but the rest of the time she was busy organizing the camp, and setting up a play school for Tabs and a few of her African friends.

Life in our camp was fairly primitive. We had neither electricity nor telephone. Kerosene lamps and candles provided all the light we needed and an old kerosene refrigerator chilled our perishables, when it was working.

We didn't really miss the telephone. In fact, isolation seemed only to strengthen our bond with the bush. When there was no way to avoid making a telephone call, we'd simply drive to one of the few places in the reserve that did have a phone: the warden's house, thirty minutes away; the Sohebele game-viewing lodge, almost an hour away; or Dr. Pierre Hugo's adjoining farm, which had a bush telephone in a box beside a tree, three-quarters of an hour away. These phones were all connected to an open party line, linked to the outside world—intermittently, and usually reluctantly—through the exchange in Hoedspruit, regional centre of the area, about forty miles away.

Once every few weeks we went into Hoedspruit for mail, food

and other supplies. There was also an open market at Acornhoek, a bit farther away, where we occasionally went for fresh rations of fruit and vegetables.

For protein we literally lived off the bush—almost entirely on impala shot by me and butchered by Charlotte. It sounds monotonous, but it wasn't. Charlotte turned the impala into delicious steaks and stews and roasts and sausages and meatballs. We even had impala kebabs and spaghetti bolognese based on minced impala.

When she marinated the meat in soy sauce for a few days and used a lot of rosemary, it tasted just like lamb. When she put in less rosemary, it tasted like beef.

Biltong was another of our bush specialities, often prepared jointly by Charlotte and me because of all the work involved. We made it in the cool of winter, mainly from impala, though you can make it from almost any game, including giraffe and even ostrich. First, using the legs, saddle and rump of the animal, we cut the meat into tongue-shaped strips. Hence the name *biltong*: from the Afrikaans words *bil* meaning rump, and *tong* meaning tongue. Next we'd sprinkle the strips with a little vinegar, salt and pepper, and spices like ground coriander seeds. The following day we hung the meat on wires under a shady tree or in an open shed, so that the cool breezes could get to it. The meat became completely dry within three weeks—and quite safe to eat for up to a year. We would often take biltong with us on long treks through the bush. Pure protein, it's an extremely sustaining and nourishing snack, as the Cape bushmen found long before the first European settlers arrived in southern Africa.

We ate extremely well. In fact, on the rare occasions when we visited friends living in so-called civilized circumstances, we found their veal and chicken comparatively tasteless.

But there were problems. The baboons were a nuisance at first. When we were away from the camp, they would break in and attack our food supplies. Once, just after Charlotte had gone to Acornhoek to stock up, they ripped the wire mesh out of a food bin, took an entire month's supply of fruit and vegetables and squashed them up against the walls, then tore up all our paintings and maps and books. The mess was unbelievable. I tried shooting a couple of them after that, but they kept coming back.

Then Charlotte remembered an old colonial remedy. She got a sack of oranges, scooped out a hole in the top of each one and poured in a little Tabasco sauce. She placed them all around the camp and we went out to watch the lions. When we got back the oranges were gone, but so were the baboons—permanently.

WHEN YOU STUDY animals, you have to adopt their schedule. Sometimes, when the moon was bright, we would drive around all night, following the lions. Then, we would go back home and, like the lions, sleep through the heat of the day, waking up in the evening around the time they would start to move about again.

The best part of a summer day in the bushveld is the still, quiet pre-dawn time, when the sky is just beginning to pale, veils of mist lie over the dew-laden grasses and the birds open up with their morning chorus. We'd often get up at first light, half past four or five, and after a cup of hot tea, set off, Charlotte, Tabs, Jack and myself.

As we drove out of camp, we might disturb a herd of kudu bulls browsing by the side of the track. These powerful antelope can jump tremendous heights. They are wary and alert, with large, sensitive ears. Sometimes if they were not too frightened by the jeep, they would stop again a short distance from the track, watching us with anxious eyes and flicking tails.

On we'd go then, and the only sound we'd hear above the rattle of the jeep would be the shrieking of the francolin as they darted ahead of us on blurred feet. Their plumage was almost perfect camouflage against the brown earth and bleached grass, except for their conspicuous scarlet heads.

I've always admired the way a mother francolin protects her young. Sensing danger, she will fly off with a fusillade of clucks and squawks, feigning injury by dragging a wing. It's a superb performance staged in the hope of luring the menace away from her brood.

Then we might see a couple of old giraffe bulls surveying us curiously over the treetops before loping off to a safe distance; or a herd of wildebeest resting in a patch of open sand, or a lone tortoise ambling along in the middle of the track.

Suddenly we might spot some fresh lion tracks in a dry riverbed. Jack and I would jump out to have a closer look. How many lions? Two, maybe three. We might follow the lions' road for a bit on foot, past an old, bare marula tree, past stumps of leadwood, then on through another dried-up riverbed. Suddenly, no more tracks, so we would have to go back a bit and find where they had branched off.

Off we'd go again in the jeep, and suddenly there they'd be —our pride, as likely as not stretched out under a shingayi. Sometimes it was difficult to pick out all the members of the group as the shade helped them to blend into the landscape. It's very easy to mistake lions for boulders; it's even possible to miss a large lioness lying down in six inches of grass a short distance away.

Achilles and Agamemnon might give us a casual glance before dismissing us as totally uninteresting. But one of the Three Musketeers might walk towards the jeep with a purposeful look. We'd all wait, absolutely silent, as he came closer and closer, swinging his tail and staring straight at us. Another Musketeer might follow him, and we'd have two of them sniffing around the jeep. These inquisitive young lions didn't seem hostile, but it was still reassuring to have the cage around us.

After several hours of detailed observation, during which I'd take photographs and make notes, we'd go back to camp to rest, knowing that the lions would stay put until sunset, when we could find them again in the same spot.

FROM THE MOMENT we discovered the white lions everything changed—and yet nothing changed. We still went on watching lions every day. I had to, for the sake of my thesis. But it was impossible to remain academically detached. I felt from the outset a growing sense of responsibility towards the white cubs.

CHAPTER FOUR

One afternoon when the cubs were five or six weeks old, Jack and I found them and their mother lolling on the white sand of the Triangle. Shortly before sundown and in the waning light, the cubs ran through part of their play repertoire: Stalk a Tail, Run and Swat, Pick-Up Sticks and Pig in the Middle. Temba, the little white male, was already showing a daredevil streak missing in Tombi and in Vela, his slightly smaller brother.

Temba couldn't resist the twitching tail of an adult lion. We watched him make an elaborate stalk on the black tip of his mother's tail, which moved as she snoozed. He squirmed the last few yards on his stomach. Then, like a domestic cat about to spring, he wiggled his bottom. A leap and he was on his quarry, giving it a sharp nip. As casual and indulgent with her offspring as always, Tabby raised her head a few inches, gave a mild mewing protest and sank back into slumber.

Run and Swat was a good game for two. On our left, Vela in brown. On our right, Temba in white. Between them, three lion-lengths of soft sand. Temba to charge . . . and off he went, bounding and prancing. As he neared Vela, they both reared up on hind legs and cuffed one another.

Tombi, with coy discretion, usually waited for one of her brothers to initiate play. But she was always ready to join them in a tug-of-war over a stick. Or in a bout of Pig in the Middle. In this game the three cubs stood in line, the two on the outside trying to nip the bottom of the pig in the middle. When one succeeded, the pig would swing round and take a swipe at its assailant—leaving its flank open to attack from the other side. The trick, it seemed, was to avoid getting caught in the middle.

Since then we've spent many hours watching the cubs at play. The adult males usually kept well clear of such sessions, and on the few occasions that Temba, the spunky one, dared to jump on Agamemnon's rump, he was swiftly warned off with an irritable growl. The cubs seldom went near Achilles. It was almost as if Tabby had some way of warning her cubs not to be too free with the adult males.

The games invariably ended in a good-natured free-for-all. But subconsciously, the cubs were rehearsing for their role in adult life. The movements they used in play were scaled-down versions of the movements of full-grown lions. The games can be roughly divided into two categories: actions lions use when killing prey, which the cubs simulated by jumping on the back of the lioness; and actions lions use on the rare occasions when they have to fight, which the cubs simulated by standing on their hind legs and clawing at one another.

FASCINATING AND lovable as we found the cubs, we could never overlook the fact that lions are potentially highly dangerous. Many of the wild animals that surrounded us were. All the camps in the reserve had protective stockades around them, but lions, and more often leopards, frequently got into the enclosures at night.

Apparently dogs are a popular delicacy with leopards, so property owners tend to discourage them on the reserve. But even if the fencing were impregnable, dogs still wouldn't be safe. A few years back, a game warden's small dog was attacked from the air in front of his very eyes. An ominous shadow . . . and whoosh, it was gone. Snatched aloft in the talons of an eagle.

We seldom saw the lions near our camp, but every few weeks during the summer, we found their tracks. At night, strangely, lions seem to lose some of their fear of human smells. But I think that the main reason for these visits was that our camp lay on a route leading to one of their principal hunting areas.

Once at midnight, I heard a familiar sound right outside our rondavel. It was the quiet, communicating *oo* sound of a lion. I crept to the door and edged it open. There they were—at least four lions. But they'd heard the door open and immediately ran away. Next day we judged from the tracks that no fewer than seven of the Machaton pride had paid us a visit.

TOWARDS THE END of the year, the first of the good rains came. Almost overnight little green daggers stabbed up through the damp soil of the plains. In a few weeks carpets of new grass had transformed bushveld clearings into verdant playgrounds for Temba, Tombi and Vela.

One afternoon I went out with Victor Hugo, a university student and son of our neighbour, Dr. Pierre Hugo. Parked at the edge of a glade, we had ringside seats for the cubs' games. We'd found them the way we frequently did these days—by watching the giraffes. Whenever we came across a group of giraffes staring curiously down into the bush, it was a fair bet they were watching the white cubs.

The cubs romped and wrestled. At one point Temba leaped up and dropped a little paw on Vela's rump, rolling him over and nipping him in the nape of the neck—in precisely the way his mother would deal with a wildebeest.

A soft rain had begun to fall, and Temba thought it would be great sport to pin Tombi down in the mud. Then Vela tried to be King of the Castle by climbing right on top of the snarling pair. The dark mud had streaked the white cubs making them look more like baby zebras than the fearsome beasts they seemed to think they were.

The elders were revelling in the sudden coolness. Achilles lay on his back, his legs spread-eagled, enjoying the rain falling on his belly. When Temba summoned up the courage to give his tail a tug, the big male merely moved off to join Agamemnon who was lying a few yards away. I'll always remember the picture those two close companions made, lying back to back, almost like book-ends, their heads held regally, half turned away, surveying their world.

Having failed to interest the big males in their play, Temba and Tombi decided to investigate a nearby tree which had been

43

The cubs spent many hours at play. Their repertoire included such games as Stalk a Tail, Run and Swat, Pick-Up Sticks and Pig in the Middle.

pushed over by an elephant. It rested against an adjoining upright tree making a ramp that the cubs couldn't resist. Vela was the first to venture up, with Tombi close behind. Last for a change, Temba charged up after them and then all three tumbled to the ground.

They tried it again. It was Vela who finally succeeded in reaching the top of the ramp. Up the tree he climbed, going higher and higher until he was almost twelve feet up. Somehow he managed to wedge himself in a fork. He looked down, shuffled uncomfortably, then gave a strangled mew, just like a domestic kitten that has got into difficulties.

Tabby had been keeping a casually watchful eye on the cubs, and now she walked over to the tree. Seeing her close at hand, Vela seemed to gain confidence. He scrambled free and slithered down the ramp towards her. Then, inevitably, over the side he went. But the six-foot fall to the soft earth didn't seem to bother him and he was soon frolicking happily with his brother and sister again.

Our observations that day underlined the concern we felt for the young white cubs. As Vic put it in his diary:

"The green fields in which these innocent tussles took place were the sharpest reminder we'd had yet of the severe handicap facing Temba and Tombi. If they stay as white as they are—and there's still not the slightest hint of any significant darkening of their coats—how can they ever hope to hunt with any degree of success? In the brown of winter or the green of summer? By night or by day?"

Over the millennia, evolution must have produced mutants of this type before, but apparently none had established a lasting strain. This could indicate that they were unable to fend for themselves.

Some zoologists believe that in the past, when lions existed in many other parts of the world there was a much greater colour variation than there is today. For example, before the Romans wiped out the lions in North Africa by rounding them up for their arenas, there would probably have been a strain of very pale, almost white lions in that area: lions would have needed that colouring as camouflage in the Sahara Desert.

Most animals carry genes known as "recessive"—that is, genes capable of producing a whole range of variations, including colour. Where this new colour proves useful to the animal, it can become dominant, as in the case of the peppered moth. Normally this moth is lichen-coloured, which makes it almost invisible on trees and even brown buildings and so protects it from predatory birds. But the moth carries a recessive gene capable of producing a black strain. In the Midlands and the North of England, where the moths spend most of their time on buildings that are black with soot, black has become the dominant strain.

Leopards have also turned up a black strain, which has persisted in certain areas. In some ways it is an advantage for a leopard to be black, since it hunts at night. On the other hand, it is also an advantage for a leopard to be spotted, because then it can hide all day in a tree with its kill, undisturbed by other predators or scavengers. So here evolution seems to have turned up two totally workable solutions, and you find black leopards and spotted leopards existing side by side.

However, I can think of no advantage to lions in being white, so I don't see this strain developing unless man steps in and does some stage managing.

One thing puzzled me at first. If a strain of white lions does exist in this part of South Africa, why has it never shown up before? Then I realized that Timbavati is almost completely uninhabited. The game warden, however observant he may be, has to patrol over two hundred square miles of wilderness, and the lions are just one of his concerns. Given high mortality rate among cubs and the tendency of lionesses to hide their young the chances of white cubs being seen in this area are very slight. Perhaps previous white cubs simply disappeared before anyone saw them. We were unusually fortunate to spot ours when they were only a few weeks old, and to be able to keep in touch with them as they grew up.

So far the trio have been luckier than most in surviving the usual dangers of growing up in a pride. Once we found Temba limping badly, and for five days, until he was well again, we fed the sub-group with impala that I'd shot. Usually the meat was snatched up by the Musketeers, but eventually the young cubs got their share. If we hadn't done this, the pride might have moved on without Temba, leaving him defenceless in the bush.

Although the cubs have grown out of the dangerous early stage, they now face the related risks of starvation or injury on a kill. On one occasion, after we'd lost sight of them for a few weeks, we found the cubs looking alarmingly thin, and Temba, always the adventurer, had a nasty gash on his muzzle. Seeing his ribs thrusting out like ridges on a sand dune, I made a confident guess that he'd stuck his nose into the dinner of one of his elders, and had got well and truly clouted for it.

CHAPTER FIVE

At this period Charlotte was helping out at the Sohebele game-viewing lodge. Sohebele camp has been considerably enlarged to accommodate tourists, and enhanced, if you happen to look at it that way, with such amenities as electric lighting, a bar and a swimming pool. Because of her childhood experiences in the bush, Charlotte had developed her own instinct for survival. It's just as well, for working at Sohebele exposed her to some extremely hazardous situations. To get there involved a seventeen-mile drive—at least an hour's journey—right through the middle of the Flop Ear pride's range. The drive home was even more harrowing, for it was usually made in the dark.

In general, Charlotte enjoyed driving in the evenings; we all did. There is a magic about the bush as the light dims and then fades altogether. The warm night air is suddenly filled with the shrieking of the cicadas, known in this part of the world as Christmas beetles because it is at Christmas, our midsummer, that their shrill chattering reaches its crescendo. Along the track, shadows move silently among the trees and the headlights keep picking up reflections from countless pairs of startled eyes— impala, kudu, steinbok. Sometimes, in a clearing, you see a hyena loitering to stare for a moment at the jeep before scuttling off into the shadows. And always, just as a small boat trails a phosphorescent wake, the jeep is followed by squadrons of darting points of light, fireflies.

Charlotte worked at Sohebele for almost three months and made that thirty-four mile drive every day. She usually took Tabs and Gracie with her. One evening as they were driving through the remotest part of the bush, in an open jeep, the engine suddenly died. Nothing she could do would get it started again.

They couldn't just sit in the jeep, because they were in the centre of the Flop Ear pride's range, and as Charlotte herself put it: "They're not nice lions at all, that pride." Some or all of the fifteen lions might arrive and decide to get into the open jeep to investigate.

The safest thing, she thought, would be to start walking, before it got too dark. So they walked, Charlotte, Tabs and Gracie, all singing at the top of their voices. They sang Afrikaans songs, Shangaan songs, pop songs, whatever came into their heads. They didn't feel like singing, but Charlotte's idea was to make sure that anything lurking in the bush would know they were there.

They must have walked for a mile and a half, which is quite a distance when it's getting dark and there are animals all around you. Finally, they came to the camp of Aniel, the local caretaker. While they were resting, Aniel went out in the bush with two or three friends, all singing every bit as lustily as Charlotte and her crew, and for the same reason. They made their way to Sohebele to tell Rod Owen, who runs the camp, what had happened. Later that night, Rod drove everyone home.

On another occasion, when Charlotte was driving our little car

The variety of wildlife at Timbavati is unparalleled. We are surrounded by species which vary from the tiniest mosquito and firefly right up to the large animals like impala, zebra, giraffe and elephant.

over the main roads (a longer route, but a slightly safer one) it broke down. She and Tabs and Gracie managed to get a lift home, and the following day the lodge people lent Charlotte a Land-Rover to tow our car back to Sohebele for repairs. So when she finished work at 10:00 p.m. Charlotte drove back to fetch our car with Gracie, Tabs, and a young Englishman named Mike. He was staying at Sohebele and had agreed to help.

They set off on the return trip, Charlotte driving the open Land-Rover, with Tabs and Gracie sitting beside her, and Mike at the wheel of the crippled car, dragging behind. When they came to a dry riverbed, they had to stop to negotiate a steep incline. Suddenly they saw a whole sea of glowing eyes coming towards them. At first Charlotte thought they were impala. But they weren't. They were fifteen lions, all running straight at the open Land-Rover—the whole bad-tempered Flop Ear pride.

Charlotte leaped out, pulled Tabby and Gracie out after her, and they all piled into the little car with Mike. Just as they shut the doors, the lions came around past the headlights and she could see them clearly. The lions climbed all over the Land-Rover, and then they started sniffing around the tiny car, literally towering over it. The windows wouldn't shut properly and the lions were breathing their hot horrible breath right in.

Then the lions began to push at the car causing it to rock on its springs, and Charlotte and Tabs got a fit of the giggles. It was so terrifying, the only thing they could do was laugh about it. The lions sniffed around for a full hour before they cleared off. At least they appeared to clear off. Charlotte couldn't be certain, because she couldn't see anything unless it was directly in front of the headlights. She couldn't tell by listening, either, because lions make very little noise.

Charlotte waited for a while, then cautiously she put an arm out, and then a leg out, and everybody coughed and talked and made a lot of noise, and nothing happened. Suddenly she jumped out, dashed to the Land-Rover, started it up, and headed for Sohebele, towing the car behind. Making that decision to run was, she says, the worst moment of her whole life.

One thing you learn in the bush is that there is a terribly narrow division between life and death. Snakes are the biggest danger. There are spitting cobra, which can blind you from a distance of ten feet, and several types of mamba. If you're bitten by a black mamba, you've got exactly ten minutes to live. We always keep a supply of serum in the camp, and normally carry some with us in the jeep.

A friend of mine who didn't take the latter precaution was bitten by a black mamba not far from his camp. He got into his jeep and drove back as fast as he could. By the time he got there he was in such a nervous state when tried to open the vial of serum that he broke it and spilled the whole lot on the floor. A few minutes later he was dead.

Tabs, even at her young age, has been exposed to danger. She and Charlotte and I often spend the night sleeping in the jeep in the middle of the Machaton range.

One night the three of us were fast asleep when Charlotte suddenly woke up and whispered: "I hear breathing." It was Agamemnon, standing less than three yards away, just looking at the jeep. He sniffed around for a few minutes and then was gone, as silently as he had come.

In the beginning Tabs was a bit nervous around the lions, but on this occasion she didn't seem at all worried. By now she had come to accept them as part of our everyday life; as my job, in fact.

And she accepts all the dangers and discomforts of living in the bush. If she gets a thorn in her foot, she doesn't come limping to Charlotte, she simply sits down and removes it herself.

She wasn't even unduly upset when we were charged by an elephant not long ago. I was driving the jeep and Tabs was in the back with Charlotte and a tracker, Mandaban. Something made them look back and they saw an enormous elephant with his trunk raised, coming straight for the car.

I stepped on the gas and went right down the nearest riverbed and up the other side, disregarding the fact that the jeep had no brakes at all at this stage. The elephant didn't bother to follow us once we got out of his path. He stayed over on the far side of the riverbed, flapping his ears and wildly waving his trunk.

It was frightening, but only momentarily so. It was all part of living in the bush.

THE MACHATON LIONS, too, steer well clear of elephants. I've seen Tabby lead her cubs quickly away, closely followed by Agamemnon, when elephants came bursting through the trees. Animals fear the known, and elephants are a known danger. But animals do not fear the unknown—even when it could be lethal. One afternoon I saw the lions with rhinos, recently reintroduced to the area after eighty years, and their reaction was quite surprising.

Tabby and her brood, accompanied by Dimples, were lying on open sand near the Machaton when two rhinos, a bull and a teenager, appeared about two hundred yards away. They came snuffling and shuffling downwind towards the lions, pausing now and again to crop the short grass. Tabby and Dimples both sat up for a brief look, then slumped to the ground and went back to sleep, obviously quite unconcerned.

Not so Temba, Tombi and Vela. All three immediately began to "stalk" the rhinos. Flattening their ears and creeping along on their stomachs, they moved from bush to bush. Still the rhinos advanced. With their poor eyesight they had no inkling that the lion cubs, two white and one tawny, were tracking them. Eventually the stalkers tired of the sport.

The cubs' behaviour was not too surprising. Unaware of any danger, they were merely playing a game. But I was amazed at Tabby's reaction. Not even when her cubs were more than fifty yards away from her, and well within a quick thrust of those highly lethal rhino horns, did she seem to show any concern.

Does this indicate that the "race memory" of animals is relatively short? That the instinctive fear which lions are believed to have for a dangerous and formidable enemy had disappeared during the eighty years that rhinos had been absent from this area? It is possible, of course, that lions never had any deep-

54

seated fear of rhinos, but we have no way of knowing for certain.

By the same token, some people believe that, in time, lions may develop an instinctive fear of man's vehicles, since in some places they are constantly hunted from jeeps. If so, this would pose an almost insoluble problem for new generations of game wardens and wildlife experts, because it is not possible to approach lions on foot closely enough to study their behaviour. It could happen, but on the evolutionary time scale it would probably take thousands of years.

BY EARLY JANUARY the heat was as intense as the grass was lush. Pans of water gleamed like broken mirrors across the landscape, and the grazing and browsing animals wandered far afield and thrived. The lions had to travel a good deal farther and work a lot harder for a living and, in turn, it became much more difficult to find them.

One moonless night I sat outside the camp with pipe, candle, compass, aerial photographs, pen and notebook, and a teakettle on the fire nearby. I wanted to record lion roars. In all, I have now collected more than a hundred and sixty nights of roar data.

That night, the first roar came at five minutes before twelve, followed almost immediately by another. In a little more than four hours, I logged thirty-three roars. They came from at least four groups of lions up to three miles apart.

Then around 5:00 a.m. I heard a single roar that sounded fairly close to camp. This was followed by a lot of snarling and growling that could mean only one thing—a kill.

Quickly I took a compass bearing and jumped into the jeep. Just before setting out, I heard Achilles and Agamemnon roaring a long way from the kill. Generally, the two big males find out about a kill from the roaring of the females. The males make their leisurely way to it, confident that they will be offered what has come to be known as "the lion's share".

In the faint light of false dawn, I drove straight through the bush and ten minutes later found the kill, a wildebeest. Six lions were wrestling over it—Golden and Tabby, the Three Musketeers and Suzie Wong. Off to one side a lone hyena waited respectfully. To the other side a pair of jackals, less respectful, kept trying to dart in. A few paces away, watching enviously from the dewy grass, were Temba, Tombi and Vela. Temba decided to try his luck, but one of the Musketeers jumped on him with a warning snarl. Instantly, Tabby left her position at the kill and led her cubs to safety.

The wildebeest had almost been demolished when, to the left, I heard a single low roar—Achilles. Only a hundred yards away, and for once without Agamemnon. Since his last roar, he'd travelled almost two miles to get to the kill. Now only fifty yards off, Achilles began to strut. Head up, chest out, he approached with the measured gait of a grenadier. Seeing him, young Suzie Wong slunk away. When he was within ten paces, her brothers and Golden followed suit.

The sun rising behind him, Achilles stood over the carcass. He lifted his head and roared so loudly that the jeep vibrated. His breath came in puffs of steam. He roared again, then bent to sniff at the tangle of skin and bones. Arrogantly, as though to indicate that what was left was not worthy of his attention, he sauntered off to urinate against a nearby bush, marking the place out as his territory.

AROUND THIS TIME, we had a couple of visits from photographers and film crews, for inevitably the news of our white lions had begun to leak out. It wasn't always easy to find the lions at short notice, especially during the rainy season, but usually an all-night vigil, listening for roars, led to the rediscovery of the pride.

Achilles and Agamemnon almost always roar in concert, and by now I could identify them because Agamemnon has a most distinctive roar. A male lion's roar begins low in his chest and wells up, exploding into a bellow followed by a series of loud grunts, often as many as thirty. The grunts sound something like the word *gum* (the bushman's word for lion, in fact), with a very gutteral *g*. Often Agamemnon's next-to-last grunt was much longer than the others.

On one occasion some cameramen and I found the males in an unforgettable setting. In the soft light of early morning they lazed on open sand with Golden, the Musketeers and Suzie Wong. Soon the sound of a waterbuck plunging through a nearby bed of reeds sent Golden off on an exploratory stalk. A cold breeze began to blow and, perhaps with shelter rather than waterbuck in mind, the Musketeers also trailed into the reeds.

Achilles rose to join the procession. As he paced purposefully away, I knew I couldn't simply let him slip from view—not with three eager telephoto lenses trained on him. When he was ten or fifteen yards from the reeds, I tried to mimic a lion's call. Pitch and volume must have been right. Achilles stopped. He turned broadside to us, feet together, great maned head high, tail curved. He listened intently.

With the trees and reeds behind him, he made a superb portrait, and the cameras clicked and rolled. Then, hearing nothing further, he continued his march and was swallowed up by the reeds.

Next Agamemnon, always the last to stir, was on his way. "Try it again," a cameraman urged.

Hearing my low imitation of a lion, the father of Temba, Tombi and Vela turned to face the jeep. He seemed even more intrigued than Achilles had been.

"Here he comes." We said it almost in unison as the enormous maned head advanced. Agamemnon strode straight towards the jeep.

"Make that sound again, and you'll have him right in here with us," someone whispered. I kept my mouth shut, and Agamemnon prowled past so close that we could almost have touched him. His burning yellow eyes were fixed on a clump of bushes beyond the jeep, and he looked rather puzzled when he found no lions waiting there. Quickly he sprayed the shrubbery, and sauntered off.

Beneath a great old tree he paused to cast one more look at the place where he thought he'd heard a lion's call. Then he, too, went off into the gently rustling reeds.

CHAPTER SIX

To understand lions, you first have to look at the species upon which they prey; then at the trees and shrubs and grasses on which their prey feed. And to understand these, you have to get to the root of the matter, literally—to soils, nutrients and micro-organisms.

To put it another way, the number of lions and other predators in any given location is controlled primarily by the number of prey. These, in turn, are controlled by the habitat—by the availability of food and water, the nature of the grass and other factors.

In this part of Africa there was once a complete, natural ecosystem. The animals evolved in their own way, each species finding a niche for itself in the scheme of things. And, by one method or another, each species helped to sustain the others, controlling its own population growth and in some cases limiting the growth of others so that a perfect balance was achieved and maintained for millions of years.

Even the predators in the area never seriously competed with one another. The leopard, for example, hunts alone at night in the thick riverine bush. Sometimes it ambushes its prey from an overhead branch and takes the kill back up into the tree to feed on it. Like the lion, the leopard is a stalker, but it uses a different part of the terrain, and in general goes for smaller animals such as duiker, steinbok, baboon and impala.

The cheetah hunts by day and relies heavily on its phenomenal speed. Cheetahs lack the powerful jaws and the extending claws of the lions and leopards. But this does not seriously handicap them. They are ideally equipped to outrun their favourite prey, the impala. And because they depend on speed rather than camouflage to pull down their prey, they hunt almost entirely in the open plains.

The hunting habits of the Machaton lions place them almost exactly between the leopard and the cheetah. They work as a pride and avoid both the thick bush and the open plains, hunting instead in the fringe of the bush. This gives them enough cover for stalking and enough room to manoeuvre as a pride. In general they go for animals like wildebeest, which are big enough to feed a pride or a large sub-group. But, occasionally they will venture onto the plains and kill an impala, thus slightly overlapping the cheetah's territory.

To sum up, the whole scheme has developed in such a way as to minimize competition and produce a very stable social system, far more stable than any of our own making.

A natural ecosystem is very much like a chain: each organism has its own role to play and is, in some way, linked to or dependent on certain others. For example, there is the aardvark. It makes holes in termitaria (anthills) in order to get at the termites, which form its staple diet. In turn, these holes are used by warthogs who sleep in them at night. Sometimes the warthogs are ousted by hyenas who use the holes as a safe place to drop their cubs. In the meantime, the surviving termites carry on their own highly organized social existence in the untouched part of the anthill.

Incidentally, warthogs normally back into anthills, presumably as a precaution against predators. One evening Charlotte and I walked past an anthill in which we spotted an aardvark hole. I looked in and a face peered back at me—a face with tusks. I suspected that the animal would come rushing out, so I shouted a warning to Charlotte and jumped out of the way. The warthog came rocketing out, closely followed by another . . . and another . . . and yet another. . . . We stood aside in disbelief as eight warthogs came bursting out of that den.

Warthogs also root up areas of grassland, exposing a certain type of corm, or bulb, on which the francolin live, so if there were fewer warthogs, there'd be fewer francolin. In turn, all sorts of

When kills were infrequent,
the cubs would look
alarmingly thin.

The affectionate Tabby
never showed the
slightest sign of preferring
her tawny cub, Vela.

Agamemnon largely ignored his cubs
and left Tabby to care for them.

A kill is served in very strict order:
first the males; then the lionesses; then the juniors;
and finally the cubs.

creatures live off the eggs of the francolin and indeed off the francolin itself.

Then there's the dung beetle. By some mysterious form of chemical communication, this extraordinary insect can detect from afar the location of fresh dung. The beetles arrive in vast numbers on the scene, and lay their eggs in a patch of dung. Then they roll the dung into balls, push the balls away, and bury them in a safe place.

Thus, these beetles break up the dung and spread it so that it can nourish the earth. Without them the dung would bake hard in the hot African sun and could not be absorbed into the soil. Presumably there is also a creature that lives on dung beetles, though I haven't encountered it yet. There's bound to be, because in an ideal ecosystem every niche is filled.

When man came along and started building cities and towns and roads and airstrips and fences, the entire ecosystem of this part of Africa collapsed. It now exists only in isolated areas like Timbavati where wildlife management maintains and fosters it in an artificial environment.

Consider the simplest, most basic need: water. In the early days if a severe drought occurred in one area, the animals would simply migrate to another, where they could find water. They can't now, because of the fences, and so we have to provide them with water artificially. When the Timbavati Reserve was formed there was one natural perennial spring in the lions' range, but there are now a number of man-made dams. Also, two of our lions' favourite watering holes, Piggy Dam and the marsh known as the Bulrushes, are windmill-fed. This is wildlife management at its most basic level.

But wildlife management goes farther and deeper than that. We must first try to understand the delicate balance in nature. For instance, it is marvellous how efficiently the animals of Timbavati utilize the habitat. The giraffe is a top-level browser and eats the leaves from the tops of the trees. The kudu, a mid-level browser, eats leaves a bit lower down. Lowest of the browsers is the tiny steinbok.

Then come the grazing animals. The buffalo is the only grazer that can comfortably handle the thick strands of perennial grass. These it eats and tramples down, opening up the lower levels of grass to other animals, such as the wildebeest, which prefers a shorter, sweeter grass.

When Timbavati was fenced off there was an immediate deterioration in the habitat which was reflected, paradoxically, by an increase in the number of impala. They are both browsers and grazers; they will eat virtually anything that grows. So within a fenced area, they soon eat everything available. As a result, the more selective grazers suffer, being forced to roam farther afield in search of food.

In good years, when there is plenty of rainfall and consequently plenty of vegetation, there is enough for all the species. But in 1964 during a severe drought, Timbavati lost many rare animals, such as the roan sable antelope. The impala demolished their food supply and the fence prevented their migration outside the reserve. A small herd of roan sable antelope is now being kept in a special fenced-off area until there are enough of them to be released with some chance of survival.

There's no point in trying to reintroduce a species to an area until you have first established what its specific requirements are, and then improved the habitat so that it is capable of supporting the species. But to do all of this successfully, there must be more research into ecology.

Sometimes a threatened species is one you would expect to be among the hardiest—for instance, the Cape vulture. In the past, the vulture parents took bone chips back to the nest for their chicks. Now, in some areas, the hyenas that once crushed the bones of a kill into small fragments have disappeared. No other predator —not even a lion—can crush bones like a hyena. And as a result, vulture chicks are dying from a calcium deficiency. Some are so weak that they fall to the ground when they try their first flight. Bits of stone and even white china have been found in nests, an indication that the parents are searching—desperately and in vain —for new sources of calcium.

MY OWN ATTITUDE to the problem of protecting wildlife has changed fundamentally as a result of my studies in America. In wildlife management circles around the world, the traditional concept of preservation, which focused on saving the animals themselves, has now given way to an emphasis on conservation, which focuses attention on the habitat. If you lose a few animals here or there through snaring or poaching, or through some farmer notching up two hundred plus lions, as one boasts he has done, it's disgraceful—but it's not that significant. These actions have no long-term effect on the animal population. What we really need to concern ourselves with is the state of the environment.

And to get the environment, the habitat, into a state that will support the widest possible variety of life, I now realize you have to accept the need for culling.

Culling is still a controversial, hot-under-the-collar word to preservationists. The very idea of shooting wild animals to conserve them seems a contradiction in terms. Yet modern conservationists know that in areas subject to periodic drought, surplus animals must be culled. In an artificial environment, culling cannot be left to predators, calf mortality rate and other natural causes.

Timbavati at present has too many impala and giraffe. If some of them are not removed, many will surely die in the next drought, but not before they have irreversibly damaged the habitat. Surplus animals, even in normal years, can wreck an environment by overgrazing or overbrowsing—to the detriment of other species as well. The overgrazed surface is trampled loose, and precious topsoil that took a hundred years to build up is washed away by the first heavy rains. Next, inferior vegetation takes over. If this in turn is overgrazed, the ultimate result is a desert.

Culling would not only improve the habitat, but it would also bring in a certain amount of revenue. Every part of the impala, for example, can be sold: the meat; the hides; the bones; even the hooves, which are sent to Japan and made into gelatin for glue. The reserve could then use this revenue for further wildlife management projects.

At the moment there is a direct clash between conservationists and preservationists. The trouble is that land-owners favouring animal preservation can wreck a whole scheme by refusing to allow any shooting on their land. This prevents any planned effort at overall conservation. I'm not specifically referring to Timbavati here. Timbavati is only one of dozens of reserves, private and national, in southern Africa, and the people who run them are by no means united in their views.

But conservation cannot be approached piecemeal. If it's going to work at all, it must be instituted on a grand scale, on a scientific basis.

And it must be done soon. Otherwise it will be too late.

CHAPTER SEVEN

Late in March the cameramen paid us another visit: Mike Holmes, a freelance writer and still-life photographer who assisted me in recording the early development of the white cubs; and Mike Burts, a film cameraman from Johannesburg.

For two full days we jolted and bounced around in the jeep, pursuing pictures that are a wildlife photographer's dream. In the dew of early morning the plains were laced with spiderwebs, woven to catch the midges, flies, mosquitoes and butterflies that flitted above the flats. One long-legged black and yellow spider had spun a magnificent web right across our path. As we approached, the two Mikes saw the spider gather up the lower part of the web—almost like a curtain being raised—and we passed safely beneath. Then the spider dropped its silky skein back into place again.

Not a sign of lions that first day. Most of the next day was no different. It was cold and grey. We peered into the riverine bush where the lions take shelter in bad weather. Still nothing. Late in the afternoon, Mike Holmes happened to glance back towards a tributary of the Machaton. A young lion sat under a shingayi watching the departing jeep. It was one of the Three Musketeers. We could get no closer and it was nearly dusk. But at least we had a starting point in the morning.

Back at camp that evening we heard lions roaring from three different places within a few minutes. Charlotte and I plotted the approximate positions on our map. Then we joined our guests for an open-air *braaivleis*, a bush-style barbecue. A leadwood fire burning down to glowing embers in a sand pit gave a warm and cheerful light.

"I'm sure the white cubs are with the middle group," Charlotte announced with her uncanny instinct for the bush.

The following morning we left camp before breakfast. Fifteen minutes later we were at the place Charlotte had advised. As the jeep clattered up an incline, Mike Burts whispered excitedly, "There they are!"

Tabby and the cubs were walking obliquely away from us about sixty yards to the right. Off to the side were two of the Musketeers, hobnobbing for the first time with Tabby's cubs.

At six months Temba and Tombi were no longer the snowy white of their early days but they were still undeniably white. I felt confident now that they wouldn't turn tawny. Parts of the pelt that are darker on ordinary lions—like the ridge of the back or the tip of the tail—were now cream or a light dusty brown on Temba and Tombi. Elsewhere they were still as white as polar bears.

Luckily Tabby chose to rest in the open for two precious minutes and the photographers worked fast. Then the extraordinary family was on its way again, the cubs trotting contentedly along at Tabby's heels. We trundled along after them.

Just before reaching a thicket, Tabby stopped in three-foot grass. Tombi, who was nearest, squatted down beside her mother and suckled briefly. So, at six months, the cubs were still being nursed, although they had eaten meat from their earliest weeks.

I alerted the photographers to the possibility of drama should one of the Musketeers venture too close to Temba, Tombi or Vela. Tabby was lying on her stomach and the cubs sat and paced, sat and paced. Temba and Tombi stood out clearly through the grass; Tabby and Vela were almost invisible.

Briefly one of the Musketeers came into view in the background. At once Tabby stood up between him and her brood, baring her teeth and giving a low rumbling growl. Feigning nonchalance but taking the hint, the Musketeer stalked down to the riverbed. Soon afterwards, Tabby and the restless cubs followed and were gone.

WHEN WE SAW THEM next, they were again with the Musketeers. This was strange. Previously, Tabby had kept the Musketeers at bay, realizing that they constituted a menace to her young. They and their sister Suzie Wong belonged to another sub-group led by their mother, Golden. On many occasions this sub-group was accompanied by Scarleg, who acted as nursemaid and helped with the hunting.

It seemed that Golden had thrown her "teenagers" out, possibly because she was expecting another litter of cubs herself. When Temba, Tombi and Vela were nine months—old enough to look after themselves—Tabby allowed the Musketeers and Suzie Wong to join her sub-group, though she has always exercised complete dominance over them. Time and again I've seen them making submissive gestures to her.

Tabby and Dimples continued to do all the hunting. They had to. The Musketeers still hadn't a clue about stalking; they were pathetically bad at it. They were virtually defenceless when they attached themselves to Tabby. But they'd have to learn fairly quickly because they were due to be thrown out altogether in four or six months.

It seemed probable that Suzie Wong, who had grown up into a very attractive young lioness, would stay on as part of the pride. I wouldn't be surprised if she mated with Achilles or Agamemnon anytime now. She is the daughter of one of them, obviously, but incest is not uncommon among lions.

Indeed, it could be one explanation for the appearance of the white cubs. I have no way of knowing how old Achilles and Agamemnon are, though I can see through binoculars that Agamemnon's teeth are well worn, so obviously he is not young. Certainly he could be Tabby's father or grandfather. Thus, if a white recessive gene exists among these lions and you have a father mating with his own daughter or grand-daughter, the chances of the white strain appearing are naturally increased.

BY NOW WE KNEW the cubs quite well. Tombi, the white female, was very like her mother, extremely casual. She was much more timid than Temba, and like Tabby, not really interested in either us or the jeep. She just accepted us and, for the most part, ignored us.

Temba was constantly in trouble; he was always getting minor wounds and injuries. On a kill he still blundered in without thinking and frequently got a good sharp clip from one of the older lions. He was not so much aggressive as foolhardy, slaphappy even.

Vela, the tawny one, wasn't nearly as adventurous as the other two cubs in the early days, but he seemed to have caught up with them and even to have overtaken them. He'd grown into a very handsome, very spunky little lion, and he had quite a respectable mane now, which was more than Temba could boast.

In this part of the world there are naturally maneless male lions as well as lions with black manes, blond manes, and rufous manes. At ten months, Temba grew the beginnings of a slightly sandy-coloured mane, but when it was nearly nine inches long it disappeared. This may have something to do with the fact that he is white—we just don't know.

BY THIS TIME we could find the lions relatively easily by scouting around their favourite resting place in the jeep. Nevertheless, I continued to walk the bush—partly to keep up my spooring techniques and mostly because I've never been able to get over the thrill of watching lions on foot. It's a completely different

Opposite: *Achilles and Agamemnon frequently sit back to back, like a pair of bookends.*

69

experience—you are in their world, on the same scale with them.

On one occasion recently, Mandaban, the tracker, and I were following spoor. When we knew we were getting close to lions, we split up and I inched forward carefully. Suddenly I caught a glimpse of white under a tree—one of the white cubs looking right at me.

This was a tense situation. I spotted Tabby nearby. If we happened to wake her, she would almost certainly charge; lionesses with cubs invariably do if someone approaches on foot. The sensible thing would have been to withdraw quietly, then return later with the jeep.

But for a few minutes I couldn't find Mandaban, and of course I couldn't call out for fear of awakening Tabby. Then I discovered that he'd walked within twenty yards of her. He had stopped a bit farther on and was looking at the two pride males, Achilles and Agamemnon, also fast asleep. They were clearly recovering from an enormous meal, fortunately, and not likely to wake up in a hurry.

He withdrew quietly, without having seen either the white cubs, thirty yards to his left, or Tabby. It was just sheer luck that the lioness didn't awaken.

Sheer luck and the natural greed of lions, for when they make a big kill, they eat enormous amounts of meat. I've seen Agamemnon so full that he can hardly stand; panting heavily, saliva dripping from his jaws, he's obviously extremely uncomfortable. He doesn't move. He simply lies there, with a stomach like a balloon that's about to burst.

This ability to gorge could be an advantage in areas where food is scarce. Lions, completely gorged, can last for about a week, if they have to, without another meal.

Here, of course, food is abundant all year round. The animals tend to eat whatever is immediately available and make no provision for the morrow. In more northern climates, animals like squirrels store food against the possibility of a harsh winter, because if they didn't they might not survive. In this part of Africa, though, the sun shines most of the time; there is no real winter, and no need to plan ahead.

70

IN JULY 1976 I was forced to shoot one of the Musketeers. It had been about three weeks since I'd seen the white lions. My field work had come to an end and I had temporarily taken on the job of game warden for Timbavati. With my new duties, I hadn't had time to keep track of the lions. Also, I was now based in a different camp, farther away from their range.

In order to find them again as rapidly as possible, I decided to sleep out on the plains. With Mandaban and a friend of his, I planned to spend the night in the back of an open pickup truck, listening for roars. (There was no way that three adults would be able to stretch out in the caged jeep.)

But the lions weren't roaring that night and eventually we all dropped off to sleep. About 2:00 a.m. Mandaban started to nudge me and whisper urgently in my ear. I woke up to find that the lions were all around us. We hadn't found them—they'd found us.

They were right on top of us: the Three Musketeers, Tabby, the two white cubs and Vela, and probably Dimples and Suzie Wong.

My first instinct was to remain as quiet as possible and not do anything. But as the minutes ticked away, the situation became more and more terrifying. They were so close. If one of them had taken it into his head to leap aboard the pickup, we'd have been finished.

In similar situations in the past I had always found that if I stood up suddenly the lions would slink away, just as they do when you approach them on foot. I decided that was the safest thing to do now. Then, as soon as they withdrew, we'd leap out and run around to the cab, where we would at least have some protection.

I whispered to the others to be ready, and then stood up, making quite a noise in the process. The lions all fled—except one of the Three Musketeers, who began by making a mock charge that landed him within six paces of the truck. I was still acutely aware of all the lessons I had learned from Jack. This was a moment to stand firm and exude confidence and force the lion to back away.

But on this occasion I had only a small rifle with me, which would never have stopped that Musketeer if he'd started to spring. I knew that, and I suppose he sensed something of my fear. For what seemed like hours I stood there, the inadequate rifle cocked and pointed at him, the animal crouched for a spring—front paws stretched out, head low on the ground, hind quarters slightly raised.

I didn't know for sure whether he was going to spring or not, but I couldn't afford to take the chance. If he had come at us, he would have landed right in the back of the pickup and would have taken at least one of us with him.

So I fired.

I've spent endless hours questioning myself about this and doubting my actions. Would he have sprung if I had held my fire for another second or two? Or would he have given up and slunk away into the bush? I just don't know. It was bad judgment going out without the proper gun; with a small gun you don't have the luxury of taking a chance. There were also two other lives involved.

So I fired.

I got him in the shoulder and he dropped. When we skinned him the next day, we found that he had a nasty festering wound near the base of his spine, which could have accounted for his aggressive behaviour. I had known this lion for more than a year and a half; I had watched him grow up and had taken over sixty photographs of him and never felt even remotely threatened before.

I was extremely sick about the whole incident.

THE FACT THAT I was so desperately upset about shooting one lion in what really amounted to self-defence underlines the huge change that has taken place in man's attitude towards shooting predators.

I discussed this subject at length with a man called Gustav Battenhausen who had a camp here in the early 1940s, when killing lions was regarded as something of a lark.

In those days, there were only three other land-owners in the area. One was a fellow I'll simply call Jan. He was fond of boasting that in his first year here he notched up eighty lions, including one that he shot while sitting at dinner. He was in the middle of his meal when he spotted a pair of eyes outside the rondavel. From their height and distance apart, he knew they were the eyes of a lion. He simply shot at the eyes and killed the lion—without even bothering to stand up.

There was another farmer, we'll call him Moss, in the Timbavati district around this time. He went out one night after some lions with a party of eight, including Battenhausen, who told me about it. Moss spotted a lion in the beam of his flashlight and fired. The lion sank down, then started to rise again, growling ferociously.

Moss started to walk towards it, and as there's nothing in the world more dangerous than a wounded lion, two members of the party fired shots into the animal. Moss turned and shouted at them: "Stop making holes in my lion skin." Then, crouched down close to the dying animal. "This is the best bait we're ever likely to get," he said.

After a few moments, a lioness came out of the bush, attracted by the roars of the dying lion. Moss put two shots into her. She ran off; then fell about fifty paces away, still very much alive. Moss walked right up to the lioness and shot her dead at point-blank range. He then killed his "bait", saying, "Well, I think that will do us for one evening."

Lowveld people were tough in those days, and they had their own very strict rules of conduct.

An unforgivable crime was to leave a lion wounded in the bush. If you wounded one, it was your responsibility to finish it off there and then.

That's what Hans did. He was managing a large cattle ranch just outside Timbavati. Since he didn't much like the isolated life, "he got himself married", as Battenhausen put it, and brought his bride down to live in the camp with him. During the honeymoon Hans went hunting one night and wounded a lioness. As he

73

was tracking the animal down, he happened to go right past his own camp.

His wife came out and joined the hunters. Hans warned her it was a very dangerous business, and told her to stay well behind. Unfortunately, they walked right past the wounded lioness. She charged and Hans's wife, last in line, was knocked down.

Hans shot the lioness right there as it crouched on top of the woman. Then he pulled the lioness off her and asked if she was all right. There wasn't a mark on her, but she said that she felt very strange. Hans took her straight to the hospital, where they discovered that her liver had been completely smashed. The woman died that night.

Battenhausen also told me about a couple who had a luxury camp, fully fenced in and equipped with a swimming pool. One day they hired a servant.

The next morning the servant got up, lit her lantern and went into the kitchen to make coffee, followed, she thought, by the camp dog. A few minutes later she came bursting into the main rondavel where the man and his wife were, saying that she had been in the kitchen with the dog when suddenly a lion had walked in.

Having calmed her down a bit, the wife explained that they didn't happen to have a dog. They went back to the kitchen and found *two* lions there. Not only that, but there were fifteen lions in all inside the enclosure, prowling around and drinking out of the swimming pool. The man got a jeep, rounded them up and forced them back out through a hole in the enclosure which had been made by elephants.

As these stories point out, lions are completely unpredictable. There are times when a pack of hyenas can chase a pride of lions off a kill. There are other times when a lioness will claw a vulture out of the sky, simply because the vulture is irritating her. People who live with lions all their lives—zoo curators, for example— always emphasize this utter unpredictability, even in captivity: it is the lion you trust most that is likely to lash out one day and gash your arm.

74

CHAPTER EIGHT

As early as May 1976, some eight months after we found the white cubs, I discovered that Scarleg had two new cubs. They were normal, tawny cubs, and very small—no bigger than large rabbits. I saw only two, but I sensed that there were almost certainly others.

Then, in August, while driving with friends near Piggy Dam, I spotted the spoor of several lionesses and cubs. We followed the tracks across the river, where we came upon four lionesses and about ten cubs. At first we couldn't count the cubs because they were all bunched together and tripping under the feet of the lionesses. I was surprised that there were so many.

The group ran off along the river bank, and stopped under a shingayi tree.

Suddenly one of my friends said, "There's one of the white ones."

I was a bit doubtful because I couldn't see any sign of Tabby. After a few minutes the cubs began to move out, one by one, from the shade and straight towards us. The sixth cub to emerge was white, only about six weeks old—every bit as white as Temba and Tombi had been at that age.

We called the new cub Phuma (pronounced Poo-ma) from the Zulu for "to stand out" or "to be out of the ordinary". After observing it a few more times, we knew it was female.

Three of the lionesses were Golden, Scarleg and Suzie Wong. The fourth one had me puzzled. It could have been either Greta or Lona, one of the two that we seldom saw with the pride. Which of the four, I wondered, had given birth to the new white cub? There was no way of telling. Cubs will suckle indiscriminately on any lactating lioness. I have had to resign myself to the fact that we are never going to know.

Once I recovered from the shock of finding another white cub, I studied more closely the remaining nine cubs in the pride. There seemed to be a distinct gradation of colour from the normal tawny gold, through various pale blond shades, to the pure white of Phuma.

I've seen Phuma about thirty times so far. Already she appears to have far more spirit than the other two white cubs. We've even observed her tripping up a Musketeer on one of the rare occasions when the two sub-groups were together. She's extremely aggressive on a kill, chasing all the other cubs off until she's had her fill, and she's very cocky towards our vehicles. She's the one that always comes closest.

In September, as they approached their first birthday, Tabby's cubs were also thriving. Seen in silhouette alongside Tombi, Temba's body seems heavier, his chest deeper, his jaw fuller. Tombi is sleeker, her face sharper, her coat slightly whiter. Vela is rapidly losing the darker spots of a normal baby lion. The three are clearly still pals. I've seen minor friction, never a serious clash.

We saw them again just before the rains came. Four vultures sitting on a tree gave us a sure sign of a kill. We parked, waited, and eventually heard a lot of growling and snapping. We found them on a wildebeest kill—two Musketeers, Dimples, Tabby and her three cubs, all as fat as butter and in prime condition.

By this time, even Phuma, at four and a half months, was past the first perilous period of a lion cub's life.

BY NOW I HAD spent two·years in the Lowveld living with the lions, and I found myself deeply involved in two issues. One was the future of Timbavati itself. The more I learn about the place, the more it seems to me that it should be preserved exactly as it is. All around us this ancient area of Africa is slowly being eaten into by civilization. But here, there has been little interruption in the pattern of evolution since long before the dawn of our species.

Opposite: *Phuma was named from the Zulu "to stand out" or "to be out of the ordinary".*

In this part of the world, almost five and a half million years ago, *Australopithecus* evolved, a discovery made by Raymond Dart about a hundred miles north of Timbavati. These predecessors of man were probably only about five feet tall and weighed no more than one hundred and thirty pounds, but they walked erect and could use their hands to construct simple tools and weapons.

About a million years ago *Australopithecus* was succeeded by *Homo erectus*, one of the first varieties of true man. He used his brain to discover the potential of fire and began to change the world in which he found himself. Thus this whole area of Africa must be regarded as one of the very cradles of the human race. It is also one of the few areas where modern man has intervened without destroying all the wild creatures around him.

In the words of King George VI, taken as the motto of the Timbavati Reserve, "This wildlife of today is not ours to dispose of as we please. We have it in trust. We must account for it to those who come after."

My other, and even more urgent, concern is the future of the white lions. They are beautiful. They were irresistible as cubs, and I am eager to ensure the survival of the strain.

From an evolutionary point of view, it might be said that the white lions are largely a curiosity. There are now white tigers in zoos in Delhi, Bristol and Washington, all bred from one white male tiger who was found in the wild, and was mated with his grand-daughter and in turn with her offspring. The propagation of these white tigers has been man-managed. Theoretically, successive generations of white tigers would never occur in the wild because it is not an advantage for a tiger—or a lion, as I have already mentioned—to be white.

On the other hand, the steady gradation from tawny to white among the Machaton pride indicates that there is a gene here that tends to work towards a white strain.

Natural selection usually prevents brother and sister lions from mating with each other in the wild. So it is unlikely that Temba and Tombi would ever mate unless they are put together in some sort of enclosure. But once they've been in such an artificial

78

environment, there would be very little chance that they would ever be accepted back into the pride.

Temba and Vela, as males, will face their most critical period when they are between two and three years old. Until they are around two they will be almost entirely dependent on Tabby and the other lionesses of the pride, who will do all their hunting for them. As the cubs approach the age of three, Achilles and Agamemnon may start regarding them as rivals, particularly sexual rivals. The cubs, whether white or tawny, would stand very little chance against the adult lions.

Temba and Vela will most likely become nomads, living either together or separately, looking for their own worlds to conquer. Temba, if he walked out of the pride alone, could well be sentencing himself to death by starvation. His white coat would stand out like a beacon at night and he couldn't possibly hope for the hunting success of an ordinary lion.

Outside the Machaton range other hazards await. To the east lies the Kruger National Park with many prides of lions of its own. To the north and south are other Timbavati prides, each with their own fiercely protective males. Southwest lie the greatest dangers of all: the guns of the farmers who think of all lions, regardless of their colouring, as a threat to their cattle and little more.

One man in the area has actually been known to lure the lions towards his fence by playing a tape recording of lions roaring. When they approach to investigate, he shoots them. Whenever I found lions' spoor near this man's land, I used to set up my own tape recordings of lions roaring and try to lure them away. It's extraordinary how well it works: they will often come right up to the jeep to see what's going on.

Another cruel threat is the trophy hunter. A white lion skin would be quite a conversation piece stretched out on somebody's living-room floor. And there's nothing to stop a relentless hunter from stalking and claiming such a trophy. Once outside the sanctuary of the reserve, the lions are unprotected by law.

The chances of Tombi and Phuma surviving in the wild seem a

little less grim. When lionesses reach maturity, they are quite often allowed to remain in the pride. Since their unique colouring doesn't seem to have aroused any hostility among the other lionesses, it is likely that they will continue to be accepted.

I've often wondered whether the best idea wouldn't be to hedge our bets and send the white male, Temba, off to a zoo now, quickly, before he is thrown out of the pride and exposed to the dangers outside the protection of the reserve; and while he is still young enough to settle down in a zoo. If we did that, it would provide revenue for the reserve for use in its wildlife management programme. The funds could also be used to purchase electronic tracking and monitoring equipment to enable us to keep in constant touch with Tombi and Phuma.

In this way we would have the best of two worlds. Breeding experiments could be carried out with Temba in a zoo, under controlled conditions. And, at the same time, we would still have two white lions in the wild to continue to study.

If Tombi is not thrown out by the pride, there would be a strong possibility of her mating with Agamemnon, and there might well be further white cubs. In the meantime Phuma would also be growing up in the wild, and we would have another chance because she too might mate with Agamemnon, or even with some other pride male—possibly Vela—who could well carry the white gene.

In this way we would at least be doing everything in our power to ensure that this is not the end, but only the beginning of the story of the white lions of Timbavati.

EDITORIAL POSTSCRIPT. LONDON. AUGUST 1977

A week before the hardback publication of his book in England, Chris McBride came to London to be "lionized" not only by the media but also by the general public whose imagination had already been caught by news of the cubs' discovery. Chris brought Charlotte and Tabitha with him, but left his seven-month-old son Robert at home in the care of Mr. and Mrs. McBride Senior.

For the three travelling McBrides, it was the start of an intensive publicity tour throughout the British Isles, a prelude to similar tours in America, Australia and their home country. I was fortunate to meet them on their first day of public appearances. All three were looking thoroughly relaxed and at home in the spacious flat hired for them by their publishers as, over "elevenses", Chris brought me up to date with the present plight of his lions.

A great deal has happened since he completed his manuscript. It all began with the disappearance of Agamemnon. It seems that, about eight months ago, the old leader of the pride just vanished— perhaps he died, perhaps he was shot or possibly he just wandered off into the African sunset. Then, Achilles—presumably because he could not bear to live amid the same old haunts without his friend—moved away to join a neighbouring pride.

The original pride was promptly taken over by two young males and by the Interloper, a mysterious lion that had appeared from nowhere to take the place of the shot Musketeer. Thereafter Temba, Tombi, Vela and their mother splintered from the pride and the risk to the young lions' survival grew enormously. Within three months, their mother grew tired of supporting them and began to abandon them for long periods. Throughout June, Chris tracked them and fed them almost every night. In order to summon them, he taught them to recognize Beethoven's Triple Concerto which he would play from a tape recorder in his jeep and beam over a three-mile radius by means of an amplifier and loud-hailer.

With Chris's unflagging devotion, the young lions might yet have prospered. However, towards the end of June, the Interloper began to court their mother, and seriously threaten their existence. The situation was desperate. Chris was forced to request the Department of Nature Conservation and Wildlife for permission to bring the young lions into captivity. On 27th July, the trio were painlessly darted with a short-term sedative and brought to a temporary enclosure near the McBrides' camp. On 12th August they were hoisted by helicopter to permanent safety in the National Zoological Gardens in Pretoria.

When I spoke to Chris, the young lions were still in isolation, under special observation to ensure that they were not suffering from any diseases that might affect the other animals in the zoo. Their present enclosure, destined to become their permanent home, does however sound idyllic: five acres no less, comprising a *kopje* or small hill surrounded by a moat. The privacy thus provided is such that the lions are often quite hidden—nice for them but perhaps not so nice for the crowds that will undoubtedly flock to see them once the enclosure is no longer in isolation.

"I couldn't be more happy with their new home," Chris told me. "They are going to be looked after by people who really love and understand lions." The finest veterinary research station in all South Africa (Onderstepoort) is close at hand. Also nearby is the Mammal Research Institute and Pretoria University's unsurpassed Wildlife Department. This means that the lions are not only going to be well cared for but that they are also going to be studied by experts in all the appropriate fields, particularly by geneticists and scientists studying the phenomenon of leucism or "whiteness".

Now, twenty-one months old, the young lions weigh in excess of three hundred pounds each, and look all set for a happy and scientifically useful future. Meanwhile, Chris assured me, Phuma continues to thrive in the bush because she has remained with the Machaton pride. As long as that pride stays unified and Phuma stays an integral part of it, Chris feels that her chance of survival in the bush is "probably quite good".

With all the excitement and activity of the last two years, it is hardly surprising that Chris has not yet managed to complete his Master's thesis for Humboldt University. "I have notes this high," he told me, and raised his hand four feet from the ground. "The trouble is I don't seem to be able to get round to organizing them. I can happily sit in the bush all day and just watch lions. Charlotte is kind enough to call it dedication, but I'm not sure it's not pure laziness. Come to think of it I suppose I'm rather like a male lion, content to let the women get on with the work."

Charlotte, it seems, designed and oversaw the building of their new camp—a marvellous reed enclosure with an extremely smart and salubrious mud hut as the central living quarters, plus tents for the children and visitors to sleep in and special quarters for the livestock. Through the chicken wire of the front entrance and the windows cut in the reed walls, the McBrides can look out over miles and miles of undisturbed bush, and observe the countless wild animals going about their daily routine. I understand that, every now and then, the occasional wild animal reverses the process and has a peep at the McBrides going about theirs.

Despite the enormous success of *The White Lions of Timbavati* (assured long before publication) and the possibility of both a documentary and a major feature film being made from it, the McBrides foresee little change in their way of life. Chris has bought a special fast-focusing lens for his camera, and also a spot meter—two instruments that he hopes will improve what appear to me to be his already considerable photographic skills. Charlotte will be able to carry on with her great hobby of drawing and painting. For the rest, they will continue to live on the meat that they can shoot and the vegetables that they can grow in their garden. Although they were looking forward to their colossal fêting in the civilized world, they were already feeling a mite homesick for the camp where they keep cats very largely to chase away the snakes, chickens to gobble up the scorpions and where the nearest doctor is a hundred miles away.

They are confident that they will return to find their home in perfect order. Charlotte has warned the native Shangaans who are looking after it that if anything is stolen, or if any animal is killed, the witch doctor will visit instant retribution on the heads of the wrongdoers. What sort of retribution, I asked. "Death," Charlotte replied, giving a warmly conspiratorial smile. "You've no idea what a strong effect that has on a person's morals."

I can't be certain of course but it does occur to me that perhaps the natives have already taken their revenge for being threatened in this way. The very day after I visited the McBrides, Chris, who had not had a day's illness since the day the cubs were first sighted, had to take to his bed. In the middle of summer, he had suddenly been struck down by a particularly heavy cold.   NDB

MERLIN'S KEEP

a condensation of the book by

MADELEINE BRENT

Illustrated by Alan Lee
Published by Souvenir Press

This spell-binding story opens, at the turn of the last century, in one of the most remote and exotic regions of the Himalayas. Here, near the ancient monastery of Galdong, a beautiful half-caste girl, Jani, has been brought up by a strange Englishman called Sembur. Jani's past is shrouded in a mystery which grows ever deeper for her when the monastery's oracle declares, among other frightening predictions, that a foreign demon on a black horse will shortly come to destroy Sembur because of an unnamed evil that he has committed.

For Jani, the demon's arrival signals the start of a long and often terrifying journey which takes her to England where she finds friendship and love, only to risk them in an inevitable confrontation with the Silver Man, the Eater of Souls.

Madeleine Brent, author of *Tregarron's Daughter* and *Moonraker's Bride*, once again tantalizes the imagination with an enthralling tale of adventure and romance.

Chapter One

Even before we reached the top of the Chak Pass, I saw far ahead of me the tall figure of Sembur begin to sway in the saddle, and knew that his heart was labouring badly in the thin air. A chill deeper than the coldness of the mountain winds touched my own heart, for Sembur was all I had.

My place was at the rear of the straggling caravan, but I touched heels to my pony and urged her forward, past the long line of plodding yaks, their big leather panniers loaded with salt.

When I came up beside Sembur I reached out to grasp his arm and spoke in the tongue that only he and I knew, the tongue he had taught me from the beginning. In time to come I was to discover that I spoke it with a very bad accent, but at this time, when I was in my thirteenth year, I had never heard it on the lips of anyone but Sembur. He called it Hinglish, and was himself a Hinglishman, which meant that he came from a country on the other side of the world.

"You don't 'alf look rotten," I said. "Put your 'and on my shoulder."

He turned his muffled head, and I saw that his colour was bad, his lips bluish, and even the sharp points of his moustache were drooping. The chill touched me again. This was Sembur, who had always seemed to me as strong and ageless as the mountains themselves. But of late I had realized that he was no more than human, and now I saw that he looked old.

He pulled himself together with an effort, and glared down at me. "What's this? What's this, eh? 'Oo told you to leave your post with the rear-guard, young lady?"

"Ah, don't go and get cross with me, Sembur. I saw you sorter swaying about and I got ever so worried. Go on, 'ang on to me a bit, till we get over the top."

"Don't want this lot to see I'm not meself, Jani." Sembur twitched his bushy eyebrows, indicating the men, their faces hooded for the cold, who were riding with us on the caravan.

I said, "Listen, you gimme your rifle to carry, Sembur, then you can lean on me an' pretend you're telling me 'ow it works while we go along." When he hesitated I added urgently, "Come on, we're not going to 'ave any trouble. Them Khamba tribesmen won't never attack in the pass, and we'll be in Smon T'ang soon." This was the name of the country where we lived. The people were known as Lo-bas, and we were returning now after a month-long trading journey into the land of Bod, or Tibet as Sembur always called it.

He nodded, and slipped the rifle from his shoulder. I knew that this was the finest rifle in the whole country, for it was a Hinglish one, with a magazine, so that the cartridges did not have to be put in one by one. I took the rifle, made sure the safety-catch was on, as Sembur had always taught me, and sat holding it in front of me with both hands, guiding my pony with my knees. Sembur rested his hand on my shoulder.

After a few moments I heard him give a little sigh. "Thanks, lovey. I'm getting a bit old for these 'igh haltitudes."

I did not answer, for I was too busy reproaching myself for not setting a demon-trap outside our tent each night, to keep the mountain demons away. I had no doubt that one of them had got into Sembur and was plaguing his heart and lungs. The trouble was that Sembur himself had forbidden me to make or set demon-traps. He said no Hinglish person would believe such nonsense.

It was sometimes difficult to make Sembur understand the people we lived with, because although we had been ten years in Smon T'ang, or Mustang as he called it in Hinglish, he still spoke only a few words of the language, and was always making mistakes.

He had taken care of me all my life, and I loved him very much, but I still thought him in many ways the strangest and funniest man I had ever known. The Lo-bas would have treated him as a fool if it had not been that they respected him as a powerful warrior. It was not just that he possessed the finest gun in the country, while they owned only a few muzzle-loading weapons. He was also a man of strong spirit, forceful and unafraid. Before Sembur's time, at least two caravans each year had been set upon by the fierce Khamba tribesmen of Bod. When Sembur began to ride with the caravan, it was different. The robbers were driven off.

I often felt very proud because I was the only girl who ever rode with the salt caravans. Earlier, when I was small and Sembur went away on a caravan, he always left me in the care of a woman called Chela. I did not like her because she used to tell terrible stories about demons, which frightened me and gave me bad dreams. Then Chela died, when I was in my tenth year. Sembur said it was something called a busted appendix, but I knew that what had really happened was that a demon had entered her and made her belly swell up very painfully until her spirit was driven out and she died.

When the next caravan was due to go, I begged Sembur to take me with him. I had started riding ponies almost as soon as I could walk, and promised I would be no trouble. Sembur was taken aback, but at last he gave me that brisk nod which meant he had made up his mind. In the morning, therefore, when the caravan assembled, I went with it.

And, even on that first journey, I was soon welcomed when the tribesmen discovered that I had what they considered a truly magical gift with the yaks. We used yaks for ploughing and as beasts of burden, we spun their hair to make our clothes, and twisted it into thick strands to make our boots. We drank their milk, burned their dung for warmth, and bled them once a year to eat their dried blood. They were too precious to slaughter when young, but in time they gave us meat and bone. However, they were slow-moving creatures, always bad-tempered, and on a caravan a yak might suddenly decide to stand stock still for many hours, like a monk in meditation. It was too heavy to drag, and nobody dared to use any painful method of goading, for fear that the creature might be the reincarnation of some dead relative. My gift was that I could persuade a yak to move, just by rubbing its nose and talking to it. I had no idea how I did this, I only knew it happened.

I was now completing my ninth caravan. Without Sembur, I might almost have been accepted for, though my skin was pale, I had eyes as dark and hair as black as any of the people of Smon T'ang. But though Sembur was respected by the Lo-bas, he could never have become one of them, for he would never dream of trying to change his Hinglish ways.

"They're all a bunch of 'eathens, this lot, Jani," he had said to me many times. "Good 'earted, mind you. They been very nice to us most of the time, I must say. But they're hignorant, see? Never been taught proper."

"Taught what, Sembur?" I had once asked.

"Eh? God bless my soul, just about *heverything*, girl! I mean, they don't even wash regular an' keep themselves clean an' well turned-out like we do, for a start and none of them can read or write, except for the monks."

I had had reading and writing lessons almost every day for as long as I could remember. Once when reading a book called the *Holy Bible*, I had asked, "Sembur, why are there some words that don't 'ave a haitch in front, but we say it just the same, like 'hangel'?"

Sembur had sucked at his pipe, frowning and nodding slowly. "Well, that's a very 'ard question to answer, Jani. Tell you the truth, it really needs someone with more book-learning than me. But *reading* is different to *saying*, so I think what really 'appens is that you get certain words like hangel and Hinglish and—er—heducation, where you put in a haitch when you're saying it, for what they call hemphasis, see?"

"Well then . . . 'ow do you know which words to do it with?"

"It's like a lot of things, Jani," Sembur had waved his pipe airily. "It comes with experience, see?"

We had one other book apart from the Bible and that was called

Tales of Jessica. It had pictures in it, and was about a girl who wore a long dress and was always doing exciting things like going to school, or to a place called the seaside, and she was very good at helping people. The picture I liked best was of Jessica waving a flag to stop a huge railway engine, because a gentleman had got his foot caught in one of the lines. I often hoped I would grow up to be like Jessica and save people from getting run over by railway engines.

Once I said, "There are lots and lots of scrolls in the Galdong monastery, Sembur, an' scrolls are like books. I wouldn't 'alf like to read something different."

Sembur had laughed his sharp throaty laugh that sounded like a dog barking. "You can't read *them*, Jani. They're all written in foreign, not Hinglish."

"Why can we only read an' write Hinglish then?"

He had given me his fierce stare, which he used a great deal on the Lo-bas. "Gawd's strewth, Jani, because we *are* Hinglish, that's why! And you better be proud of it."

"I dunno, Sembur. Sometimes I wish I wasn't. I mean, when the other children don't like me and act rotten to me because of being different. Grown-ups too, sometimes."

Sembur had sighed. "I know, lovey, I know," he said gently. "Still, you got to make allowances for 'em. It's just hignorance. They're always seeing omens everywhere. Only needs a yak to fall down a crevasse, and they'll see 'alf a dozen omens to say it's all because of two foreigners living in the village." He shrugged. "Still, all we 'ave to do when they turn funny is clear off for a few days, an' they soon forget about it."

If the omens were bad and it seemed wise for the two of us to go away alone into the hills for a while, the High Lama of Galdong would send for Sembur. His name was Rild, and he was very important. I had met him three times to speak to, on occasions when he had sent for Sembur and had needed me to translate. I liked him, because although he gazed through me or past me he always smiled and spoke gently to me. I remembered the first time he had spoken to me in his thin high voice as we stood before him

91

in a lofty chamber with butter-lamps flickering along the walls.

"You will inform Sembur that all omens declare that the strangers among us are opening ways for new demons to descend on us."

"I will say this to him now, High-born."

When I did so, Sembur growled, "Tommyrot, the lot of it. Ask 'im why all these hextra demons turn up in winter, when there aren't any caravans that need guarding."

"I can't say that to 'im, Sembur!" I turned to Rild. "Forgive me, High-born. He is of slow wit, like a yak, and there is need for me to explain as to a small child. He will understand."

The High Lama went on to explain that if Sembur and I did not leave Namkhara of our own accord for a while, and live alone in the hills, then we would be driven out of the village.

Sembur took me home. He had been ready to break one or two heads with a cudgel when the men came to drive us out, but they did not come. Instead, a dozen or more women descended upon us, waving sticks. Sembur was aghast and furious, but quite unable to stand firm against the women. Within a few minutes he had packed our tent and our few belongings, and we were gone.

Since then we had been sent away from Namkhara twice more but we had always gone without argument or fuss. Our exile never lasted longer than a few weeks, for in the world of demons all things changed with the new moon. When we returned to Namkhara we were always welcomed in the most friendly fashion.

When I thought about it, I realized that Sembur would never change, but stay exactly the same as he had always been, going right back to that other world at the very beginning of my memory that was like a half-remembered dream. I always assumed that my parents had died in that other world. I did not remember them, and I suppose I had given little thought to the past until my tenth year, when for a short time I became intensely curious, pestering Sembur to tell me about my mother and father. For the most part Sembur managed to avoid my questions, but at last I pinned him down.

"Well, Jani, what makes you think *I'm* not your Pa? That's what all the Lo-bas reckon."

"It just doesn't seem like that, some'ow. Are you my Pa, honest?"

"I'll tell you one day. When it's safe. If I'm not careful you might be in danger."

"All right, but what about my Ma? Is she dead, Sembur?"

He nodded, and I saw him swallow hard. "Yes. I'll explain everything when you're a bit older, lovey, I promise."

I had sulked for a while, but then my curiosity had waned. Sometimes, however, half waking from a dream of great rooms and silken rugs and soft arms holding me, I would remember Sembur's promise, and feel impatient for the time when I would know all that was hidden.

BY THE TIME we had descended from the top of the pass to ten thousand feet, Sembur looked better. His breathing was easier, and there was no longer that frightening blue tinge to his lips. He took the rifle from me, slung it on his shoulder, and turned in the saddle to look back along the straggling column of yaks and ponies. The walls of the pass were high here, protecting us for a while from the harsh mountain winds.

Behind us the peaks were grey and white. Before us the trail wound steeply down through brown foothills towards the patch-work of green fields covering the flat plain. Below us the river was a thread of silver twisting through the fields. Beside it was the road to Namkhara, and at the point where the river widened into a moon-shaped lake stood the monastery of Galdong, six great terraces of dull red stone topped by four needle-like gold spires.

The monastery stood in a courtyard surrounded by a high wall with an arched gateway. In the courtyard I could see little red dots moving about. These were the lamas in their tall red hats. Sembur called them an idle lot. He thought it a disgrace that they sent the holy women out to work in the fields while they did nothing but spin prayer wheels and meditate and write in huge scrolls.

We rode down into the valley with our slow-moving caravan. Beside me, Sembur said briskly, "Shoulders back, Jani. Sit up straight in the saddle, there's a good girl."

I stretched to ease my aching muscles, and with an effort drew myself up. "Sorry . . . I'm 'alf asleep."

"I know, lovey, I know. But I told you before, if people see you're all fagged out, they're not going to 'ave any respect."

Ten minutes later our caravan trailed through the wide gates of the monastery's outer wall and into the courtyard. Lamas and monks were assembled there, waiting for us. The lamas wore their hats and the monks were bare-headed, some of them very young, for boys could be entered into the order of the Galdong monastery when they were only nine.

Three of the lamas had very long trumpets, longer than the height of a man, made of copper decorated with silver, coral and turquoise. The bell of each trumpet rested on the shoulder of one of the boy monks, and the lamas were now blowing the trumpets while other lamas beat on drums and cymbals. All this was done to drive away any demons we might have brought in from Bod.

I always enjoyed the demon-chasing, but Sembur thought it was all very stupid. He watched coldly, giving an occasional sniff, and said, "They got no more sense than a bunch of kids."

As the noise faded, three lamas bearing blank scrolls and quills began to examine our load. Sembur and I would be paid for our work according to the value of the caravan, and I thought that if we were lucky we would get paid at least fifty rupees for this trip. Apart from the usual load of salt, we had bales of beautiful silks and rich brocades which had been traded in Magyari by the yellow men who came from beyond the land of Bod. We also had some sacks of their tea, which the noble families of Smon T'ang liked very much. The ordinary people preferred the tea that came from the south, from the land of India.

I used to find it hard to understand why we were not among the very poorest of our village, for we earned almost nothing except what we were paid for "escort duty", as Sembur called it. But then, when I was about nine, I realized that Sembur had some secret source of money. We had seemed to be getting steadily poorer for some time when Sembur put me into the care of Chela and travelled south to India. To the Lo-bas he gave the impression that he had gone to get more cartridges for his rifle, and indeed he returned three weeks later with more than forty clips. But he also brought back a whole bag of silver coins, which he hid in a secret hollow dug out beneath a big stone beside our hearth.

This hoard was enough to keep us for several years, and I guessed then that Sembur had brought back money in the same way on the only other occasion he had made the journey south, when I had been just a little girl. I said, a little awed as I stared at the second bag of silver, "Gawd, Sembur! How d'you get 'old of it all?"

"Don't say 'Gawd', young lady. I'll 'ave no bad language, thank you very much."

"You say it."

"That's different. And anyway, I didn't ought to."

"All right. But where d'you get all that money?"

Sembur finished setting the stone in place above the secret hollow, then rose to his feet. "When we first came 'ere, I brought one or two things that belonged to your Ma. Bits of jewellery, see? They're yours by rights, but I've 'ad to sell a couple of bits to keep us going."

"Coo! Is there much left?"

"Enough for a nice little nest-egg when you grow up."

"Can I 'ave a look, Sembur?"

"When you're a bit older, and if you're a good girl. But you got to keep it dead quiet, Jani. Not a word to anyone. Understand?"

"Yes, all right, Sembur. I promise. Cross my 'eart."

I had kept my promise. Indeed, until now when we stood in the courtyard of Galdong, waiting for the lamas to value the caravan, I had not thought about the money or the jewellery for a long time. I was talking to my pony, Pulki, telling her that I would give her a big feed as soon as we were home, when I heard Sembur say in a low, wary voice, "'Allo. Look what's turned up 'ere."

I turned my head and saw a plump, round-faced young lama making his way towards us. This was Mudok, the chief secretary to Rild, the High Lama of Galdong, and I felt my heart sink. It seemed that we were to be summoned to Rild's presence, and this would surely mean that the omens were against us once more.

Mudok halted in front of us, glanced at Sembur, then looked at me and said, "The High Lama will now speak with Sembur."

"I will tell him, Reverend One." I added quickly, "Is it that the omens speak ill of us?"

"It is not as before," Mudok said, frowning as if puzzled. "It is another matter, arising from a vision of the Oracle."

I was startled, and hastily explained to Sembur. We collected our pay and then anxiously followed Mudok up the broad steps and through the great doorway of the monastery.

Chapter Two

Little daylight entered the monastery, for most of the windows were shuttered. Every hall and corridor was lit with scores of butter-lamps, the little flames dancing and flickering on silvery statues of gods and goddesses as we passed. The air was sickly with the scented fumes of incense. Somewhere a big gong was booming faintly to a steady rhythm.

We came at last to the ante-room. Mudok took two *khabtas* from a number which hung in a big iron ring on the wall and handed one to each of us. It was impossible for us to enter the presence of the High Lama without these narrow white scarves, for no ceremonial greeting could take place without the offering of a *khabta* from the lower-born to the higher-born.

Mudok then threw open a big door and beckoned us forward. Daylight poured into the High Lama's room from a huge arched window. The walls were hung with gold brocade, and white goatskin rugs covered the floor. A great golden Buddha towered against the eastern wall. Rild himself sat with his back to the window, cross-legged like the Buddha, on a low platform which was painted with strange beasts in green and gold. He wore no hat, and his head was smooth and domed above the quiet eyes.

We halted in front of him, holding out the white scarves in a token offering, and bowed. The High Lama waved a slender hand in acknowledgement, looked at a point somewhere between the two of us, smiled faintly and said, "I greet you with a blessing."

96

I said, "May your blessing aid our release from the wheel of rebirth, High-born."

I nudged Sembur, who drew himself up very straight, hands by his sides, heels together, and said loudly and rapidly, "Very happy to see you in good 'ealth, sir."

"He says he is grateful for your blessing, High-born."

Rild nodded absently. Five minutes passed, and not a word was spoken. Then, at last, "The Oracle has seen a demon who has put on human form," Rild said in a sing-song voice. "The demon is coming from the south, to take Sembur and destroy him."

I felt the blood drain from my face. Beside me, Sembur said sharply, "What's up, Jani? What's 'e say?"

I turned to him and translated Rild's words. I knew Sembur did not believe in oracles, but to my astonishment he stared down at me from narrowed eyes for long seconds, then said slowly, "Does 'is nibs know what this demon looks like, Jani?"

I said to Rild, "He begs to ask if it was given to the Oracle to see a likeness of this demon, High-born."

Rild stared at nothing for a while, then closed his eyes. There was silence. I heard Sembur stir beside me, drawing breath to speak, and I turned my head quickly, putting a finger to my lips.

Several minutes passed, then the door to our right opened and a young woman wearing a white robe entered the chamber, followed by Mudok, who carried a silver tray with a plain glass bowl and flask on it. The flask was almost full of some inky black liquid. The girl moved to stand before Rild, and bowed. Her mouth hung open a little, and her face was without animation.

Rild opened his eyes and said, "I have summoned you to look again into the darkness, child, for the likeness of the demon who comes from the south."

I realized then that this girl was the Oracle. "I will look, High-born," she said, and turned towards Mudok, who was pouring the black liquid into the bowl. When he had finished, he held the bowl in front of the girl. She bowed her head slightly, staring down upon the shiny black surface of the liquid. After a few moments her eyes opened very wide, and her whole body seemed to grow stiff. When

97

she spoke, her voice was high-pitched. "He rides a black horse. He has taken the form of a man from the same land as the man who is called Sembur. The demon comes to take Sembur and destroy him. It is . . ." the girl's voice faded for a moment as she hesitated, then, "it is a warrior who comes, sent because . . . because Sembur has done an evil thing."

There was a silence. Rild said very softly, "Tell me the look of this demon, child."

She stared down at the liquid blackness, and I felt a shiver of awe touch my spine. "Long boots," she said musingly. "White fur to cover his body, and a gun that rests in a case tied to the saddle." Her lips curved in a strange smile. "He is young, this demon. Black hair, tight-twisted, and eyes like a clear sky at dusk. Proud . . . too proud. But his pride will be broken." She began to speak more quickly, and her breathing became laboured. "He will go down into blackness, and then will come the bloodless one, the Silver Man, the Eater of Souls . . ." she was panting now, and gabbling in a shrill voice so that her words were hard to follow, ". . . and there is the debt to pay, and in the Year of the Wood-Dragon they will come to the Land of Bod, to seize the teardrop that fell from the eye of the Enlightened One—"

Her voice rose to a shriek, then ceased abruptly. Her body quivered like a plucked bow-string, and flecks of foam appeared on her lips. Then her lungs emptied with a long sigh, her body loosened, and the life went out of her face.

Rild moved a hand. The girl bowed and turned to leave the room, followed by Mudok with the tray, bowl and flask. I felt suddenly cold, though the room was warm. Much of what the girl had said was meaningless to me, but it was clear enough that somebody very dangerous was seeking Sembur to do him harm.

Rild was speaking. "You will inform Sembur that he must leave Smon T'ang, so that our land is not tainted with the disputes of those who are not of our kind—"

At the same time Sembur was muttering to me urgently, "What did she say? Come on, girl, don't just stand there like a goat with gout! What's she been saying?"

98

I pressed my hands to my head and whispered frantically, "For Gawd's sake shut up, Sembur! I'll tell you *later*." I bowed to Rild, and said, "Forgive me, High-born."

For the first time he looked directly at me, and I saw amusement in his eyes. Then his gaze became remote again and he went on, "It is seven nights now since a star fell in the south, and the Oracle has declared that this heralds the coming of the foreign demon before the moon is full."

I realized this meant the demon could appear at any moment now. In a shaky voice I said, "Where are we to go, High-born?"

"That is a question for Sembur." Rild's pale eyes studied me for a moment. "It is permitted that you remain, child. You may become a novice here, and study the True Way."

I said nervously, "No, High-born, I must go with Sembur."

The High Lama gave a faint shrug. "Each one must acquire whatsoever karmic burden he wills. Go with my blessing, child." Again his hand moved slightly, then his eyes closed, and it was as if Sembur and I were alone in the chamber. The door opened and Mudok appeared. He did not speak. When he turned we followed him out through the maze of halls, stairs and corridors until at last we emerged into the wintry sunshine again.

I must have begun to weep without knowing it, for there were tears on my cheeks. As I rubbed them away I said, "I'm sorry, Sembur. I mean, I'm sorry I said for Gawd's sake an' told you to shut up. I 'ardly knew what I was doing."

"Never mind, lovey," Sembur's voice was gentle as we made our way to where we had left our ponies. "The 'Igh Lama was saying I've got to clear off, wasn't 'e?"

I nodded. "It's because they don't want that foreign demon 'ere, causing a lot of trouble."

Sembur nodded bleakly, "Tell me all about it as we ride on 'ome, Jani."

Although I could not repeat what the Oracle had said word for word, I was certain I could give Sembur the exact sense of it, with nothing missed out. He listened carefully, and continued frowning into space for a long time after I had finished.

I said, "So you reckon this foreign demon might really be coming 'ere from the south?"

"Not a demon," Sembur said slowly. "But a somebody. Somebody looking for me."

There was a tight feeling in my chest as I said, "She spoke about 'im coming to kill you for doing something wicked."

Sembur was thoughtful as we rode.

"D'you trust me, Jani?" he asked.

"'Course I do."

"I never did this bad thing they say I did, but nobody's going to believe me, except you."

"I don't care what 'appened, anyway. If this feller comes 'ere to take you away, I'll get your rifle and I'll kill 'im."

"You can stop that kind of silly talk this minute, young lady. I won't 'ave it."

I gave him a scowl. After a while, thinking back to what the Oracle had prophesied, I said, "What d'you think she meant about 'im being too proud, and 'is pride would be broken?"

Sembur shrugged. "Sounds more like this other bloke's trouble than mine, so I'm not going to worry about it."

We came into Namkhara. By now the shadows were growing long and to the south the great peak of Annapurna took fire from the dying sun. In the middle of the village Sembur and I turned off towards the two-storey house of rough stone and rammed earth. Then we took our ponies into the small stable across the street from the house, fed and watered them and gave them a good rub down. This was a habit ingrained in me by Sembur. "There's a right way of doing things, Jani. Don't matter 'ow tired you are, first you take care of your 'orse, your rifle, your subordinates, then yourself."

Afterwards we walked across the street into our home. It was a very nice home, for Sembur had worked hard to make many improvements over the years. There was a living room, a small kitchen with an iron stove, and a bedroom with a curtain partition put up three years ago by Sembur because I was growing up, he said. Rugs covered the stone floors, and we had beds, tables and

100

chairs, as well as some big cushions and several boxes for keeping our spare clothes and other belongings.

As soon as we entered, Sembur spread an old blanket on the table and began to clean his rifle carefully. I opened all the windows to air the rooms, then I made a fire of dried yak-dung in our big living-room fireplace. I lit another in the stove in the kitchen, closed the windows, which were covered with yak-hide, lit some butter-lamps, then went out with a leather bucket to fetch water for Sembur's bath from the stone cistern.

While the water was heating in a big iron pot on the stove, I went into the kitchen and made a big bowl of *tsampa*. This was the main food in Smon T'ang, and in Bod also. It was made by heating barleycorns in an iron pan until they popped, then grinding the corn very finely. This fine corn was finally mixed into a paste with tea made with rancid butter. I liked it because I had always eaten it, but Sembur never got used to the taste.

By this time Sembur had taken his bath and there was more water hot enough for me to take mine. I lifted the pot from the stove, carried it into my room, and filled the tub on the floor.

Less than an hour later I had put on a clean vest and drawers of thick wool, my red tunic, quilted trousers, and indoor shoes, and Sembur and I were sitting at the table near the fire, with well-filled bowls of *tsampa*. I pressed my palms together, closing my eyes tightly as Sembur said solemnly, "For what we are about to receive may the Lord make us truly thankful."

We both said "amen", then began to eat, and almost five minutes passed before either of us could spare time and attention to talk. Then Sembur looked across the table at me, gave a sad little smile, and said, "You're a good girl, Jani. I wish I could 'ave done better for you, lovey."

I looked up in surprise, and said, "I don't see 'ow we could've done better. We've got a nice place to live, and we eat well."

"Well, that part's not too bad, I suppose. But you're growing up now, and . . . well, I ought to 'ave done something about your future, except I've never been able to think what to do." He shook his head, troubled. "That's where heducation comes in. If I was a heducated man, I'd know what to do. I only 'ad a bit of schooling as a boy-soldier, that's all, and after that there was just the army." He looked at me sharply. "Nothing wrong with the army, mind you. Teaches a man to be disciplined an' self-reliant, but it don't teach a man 'ow to bring up a little girl." He grimaced. "Still, I done me best, Jani. Some day, when you might feel a bit badly towards old Sembur, just try an' remember I done me best."

I slipped down from my chair, went to him, put my arms round his neck and pressed my cheek against his. Suddenly I felt sad and afraid, more for him than for myself, though I was not sure why. I said, "Don't talk daft. I'm ever so lucky the way you've always been kind an' looked after me. I wouldn't ever think bad of you."

He patted my shoulder. "Come on, let's 'ave some more *tsampa*, Jani. We got a lot to talk about tonight."

I refilled our bowls from the kitchen. We said little during the rest of the meal or while we were washing up together in the little kitchen. When Sembur was settled in his fireside chair with a mug of tea, and I was sitting in my favourite position on a cushion beside the hob, he said, "Right, then, Jani. What did that oracle-girl say? Tell me that last bit again."

"Well . . . it was a bit confused. There was something about the foreign demon going down into blackness, and then she talked about someone without any blood, a silver man, called the Eater of Souls, and they were going to come to Bod in the Year of the Wood-Dragon to take the tear-drop that fell from the eye of the Enlightened One." I had closed my eyes, remembering, and now I opened them. "Sembur, that's what they sometimes call the Buddha 'ere, because he sat under a tree and suddenly got enlightened."

Sembur gave one of his sniffs. "When's the Year of the Wood-Dragon?"

"Um . . . let's see." I counted on my fingers. "It's another seven years off. That's 1904, the way you count in Hinglish."

"Right, then we can forget about it, lovey. Now let's tackle this in a soldierly fashion, eh? First, information. It's expected that a young man, a soldier, probably an officer, is on 'is way to

Mustang, looking for me to take me back. We 'ave a rough description of said young man. Now, if said young man succeeds, I'm a goner. They'll 'ang me or shoot me." Sembur rubbed the bowl of his empty pipe against his nose, then went on. "Intention. To be gone from 'ere before said young man reaches Namkhara, and to settle somewhere in another country, where nobody can find me." Sembur looked at me. "Now we come to method," he said slowly, a hint of tiredness in his voice. "No way to go but north. Get right across Tibet and into China."

It was hard to think of leaving our home, but I smiled and tried to sound cheerful as I said, "Sooner we go the better, Sembur. It's nearly winter. Another day or two an' we'll never get through the passes into Bod." An idea came to me. "We ought to buy a couple of yaks. They could carry a lot more of our things, and we wouldn't 'ave to load the ponies 'ardly at all."

Sembur looked away. "I can't take you with me, Jani. It's not fair. They'll let you stay all right, as long as I clear off."

"No!" I was on my feet, my lower lip trembling so much that I found it hard to speak clearly. "No, Sembur, I'm not 'aving that! You'll never get there alone, Sembur. You . . . you'll die!"

He gave a sudden grin. "I've 'ad me time now, Jani, so it wouldn't be anything to cry over. I'll 'ave me boots on and I'll be going forward, an' there's no better way for a soldier to make an end."

I knelt on the rug beside his chair, and took his hand. I felt calm and very determined.

"Sembur," I said, "I told you what Rild said about me being taken into the monastery. That's what they'll do if you leave me 'ere. They'll shave all my 'air off, an' stick me in a nun's robe, and I'll be miserable all me life."

He chewed on his pipe-stem, and rubbed a hand fiercely back and forth across his short-cropped grey hair. "That's all very well, Jani, but I'm right up a gum-tree. Whatever I do, it's going to be bad for you one way or another."

"Tell you what," I said quickly. "I got a good idea. If we leave for Bod in the next couple of days, we'll get through the passes.

We know the merchants in Magyari so we won't be complete strangers. Now, p'raps this foreign demon will guess we've gone there, but 'e can't chase us for another four or five months, because of winter." I went on talking urgently, reminding Sembur that the people of Bod were enormously secretive. A stranger trying to track us down in that country would have a hopeless task.

By the time I had run out of good reasons for my plan I was breathless. Sembur looked down at me, and I was glad to see a twinkle in his eye. "You're a chip off the old block, you are. That took me back a few years, listening to you just now."

I did not know what he meant, but with a huge inward relief I knew that I had won him over, and he would not leave me behind. I said, "When d'you think we'd better leave, Sembur?"

He rubbed his chin. "The sooner we get through the pass, the better." He gave my hand a little squeeze, then got up, moved to the hearth, picked up the long iron poker and used it to lever up the stone which hid our secret hole. In it was the remaining ammunition for the rifle, a leather bag with a drawstring neck containing all our money, and an old tobacco tin.

We counted the money, put aside what I thought we would need for buying two yaks, and returned the rest to the bag. Sembur then opened the old tobacco tin, and we stared down at it as we knelt side by side. I knew that at last I was looking at my mother's jewellery. There were two earrings, each made of a large red stone set in a droplet-shaped piece of gold, a ring with three square green stones, and a gold brooch shaped like a peacock's tail, set with six diamonds. There were two empty settings on the brooch.

"Wicked to break up that brooch, but I didn't dare try an' sell it complete," Sembur said quietly. "Sold a diamond each time I travelled down into India to raise money."

I said, "Was all that my Ma's jewellery, Sembur?"

"That was only a bit of it. A few pieces."

"She must've looked nice wearing it."

"She was the most beautiful lady I ever saw, Jani."

"Coo, then I must be beautiful! You once said I looked like a miniature of her."

"Don't get big 'eaded, young lady. Remember that story I've told you about being an ugly duckling. *Maybe* you might turn into a swan, but don't be too sure."

I giggled. I had long since given up hope of changing from an ugly duckling. My eyes were a funny shape, while my nose was narrow instead of being broad and flat like all the other faces in Namkhara.

Sembur shivered suddenly as if somebody had walked over his grave, and began to fit the lid back on the box.

"Do you always shiver when you look in that box?" I asked.

"Do I? Yes, I suppose I do. It's just . . . memories. Now then, while I pack these back in the 'ole suppose you get the 'oly Bible. Then you can read to me for 'alf an hour before we go to bed."

Later, after I had kissed Sembur goodnight, and tucked in his blankets, I took the lamp and went to my own bed, thinking as I snuggled down that it was a pity Sembur would not let me get demon traps to protect us. They might even avert the coming of the foreigner prophesied by the Oracle.

But this was a foolish thought, as I was to learn. It would have taken more than skull-bone, horn, and enchantments on strips of leather, to stay the man I was so soon to meet.

Chapter Three

It was the next afternoon, on the road between Namkhara and the village of Yamun, that I came face to face with him. Sembur and I had risen early, for there was much to be done. Throughout the morning we were busy with preparations for the journey. When the sun had passed its high point I set off on Pulki for Yamun to buy the two yaks. They would be cheaper in Yamun, for the people there, unlike almost everyone in Namkhara, would not yet know that we had to leave Smon T'ang, and so it would be easier to make a good bargain. I was thankful I had persuaded Sembur that he could not spare the time to come with me, for he was not good at haggling and seemed unable to grasp the way of doing it.

There were a few people on the road that afternoon. Some were travelling between Namkhara and Yamun, as I was, and some were turning east where two trails joined, making for the more distant village of Gemdring. Pulki was walking steadily, and I was lost in my thoughts when I heard a man's voice calling me.

He was speaking in the tongue called Gurkhali, used by the small men from Nepal. Sembur could speak it a little, because many of these men became soldiers with the Hinglish army, and Sembur had once been in charge of almost a thousand of them. During the long evenings he had taught me some Gurkhali, and I found that much of it was like the tongue of Smon T'ang.

Pulki stopped and turned at my touch. It was then I saw the man on a great black horse riding easily towards me, and I knew that this was the foreign man whose coming had been seen by the Oracle. He wore a short coat of white lamb's fur, and breeches of a heavy brown cloth, tucked into tall leather boots. His hands were gloved in soft brown kid, and he wore a cap of thick felt with ear flaps which were buttoned across the top. Both saddle-bags were bulging, and behind the saddle was strapped a large canvas-covered roll which would hold his tent and bedding. In front of his right leg was a long holster with a rifle in it.

All this I remembered later, but at the moment of first staring up at him I was aware only of his face. It was a face that sun and weather had made darker than my own. The eyes, as cold and haughty as the eyes of a snow leopard, were deeper blue than Sembur's, the nose as thin and ugly as mine, jutting above a long tight mouth.

He said in Hinglish, but not the proper Hinglish that Sembur and I spoke: "Good God, it's a girl. I thought it was a boy." Then, in slow Gurkhali: "Can you understand me?"

My heart seemed to be trying to climb into my throat. I could not have been more frightened if a true dragon-demon with a tongue of fire had appeared before me. Even so, it was a strange

106

kind of fear, with an almost painful excitement in it. Perhaps this was because he was the first Hinglish person I had ever seen, apart from Sembur. There was no scrap of warmth in his face, yet I felt an impulse to reach out and touch him, and talk to him.

With an effort I gathered my confused wits. This man was a soldier, come to take Sembur away to be hanged or shot. He was a mortal enemy, to be deceived.

I said slowly, in Gurkhali, "I speak this tongue a little, honoured sir."

He took off his cap. "I seek a foreign man," he said. "A man who has lived many years in Smon T'ang."

I saw with surprise that the stranger was younger than I had first thought, perhaps twenty-two or three, but with the confidence of a man ten years older. His hair was as black as mine, but clung to his head in short, tight curls, making him look very like the fire-demon carved over the entrance to the small shrine by the gatehouse of Namkhara, except for its two double fangs.

He continued slowly in Gurkhali, "I have spoken to men in the hills to the south. They say such a man has passed through their village. Two, three times. He carries a fine rifle." The stranger touched his own rifle. I did not look at him but pretended to be more interested in the beautiful black horse than in what he was asking. A touch of impatience came into his voice as he went on, "They have told me that the one I seek is from the town of Namkhara. Do you know of such a one, girl?"

I said idly, "There is a foreign man who has lived here many years, sir. A big man, who was a soldier, it is said."

"Yes. The one I seek was a soldier. Where shall I find him?"

Still looking at the horse I said, "I am from Namkhara. Once the man you speak of lived near me. But last winter, he went away to live in a small village."

"Where?"

"To Gemdring." I pointed to where the trail forked away from the road between Namkhara and Yamun, and tried to make my mind blank so he would not see I was frightened.

"How do you know he still lives there?"

"I do not know. It is half a year since I saw him."

There was a little silence, and then the stranger said, "Look at me, girl."

It was not easy to obey. I felt that if he suspected I was lying, he was a man who might very quickly have the truth out of me. I jumped as his black eyebrows came together and he said suddenly. "Are you telling the truth, girl?"

Panic touched me. I reached out my hand towards the big black horse as I began an answer which I knew would sound halting. "Sir, I—"

He cut in sharply. "Get your hand away from his muzzle! He'll have it off if you're not careful."

That changed everything for me. I could not hold back a giggle as I put my hand firmly on the cold damp nose and said, "We are friends, sir. He will never hurt me." The black horse edged forward, nudging and butting my hand. I could feel the strong spirit of him, and knew he would be dangerous to all but his master, and to the few who felt true love and respect for him.

The man on his back said in Hinglish, "Good God, what on earth's got into you, Flint? Has the child bewitched you?"

That made me laugh again, but inwardly, so the man would not know I had understood. Meanwhile I said in Gurkhali, "It is you who has not spoken truly, honoured sir, not I. You told me that your horse would bite my hand off. That was an untruth."

His lips drew into a tight line, and he looked down at me with dislike. "How far is Gemdring?"

I pointed along the trail away to the east. "You will come there before sunset, sir."

Without another word, he clapped the cap on his head, gathered the reins, touched heels to the great horse, and wheeled away. I watched him as he moved off down the trail. He rode straight-backed, as if he were lord of every village in the valley. Somewhere in my whirling thoughts I decided that he was a good horseman and that Flint would be happy with such a master.

When he passed out of my sight beyond a shallow fold of ground, I turned Pulki and started back towards Namkhara at a fast trot. There would be no going to Yamun to buy yaks for our journey. However, I had won us a good advantage. It would take the Hinglishman time to learn the truth, return to Namkhara, and discover at last that we had gone north to Bod. We would have a lead of two days at least, and surely no stranger would dare to venture the Chak Pass alone, with the snows of winter so close.

WE CAMPED at sunset in a broad gully at the foot of the pass, where the thin earth had not yet given way to rock, and there was some scanty grazing. While we heated some *tsampa* and ate a few pieces of the yak-meat I had cooked before leaving, Sembur and I spoke hardly at all. I knew that having to leave in haste had distressed him. He liked to think carefully and take his time in all he did. As it was, we had left Namkhara less than two hours after I had arrived home.

Later, as we lay in the little black tent, warm in the thick woollen sleeping-bags, Sembur said, "Did he say what 'is name was, this feller?"

"No. All he did was ask questions. Once he said something in Hinglish, to the 'orse, but it was funny Hinglish."

"I expect it was posh. He'd be an officer, see, a heducated person. What was he like, Jani?"

"I dunno. He didn't like *me* much, and he was proud, like the Oracle said. But I didn't mind that. I sort of liked 'im, really."

I heard Sembur sigh, and a few seconds later I fell asleep.

As the rising sun struck the golden spires of Galdong, we rose, ate a good hot breakfast to help us through the day's climb, and set off up the pass, leading our heavily laden ponies, Pulki and Bugler. It was a journey we knew well. There was a lower ridge at about ten thousand feet. We hoped to get beyond this today and drop down into a sheltered valley where we would camp for the night. Next morning we would start the climb to the true crest of the pass. There we would follow the twisting trail for over a mile across the great wall of the Himalayas before starting the descent into the land of Bod.

We hardly spoke at all that day, for we were saving our

strength. Towards the end of the afternoon I became worried about Sembur, for his colour was not good and he seemed unable to get enough air. I made him lie down while I lifted the panniers and bed-roll from his pony, and strapped them on Pulki. Then I made Sembur mount Bugler and ride.

I slept uneasily that night, wondering how we would manage the next day's journey, which would be harder and would take us another five thousand feet higher. My fears were not calmed when I woke to find that the sky was heavy with the threat of snow.

I was fretting to be on the move, but forced myself to be patient while we made breakfast and fed the ponies from the sacks of mixed buckwheat and crushed barley we had brought with us. All that morning we moved steadily up the ever-winding pass. At midday we reached a point a mile short of the true crest. Here it was possible to look down across the valley below, where we had spent the night, towards Galdong. I stood for a moment, saying a silent goodbye to the land where I had grown up.

Something moved. Far, far away on the small slope which ran down from the lower ridge into the valley, a black and white dot moved along the trail. Black horse. White fur.

I narrowed my eyes, trying to see more clearly, but there was no need. With sinking heart, I knew that Sembur's pursuer was no more than half a day's march behind. He could have rested only two hours in Gemdring before setting out for Namkhara, where they must have answered his questions quickly just to be rid of him.

I did not tell Sembur what I had seen, for it would only have made him feel hopeless. I said, "We're doin' ever so well, Sembur. Soon be going across the top, and after that it's easy."

He paused, and leaned on his pony. I knew then it would be all he could do to get through the pass.

During the next hour we trudged on slowly up the pass, leading our heavily burdened ponies. Suddenly something cold touched my cheek, then my brow, my chin. Great flakes of snow were falling. "Keep . . . going, Jani!" It was a rasping whisper from Sembur. "Get through . . . 'fore it's too late."

We took half an hour to reach the top, and by then the snow

110

was halfway to my knees. The huge soft flakes were like icy butterflies flung into our faces, and it was impossible to see more than a few yards ahead. Sembur was staggering, and even above the wind I could hear the awful sound as he struggled to drag enough air into his lungs. Terror struck into me, for I knew now he could never stay on his feet for that long mile across the top. Yet if we did not do it within the next hour we would die, for the snow would soon be thigh-deep.

I took my knife from its sheath on my belt, looped the reins over my arm, and called, "Sembur! 'Ang on a minute!" Head down against the wind, I pushed through the snow towards him and cut the straps which held Bugler's load. Sacks and panniers fell to the snow. The vital tent and bed-rolls were on my pony.

"Get up on 'im, Sembur!" I called. "Up on Bugler. Oh, for Gawd's sake don't argue now! Get up!" Somehow Sembur dragged himself into the saddle, slumping forward. I took the ponies' reins and plodded forward into the driving snow once again.

Some time later, there came a moment when I knew that we could never get through the pass against this blizzard. And in the same moment I remembered the cave. It lay on the east side of the pass, about a hundred paces from the trail and up a slope which ended in a great upthrust of cliff. Here there was an overhang, with the entrance to the cave beneath it. Sembur and I had explored the cave once, during a summer caravan. The Lo-bas would not go near it, except to throw in an offering, because they believed that wood-demons lived there.

I was peering through the swirling snow, trying to pick out the overhang, when a figure loomed through the heavy yellow light that encompassed us. At first I thought it was a strange squat horse, and then saw it was a bear. I did not feel afraid, for I knew the bear was simply making its way down the pass, but Bugler gave a whinny of terror and I felt a sudden painful wrench as the reins were torn from my hand. The pony lunged sideways, Sembur was flung from the saddle and the next instant Bugler was gone, vanishing into the blizzard back in the direction of Galdong.

111

I stood knee-deep in the snow, close to sobbing with panic. The bear, still on its hind legs and with an air of apology, shuffled on its way.

Keeping tight hold of my pony's reins, I moved to Sembur, bent over him, and shouted, "Come on, we'll just 'ave to get to the cave and 'ope the snow don't last!" He did not stir. Crouching, I saw that his eyes were closed and his face twisted as if in pain. I knew he could not have hurt himself falling into the snow, yet he was unconscious, and did not respond even when I gave his face a hard slap.

I think I cried with despair then, but I remember nothing more until I found myself moving slowly up the slope towards the overhang. I was leading my pony. When I looked back I saw that I had taken the coil of rope from Pulki's saddle, tied it round Sembur's shoulders, and fastened the other end to the pommel. Sembur was on his back, sliding along through the snow.

There were three holes giving entrance to the cave, two barely large enough for a man to crawl through, the third more like a rough doorway, and high enough for a horse to pass. Inside, the cave was perhaps fifteen paces across, but ran back twice that distance into the cliff.

It was a huge relief to be out of the wind and the driving snow. First I lit two butter-lamps. Then I unrolled Sembur's groundsheet and struggled to roll his limp body on top. Then I spread his sleeping-bag over him.

Over the years, travellers had thrown hundreds of offerings into the cave to please the wood-demons. There were roughly-carved wooden statuettes, and effigies of straw, paper and twigs. There was also a carpet of tiny bones from small creatures, which showed that many a snow leopard had made the cave his home.

I lit a fire near the entrance, then I went out and gathered snow in a pan until I had enough water to make some *tsampa* on the fire. While the *tsampa* was heating I hobbled my pony, took off his saddle, then set out all we had left of our possessions.

There was our bedding, our tent, and our leather bag of basic kit, with food for nine or ten days. There was also Sembur's rifle and the pack from his back which contained his spare clothes and special possessions including our small bag of silver coins, the tobacco tin with the pieces of jewellery, and our two books, the Holy Bible and *Tales of Jessica*.

I spent a little while talking to my pony. Then I sat beside Sembur and rubbed his hands while I talked to him.

After a few minutes he gave a long sigh and said in a thick voice, "Jani, go back . . . down to Galdong. Take what you need, but 'urry . . . 'fore it's too late. I'm a goner."

My spirit broke then and I hunched forward as I knelt beside him. "Sembur, I *can't*," I sobbed. "I can't leave you 'ere . . . 'an even if I could, I . . . I'm too tired."

I felt his hand touch my knee. Through my tears, I saw that he had closed his eyes as if in pain. Head tilted back, he whispered, "Ah, sweet Jesus 'elp 'er now." I heard the hiss of the *tsampa* boiling over, and scrambled up to take the pan off, wiping my eyes on my sleeve. I poured the *tsampa* into our two bowls and carried them to where Sembur lay.

He could not sit up, but by supporting his head I was able to give him a few spoonfuls before he became too exhausted to take any more. When I had eaten my own bowl of *tsampa* I went out to look at the weather.

I should have been relieved to find that the snow had stopped, but somehow I felt too tired to care. It was as I turned to go back into the cave that I glimpsed movement from the corner of my eye. At first I thought the bear had returned, but as I stared down the shallow slope which rose from the pass to the cave, I saw the foreign stranger leading his black horse. He was following the deep groove made in the snow by Pulki when he dragged Sembur up the slope. As I watched he lifted his head and saw me.

I suppose there was no room left in me for fear or despair. I stood still, and he came on steadily, passing from the deep snow to the thin scattering under the overhang. Eventually he stamped snow from his boots, put a gloved hand under my chin, and tilted my head to look at my face.

"You're a convincing little liar, aren't you?" he said in

113

Hinglish, and I knew that at Namkhara he must have learned I spoke the same tongue as Sembur.

I said tiredly, "I couldn't 'elp it, Mister. Sembur said you'd take 'im away to be 'anged. I got nobody else but Sembur."

He took his hand away and looked past me. "Is he in there?"

I nodded. "Yes, Mister. But he's sick. Being 'igh up made 'is 'eart go funny."

He moved into the cave and I followed him to where Sembur lay. When he spoke, he said Sembur's name strangely. "Ahressembur?"

Sembur opened his eyes. For a moment or two he stared blankly, then I saw his body gradually stiffen beneath the blanket until he lay rigid. He said, "Sir?"

"Captain Gascoyne, Third Battalion, 2nd Queen Victoria's Own Gurkha Rifles. I have orders to place you under arrest and take you to Battalion Headquarters at Gorakhpur. From there you will be taken under escort to Delhi, to stand trial for theft and murder."

"Yessir. I beg to report . . . unable to move, sir."

"I know of no way to ease your condition except by getting you to a lower altitude."

"Perhaps . . . tomorrow, sir. After I've 'ad a rest."

"Very well. And don't lie at attention, it doesn't impress me. You're a disgrace to your calling."

That woke me from my stupor. I kicked the stranger on his booted leg as hard as I could, and shouted. "You leave 'im alone!" He looked at me tight-lipped, turned and went out of the cave, limping slightly.

Sembur said painfully, "Be'ave yourself, Jani. Please. Nobody can do me any 'arm now. But I want 'im to look after you, so be polite to 'im, lovey . . . please, for my sake." I dropped to my knees and hugged him, crying silently, for I knew Sembur had just told me that he was going to die.

"None of that now." A little strength came back into his voice. "No tears. Don't make it 'ard for me, Jani."

The stranger returned, took off his cap and fur jacket and began

114

to heat something which smelt very good over a spirit stove. Sembur seemed to be dozing.

I remembered his words, and said, "I'm sorry I kicked you, Mister."

He looked at me, unsmiling. "Have you eaten?"

"I 'ad a bit of *tsampa*."

"Fetch your bowl and have some of this."

There was some kind of hot stew in the pan. I said. "Can I try giving a bit to Sembur?"

"I wasn't proposing to let him go without. Fetch the bowl."

"Thanks, Mister."

I roused Sembur, and he made a big effort to eat. When he had finished the stranger said to me, "Have you been through this pass in winter?"

I shook my head. "Can't get through in winter. If it starts snowing steady now, we'll be stuck 'ere."

"Thank you." The words were polite, but the way they were spoken made me feel as if he scarcely knew I was there.

I laid out my groundsheet and sleeping-bag, then got wearily to my feet and picked up our canvas bucket. The stranger turned towards me. "What are you doing?"

"Going to get some water. I got to see to me pony before I go to bed." The cave swam suddenly, and I wearily rubbed a hand across my eyes. "We lost all the feed we were carrying, so I got nothing for 'im to eat."

The stranger studied me, and for the first time a tiny hint of warmth came into his eyes.

"I found the stuff you dropped to lighten the other horse. It's over there, behind Flint."

"Coo, thanks, Mister. I'll go and feed 'im now."

"I'll see to both horses. Go to bed, girl."

"I 'ave to see to Pulki meself. Sembur always says—"

"Don't argue. Go to bed."

I took off my boots, wrapped my spare blanket about me, and wriggled into my sleeping-bag. Several times during the night I half awoke, my mind confused. Once I came awake to hear voices.

The stranger and Sembur were talking, not urgently but in a slow, almost idle fashion.

"For my report, would you care to tell me if it's true that you killed the Maharani and her husband?" the stranger was asking.

The question seemed to hang in the air for a moment, then Sembur answered, "Yes, sir. That's quite correct, in a manner of speaking."

"And took the jewels from her body? The jewels of which some still remain in this box I've found in your pack?"

"Yes, sir. I took 'em."

"And ran away?"

"Quite so, sir."

Chapter Four

I lay feeling a remote astonishment. What Sembur said he had done was quite impossible. I heard the stranger give a little sigh, as if puzzled, then he said, "And that's the whole truth?"

"Ah . . . now that's a hard question, sir, because nobody knows the 'ole truth about anything, I reckon."

"I should have thought you of all people would know the whole truth about that night. Why did you do such a terrible thing?"

"Private reasons, sir."

The stranger gave a grunt of impatience. "I'm damned if I can make you out, Sar'major."

"I wouldn't bother, sir. Not important really. Can I 'ave a word with you about the child, sir? About Jani?"

"Yes, I think you'd better. To start with, who is she?"

"I lived with an Indian woman in Jahanapur, sir, when I was serving with the Maharaja's forces there. Jani was born about two years before . . . before I left. I took 'er with me that night."

"We know you lived with a woman called Parvati, but there was no record of her bearing you a child."

"There's no record of *any* child being born in Jahanapur,

117

outside the palace, begging your pardon, sir. It's an Indian state, not like at 'ome."

I did not hear what was said next, for my mind was struggling with a new puzzle. If my feeling that Sembur was not my father was right then Sembur was lying to the stranger. I had never known him lie before, and could see no reason why he should do so now. My mind drifted back to the conversation again.

"What do you want me to do about her?" The stranger's voice was cool and wary.

"Take 'er back to Gorakhpur with you, sir." There was an urgent pleading in Sembur's voice now. "Try and get the Widows an' Orphans Association to take care of 'er."

"She should be taken back to her mother, surely?"

"Parvati's dead, sir. I got word last time I went down over the border to get some ammunition and one or two things." Sembur's voice was hoarse and shaking. "Sir, try to get 'em to send 'er 'ome to England for some schooling. She'll be safe there."

"Safe?"

"Well . . . I mean, think of the kids you've seen in Calcutta, sir, living in the gutters. For pity's sake don't let that 'appen to Jani, sir. If you could just—"

"All right, man, all right," the stranger broke in sharply. "I'll do what I can."

"Thank you, sir. Greatly obliged . . ." Sembur's voice trailed away as if he had used up the last of his strength. I felt nothing. Sembur was dying, and had put me under the care of this Hinglishman, this strange soldier who made it clear with his every look that he disliked me. I should have been torn with grief and afraid of what was to come, but I was empty.

I slept again, to be woken by a hand gripping my shoulder, shaking me. I opened my eyes and looked up into the face of the stranger. It was a face hard as stone, and yet I had a sudden insight which astonished me. The Hinglishman was not angry with me. His fierce glare hid some kind of dismay and uncertainty.

He said stiffly, "Jani, I'm sorry but I have to tell you . . . I'm afraid your father died during the night."

118

"My father?" I sat up and looked towards the place where Sembur had lain, but he was no longer there. The stranger said, "It happened a couple of hours ago, I took him out at first light."

Slowly I dragged myself to my feet. "Where is 'e, Mister?"

"Outside. I was able to find enough rocks to make a cairn."

I went out and looked at the long low pile of stones, knowing there was something I should do. I went back to fetch the Holy Bible from Sembur's pack. I wished I could cry, but no tears would come. The stranger followed me out again, and when I knelt down by the cairn, he took off his cap.

I opened the Bible at Ecclesiastes, Chapter 3. I read very slowly. *"To every thing there is a season, and a time to every purpose under the heaven: A time to be born, and a time to die; a time to plant, and a time to pluck up that which is planted . . ."* I had to pause, and lift my head to swallow. A winter sun glittered on the blanket of snow. A great eagle flashed over the pass and dipped out of sight. *". . . a time to weep, and a time to laugh; a time to mourn, and a time to dance . . ."*

I fell over sideways. When the blackness went away I found that I was back inside the cave and the stranger was supporting me with one arm round my shoulders. There was a fine chain round his neck, with a thick silvery disc on it, which fell from beneath the collar of his shirt as he bent over me. "Jani? Are you all right?" he said.

I clung to his hand. At last I whispered, "I'm all right. Just ever so alone . . . I dunno why." I touched the silver disc and said, "Can I 'ave this to 'old, please?" At once I felt ashamed for having said such a thing.

"This? All right." He unclasped the chain, wrapped it round my wrist, and pressed the medallion into my hand. "Like that?"

I nodded, no longer feeling that dreadful sense of being completely alone. He said, "Are you ready for breakfast now?"

"Well, yes please." I pulled myself together. "We'd better 'ave a talk about what we're going to do now, Mister, because when it snows again we'll be cut off 'ere for the winter. There'll be nothing for the 'orses to eat. We'll 'ave to slaughter them an' freeze the meat to last us about three months till spring. So it's best if we can get back down the pass before it snows again."

His eyebrows went up, and for the first time I saw the stern, foreign-demon face break into a grin.

After a few moments he said as if to himself, "How you'd shock them in England. Such grim realism so young." He gave me a little nod, as if he did not totally dislike me now, and went on, "I've been very much aware of the situation, Jani. Certainly I've no wish to spend the next few months in this cave, and it would break my heart to slaughter the horses." He looked down at me, frowning thoughtfully. "Now, assuming we get back down the pass to Galdong, we'll press on south, through Nepal. There's a hospital at Gorakhpur run by nuns, and they can make arrangements for the Army Widows and Orphans Association to take care of you." He paused, thinking. "We ought to reach Gorakhpur in less than three weeks. Do you think it's going to snow soon?"

I glanced towards the cave entrance. "Not today, but we'd be wise to start as soon as possible."

"Will you be strong enough?"

"Yes, Mister. I'll manage." I called him Mister because I had only heard his real name once, when he first spoke to Sembur, and I had already forgotten it.

He stared at me hard, then nodded slowly. "All right, Jani. After breakfast."

When we led the horses out I knew we had left no time to spare. The sky to the north was heavy with the threat of more snow. I stood by the cairn for a few moments, silently saying goodbye to Sembur and thanking him for looking after me. As I did so I remembered the moments when I had lain half-asleep hearing Sembur calmly admit that he had killed a Maharani and her husband. The idea that Sembur would kill any woman was unbelievable. But then, he had told Mister I was his daughter, and I could not believe that either.

I looked at the pile of rocks under which Sembur lay, and thought that whatever the truth might be, it no longer mattered to anybody now but me.

Chapter Five

Just to sit in the saddle was hard work, for we were constantly lurching and slithering. Beneath the walls of the pass the snow was up to three feet deep, and I marvelled at the way Mister thrust on against it, forcing a narrow path for us to follow.

After several hours of cruel struggle, we reached the small village of Galdong, which lay west of the monastery. Mister would have paid a gold piece for the two rooms we rented for the night, but I was so shocked at his stupidity that I forgot myself.

"A piece of *gold*?" I said quite rudely. "You gone barmy or something?"

"It's only a half sovereign."

"Don't let 'er see it!" I snatched it from his hand before the woman I was bargaining with returned with her husband in support. "Let's 'ave a silver rupee, quick!"

When the woman and her husband appeared I politely pointed out the poverty of their home, the lack of all things necessary to persons of quality, and the extraordinary goodness of our hearts in condescending even to consider spending a night or two under their roof. When the bargain was closed for the one silver rupee and we were alone, I saw Mister laugh for the first time. "You're a card, Jani. You're really quite a card."

I did not entirely understand what he meant, but felt rather proud of myself for having made him laugh. It wiped away all his sternness and arrogance and gave me new heart.

We saw that the horses were comfortable, took turns to bath in a tub, ate a big meal, then slept the night through. As I expected, the High Lama had heard of our arrival at once, and in the morning he sent for me. Mister frowned when I told him, and said, "I'd better come along."

"No, you can't if you 'aven't been invited. Anyway, Rild's just going to ask about Sembur. Then he'll say I can stay on 'ere and become a nun if I like."

"And do you like?"

I shook my head. "No. And anyway I can't become a nun 'ere because Sembur says they're a lot of 'eathens. An' I wouldn't do anything to upset Sembur."

Mister gave me one of his long frowning looks, as if trying to puzzle something out. He said at last, "Well, whatever Sembur did, you're fortunate to have had a father who inspired such loyalty."

"Sembur wasn't my Pa. And what you and 'im were saying when I was 'alf asleep, that wasn't true either. Sembur never killed those people an' stole their jewels."

"You're saying Sembur was a liar when he confessed?"

I felt trapped, and a sudden rage against Mister swept me. "No 'e wasn't a liar!" I stormed. "Sembur just told you all wrong that night for some special reason. And if I was big enough, I'd '*it* you." With that I turned and stalked away, making for the monastery.

My audience with Rild went just as I had expected until suddenly, after a silence, he closed his eyes and murmured, "Your way is dark to me . . . but I see the woman in red who will be your friend, and through her will come the one to fear, who will be your enemy, the Silver Man—" He broke off with a hiss of indrawn breath, eyes opening suddenly very wide with shock. I had thought it impossible for the High Lama's calm to be disturbed, but now it was as if he recoiled from the sting of a scorpion. "Ahhh. . . ." he breathed. "Within the bounds of earth and incarnation I had never thought to feel such power."

I saw his lips moving as he murmured mantras to bring quietness to his mind. Then he spoke again, "With the turning of the stars you will come to us again, child. Till then, go with my blessing."

On leaving the monastery I took scarcely any notice of Rild's words, for I was busy thinking about preparations for our journey south. When I returned to our lodging I found Mister rubbing down the horses. I began to help in silence, then swallowed my pride and said, "I'm very sorry I was rude to you, Mister."

122

He gave me an amused look. "That's all right. Let's make a
start for the south as soon as possible."

BY THE SIXTH DAY I felt completely myself again. There was still
an aching emptiness within me for Sembur, but I had stopped
wondering about my own future, and pretended that Mister and I
would simply go on and on, through mountains and foothills,
across tumbling rivers, our journey never ending.

As the days passed, we had fallen into a simple pattern. Each
morning I would make a good hot breakfast while Mister folded
our tents and attended to Flint and Pulki. As we busied ourselves
with our tasks, or rode on our way, we would sometimes talk a
little. But he would never talk about himself. Our silences were
not unfriendly, though. It was more that we had little to say to
each other as we came from different worlds. Before sunset we
would make camp, and wash the dust and sweat of the day's travel
from us before making our second and last meal of the day. This
was the time I liked best, when we sat by our fire in the dusk, and
all the world was quiet but for the shuffle of a hoof, or a little
snort from one of the animals.

From Smon T'ang we crossed the border into Nepal and
moved steadily south, descending from the high country where
fir and birch and the huge-bloomed rhododendrons grew, to the
slopes where the wind blew more gently among pines, oaks and
walnuts. We swung east to Pokhara, where Mister re-filled our
panniers with fresh stores, then moved south again for the Indian
border.

One day, when it was my turn to wash first in the bucket of
water we had heated, I looked at the silver medallion hanging
against my chest, as I always did now, for it had become a kind of
talisman for me. Summoning up my courage, I said, "Can I ask
you something, Mister?"

He looked up from the razor he was taking from its leather
case and said absently, "Why not?"

"I'm not sure if it's polite."

"Try asking, and I'll let you know."

"I was wondering what this medallion is."

He came towards me. The thick silver disc, about twice the size of my thumbnail, was inset with a gold star which had five points. On the back was a spiral of tiny little squiggles and curlicues, and I realized that this must be some kind of writing. I said, "Is it a foreign language, Mister?"

"Yes. A language of India, called Hindi."

"What's it say?"

"Oh, it's a poem of some sort. Nothing important."

"Did someone give it to you?"

He gave me one of his heavy scowls. "A lady. Now stop asking questions."

I liked his scowl and did my best to imitate it. "You've got a long nose," I said, "an' hooky eyebrows, an' you look like a foreign demon."

His face shifted in a funny way, and he said, "I thought you were supposed to be polite to me."

"Oh. Yes, I am, but sometimes I forget. Beg pardon."

"Don't mention it," Mister said.

Almost from one day to the next the air became warm and moist, and we found ourselves moving through country quite unfamiliar to me. For a whole day we travelled along a trail through a forest, passing small villages where dark-skinned people stared at us as we went by.

As long as I was able to shut out of my mind the fact that our journey would come to an end, I was happy during this time. I could not have said why. Perhaps, with Sembur lost to me, it was because I was so glad to be in Mister's care for a little while.

On the fifteenth day I woke in the night feeling ill, my heart palpitating. When morning came I barely had strength to stand and I knew I had fallen victim to a disease demon. Mister felt my pulse and forehead, and bit his lip.

"You have a fever, Jani," he said shortly. "We've done well, but we still have another three days to go." He laid me down on my bedding, and drew a blanket over me. "You rest while I get breakfast and strike camp."

124

That morning I rode tied to Pulki's back, lolling and lurching in the saddle. At some time during the afternoon I realized that I was on Flint, with Mister seated behind me, his arms supporting me on each side. Or perhaps it was a different day, for often I seemed to drift away to a place where time stood still.

It was presumably the third day when I roused to the chatter of a tongue unknown to me. The disease demon was still with me. I was in a small cart, and I seemed to be lying on a mattress of straw. I could hear Mister's voice speaking warningly, as if telling the driver to go carefully. Vaguely I realized that we must have reached a village where he had hired a cart and driver. After another time of blankness I heard a whole medley of sounds and knew we were in a town.

Then the noise was left behind. The cart stopped. Mister lifted me out and carried me through a big doorway into a cool place. Somebody spoke to him. I heard his voice, sharp and demanding: "I don't give a damn about the proper channels. Get this child into nursing care at once."

Then everything faded, and I went far away again to the distant place where nothing happened and time did not move.

I CAME BACK to the world unwillingly. I lay in a bed with white sheets and was wearing a faded flannel nightdress. The room was small, and a lady all in black except for a white peak to her hood, was standing by my bed. I was to learn that I was in the Gorakhpur Mission Hospital and that lady was one of the Hinglish nuns who ran it.

She smiled and said, "Well, you gave us all quite a fright. It's been five days now, you know. How do you feel this morning?"

"A bit . . . a bit weak. But all right, thank you, Miss."

"You call me Sister. Sister Ruth."

"Yes, Sister. I'm Jani."

The nun picked up a board with a paper fastened to it at the foot of my bed. "We have you entered as Jane. Jane Burr."

I wondered why someone had chosen that name for me. No doubt Jane was the Hinglish way of saying my first name, but in

Smon T'ang I had never had a second name, and could not think why they should call me Jane Burr. The nun was saying, "We expect to have you up in a few days now, and off home to England within a month."

I said, "Please . . . where's Mister?"

"Who, dear?"

"I . . . I forget 'is name. The gentleman 'oo brought me 'ere."

"Oh, the young captain. He left three days ago, Jane. He had orders to report to Calcutta, and he went off by train, with that lovely horse in a horse-box."

I had known he would be gone, back to his own world, and that I would not see him again. Yet to be told so was like the shock of an unexpected blow. I was now truly alone. I turned on my side, sliding my hand up to my throat where it felt as if a great lump had suddenly risen. My fingers touched something small and round beneath the nightdress. I fumbled at my neck, found the slender chain, and drew out the medallion with the inset gold star.

I turned the medallion over and peered with tear-blurred eyes at the spiral of tiny writing on the back. A thought came to me, and I whispered, "Sister . . . excuse me, but . . . do you 'appen to know what this Hindi inscription says?"

"I don't read Hindi myself, dear," I heard her say brightly. "But one of our sisters does and she wrote it down for you." She turned over the little board she held, and looked at a piece of paper clipped to the back. "Apparently it's more poetic in Hindi, but it means something like this:

Here is a token to remind you of a friend.
It may not bring you good fortune,
Or protect you from fate or from your enemy.
It is for remembrance only.
Keep it until a friend has need of it,
Then give it gladly and go your way."

I turned my face into the pillow and let the tears come. There was heartbreak in me, but gladness too, for I held the medallion gripped tightly in my hand, this token which said I was his friend. I would never ever be quite alone.

Chapter Six

I first set eyes on England three months later when we landed at Southampton in a steady drizzle of rain.

I no longer called this country Hingland, because I had noticed that other people did not use an extra aitch for emphasis, as Sembur had done. In fact I spoke very little, for I was very afraid. In *Tales of Jessica* I had read at least a little about the world outside Smon T'ang, and Sembur had told me many amazing facts. But it was one thing to be told about a great iron locomotive or a sea reaching to the horizon; to experience such unbelievable sights is very different.

Throughout the journey I was in the care of a Miss Foot, who had been a governess in India and was now going home. She was being paid a small sum by an army charity to escort me to London, where a place had been found for me in an orphanage. She was a thin lady with grey hair and a nose like a beak. We hated each other.

She would talk about me, while I was sitting beside her, as if I were not there. ". . . We all have our cross to bear, Mrs. Stoddart, and Jane is a great burden to me. I had hoped for peace and quiet on this voyage, but—*don't* cross your feet, Jane!—I have very little peace, I assure you. The child is a half-caste, of course. Her father was a common soldier who married an Indian woman in Jahanapur, then perpetrated some dreadful crime—*don't* hang your head like that, Jane!—I beg your pardon, Mrs. Stoddart? Oh, yes, I was *amazed* that the army should send a half-Indian child to England, but it seems *somebody* exerted a great deal of influence and also paid her fare—keep your *knees* together, Jane!"

I put my knees together and sat up very straight, hoping to avoid any more complaints. If somebody had paid my fare to make sure I was taken to England it could only have been Mister. He had honoured his promise to Sembur.

On a grey day in January I saw the last of Miss Foot and entered the Adelaide Crocker Home for Orphan Girls, in a part of London called Bermondsey, where I was to spend the next two and a half years. For me, once I had grown used to the life, they were not unhappy years.

The number of girls varied from sixty to seventy, and their ages from five to fourteen. The principal was Miss Callender, who looked rather like Miss Foot but was very different. Of the grant made each year to the orphanage under Adelaide Crocker's will, Miss Callender spent every possible penny on food. Our clothes, though, were dreadful because Miss Callender hated to spend money on them. Old dresses were remade, patched, turned, and remade yet again for as long as the threads would hang together. Our boots came to us secondhand from a school for young ladies, and were repaired again and again. They all had the toes cut away so that they would fit a wide range of feet.

The seasons came and went, and the orphanage became my world. We had lessons every day, and were taught reading, writing, sums, sewing, knitting and crochet. The older girls were expected to look after the small ones, which meant that we were always busy.

When a girl became fourteen, a position was found for her, usually in service, but sometimes with a dressmaker or in one of the East End factories, or very occasionally on a farm. I stayed until I was fifteen, a year longer than I should have done, because Miss Callender found me a special help with the smaller children. I might even have remained to become a kind of unpaid assistant, if I had not fallen out with an unpleasant girl called Big Alice who was in charge of another dormitory. She was always sneering, and one day I lost my temper and hit her. It was the first time I had done such a thing, but a great fuss was made about it, and Miss Callender decided it was time for me to go.

Although I had always tried hard with my sewing, I had no gift with a needle, neither did I want to go into a factory, for I had heard grim tales about conditions in such places. I imagined that I would go into service, but to my great joy Miss Callender sent for me one day, and said she had found me a place helping on a farm in Hampshire with a Mr. and Mrs. Gammidge. They

128

had paid for my railway fare and would meet me that Saturday at Tenbrook Green Station.

Miss Callender concluded our talk by saying that she was sorry to lose me, and by wishing me well in what she described as my new life.

MY NEW LIFE lasted exactly two weeks and three days. Mrs. Gammidge was a quiet, stolid woman who worked hard. Her husband was cheerful but lazy, a lanky man with a long face and a jumble of big white teeth.

On the second day, when we were getting grain for the chickens from the shed where it was stored, Mr. Gammidge put an arm round me and pressed his hand on my bosom. I pulled away, startled, realizing that I had an awkward problem to cope with, and one that was new to me.

From then on, almost all my thoughts were devoted to avoiding being left alone with Mr. Gammidge. Once, when he cornered me in the barn, I had to stamp on his foot hard to get away. It ended when I came down at half-past five one morning to light the fire in the big range, and found Mrs. Gammidge there before me. She turned from the sink, where she was washing up one or two plates, and said quietly, "Goo an' pack yer things, girl, I'm wanting 'ee gone 'fore Muster Gammidge come down."

I made no pretence of being puzzled, and said, "I'm sorry, Mrs. Gammidge. I 'aven't done anything to make 'im think—"

"I know. 'Tes no blame to you, girl." She gave a weary shrug. "He's allus been like that. It's a lad we need, and it's a lad we'd 've had, if it weren't for Vicar sayin' we should tek an orphanage girl."

I went up to my tiny room and packed my belongings in the small canvas sack I had brought with me from the orphanage. The task did not take long. I was wearing a skirt and a flannel blouse which had once been a man's shirt. My silver medallion hung round my neck next to my skin, as always. Now I put on my well-scrubbed but rather frayed straw hat with a ribbon round it, a special treasure Miss Callender had provided, and went down to the kitchen.

Mrs. Gammidge sat in a wooden rocking chair, gazing at the fire in the range. As I entered she spoke without looking round. "That on the table, 'tes for 'ee, girl. A packet o' bacon san'wiches an' a sixpence. Best I can do."

"Thanks ever so much, Mrs. Gammidge. I'm sorry about . . . everything."

She shrugged, still gazing into the fire, but said nothing, and after a moment or two I went to the door and let myself out, the canvas sack on my back.

I set out for Bournemouth where I had been told there were lots of gentry and big hotels so that, with a bit of luck, I might find a job there as a chambermaid. It was thirty miles away.

I walked seven miles that morning, not hurrying and keeping to the greensward beside the road as much as possible, so that there would be less wear on my boots. At noon I ate one of the three thick bacon sandwiches Mrs. Gammidge had made for me, and two hours later some wild ponies came close. After a while, I was able to rub their noses, chatter to them and give them greeting from my old friend Pulki.

That night I slept under an old yew whose low branches formed a shelter to keep the dew from soaking me and next morning I woke with the birds, very hungry. I walked to a brook I had noted the evening before, washed as well as I could, combed my hair, and then thankfully but very slowly ate my second bacon sandwich. I was keeping the last one, and my precious sixpence, in reserve, for I had no idea how long might pass before I could earn myself a meal.

Throughout the morning I went on at a good pace, and judged that by noon I had walked ten or twelve miles. I felt sure that I had not far to go now before reaching the coast, for I could smell a difference in the air, and was sure it came from the sea. I was very hungry again, and very tired. I rested for an hour as the sun moved overhead, then set off once more.

Passing through a narrow glade, I was startled suddenly when a voice quite close to me called, "Stop!" The word was spoken not very loudly and rather shakily. When I stopped and looked to my left I saw a man standing in a patch of grass. He wore a tall black

130

hat, check trousers, a frock coat, and gold-rimmed spectacles. In his
hand he held a large note-pad. He was standing in a strangely
awkward way, one foot advanced and with his weight on it, as if he
had stopped suddenly in mid-stride.

As I stared, the man lifted his tall hat, and I saw that his hair was
grey and rather thin. He said rather breathlessly, "Pray forgive me,
young lady, but I should be greatly obliged if you could assist me."

I began to move towards him.

"Oh, stop, please stop!" he croaked anxiously, waving his hat.
"Don't come any nearer." I stopped short, completely bewildered,
and he gave a sigh of relief. "The—er—the fact is," he went on,
"I am standing on a poisonous snake, of the *Viperidae* family, an
adder. If you approach with caution, you will observe that the
creature is trapped under the instep of my right boot. At first, and
most fortunately, it was trapped very close to the head. But we have
been in this position some time now, and I believe he, or possibly
she, has been slowly gaining more freedom."

My stomach felt cold. Unfortunately my small gift for coaxing
the best out of animals did not extend to the serpent. However, I
put down my sack, went quickly forward, and dropped to my hands
and knees. The snake was about twenty inches long. Its arrow-
shaped head and perhaps three inches of thrashing body protruded
from beneath the instep of the boot. It was clear the snake would
soon gain enough of its own length to strike into the man's leg.

The hesitant voice said, "I think you had best move away, young
lady . . . my head is swimming and I fear I may fall . . ."

I glared up at him, and my face must have been as pallid as his
own, for I had decided what I must do, and it terrified me. "Don't
you dare fall down!" I said furiously. "Don't you *dare!*"

I moved round to his right, where the main body of the snake
emerged from under his boot. Nerving myself, I gripped the scaly
body with both hands near the tail.

The man said, "No, really, my dear child, . . . you mustn't . . ."

"For Gawd's sake shut up!" I snapped, the sweat running into
my eyes. Then I added "sir" to make amends. "Listen" I said,
"when I say *Go*, you lift this foot an' take a big step forward, see?"

"But . . . but the creature will turn on you and—"

"Don't *argue!* One, two, three . . . *go!*"

The man lunged clumsily forward. The instant his right boot began to lift I straightened from my crouch like a spring, swinging to my right and hurling the viper away from me with all my might. It soared through the air to fall amid bushes twenty paces away.

I dropped to my knees, shaking in every muscle. When I looked up I saw that the man had sprawled headlong in the thick grass. He began to crawl towards me, his leaden face full of anxiety. "Child . . . are you unhurt?"

"It's all right, 'e didn't get me."

The man gave a great sigh, then rested on all fours, his head hanging low. I got up, picked up his hat and the large note-pad, which I noticed had a drawing of a butterfly on the open page, then said, "We'd better get out of this long grass, 'adn't we? There might be more of 'em."

"They . . . are not hostile," he gave me a painful smile, "except when one is so foolish as to step upon them." Slowly he got to his feet. I judged him to be about sixty, a tall man with a wide mouth and very small turned-up nose which gave him an almost comical appearance. His eyes were brown, kind, and friendly.

After a moment or two he seemed to come to himself. "Oh, pray forgive me. I am Graham Lambert of Merlin's Keep, Larkfield."

I dropped him a curtsey, as we had been taught in the orphanage. I now always used the surname which had apparently been Sembur's real name. I said, "I'm Jani Burr." I could not help a slight giggle. "Of nowhere special."

Mr. Lambert gave a little bow. "Your servant, Miss Burr. I am . . . profoundly grateful." He swayed and I caught his arm to steady him. "I'm sorry, my dear. I have a heart which is inclined to sulk if called upon to do more than it deems necessary."

"Are you far from 'ome, sir?"

"About . . . two miles. Just this side of Larkfield. I have a gig close by." He pointed vaguely.

I put my arm round him and made him lean on me as we moved slowly in the direction he had indicated. There, on a grassy patch,

132

a beautifully groomed horse stood grazing in the shafts of a two-wheeled carriage.

With much pushing and heaving I managed to get Mr. Lambert into the gig, and put my canvas sack in beside him. I hesitated, then said, "Would it 'elp if you 'ad something to eat, sir? I got a sandwich you can 'ave." I raked in the sack, and took out the last of Mrs. Gammidge's bacon sandwiches.

He whispered, "Thank you . . . no, my dear. Most kind . . ." Greatly relieved, I put it away. In the same croaky whisper he said, "Can you . . . drive the gig?"

"I don't think I'll 'ave any trouble once I've 'ad a word with your mare, Mr. Lambert. What's 'er name?"

"Oh . . . ah . . . Sally."

I moved up to stand where she could see me, and scratched her ear, talking to her first in English but then in the tongue of Smon T'ang, which was better for animals because it was more polite and dignified. I asked her to take us home, rubbed cheeks with her, then climbed up beside Mr. Lambert and took the reins. I had never driven a cart before, but once I concentrated on letting her feel me through the reins, it was very easy.

Our route led away from the forest and along a lane that twisted and turned between thick hedgerows of hawthorn. After ten minutes we descended a hill and saw a village below, a pleasantly rambling pattern of little houses with slate or thatched roofs, and a church with a square tower.

Suddenly, ahead on our left, I saw two huge pillars. Sally turned in between them. We trotted briskly along a gravel drive which curved to the right, away from a line of big elms.

Then I saw Merlin's Keep, and in the same moment a blue-grey bird with a white-banded tail flashed across the drive in front of us —a merlin, though I did not know it then. The house was of grey stone and mellow brick, its front made up of a centre span and two short wings which slanted forward from it. Strangely, it seemed the centre span was curved, as if it formed part of a circle.

We drew to a halt on stone flags at the foot of some broad curved steps and, at that moment, the big front door opened and a woman

133

came flying down the steps. Her wine-coloured satin dress swirled and rustled. Her hair, piled high on her head, was rich auburn, almost red. She was in her late twenties, with a strong handsome face and grey-green eyes which were wide and full of anxiety as she strode towards the gig. Behind her came a thin, older woman wearing a dark dress.

A little beyond where we had stopped, a strapping young gardener was working on a flower bed. The lady in the red dress turned towards him. "William! Here, quickly!" She looked up at me. "What happened?"

I was still supporting Mr. Lambert. "I found 'im in the forest, Miss. Trod on a viper, 'e did, and couldn't move. He never got bitten, but I think his heart's gone a bit wonky."

"Father? Father, do you feel very bad?" She had taken his hand and was holding it, her voice warm and gentle as if she were speaking to a child.

Mr. Lambert sighed. "Such a stupid thing, Eleanor dear. This child saved my life, I'm sure. . . ."

The lady looked hard at me for a moment, then said, "Wait here, please." She turned to the thin lady. "Give me a hand to help Mr. Lambert down, Burkey. Steady now. All right, Father, we've got you." She turned to the young gardener. "William, please fetch Dr. Vine at once."

A minute later I was alone. I got down from the gig, lifted out my canvas sack, and looked about me. All was quiet again. I made a little fuss of Sally, thanking her for being a good girl, then went and studied the house. I had never been as close as this to a gentleman's house, and I was intrigued despite my tiredness.

Five minutes passed, I looked at the sun. If I wanted to get to Bournemouth before the light failed the sooner I started walking again the better. I picked up my sack and set off, but had gone no more than a hundred paces when I heard a cry behind me. Looking back, I saw the lady in the red dress, waving as she approached.

"What on earth are you doing, Jani Burr? Didn't you hear me ask you to wait?"

"Yes, Miss. But I got to get into Bournemouth."

134

"Where are you going in Bournemouth?"

"I dunno yet, Miss."

"I see." Her grey-green eyes gave me a searching look. She said, "Jani, I want you to come into the house. My housekeeper will give you something to eat. Then I want you to tell me something about yourself. Afterwards, if you wish, I'll have you driven into Bournemouth, so you'll lose no time. What do you say?"

"Thank you very much, Miss."

I walked beside her across the lawn, up the steps into the house, through a panelled hall twice as big as my whole home in Namkhara, then down some stairs and into a huge kitchen. Here, the thin lady was giving orders to a maid, while another maid sat at a long scrubbed table cleaning silver cutlery.

"Now," said the lady in red briskly. "This is Mrs. Burke, our cook-housekeeper, this is Annie and this is Meg. They will look after you, and I'll see you in my study later."

During the next hour I discovered quite a lot about Merlin's Keep and the Lambert family, for Mrs. Burke chatted almost unceasingly, and whenever she paused for more than a second or two either Annie or Meg would seize the chance to put in a few words. I learned that Merlin's Keep had been built sixty years before by a rich man with a passion for falconry, his favourite bird for this sport being the merlin. The house had been designed as a squat tower three storeys high, like a castle keep, with two long triangular wings, so that if anybody could have seen the building from above it would have looked something like a bird in flight. There were still merlins in the nearby pine woods.

While they talked I washed my hands and face at the kitchen sink, then sat down to a plate Mrs. Burke set in front of me with cold meats, tomatoes, lettuce, and small new potatoes.

I learned that Miss Eleanor Lambert was Mr. Graham Lambert's daughter, and these two were the whole family, since Miss Eleanor's mother had died giving birth to her, and Mr. Lambert had never remarried. Mr. Lambert was a naturalist. "Writing a book on butterflies, so 'e is," Meg put in impressively. "A book wi' pictures painted by 'is own self."

135

Miss Eleanor was no less clever, for she knew all about wild flowers. "Very high up in wild flowers she is," said Mrs. Burke, who had put on an apron and was mixing something in a big basin. "What they call an authority on them, see?"

"Paints 'em, like 'er father does butterflies," chimed in Annie.

"Ooooh, they're clever, mark my words," said Mrs. Burke.

They talked more between themselves than directly to me, and it soon became clear that this was a happy household. I began to hope, though scarcely daring to, that Miss Eleanor might offer me a position in service, as a kitchenmaid, perhaps.

Some time after I had finished eating, a man called Mayes came downstairs. He was about fifty, a quiet man with a soft voice, and I learned that he was Mr. Lambert's manservant. Mayes said that the doctor had been, had left some pills for Mr. Lambert who already looked much better and was making little jokes about his adventure. And Miss Eleanor was ready to see me now.

I felt very nervous. Miss Eleanor's study was in one of the angles of this strangely designed house, and was shaped like a triangle with one corner cut off. The walls were panelled in dark wood up to one third of their height, with a nice cheerful yellow wallpaper above. Miss Eleanor sat behind a large desk. There was an easel in one corner by the big window, and a long narrow table with paints, cartridge paper and half-finished sketches.

As Mrs. Burke ushered me in she said, "A nice snack she's had, Miss Eleanor. And asked if she could wash herself an' tidy up before she sat down to it." She gave a nod of approval.

"Thank you, Burkey. Off you go." When the door closed, Miss Eleanor gave me a thoughtful smile, and pointed to a chair near the desk. "Sit down, Jani. What have you got in that little sack?"

"Just my belongings, Miss."

"May I see?"

I felt ashamed as I set them out on the desk. My spare undergarments and dress were clean but very rumpled, and the buttermuslin wrapped round my last sandwich was becoming greasy. Miss Eleanor pointed. "Is this the famous bacon sandwich you offered my father?"

136

"Yes, Miss. Well, I dunno about famous."

"And what are these?"

"The 'oly Bible and *Tales of Jessica*. They're my books, Miss I covered 'em in brown paper."

She looked taken aback. "Where do you come from Jani?"

"Well, first of all from Smon T'ang, Miss. It's a country in the 'Imalayas, north of Nepal and south of Tibet."

Her eyes narrowed. "Are you joking?"

"No, Miss. Honest."

"You speak the language?"

"Yes, Miss."

"Say something in it, please."

"Which kind, Miss? There's a posh kind for talking to 'igh-up people, like lamas, and there's an ordinary kind."

Her lips twitched, "Let me hear the posh kind."

When I had spoken a dozen or so words she asked, "What have you just said?"

"Well, it sounds sort of funny in English, Miss. I said, *Gracious lady, I thank you with 'umble gratitude for the 'ospitality shown me by your 'ouse. May your kindness gain you much merit to aid your release from the wheel of rebirth.*"

She gasped and sat back in her chair. "Good Heavens above! I apologize for doubting you, Jani. How did you come to England?"

"It's ever such a long story, Miss."

"Never mind. Tell me."

When I had finished, Miss Eleanor looked down at her hands. "You have a gift for précis, Jani. Why did you have to leave the orphanage? You said something happened, I believe."

My heart sank. I had been trying very hard to make a good impression, but now my answer to this question would surely destroy all hope of gaining a position here at Merlin's Keep.

"Well, Miss, there was this girl called Big Alice," I said. "One day I was telling some of the little girls I looked after a story. It was about someone 'oo 'ad brought me down, safe from a cave on the Chak Pass, someone ever so special. An' this girl Big Alice, she sniggered and said something 'orrible about 'im."

137

Miss Eleanor looked at me curiously, head tilted a little. "Go on, Jani."

"So I clouted 'er on the nose with my fist, as 'ard as I could, Miss. She didn't 'alf bleed." I could hear the satisfaction in my voice, but no longer cared. It was all over now anyway.

Miss Eleanor pressed her hands over her mouth and made a funny snorting sound. Then she looked up with an expression of excitement. "Jani. Would you like to stay here at Merlin's Keep?"

Suddenly my eyes felt wet. I said fervently, "I'd like that more than anything in the world, Miss."

"I'm not taking you into service," Miss Eleanor said. "Oh, you'll start off below stairs, of course. You'll be more at home there to begin with, and I don't want to go too fast, but you have a brain, and character. I'll not see you wasted. And it will please my father, too." She slapped her hands emphatically on the top of her desk. "I'm going to make something of you, Jani. I'll give you lessons in everything you've missed. I'll teach you to talk properly, I'll make a young lady of you. Can you write, Jani?" I nodded dazedly. "Good! You shall become my secretary in the long run. Heaven knows I need one."

"Miss . . . please, Miss Eleanor." I felt confused and frightened. "You'll only make trouble for yourself, Miss, if you teach me 'ow to be a young lady an' mix with the gentry. They don't like someone that's 'alf Indian, I found that out on the ship. They'll think badly of you."

Miss Eleanor's grey-green eyes opened very wide, and though she spoke quietly I could hear a whiplash in her voice. "I have never allowed myself to be troubled by what others may think, Jani. I think you have the character to overcome racial prejudice, and you can be quite sure that you will have total support from both my father and myself."

I felt a strange peace come upon me, as if suddenly all my burdens had been shifted to other shoulders, far stronger than mine. Suddenly from the past a memory came drifting into my mind. I was standing in the sunlit chamber of the High Lama. His eyes were closed and his voice quiet as he said, ". . . *Your way is*

138

dark to me . . . but I see the woman in red who will be your friend. . . ."

Now I sat looking at the woman in red, Miss Eleanor Lambert, who would be my friend. There had been something more Rild had said . . . what was it?

Miss Eleanor was saying, "Mind you, we shall have to see how we get along together, so you'll be on trial for a while, but I'm sure I've judged you rightly."

"I'll try very 'ard, Miss." I meant it. Rild's voice faded from my mind. Three long and wonderful years were to pass before I remembered those words of his I could not now recapture.

It was then that the Silver Man would come into my life, the one who would be my enemy.

Chapter Seven

During my first six months at Merlin's Keep I did housework and kitchenwork with Meg and Annie every morning from six o'clock till noon. After we had served a light luncheon, and taken our own in the servants' hall, there followed three hours of lessons for me, either with Miss Eleanor or Mr. Lambert.

In the evenings I would take turns with Meg and Annie, two of us serving dinner, the other helping Mrs. Burke in the kitchen. After dinner I was free to spend whatever time I wished in studying for myself in the enormous library.

Amazingly, Annie and Meg were not in the least jealous of my privileges, in fact they pitied me and were always warning me of the danger of getting brain-fever. Both were courting, and both married within a few weeks of each other, six months after my arrival. This was the time, with new servants to be engaged, that Miss Eleanor chose to move me from below stairs to above stairs.

Mrs. Burke sniffed a little, and made dark remarks about the Good Lord having appointed us to our station in life, but within a week she was calling me Miss Jani and behaving as if she had never in her life seen me scrub out a pot.

For the first few days it was a great ordeal for me to sit at table with Mr. Lambert and Miss Eleanor and to retire to chat in the drawing room afterwards. It was an even greater ordeal for me to start calling her simply Eleanor. Within a few days, however, the awkwardness vanished. "Good girl, Jani," she said at breakfast one morning when I used her name quite naturally without even thinking about it. "That's another big step you've made."

My lessons continued, but for longer hours now that I had no other work to do. We also spent a great deal of time out of the house, much to my pleasure. Eleanor liked riding. She had no knack for co-operating with a horse, but simply dominated it, being filled with such powerful certainty it would obey her that the creature almost always did so. We played tennis, joined in the village activities, walked or bicycled for hours with sketch books and paints, looking for wild flowers. I loved to help Eleanor in whatever she did, whether it was cataloguing her flower paintings, checking the names in Latin, visiting a sick or bereaved villager.

Soon it became hard to remember she was not my elder sister, for that is exactly how she behaved with me, and I adored her. If Eleanor treated me as a younger sister, Mr. Lambert treated me as a younger daughter. When we met at breakfast he would kiss me on the cheek, as he did Eleanor, and wish me a happy day. At bedtime he would do the same, and say, "God bless and keep you, child."

Many a time during the summer I would take the gig and drive him out into the country, searching for some creature or plant he wished to study and sketch. Whenever we returned to the gig after walking in the New Forest he would make the same little joke about the pretty girl in the straw hat, with no toes to her boots, who had offered him her last bacon sandwich. This kind of thing, telling the same story or making the same joke, sometimes annoyed Eleanor, but I never minded with Mr. Lambert.

If I had to decide on a moment when I first felt certain that I had put behind me my early difficulties and awkwardnesses, it would be the day a few weeks after my sixteenth birthday when I was officially presented to the gentry of the parish at a summer garden party given by Eleanor. The new "Indian" girl the Lamberts had taken

140

up had of course been much discussed by the community, and I
knew very well that not everyone was well disposed towards me.

On the day of the garden party I was so frightened I kept fearing
I would faint. I wore a dress of very pale apple-green ninon over a
silk foundation, with a bertha collar.

On Eleanor's advice I had kept my hair shorter than most girls
wore it. Indeed, she had cut it for me herself. I had a short thick
fringe across my brow, and on either side the black hair fell straight
to the level of my jaw, framing my face.

Eleanor studied me in the looking-glass. "If you didn't look like
a frightened doe, you'd be very beautiful. Nobody's going to eat
you, Jani."

"Oh Eleanor, you should have *told* them you were going to
present me today, then people who didn't want to come could have
stayed away."

"Which is exactly why I didn't tell them," Eleanor murmured,
still studying my reflection. "Yes, I'm glad we've done your hair
this way. It emphasizes the Indian part of you which is what will
worry the squire and his cronies, so let's hit them in the eye with it
and make no pretence."

It was not until all the guests had arrived, and were strolling and
chatting on the lawn, with the maids moving among them serving
tea and sandwiches, that Eleanor came to the house to fetch me.

She linked her arm in mine and began to take me round the
lawn, introducing me. My face felt frozen, and my legs were trembling, but I tried to smile and look each person in the eye as I
touched hands in the rather feeble way that was correct. "How do
you do, Mrs. Markham? Good afternoon, Mr. Sangford." Here was
the Vicar's daughter. "How nice of you to come, Dorothy."

There came a moment when I felt Eleanor tense slightly, then
she turned so that we moved directly to where two gentlemen
stood chatting. "Squire Tarleton, Major Elliot, I should like you
to meet a young friend who is very dear to my father and to me,
Miss Jani Burr."

"How do you do, sir?" The squire screwed up his heavy red face
doubtfully as I dropped a small curtsey to him.

"H'mm! Hallo, young lady." He looked down into his teacup as if seeking inspiration there.

Major Elliot was a tall, dried-up man. I knew from Eleanor that he had spent several years in India with the British army. He looked at her and his lips tightened. "I'm bound to say, ma'am, that in our society a person of mixed blood—"

"Quite right, too, Major." It was Mr. Lambert who had strolled into our little group, "They are indeed to be envied, but we cannot all expect to be so privileged."

"I beg your pardon?" the Major began blankly, but Mr. Lambert went on speaking without pause. "How chastening it is to think, Major—" his usually quiet voice had become remarkably penetrating, so that people all around fell silent in surprise "—that she carries the blood of a people who had achieved a high state of civilization when your ancestors and mine were still wearing half a goat-skin and a few daubs of woad."

The Major said, "Eh?" But nobody heard him, for Eleanor now came in with a voice she could have used for hailing a ship, "Oh, I can well understand your high admiration for the Indian race, Major. No doubt it stems from your personal experience. You have had the pleasure of seeing the Taj Mahal, have you not? What amazing architects and masons. to produce such a beauty."

I kept my face straight and solemn, but inwardly I was giggling, and all my fears were draining away.

". . . and of course," Mr. Lambert was saying now, "it is not only for her inheritance of intelligence that we should envy Jani, as I am sure you would be the first to observe, my dear Tarleton . . ."

"Me?" The squire grunted in surprise.

". . . for you are the first to admire a physical skill, my dear fellow. You have seen her ride. You were watching her last week, Eleanor tells me."

Squire Tarleton stood gazing blank-faced, rubbing his chin. I had the feeling that he was trying to catch up with events which had moved much too fast for him, "Yes," he said at last with a judicial manner. "There's a great deal in what you say."

Then he crooked his arm at me and said with an air of cheerful

142

acceptance, "All right, young Jani, let's take a walk to the stables and look at the horses, hey? And you can tell me where you learnt to ride."

It would be untrue to say that from this moment on I was completely accepted in Larkfield, but this was the critical point. Most people followed the squire's lead. Others were swayed by an extraordinary rumour shortly afterwards.

It was whispered that Jani Burr was really an Indian princess, her parents being a Rajah who ruled one of the states of India and a beautiful Englishwoman, daughter of a nobleman. It appeared that Jani had been kidnapped as a child by a wicked relative of the Rajah. Her mother had died of grief, the Rajah had given up everything and gone away to become a holy man, and the villainous relative now ruled the princely state. But Jani had been discovered in Tibet by an agent of the British Government and brought to England where her true identity was to be concealed until she came of age and the army in India would throw out the usurper.

On the day Eleanor first found the village buzzing with this rumour she came straight back to Merlin's Keep, where Mr. Lambert and I were playing croquet on the lawn, went up to her father and hugged him, her green eyes sparkling with mischief and joy. "Father, you clever old thing for starting that rumour about Jani."

"Rumour? Come now, Eleanor, I don't spread rumours."

"You didn't spread it, Father, you started it. I know your style too well to be taken in. But it's a lovely rumour! Our Jani, an Indian princess, incognito!"

I said blankly, "A what?"

Eleanor took my arm, still bubbling with merriment and delight. "I'll tell you in a moment, dear. Father, how did you manage it?"

Mr. Lambert sighed, laid down his mallet, and began to polish his spectacles.

"Really Eleanor, you do run on," he said gently.

He would never confess to having started the rumour, but as I came to know him ever more closely with the passing of time, I was quite sure Eleanor had made no mistake. Mr. Lambert knew the power of snobbery in the world we lived in, and he had made good

143

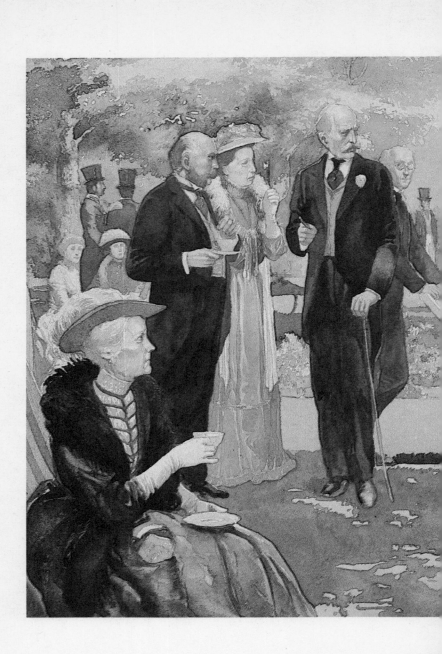

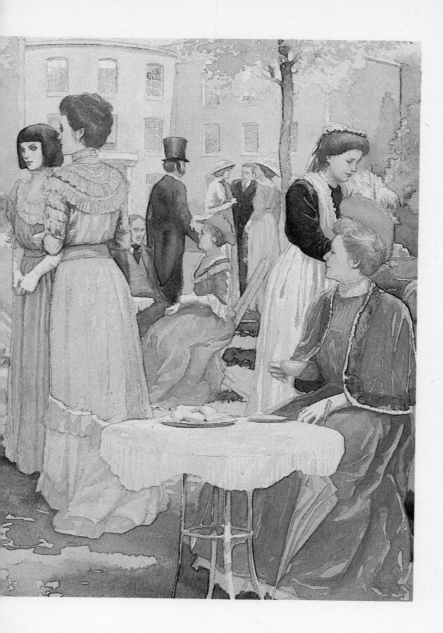

use of it. In time the rumour faded, but the effect of it remained, to give me good standing in Larkfield at all levels.

Eleanor was gradually accumulating material for a book on European wild flowers, and took me abroad with her twice during my third year at Merlin's Keep, once to Austria and once to Italy. I had worked hard to make myself a capable secretary, and was able to take notes at Eleanor's dictation while she made colour sketches.

We no longer speculated much on the mysteries of my past, for as Mr. Lambert said, "One cannot make valid deductions from insufficient data." But one small puzzle we did solve was the question of Sembur's name. Since I had been registered at the hospital in Gorakhpur as Jane Burr, presumably by Mister, we took it that "Burr" was the correct surname. And I had heard Mister speak of him more than once as "Ahressembur".

"I fancy," said Mr. Lambert, "that 'Sembur' was a baby-talk corruption of RSM Burr, or to put it in full, Regimental Sergeant-Major Burr. Would you not agree?"

I said eagerly, "Yes, I'm sure you're right, Mr. Lambert."

"Now, it would be very odd," he went on, "for a child to address her father by a corruption of his military rank and surname. How does a child come to know a name? By hearing it spoken, of course. So I think we can make the strong assumption that during your babyhood RSM Burr was present in some capacity, and people referred to him as RSM Burr. I believe we can therefore be certain that he did not speak the truth in claiming to be your father, which gives excellent reason to believe that his confession to murder and theft was also false, though we can never hope to guess why."

We were having tea on the lawn when this conversation took place, and I was so full of delight at the way in which Mr. Lambert had argued for Sembur's innocence that I got up from my seat, put my arms round him and kissed him on the cheek.

A WEEK OR TWO before my third Christmas at Merlin's Keep, a great shadow was cast across Eleanor's life and mine.

It was then, without warning, that Mr. Lambert died peacefully

146

one night in his sleep. To say I was heartbroken tells little of the grief I felt, for with his passing I lost not only a man who had treated me as a daughter, but also one who had been a wonderful companion and friend. In my sorrow I did not forget that he was Eleanor's true father, and I fought hard to keep my feelings under tight control, for Eleanor needed comfort, and it was to me that she turned while showing a stoic face to the rest of the world.

I had never thought to see my strong, brisk, fearless Eleanor so dazed and shaken. I was thankful to lift from her shoulders all the sad tasks which had to be dealt with on such occasions, and I think in the end it was this which enabled me to pass through my time of grieving more quickly than Eleanor.

When the Will was read, I discovered that Mr. Lambert had left me a legacy of two thousand pounds. I felt guilty at the idea of such an inheritance, and at once begged Eleanor to take it. "Don't be silly, dear," she said gently. "Father spoke to me about it a year ago, and I fully agreed. He was a man who lived a happy life, Jani. And you gave him almost another three years to live it."

In March, Eleanor decided to go away on one of her trips abroad, to seek and paint wild flowers in Greece. I was torn between the wish to go with her and a feeling that she might prefer to go on her own. We talked about it as we walked a frosty footpath to the village for exercise one morning.

"I've been leaning on you for too long, Jani, and it simply won't do," she said. "So I shall go away alone, and work very hard for a few weeks, then come back home and be my old self again. Are you sure you can manage while I'm gone?"

"Don't worry, I shall enjoy having lots to do. If I need advice on anything I'll go to David Hayward."

David Hayward had come to Larkfield eighteen months ago, taking over the veterinary practice, and had quickly become a welcome visitor at Merlin's Keep.

"Yes, do that," said Eleanor. "David is very reliable."

I sighed. "I do wish you hadn't refused him when he wanted to marry you last year."

I saw her flush, and she said, "Oh, stop nagging. David can't be more than a year older than I am. It's quite unsuitable. I became an old maid years ago, and I'm perfectly happy."

"Well . . ." I took a hand from my muff and slipped it through her arm as we walked. "I hope he asks you again, anyway."

Eleanor laughed. It was the first time I had heard her laugh for many weeks, and the sound made me glad. I hoped that she would soon come back to Merlin's Keep strong and happy once more, her sorrow transformed to loving memory. Then perhaps she would marry David after all . . . and perhaps some handsome and exciting man would fall in love with me and want to marry me, and perhaps we would share Merlin's Keep, and everything would be quite wonderful. . . .

Chapter Eight

A voice behind me said, "Miss Burr, I should like to make a proposal."

It was a fine day in July, three months after my eighteenth birthday. I had ridden my horse Nimrod through the village and then up Goose Hill to where I had dismounted to let him wander while I sat gazing across at Merlin's Keep and the village below it.

I came to myself, startled for a moment, then smiled and managed to stop myself looking round. "A proposal? Oh, sir, this is so sudden."

For almost as long as I had known David Hayward he had been teasing me with pretended proposals of marriage. He came into my view now leading his big grey, Smokey, gave it a slap to go and join Nimrod, then dropped down beside me on the dry grass. "Hallo, young Jani. Mrs. Burke said I'd find you up here."

"I'm getting less young all the time, David. You'd better be careful, in case I say yes when you propose."

He laughed, then looked at me thoughtfully, his head on one side. "Well, if I do it again, you'll know I'm serious."

I knelt up and glared at him. "Don't talk like that! You know very well you want to marry Eleanor."

He spread a hand. "She won't have me."

"Well, you must just try again when she gets back from Greece."

I liked David. His hair was thick and brown, his face quiet and rather nondescript except when he smiled, but then the warmth that lit it made him almost handsome. The youngest son of a titled landowner in Lincolnshire, he had left university to take the long training of a veterinary surgeon because his great ambition in life was to heal animals. A quiet, serene man, he showed politeness to all, deference to none. Within a few weeks of setting up in practice in Larkfield, he had discovered through Eleanor that I had a way with animals. At first, he had been sceptical, but he had lost no time in putting me to a practical test at the earliest opportunity. I had pacified Mr. Sangford's big Airedale when it was mad with the pain of a poisoned foot and would let nobody come near.

Since that day it was rare for more than three or four weeks to go by without David asking me to help with one of his patients.

Now he grinned and got to his feet, "I forgot to tell you my proposal, Jani. What I'm proposing is that you come along with me to Stafford's Farm and talk to his cow Mabel, while I get her womb back in."

"Oh, so that's it. But you'd better not make proposals of that sort to any other young lady, David."

He drew me to my feet, and we called Nimrod and Smokey to come to us. Moments later, we were cantering down the grassy slope of Goose Hill. And, as we fell into an easy trot on the footpath at the bottom, he said, "Is everything all right at the house, Jani?"

"Yes, thank you. Mrs. Burke and Mayes keep everything running smoothly."

"Well . . . if you haven't any household problems, what's wrong?"

I looked at him, a little startled. "Why do you think there's something wrong?"

He shrugged. "I've come to know you quite well, and I think I can tell when you're worried, even when you try to hide it."

I hesitated. "Perhaps I'm worrying about Eleanor a little."

"Ah." He looked at me quickly. "Why, Jani?"

"I expect I'm just being silly. For the first month she was away she sent me letters every week. But then she wrote saying she had met an Englishman who was staying at the same hotel, and she was always trying to avoid him. And after that her letters became . . . I don't know. Strange. She'd start to write something, then she'd jump to a fresh thought so suddenly you could scarcely follow her."

I paused for breath, a little embarrassed. Now that I had begun to voice my fears, I was almost gabbling them. I thought David might smile at them, but he said soberly, "Go on, Jani."

"Not long after that, her letters became even more strange. They were very short and she spoke of this man suddenly as if they had become friends. When she moved from Trikkala down to Corinth it seems he was still with her."

"She's not a child," David said quietly. "If she's made friends with the man, it's because she wished to."

"But Eleanor wouldn't travel alone with a man. I know everyone says she's unconventional, and it's true in some ways, but in other ways she's very correct about standards of behaviour. Oh, it's so difficult to explain . . . She was going to be away for six or eight weeks, but she's been gone more than three *months* now."

We turned at the corner of the copse and began the gentle climb to Stafford's Farm. David said, "Perhaps she's in love. That could account for everything, I suppose."

I felt in my pocket for the two rather crumpled pieces of writing paper covered in Eleanor's bold hand, and passed them to him. "That's the last letter I had from Eleanor. It came about a week ago."

I had taken it up to Goose Hill to read again in the hope of wringing some previously unnoticed shred of comfort from the letter, but my hopes had been in vain. It read:

Dearest Jani,
    Your letter came on Thursday, I think. I hope you are well. I have no notes for you to type. Why have I done no work this past week, or is it longer?
    So deep, the Corinth Canal. I was seized by vertigo, and could

150

have cast myself down from the bridge, but Mr. Quayle was holding my arm. What shall I do? It has been very hot and he has advised me to rest.

Keep well and strong, and always be yourself, Jani. Greece is so beautiful. I'm sure you would enjoy it.

I am writing this letter before going to bed. Please pray for me, Jani.

With fondest love,
Eleanor

We had halted a stone's throw from the farm while David read the letter. I saw his frown deepen as he read it through twice, then he handed it back to me.

"I just wanted you to see that she isn't behaving oddly because she's in love," I said. "It's not that sort of letter, is it?"

"No. Far from it. There's an underlying note of desperation."

"That's how it seemed to me. But what can be wrong? And if there *is* something, why doesn't she say?"

He nudged his horse into a walk, and I fell in beside him again. "I've no idea, Jani." he said grimly. "None at all. This fellow Quayle must be the Englishman she met earlier?"

"Yes."

"If it was anybody but Eleanor I'd think Mr. Quayle was one of these parasites who ingratiate themselves with lonely women. But she'd spot that kind in a flash."

We were nearing the cowshed now, and Mr. Stafford was coming towards us, calling a greeting.

Veterinary work was usually a messy affair, and Larkfield had taken some time to get over the shock of knowing that young Jani Burr was often involved in such unseemly matters. The Reverend Wheeler and several ladies had remonstrated with Mr. Lambert and Eleanor for permitting it. What Eleanor and Mr. Lambert said, I never knew, but my activities as an animal nurse soon became just one more eccentricity of the many displayed by the folk at Merlin's Keep.

I now stood talking to Mabel the cow while David made his

preparations, then coaxed her to kneel and be still while we helped her. She almost went to sleep, so he and Mr. Stafford had little trouble in pushing the calf-bed back into her, and she continued dozing even when I went back to help him stitch her.

When we had finished, and enjoyed a glass of homemade lemonade with the Staffords in their cool kitchen, David insisted on escorting me home. We spoke very little on the way, and not at all about Eleanor until we reined up outside the stables, then he said quietly, "I think you're right to be worried, but there's nothing you can do except wait for Eleanor to come back."

I shook my head slowly. "No, I've been thinking about it all the way back from the farm, and I know what I must do. I'll wait just ten days, till the end of the month. If by then I haven't had a letter from Eleanor to say she's returning, I must go out to her."

"Go out? To Greece?"

"I have my own money, and Mrs. Burke can look after the house. I must *see* Eleanor, and *talk* with her. I don't know what's wrong but I'm sure she needs help, so I must go to her. I'm all she has left, now that her father's dead."

I had dismounted as I spoke. David stared down at me with a wondering look. "What you say strikes me as being very sensible. Will you discuss this with me again a week from today?"

"Yes. Yes, I'll do that, David."

He regarded me soberly for a moment or two. "Few people remain grateful for long, Jani. You're certainly one of the few."

I scarcely paid attention to his words, for I was busy with a thought of my own, and said, "David, when Eleanor comes back will you ask her to marry you?"

He laughed, and gathered the reins. "Well, I'll ask one or other of you, Jani. I haven't quite made up my mind which."

He was teasing me again, and I was able to laugh with him, for I felt relieved, almost happy, now that I had come to a decision and made up my mind to act.

I spent the rest of the day trying to work out how best to travel from Bournemouth to Athens.

When I went to bed that night I read Eleanor's letter again, and

152

as happened every time I did so, one line in particular held my eye. *Please pray for me, Jani.*

Carefully I took out my worn Bible from the chest of drawers where I kept it, knelt beside the bed, and began to turn the pages. I knew I was not very good at praying, but I would now attempt to do so every day until Eleanor and I were together again. When I had finished, I read through the Twenty-Third Psalm aloud. Then, I got to my feet. In doing so I must have knocked the Bible for it slid off the counterpane and fell to the floor. In my haste to pick it up, I stubbed my toe on the leg of the bed.

When the pain eased I picked up the Bible, and sat on the bed to examine it, fearful lest it was damaged. To my relief I found that the binding had held. However, when I looked at the endpapers, the sheets which were glued down to the inside of the leather-bound covers, I saw that the back one, brown with age, had split down the inner side. It was a curiously straight slit, more like a cut than a natural tear. And beneath the endpaper, resting between it and the board of the cover, there seemed to be a sheet, or several sheets, of very thin paper, folded once.

I sat very still, staring at them. It dawned on me that here was something which had been deliberately hidden in the Bible, either by Sembur or by whoever had owned it before him. Carefully I edged the folded papers out. There were nine sheets of flimsy rice-paper, the kind of paper I had sometimes seen in Namkhara. One side of every sheet was crammed with tiny writing.

My heart jerked as I realized that it was signed on the last page in Sembur's usual large and ornate hand. I drew a deep breath, and began to read.

Dear Jani,

Today you were seven years old and I have decided to spend my evenings these next few weeks writing down your story. Perhaps you will never read this but I must write it down all the same.

Your father was Captain Francis Saxon, of the First Battalion, 2nd Queen Victoria's Own Gurkha Rifles. He was seconded to the State of Jahanapur, with the rank of Colonel, to command the

Maharaja's armed forces, three companies of infantry and one battery of artillery. It was to do with politics, because some of the Indian Princes are friendly to us and some are not, but I won't go into all that.

I was the only British RSM in any Gurkha regiment, which was something special, and I was nearly due to retire, so when your father asked if I would sign on for seven years as RSM of the Jahanapur army I was very pleased as I have no family in England to go back to. Also he was the best man I ever knew.

The ink took on a slightly different shade at this point, as if Sembur had stopped writing for a while and then begun again with a thicker mixture. I was to find there were many such changes during the time it took Sembur to compose and write down his strange and terrible story. I read on:

The Maharaja was a good ruler. His daughter Sarojini had been to school in England and Switzerland. They were both popular with the people. We had some trouble with a man called Chandra Ghose, who was the half-brother of His Highness. Ghose wanted the throne of Jahanapur, and tried to start a rebellion, but your father soon put a stop to that. I wish His Highness had ordered Ghose to be shot, but he pardoned him.

Well Jani, I must try to keep this short. Colonel Saxon and Princess Sarojini fell in love. It was really something made in Heaven as the saying goes, I only wish I had the words to tell you. Her father, the Maharaja, was very pleased, and so was some high-up man from the Viceroy's Office who came to see the Colonel.

I looked up from the cramped writing. Colonel Saxon, my father? Princess Sarojini, my mother? I recalled the story Mr. Lambert had put about in Larkfield, to make people think I was an Indian princess. Now it seemed his story was partly true, except that he had reversed the nationalities of my parents. I read on.

Some people in Jahanapur were against the marriage because of religious reasons, but your father didn't bother much about such things. He said it would please the people if they had a wedding in

154

Indian style as well as Christian, so they did that. You were born nearly a year later, Jani. You were fifteen months old when the Maharaja died and your mother became the Maharani, which meant she was the ruler of Jahanapur.

Chandra Ghose, her uncle and the one who made trouble before, he acted like he was very pleased for her to be Maharani. We didn't trust him, but your father controlled the army, so there was nothing Ghose could do we thought. We was wrong.

I've got to come to a terrible bit now, Jani. I still have nightmares about it and always will. You and your parents lived in the palace of course, and I lived in a nice bungalow between the palace and the barracks, with a woman called Parvati to do housekeeping for me.

Parvati . . . I recalled that in the cave at the top of the Chak Pass I had heard him tell Mister that Parvati was his wife. Perhaps it had been true. I focused on the laborious writing again.

The Maharani's personal maid Pawala came for me one night, bringing you with her. She said her mistress and the Colonel was both dying. The Colonel had said I was to come at once and tell nobody. We left you with Parvati and went to the palace.

As soon as we reached the bedroom I saw they was done for, your mother and your father. It was poison, I didn't know what sort or how it was given them. Pawala said it was two things, something from the gland of a frog, and very finely chopped whiskers from a tiger. She said they act like steel splinters, I don't know, but I never saw such agony. Their muscles kept going into spasms so bad I thought their bones would break. I'm sorry but I have to tell you how they was suffering Jani or you will think bad of me for what comes next.

The Colonel was on the floor, with blood running down his chin. The Maharani was near him, poor girl, and he was holding her wrists because she had gone over the edge and kept trying to tear her own stomach out with her nails.

Sitting at the desk, I cringed and felt the blood draining from my cheeks. Sembur had no gift for words, but his simple telling conjured up a scene so dreadful that I had to screw up my courage to go on reading.

Your father gasps at Pawala to go. Then he says between spasms, we're finished, Sergeant Major. For the love of God give my darling rest.

At first I did not understand, and then I did. Sir, I can't I says to him, I love her like a daughter. Then help her God damn you he says in a kind of screaming whisper.

When I come from the bungalow I had put on my belt with the bayonet in it, so now I took it out and knelt down, and slid it in quick under the second rib, and she went limp and quiet right away.

The Colonel let go her wrists and fell over sideways, both hands holding his stomach now and he said, Thank God, you have never served me better Sergeant Major. I said, Sir, I will turn out the army and have that dog Ghose hanging in the palace square at sunrise.

Don't be a fool he tells me. The army will not follow you against Ghose, not with the Maharani dead.

I knew it was true. They would know Jahanapur needed a new ruler quickly before one of the border states laid claim to it. Then I remembered the rightful new ruler was you, Jani, but you was only two, so Ghose would act for you and you would not live long enough to grow up. Your father had worked that out all right even with all the pain. He said, you have to get Jani away. I promised Her Highness. Go north. Have Parvati bring you news of what happens here, then use your discretion. You will need money. Take the jewellery Her Highness is wearing.

Then suddenly he says to help him because he could not hold the bayonet himself, and so I did, same as I had done for your mother. God forgive me for what I did that night but I still don't know what else I could have done.

My poor Sembur. I sat weeping silently, for my mother and for my father, for Sembur himself. As soon as I could see again I went on reading, there could be nothing worse to come.

I took the jewellery and went north with you as ordered. A week later Parvati came into the hills where I was hiding. She said Ghose had put out the story that I had gone to rob the Maharani because I wanted to run away with Pawala, but I had been caught in the act and had brutally killed both the Maharani and her husband. They said Pawala had confessed to all this before hanging herself in her prison cell in shame for what she had done.

Parvati said the army did not believe it but they pretended to because with Her Highness dead they would be relying on her successor for their pay. She said the British army had been informed and a reward had been posted for me. All the palace staff had been dismissed and Ghose had moved in.

I was not surprised at any of this, Jani. What did surprise me was that Ghose did not give out that I had took you with me. I suppose he thought it would not fit in with the story he had told about me murdering your mother and father. So instead he gave out that you was quite safe in the palace. Parvati said they might soon get hold of a girlchild from somewhere and pretend she was you, then she would die of a fever or something. But she said Ghose would never stop looking for you to destroy you because you was the rightful ruler of Jahanapur.

I brought you here to Mustang so nobody would ever find us and I went down to meet Parvati again two years later, near the border. She said the child had died and that Ghose was ruling Jahanapur and everything had settled down, but the British was still after me.

We met again after another two years and nothing had changed, but she never kept the next appointment. She did not send any message so I think she must have died.

Well now I have put it all down, Jani. Perhaps I will tell you all this when you are a big girl, then we can decide together, but I just wanted to put it down in case anything happens to me. I can't think of any more to say so will close now.

　　　With love,

　　　　　Sembur (RSM George Burr)

My head was throbbing. I crossed my arms on the desk and rested my head on them. I wished desperately that Sembur had described my mother and father, for then I could at least have pictured them. As it was, the two who had died so terribly were as strangers to me.

Poor Sembur. Even at the last he had struggled to protect me from the smallest chance of discovery by Ghose. He had implied to Mister I was his own child, and that Parvati was my mother. He had begged Mister to see that I was sent home to England, where I would be "safe". Now I understood what he had meant, and as I recalled that conversation in the cave as he lay dying I understood, too, why he had appeared to confess to robbery and murder under Mister's questioning.

"... Is it true that you killed the Maharani and her husband?"

"Yes, sir. That's quite correct, in a manner of speaking."

"And took the jewels from her body? ...."

"Yes, sir. I took 'em."

"And ran away?"

"Quite so, sir."

It had not even been necessary for Sembur to lie. He had simply held back some of the truth, to make sure my identity was not suspected. And in doing so he had knowingly died with the stain of brutal murder upon him.

Chapter Nine

At half past eight on the morning after my discovery of Sembur's letter I was sitting at David Hayward's breakfast table, my throat dry from having talked almost without stopping for the best part of half an hour. I had ridden out to his large rambling cottage just as soon as I had had my own breakfast. I had found David in his shirt-sleeves, with the morning paper propped against the milk jug, sitting under a trellis at the side of the cottage.

He had interrupted me only twice as I told my story, to have something made clear. Now he was reading the last page of Sembur's letter. I sat fidgeting with my riding crop, waiting. He lifted his head, then smiled ruefully. "Your story seems to raise a daunting number of issues. What in particular is worrying you?"

"Only one thing." I sat forward on my chair. "Sembur. I have to clear his name."

David leaned back, hands linked behind his head, and stared at me. "I'm not surprised that of all the issues raised by this letter the most important to you is clearing Sembur's name." He hesitated. "Yesterday you were worried about Eleanor, I think rightly. She's alive and Sembur is dead. Clearing his name isn't urgent. Shouldn't Eleanor come first?"

I stared. "Of course she must! I'm still going to Greece if I don't hear from her, but I thought perhaps something could be going on for Sembur while I'm away. If I go."

"Oh, Jani." He laughed and handed me back Sembur's letter. "I think we should go to Major Elliot with your story."

"The Major?" I was a little surprised.

"Yes, I know he's pompous, Jani, but he's very knowledgeable about the army and about India. If he decided to take up the cause of clearing Sembur's name, I think he would relish a full-scale campaign. And your new standing as daughter of a Maharani and a Colonel will have a splendid effect on him."

"Well . . . if he believes it."

David stood up and touched the letter I held. "I've never yet read anything with a greater ring of truth. I'll have a note taken to the Major this morning. You'll hear from me later, Jani."

WE SAW MAJOR ELLIOT that same afternoon, in a study where the walls were hung with spears, guns, and the stuffed heads of wild animals. He greeted us, then moved to a large ornate desk and sat down. "I gather from your note, Hayward, that Jani is seeking my advice in a matter of some importance." He placed some writing paper in front of him, and picked up a pen. "Very well," he said, "you had better tell me all about it, Jani."

Once again I told my story and showed the sheets of rice-paper covered with Sembur's cramped writing. The Major kept interrupting with questions, and would then make me pause while he wrote notes. But he displayed no emotion whatsoever, not even when reading Sembur's letter. When I had spoken my last word, however, he moved from his desk to stand looking at me, his faded blue eyes sparkling with zest.

"No doubt at all," he said, his creaky voice a little higher than usual. "I recall the case, of course. It made a big stir. Couldn't understand it. And old Baggy Ryman, he'd known this chap Burr as a sergeant years before, in Lahore. Baggy said he wasn't the murdering type at all. Fishy. All very fishy. But he bolted, d'you see, so what else was there to think? However, at last we've got to the bottom of it, hey? Splendid, splendid!"

He fell silent, still gazing at me, and now there was a hint of embarrassment in his look, a slight flush to his cheeks. Suddenly he picked up my gloved hand, and made a small bow over it, saying, "I am truly honoured that you should have come to me for advice, Your Highness."

"Oh no, please, Major!" I rose to my feet, and drew my hand away. My cheeks were hot, and I felt a complete fool as I shot a frantic glance at David, who had risen as soon as I stood up. "Please call me Jani," I said, floundering. "I don't want to be . . . oh, really, don't sit there grinning like that, David!"

"Eh? No indeed." Major Elliot gave David a very frosty glare. "Now look here young Hayward, you don't seem to understand that as Maharani of Jahanapur, this young lady is ruler of some two million souls. That is no cause for amusement."

The Major turned back to me. "If you wish to remain incognito, as it were, and not to assume your proper style and title, I shall of course respect your wishes—ah—Jani. Perhaps that would be best for the moment in any event, until the Foreign Office has looked into all this and confirmed your right to Jahanapur. Meanwhile I agree with you about clearing Burr's name, poor devil. Now that's where we should start, if I may advise you. I'll go up to town this week, and talk to some old friends in the War House and the Foreign Office." He lifted a triumphant finger and beamed at me. "I shall also go to see Lord Kearsey! How about that?"

"Lord Kearsey?"

"Lieutenant-General Lord Kearsey. He's Colonel of the regiment. If we give him a chance to wipe out this nasty stain in the regiment's history, he'll go at it like a rogue elephant."

He turned to pace across the room, rubbing his hands together, and I realized that David Hayward had judged him correctly. Major Elliot still relished a campaign. "By George," he said slowly, "I'd like to be in the battalion mess the night that news of Burr's innocence reaches them!" He looked down at me, a gleam in his eyes. "I know what they'll do, Jani. They'll send a party of Gurkhas up through the Chak Pass to bring that old soldier home, and they'll bury him in their own military cemetery where he belongs."

It was then, quite unexpectedly and with scarcely a sound, that I began to weep as I stood there, the tears rolling down my cheeks. Major Elliot stared aghast, and looked frantically at David. "What happened, Hayward? Did I say something wrong?"

David put a clean handkerchief in my hand, and tucked my other arm under his as he spoke. "I think you said something exactly right, Major. Thank you for your help, and we'll leave you to carry on as you think best."

WHEN THERE WERE only four days left of the time I had allowed, a letter came from Eleanor, on the writing paper of a hotel in Athens.

> Dear Jani,
>
> Mr. Vernon Quayle and I were married in the Anglican church here yesterday, and we shall leave for England in two days' time.
>
> We expect to reach Bournemouth on Monday 29th, by the train arriving at three o'clock. Please have us met, and make suitable arrangements for our taking up residence at Merlin's Keep.
>
> Yours sincerely,
> Eleanor Quayle.

It might have been a letter from a stranger. I read it a dozen times in the hour I spent waiting for David to call, for this was the day I had agreed to talk with him about my journey. But there would be no journey now.

I was in the stables, grooming Nimrod and pouring out my anxieties to him, when David arrived. I showed him the letter. He read it through, his face startled at first, then becoming impassive. At last he handed it back to me, rested a hand on Nimrod's withers and stared down. "Well . . . that's it, then."

I touched his hand. "I'm so sorry, David."

"Thank you, Jani dear. And you're worried, too, I fancy."

"Yes. I'm frightened."

He shrugged and gave a wry smile. "Don't let your imagination run away with you. Mr. Vernon Quayle is probably a very nice man. I'm sure Eleanor wouldn't have married him otherwise." He paused. "I'm sure this won't affect your situation, Jani."

"I hadn't thought about that. I've never taken my position here for granted."

He nodded. "No, I didn't imagine you had. But I'm quite sure you'll be staying on here with Eleanor. I've often heard her say she couldn't do without you. New husband or not, she needs you, Jani."

For the next two days I was very busy, for there was much to be done. Mrs. Burke, Mayes, and the maids all received the news with more unease than enthusiasm. I decided that Eleanor would prefer to retain her own bedroom, which was very large, for herself and her husband, so I arranged to have the big bed moved in from Mr. Lambert's old room. The house was cleaned from top to bottom.

On the Saturday morning before their arrival, I found time to drive into Bournemouth, and buy a lovely four-piece silver tea and coffee service. This was to be my wedding present to Eleanor and her husband.

On the Monday afternoon Mayes drove me to Bournemouth station in the landau. William, the young gardener, followed us with the gig.

The train came in no more than a minute late, and I stood on tiptoe, craning my neck, stupidly worried that I might miss Eleanor amid the bustle of alighting passengers.

My heart leapt as I saw her, rich auburn hair glowing beneath a green straw hat I had helped her choose before she went away, and I almost ran as I hurried through the crowd on the platform.

162

I was vaguely conscious of somebody beside her, but I had eyes only for Eleanor, and called her name as I drew near.

She was staring at me from a rather drawn face but suddenly her eyes lit up and she threw out her arms. "Oh, Jani! Jani!" We hugged each other, and my hat was pushed all askew, for she was taller than I, then she stepped back, clutching both my hands.

"Jani, how good to see you,—oh!" I saw the animation suddenly vanish from her face. She loosed my hands almost guiltily, and said in a flustered fashion, half-turning to the figure beside her, "Oh, forgive me, Vernon. This is Jani." Without looking at me she continued, "Jani, this is my husband, Vernon Quayle."

His hair was silver grey, and spread thinly over a skull that seemed too large. The long face was strangely unlined, the eyes remote, grey as cobbles. He carried a hat in his hand and wore a rather ill-fitting suit, also of silver grey.

Time seemed to have stopped. Suddenly my memory opened the gates of a cold and paralysing fear. I remembered the Oracle of Galdong who had looked into the pool of darkness and spoken of the Silver Man, the Eater of Souls, the bloodless one. . . .

I knew he stood before me now. Somewhere deep in my being I felt sure that I was looking at the Eater of Souls. Bloodless he was, for his face was unnaturally white. Even as I stared, with horror creeping through me, I remembered how Rild, normally so quiet and serene, had given a little gasp of shock, and whispered, "*. . . within the bounds of earth and incarnation I had never thought to feel such power.*"

Vernon Quayle said, "Good afternoon." In contrast to his appearance he had a beautiful voice, quiet and mellow, but I heard no trace of warmth in it. I dropped a little curtsey and said, "Good afternoon, and welcome to Larkfield, Mr. Quayle. You have my warmest congratulations."

When I put out my hand he merely touched it with cold fingers, yet I had to repress a shiver and make a positive effort to withdraw my hand naturally rather than snatch it away.

"I have three trunks of important chattels in the van," he said.

"William will see to it, Mr. Quayle," I said. "If he can't get it all on the gig, he can make another trip."

When we took our places in the landau I sat facing Eleanor. Vernon Quayle sat beside her and took her hand. I hoped this was a gesture of affection, but as we drove through Bournemouth and out onto the Larkfield road he said no word to her but simply looked about him, silver head turning slowly this way and that, the empty grey eyes gazing without seeming interest. I waited for Eleanor to speak, but she sat stiffly, with an embarrassed air, giving a timid smile when she caught my eye. Somehow I managed to keep chattering away about nothing in particular during the drive home, but it was a heavy ordeal.

We came to Merlin's Keep, where Mrs. Burke and the other servants appeared on the steps to welcome their mistress and new master. This should have been a happy and exciting moment, but everybody seemed ill at ease, except for Vernon Quayle himself. He eyed the staff absently as they were introduced in turn, but seemed much more interested in studying the house itself. I had planned to have a refreshing cup of tea brought to us, but as we entered the big hall Vernon Quayle said, "I should like to see the house, my dear."

"Of course, Vernon."

I set my teeth and said as cheerfully as I could, "Won't you have a cup of tea first, Eleanor? You must be so tired."

Vernon Quayle gave me a long slow stare, and Eleanor said quickly, "No, dear, no, I'm not at all tired, thank you."

During the next twenty minutes we made a brief tour of Merlin's Keep. When we were upstairs, he said in his fine mellow voice, "We shall require separate rooms." He glanced round the big bedroom I had made ready for him and Eleanor. "No doubt this will suit you well enough, my dear. I will take the east-facing bedroom across the passage." He looked at me. "Perhaps you will see to it."

"Certainly, Mr. Quayle."

Eleanor said, "I do hope you will find a room suitable for your study, Vernon. There is mine, of course, or the room that was my

164

father's study, or Jani's office, all on the ground floor, as you have seen." She sounded nervous, and I could have wept.

Her husband said, "None is suitable, Eleanor." He gazed at a flight of stairs leading up from the passage where we stood. "Does that go up to the servants' quarters?"

"Not exactly, Vernon, though it leads to the same floor. Their quarters are in the two wings, each with a separate staircase. This leads to what we call the Round Room."

The Round Room had no connection with either wing, and the stairs we now mounted provided the only access to it. The room rose slightly above the level of the rest of the roof, and had four windows. One was wide and deep, looking out from the back of the house over the grounds. The other three, equally spaced round the circular room, were high up near the ceiling and slot-like in shape. Mr. Lambert had always suspected some architectural error, for in fact the room was not really round, but bulged on the southern quadrant.

Vernon Quayle stood in the middle of the newly cleaned but unfurnished room, gazing slowly round him. "This will do admirably," he said, and looked at me. "Perhaps you will be so good as to have a furniture maker call at the earliest opportunity."

"Very well, Mr. Quayle." I felt suddenly that I must get away if only for a few minutes, for I could scarcely bear to see Vernon Quayle and Eleanor together. "Please excuse me while I attend to the changing of your bedroom."

Later, after practising some cheerful smiles in the looking-glass, I tapped on the door of Eleanor's room.

Entering at her call, I found her sitting at the dressing table, hands in her lap. She still had not taken off her hat or jacket.

"Where is Mr. Quayle?" I said.

She looked down at her hands, "He's up in the Round Room."

I moved towards her. "Take your hat and jacket off, dear, it's so warm. Come along, let me help you." She sat listlessly as I drew out the pin and lifted the hat from her beautiful hair, then suddenly she caught at my hand and gasped, "Don't leave me, Jani! Don't ever leave me, please promise!"

My nerves jumped with shock, then I put my arms round her and held her tightly to me. "Of course I won't leave you," I whispered fiercely. "Never, never, never while you need me. Oh Eleanor, what is it? What's wrong, dear?"

For a moment she clung to me, then twisted suddenly away and stood up, her head cocked as if listening, a puzzled frown between her eyebrows. "What did you say, Jani?" she asked after a moment or two.

"I asked what was wrong."

"Wrong?"

"Yes. You begged me not to leave you, and you seemed so distressed."

"Did I?" She stared at me in what seemed genuine bewilderment. "Oh dear, I seem to do such funny things these days. I'm so sorry."

I stood undecided, with the feeling that I was trying to cope with something I could not begin to grasp. At last I said, "I'll make some tea, and fetch it up here, shall I?"

"Yes, dear. That would be nice," Eleanor said absently.

I went out of the room, now knowing for certain that something quite dreadful had happened to my dearest Eleanor.

Chapter Ten

I had promised Eleanor I would never leave her. Within seven weeks I had broken that promise, not of my own failing but because she herself made it impossible to keep.

In only a few days the easy and pleasant atmosphere I had always known at Merlin's Keep was changed to one of sombre unease. At the end of a month, Mayes left to live with a widowed sister in the Midlands. In his place Vernon Quayle engaged a man called Thorpe, who spoke scarcely at all, and appeared to have a grudge against the whole world. Mrs. Burke stayed on only because I begged her to.

Less than a week after Vernon Quayle entered Merlin's Keep,

workmen were busy in the Round Room, under his constant super-
vision. Later the furniture he had ordered to his own design was
delivered and installed.

Neither I nor any of the servants climbed the stairs to the Round
Room during this time, for Eleanor said that this was her husband's
private domain. I was shaken when I discovered that it was Eleanor
herself who kept it cleaned and dusted.

Vernon Quayle spent much of each day in the Round Room,
and often summoned Eleanor to be with him, sometimes for
several hours. I could not imagine why, for at other times they
seemed to have little to say to each other. He always spoke civilly
to her, but I never heard them converse on any general subject.
At table he could sit completely unembarrassed throughout a
whole meal without uttering a word, while Eleanor and I talked.

I say that we talked, but it was not as before. In the old days,
when all three of us were constantly busy at our various pursuits,
there was always news and gossip and discoveries to be exchanged.
But now Eleanor did nothing. Her notes, manuscripts and
paintings gathered dust in her study. Once her energy had seemed
boundless. Now she rose late, went to bed early, and seemed to
spend most of her waking hours in an uneasy dream.

Sometimes, fleetingly, I would catch a glimpse of the old
Eleanor. Twice when we were alone, she unexpectedly caught my
hand in a desperate grip and said, "Help me, Jani!" Yet almost
before I could cry, "Tell me what to *do!*" the moment was gone,
and she would look at me blankly as if she had not spoken.

When Vernon Quayle was not in the house he was out walking
or riding alone. On these country journeys he carried a haversack
containing a number of small glass bottles. Eleanor had said
vaguely that he was interested in botany, but it was from the
village folk I discovered he was solely interested in collecting
herbs and small insects. In Larkfield there was much whispering
and shaking of heads over Vernon Quayle, and over "poor Miss
Eleanor". Once when I was in the smithy and he rode past, I saw
a woman furtively point crossed fingers at his back in the
ancient gesture to ward off the Evil Eye. I shivered, wondering

what instinct made her regard Vernon Quayle in such a light. She was not alone in this, as I found when I went to have tea with David Hayward one afternoon.

"They all think Quayle's some sort of warlock," he said. "Old Mrs. Spicer vows that he just looked at her goat and it died in the night. Mind you, if spoken to, he's civil enough. For the rest, he goes his own way, ignoring gentry and village folk alike. That's his own business, I suppose." He looked at me. "Have you told Eleanor about your discovery? I mean, Sembur's letter, and all about your mother and father?"

"Yes. I read her the copy I made of the letter." Tears were very close. "I thought she'd be so excited, and that we'd laugh together about my being a Maharani. But she just smiled and said, 'How interesting, Jani dear.' That was all."

David bit his lip, and I realized that what I had just told him must have given him a clearer picture of how Eleanor had changed than anything else. He said, "Does Quayle know all about you?"

"He knows what is in the letter, because he was there when I read it out to Eleanor at dinner one evening. He never seems to listen, but he must have heard."

David looked at me incredulously. "You told the whole story of Sembur's letter, and Quayle didn't ask a single question? Good God, the man can't be human."

We spoke little more until it was time for me to go. "Have you heard anything from Major Elliot yet?" David asked as he helped me mount Nimrod.

"Oh, I'm sorry, I should have told you," I said contritely. "He wrote to me after he had seen what he calls 'the right people' in London. It seems it might take weeks before I hear anything further because London would want to discuss the political significance with Delhi. Apparently, Chandra Ghose, the man who Sembur claimed was the murderer of my parents, was killed two years ago while hunting. There was immediate civil strife in Jahanapur, but the British army restored order. They also put into power there a man called Mohan Sudraka, a distant relative of mine. Apart from

168

all that, Lord Kearsey, the gentleman who's Colonel of the regiment, is apparently *very* eager to have Sembur's name cleared, and that's all I care about."

Three days later Vernon Quayle astonished me by appearing in the drawing room after dinner. I had never known him to do so before. Eleanor and I were seated by the open French window enjoying the cooler evening air. I was busy pasting into my scrapbook some items of interest from *Country Life*, while Eleanor held a tambour frame on her lap, her skeins of silk in a box at her elbow, and was embroidering a flower design on a silk shawl.

We were both startled when the door opened and he walked in. I made myself smile at him. He pulled an armchair forward a little to sit facing the window, ignored Eleanor, rested his chin on clasped hands and gazed at me curiously for several seconds before saying in that mellifluous voice: "I understand that when you lived in Smon T'ang you visited Tibet on several occasions."

I put the brush back into the paste-pot and wiped my fingers. "Why, yes, Mr. Quayle. We called it Bod."

"I take it your route was through the Chak Pass rather than the Sharba or the Kore?"

I was bewildered. "Yes, the Chak isn't quite so high as the other two. But how ever do you know about them?"

"I have visited Tibet," he said absently, in the same way that he might have mentioned visiting Bournemouth. "But I do not know the area in which you travelled."

"I never knew it very well myself, Mr. Quayle. We just followed the old trade route to Magyari."

"Then you must have passed within a few miles of Choma La, the great monastery there. Have you been inside it?"

I half smiled. "Oh no, Mr. Quayle. I would never be allowed inside, except by command of the High Lama."

He gazed across the garden. "What do you know of Choma La?"

"I hardly know anything about it, except that the Dalai Lama visits it once a year for a special festival."

He half closed his eyes. "But surely when you were on the trail to Magyari, your companions must have spoken about it?"

I shook my head. "I suppose they did, but I was too busy coaxing the yaks along to pay much attention."

Without another word Vernon Quayle rose to his feet and walked from the room.

There was silence for perhaps half a minute, then Eleanor said vaguely, "Perhaps I should use a paler green for the leaves of this design."

I had always been very careful never to question anything Vernon Quayle did, but now I could not resist saying, "Eleanor, why do you think he asked me about Choma La?"

She chafed her fingers as if they were numb. "Oh, he has so many interests. He studies the natural sciences, astronomy, mathematics, metaphysics . . . so many subjects and all quite above my head, Jani."

"Oh, you can't say that. You're a scientist yourself."

"I used to dabble a little. But Vernon's knowledge is quite remarkable. There are reaches of the mind, Jani, which . . ." Her voice trailed away. I saw her eyes suddenly fill with tears, and she went on agitatedly, "He collects intangible things. All intangibles are potent. Light and dark, order and chaos, good and bad. It is a matter of understanding how to—"

She stopped abruptly in mid-sentence, and gazed fixedly at her hands, clenched together in her lap. I ran to her and put an arm round her shoulder, pressing my cheek to hers. She felt cold.

"Eleanor, Eleanor dear," I whispered. "I know you're unhappy. Please tell me how I can help. Is it—?" I hesitated, then plunged on recklessly. "Is it your husband? I'll take you right away if you want me to. But you must *speak*."

She turned her head, and it seemed that far away in the depths of her grey-green eyes I could see the old Eleanor looking at me with desperate appeal. Then slowly she shook her head. "No," she said softly, "not you, Jani. I'll not bring you down."

After a few moments she sighed, and picked up the tambour frame.

"What do you think?" she said, wrinkling her brow. "Would it be better to use a paler green for the leaves?"

170

TEN DAYS LATER, at a few minutes before noon, I was in my little office when Vernon Quayle entered. My office was a very special place for me, and I hated his intrusion. I said, "Can I help you, Mr. Quayle?"

"I should be obliged if you would assist me for half an hour, Jani." He turned away. "In the Round Room now, if you please."

I blinked at the empty doorway and listened for the sound of his footfalls, but heard nothing. I had never known man or woman move so soundlessly as Vernon Quayle. I tidied my desk, then made my way upstairs, a flicker of uneasiness stirring within me.

I would never have believed that a room I knew could have been so transformed. The floor was now tiled in white, the furniture stark and strange, made of glossy black wood, with nothing upholstered. Two quadrants of the room had been fitted with shelves to hold hundreds of books. Another quadrant held a curving bench with a sink and a long tap which swivelled above it. On the bench were several racks of test-tubes, and a Bunsen's burner. Above, on shelves, were dozens of glass bottles holding powders and substances of various colours. The fourth quadrant of the Round Room had been fitted with a rack which held a number of scrolls, and beside it an ancient-looking star-map hung on the wall. The centre of the tiled floor was clear, but round the edges of the room were long rugs, strangely patterned and glowing with the rich colours of the East.

There was more, much more, for the Round Room was very large, but I could not take it all in, for something was disturbing me. And then it came to me. As I have said, the room itself was not symmetrical but a somewhat misshapen circle. Now I saw that this theme was echoed everywhere. In the furnishing, in all the decoration, there was a slight but positive distortion. No single thing seemed quite round or square or straight. The whole effect was one of leering ugliness which affronted the senses.

Vernon Quayle said, "Sit down, please." As I obeyed he moved to open a small cabinet. A moment later he turned from the cabinet, and as I saw what he carried I froze.

In his hands he held a round tray on which stood a small bowl

171

of flint glass, and beside it a tall flask of inky black liquid. He set the tray on a semi-circular desk, seated himself, poured the black liquid from the flask into the bowl, and set the bowl down on the desk in front of me.

"Take the bowl in both hands, if you please," he said abstractedly, "and simply look at the surface of the liquid."

I sat upright, every muscle stiff, gripping the arms of my chair, and when I could find my voice I said hoarsely, "No!"

"I beg your pardon?" His faded grey eyes were as cool as ever, his voice as mellow, but I saw that his mouth had tightened.

"No, Mr. Quayle," I repeated doggedly. "That's what they use in Galdong to make the Oracle go into a trance."

He ran a hand over his thin silver hair, and made a languid gesture towards the bowl. "This is merely a device for enhancing the memory. I am interested to learn more of Choma La, and I believe you may know more about it than you can now recall. The black liquid offers a focus for the mind, which in turn allows the doors of memory to be opened. It is a simple scientific operation."

I stood up, my heart pounding. "Does Eleanor do it? Have you made her look into the ink?"

I could almost feel myself shrivel under his gaze. "You are impertinent," he said. "What my wife does is no concern of yours. Take up the bowl, please."

I shook my head. "I don't wish to offend you, but I'm not going to do it. I hate anything of that sort. I lived with it in Smon T'ang and I think it's bad and unhealthy."

Vernon Quayle's shoulders moved in a tiny shrug. "I had thought you too intelligent to use meaningless words like 'bad'. Very well, I shall not press you."

I moved to the door, and hesitated there, trying to find something to say, but there was nothing. I did not intend to apologize.

I do not know if Vernon Quayle decided to be rid of me because I refused to obey him in the Round Room or because he sensed my hatred. The blow fell one evening a few days later when I had persuaded Eleanor to play a game of croquet with me on the lawn after dinner. The sun was touching the tree-tops to the west when Vernon Quayle came from the house, walking silently across the lawn to where I stood watching Eleanor as she prepared to make a stroke. She was unaware of his approach, so I said softly, "Eleanor." She looked up, gave a little start, then began to bite her lower lip anxiously.

Vernon Quayle halted a few paces away, looked at me and said as if making some casual remark about the weather, "I have decided that it is inconvenient for us to retain you here at Merlin's Keep any longer, Jani. Perhaps you will be so good as leave within the next two or three days."

Eleanor looked suddenly like a ghost, and I felt my own face must have mirrored hers, for I was cold with shock. Struggling against it, I tried to speak calmly. "I don't understand, Mr. Quayle. Why do you want me to go?"

"You are not in a position to demand reasons," he said, without any hint of anger, "but I will extend you the courtesy of replying. Quite simply, now that Eleanor is married, she has no need of a female companion."

I pressed my heels hard into the soft grass, and said very politely, "Excuse me, Mr. Quayle, but it was Eleanor who invited me into this house. I won't be told to go by anyone but Eleanor."

The bleak grey eyes with their huge pupils bored into me. "Eleanor?" he said softly.

I looked, and saw her pale face working as if she were under some dreadful stress. Then she said in a harsh, frantic voice, "Go Jani. You can't stay here." Her splendid eyes fixed on me suddenly with a wild glare. "Go!" she cried again. "I don't want you here! For pity's sake, *go* when I tell you!"

She turned, caught up her skirt, and began to move towards the house at a stumbling run, a hand to her face.

"I suggest to you," Vernon Quayle said quietly, "that the longer you remain, the more my poor wife will suffer. Your presence here is obviously a cause of distress to her."

I knew then that I was defeated, for this man held Eleanor

helpless as a puppet, and it was she who would pay for any defiance I showed. I made no attempt to hide my hatred as I said, "If I am gone by noon tomorrow, will that be satisfactory?"

"That will do very well." He turned to stroll away in the direction of the rose garden.

I spent the rest of that evening sorting out my belongings and packing them in the two trunks Mr. Lambert had bought for me when I made my first trip abroad with Eleanor.

Following a plan I had worked out during the night, I drove out to Stafford's Farm the following morning and was back before breakfast time. Mrs. Burke sent breakfast up on a tray, but I could only pick at it for I had no appetite.

Afterwards I sent for the young gardener, William, and had him carry my luggage down to the hall. I said goodbye to the servants, then went to the stables and spent ten minutes saying goodbye to Nimrod and the other horses. Then I went up to my room, put on my hat and gloves, walked along the passage to Eleanor's room and tapped on the door. All this time I was being very brisk and businesslike, for otherwise I would have cried my heart out.

I went in when Eleanor called, and found her sitting in a chair near the window, a glass of milk on a table at her elbow. She wore a dark blue dressing gown buttoned to her neck, her long auburn hair was loose, her face wan. Somehow I managed a smile.

"Jani," she said. "I'm so glad you've come to say goodbye. I was afraid you . . . might not want to."

I took off my gloves, held her cold hand, and bent to kiss her cheek. "Never think such things. You'll be in my thoughts every day. And I didn't come just to say goodbye, Eleanor dear, I wanted to say thank you again. I grew up without a mother or sister, but you've been both to me, and the dearest of friends as well."

Her mouth began to tremble, and she looked away. After a moment or two she said, "Where will you go?"

"Oh, that's all settled. You know the little cottage just before you reach the farmhouse at Stafford's Farm?"

174

"Where Tom Stafford's father lived?"

"Yes. It's been empty since he died last year. There are just the two rooms, one up, one down, and a kitchen, but that's quite enough for me. I went to see Mr. Stafford this morning, and I can have it for two shillings a week." I gripped her hand hard. "And if you ever need me, just send for me, Eleanor dear. Nothing and nobody will stop me coming."

She pressed my hand to her cheek and gave a strange little laugh. "My fiery Jani, who hit Big Alice on the nose when she spoke ill of her friend Mister. Do you remember telling me, that first day?"

I nodded, "I thought you'd send me away because of it."

"I'd sooner throw away gold, Jani. Such friendship can't be bought. I could only win it from you, as Mister did."

I released her hand and groped for the clasp of the chain at the back of my neck, beneath the collar of my dress. "Do you remember the gift he left me, Eleanor? The silver medallion with the poem in Hindi?"

For a few brief moments Eleanor had shown a glimpse of her old self, but now her animation faded as if her energy had drained away. "Why, yes, I recall something of the sort, dear," she said vaguely, rubbing her temple. "What was the poem about?"

I held the medallion in my hand now, looking at it, and spoke the translation I had never forgotten.

"Here is a token to remind you of a friend.
It may not bring you good fortune,
Or protect you from fate or from your enemy.
It is for remembrance only.
Keep it until a friend has need of it,
Then give it gladly and go your way."

I took Eleanor's hand, and dropped the medallion and chain into her palm. "Please wear it for me sometimes," I whispered.

"Oh, Jani . . ."

The door opened and Vernon Quayle entered. He said, "Good

175

morning, my dear. Good morning, Jani. I see you are about to depart."

I said, "Good morning, Mr. Quayle," and left it at that, hoping he would go, for I did not want to make my farewell to Eleanor in his presence. To my disappointment, he closed the door and walked across the room. Eleanor's hand was still held out, with the medallion in it. Vernon Quayle stopped, and his eyebrows lifted slightly as he said, "What is this, Eleanor?"

I answered for her. "It's just a present from me, Mr. Quayle."

"May I see?" He reached out, and as he picked up the medallion from Eleanor's palm I saw a tremor pass over his putty-white face and heard a tiny hiss of indrawn breath. He raised the medallion almost defiantly, as if he wished to drop it but would not. Then he placed it on the table. Without taking his eyes from it he said, "Where did this come from?"

I said, "It was given to me by a friend."

"And before that?"

"I only know that it was given to him by a friend."

"Yes, indeed," Vernon Quayle said slowly. "A potent talisman. When you wish to find one who is lost, you may come to me with it."

Those strange words were spoken so casually that I thought I must have mis-heard him, and said, "I beg your pardon?"

He gave a half shake of his head. "I am sure you will recall what I said when the time comes." He nodded towards the medallion. "You will take it with you, please. Eleanor is touched by your kindness, but the gift is . . . unsuitable."

Every instinct in me urged me to argue, to insist that Eleanor should decide for herself. But she sat with head bowed, the lovely hair falling forward so that her face was partly hidden, and she did not look up. I picked up the medallion and chain. "Goodbye, Mr. Quayle," I said, and then moved to kiss Eleanor on the cheek again. "Goodbye, Eleanor."

She whispered something I could not catch, but she did not lift her head. Then I turned and walked from the room without looking back, for I could not bear to.

176

Chapter Eleven

Within a week I had made Withy Cottage into a very pleasant home. Time did not hang heavily on my hands. I began to help David Hayward more frequently.

One afternoon, when he and I were sitting on bales of hay after successfully struggling to deliver a foal from one of Tom Stafford's shire mares, I said, "David, could I learn to be a vet?"

Buttoning his shirt, he gave me a tired but satisfied smile. "You'd have to overcome a lot of prejudice," he said slowly. "But you'd make a marvellous vet, Jani. The only thing is, you'd have to go away to college and be properly trained, which takes seven years."

"Oh, I don't want to go away."

He said soberly, "Would you be interested in a partnership?"

"With you? But I don't really do anything, David. Oh, I know it helps if I talk to the animals when things are difficult, but I'm not qualified, and I couldn't take money for it."

"I was thinking of a more permanent partnership." He wiped his brow with a forearm. "Would you marry me, Jani?"

He had said it often before, but this time I knew he was not joking. Strangely, I was neither startled nor embarrassed by his words, only a little proud and a little sad. I answered at once, "Oh, David . . . you know you don't love me."

"Love? Well, that's hard to pin down, Jani. I enjoy being with you, I feel completely at ease with you, and there's nobody for whom I have a higher regard."

"But you love Eleanor," I said gently.

"You mustn't say that." His voice was a little sharp. "Eleanor is married now."

"I'm sorry. I didn't mean to offend you."

"You haven't offended me, Jani dear." He was fumbling with one of his shirt cuffs, trying to button it, but his fingers were clumsy with fatigue. His face was thoughtful as he said, "I believe you are as content in my company as I am in yours. Do we really need more? Is love something else, do you think?"

I got to my feet and went across to button the cuff for him. As I bent by the bale of hay where he sat, Mister's silver medallion slipped from the neck of my blouse and hung suspended on its chain.

I said, "Yes, I think love must be something more, David, and I think in your heart you know it."

He studied me curiously, then took my hand. "Perhaps you're right, Jani," he said. "But I wonder how you know that love is something more?" He gave a slow smile, and lifted his other hand to touch the medallion with a finger. "You know, I've sometimes had the odd feeling that Jani Burr is in love with that mysterious Mister of hers."

I gave a gasp of surprise and was about to laugh, but without warning I felt the colour suddenly flooding up my neck and making my cheeks burn.

Pulling my hand away, I snapped, "Oh, don't be ridiculous, David! I was only twelve when I knew Mister, and he called me a liar, and I kicked him, and he didn't like me, and I didn't even bother to ask his *name*, so—"

David lifted both hands, palms out. "Peace, Jani, peace. I didn't mean to upset you."

"I'm not in the least upset," I began angrily, then my annoyance suddenly faded. "Yes I am. I'm all hot and embarrassed! Oh David, I couldn't be so silly, could I?"

"As to be in love with Mister?" He laughed and shook his head. "Heaven knows, Jani. There's not much point in dwelling on it. I should imagine there's very little chance you'll ever meet again." He shrugged and stood up.

"I suppose not, but I would like to see him. I'd even be glad just to discover his name."

I did not know then how soon I was to hear it.

IN THE THIRD WEEK of September I was in my little garden soon after breakfast one morning, pruning a loganberry bush which had finished fruiting, when one of Major Elliot's stable-hands arrived on horseback. The boy touched his cap and handed me an envelope.

178

The letter read:

Dear Jani,

Sir Charles and Lady Gascoyne are in Bournemouth and would be grateful if you would receive them. I propose to conduct them to you at three o'clock this afternoon, if that is convenient to you.

I have the honour to remain your obedient servant.

J. R. Elliot (Major)

The Major did not waste words. I assumed that this must be something to do with his activities concerning Sembur. I hurried indoors, wrote a brief note to say I would be happy to receive the Major and his companions at three, and sent the boy off with it.

At one minute past three, Major Elliot came riding up the lane, followed by his best carriage. I greeted him as he dismounted. "Afternoon, Jani," he said, "Shan't be staying myself. This isn't quite to do with RSM Burr, you see. More of a side issue. The Gascoynes will explain. Ah, there you are, Sir Charles."

The footman had assisted a lady and gentleman to alight from the carriage. The Major bowed to me again and said, "Your Highness, may I present Sir Charles and Lady Gascoyne." He turned to my visitors. "Sir Charles, my lady, may I present Her Highness the Maharani of Jahanapur."

There was perhaps a minute of vague confusion during which I shook hands with both my visitors, ushered them in, thanked Major Elliot and said goodbye to him, then invited Sir Charles and his wife to be seated on the couch I had bought secondhand.

Sir Charles was a man nearing sixty, heavily built, his hair thick and dark with grey streaks, his face square and stern. His wife was a good ten years younger. She had dark eyes, black hair untinged by grey, and a thin high-bridged nose which gave her the look of an eagle. Yet in her eyes there lay some deep sorrow which had brought gentleness to her face.

I said nervously, "May I fetch you some tea, Lady Gascoyne? I'm afraid I shall have to leave for a moment while I prepare it."

She did not answer at once. They were both staring at me intently. Then she gave a little start and said, "Oh, thank you, but I would prefer not to have tea just at this moment, Your Highness."

179

Sir Charles took a large envelope from a pocket inside his coat, opened it, and stood up to hand me a photograph.

I took the photograph wonderingly and looked at it. Two people stood against the background of a fountain, and a white clematis-hung wall beyond. The man was of medium height with a strong humorous face, wearing an army uniform but hatless. Beside him, wearing a sari, her arm linked through his, was . . . myself.

The room seemed to spin about me, and I braced myself, waiting for the dizziness to pass. When my vision cleared I studied the photograph again. I said, "This is my father and my mother?"

"It is Colonel Francis Saxon and his wife, the Maharani of Jahanapur," said Sir Charles, "taken shortly after their wedding. This photograph appeared in the *Tatler* in May, 1884. I think that if any vestige of doubt existed as to the veracity of RSM Burr's letter, the likeness between you and your mother is the final proof. Forgive me, but you have become very pale, Your Highness. Won't you please sit down?"

"Thank you, sir." The photograph still in my hand, I moved to the small armchair. "But . . . please do not address me by my title. Almost everybody calls me Jani."

"As you wish," Sir Charles said gruffly. He sat down again. After a rather long and awkward silence, I said, "Forgive me, Sir Charles, but is there a particular reason why you have come to see me? Are you from the government?"

He shook his head. "This is an entirely private visit, though in fact I have been a diplomat all my life and retired from the Foreign Service only a year ago. It was a friend who is still in the service who passed on Elliot's story to me because he well knew that my wife and I would be interested." He hesitated. "Does our name, Gascoyne, mean anything to you?"

I shook my head, perplexed.

His wife leaned forward, "Jani . . . do you possess a little pendant, a silver medallion inset with a gold star?"

I stared, "However did you—? But of course, Major Elliot will have told you." I slipped a finger under the collar of my dress and drew out the medallion. "This is what you mean—oh!"

180

The last word was a gasping cry of astonishment, for even as I held the medallion suspended from my finger a vivid flash of memory darted across my mind. "Gascoyne! Of course, *that* was his name! He only said it once, to Sembur, and I was very tired at the time. Captain Gascoyne, I think he said, of . . . of a Gurkha Rifle Regiment."

As I spoke I felt the first true joy I'had known since Eleanor's homecoming, but in the next instant it was wiped away, for Sir Charles said in a low voice, "Adam Gascoyne is our son . . . or was our son. We do not know what has become of him."

I stared stupidly. "Do you fear he may be dead?"

Sir Charles nodded. His wife braced herself. "We are hoping," she said, "that you may be able to tell us something of him."

"I? But Lady Gascoyne, it was six years ago!"

She said quietly, "It is more than eleven since I last saw him, Jani."

I shook my head. "How dreadful. But . . . why haven't you seen him?"

"A quarrel," Sir Charles said harshly. "Adam and I quarrelled."

Lady Gascoyne put a hand over her husband's. "Charles," she said gently, "please do me a great service. Please go and walk in the garden while I talk to Jani."

He nodded sombrely and got to his feet. As I rose to open the door for him he paused and looked at me with a weary sadness. "You'll think badly of me, my dear," he said, "and you'll be right to do so. I'll say only one thing in extenuation of myself, which is that my foolish and stiff-necked pride has been equalled only by that of my son."

When I closed the door behind him, Lady Gascoyne patted the couch beside her.

"Come and sit with me, Jani."

I went to her and put the medallion in her hand. "You must have this. Do you know what the poem says?"

"Oh, yes." She gave a pale smile. "It was given to me when I was not much older than you, by the man I loved. We could not marry because he was not considered a suitable match for me. He went

181

away, and I never saw him again. Fifteen years later he was killed on the Northwest Frontier."

She fell silent, gazing distantly down at the medallion on her palm. I did not know what to say, and after a few seconds she went on. "I married Charles. He has been a successful diplomat and I have learned to respect him, admire him . . . yes, and to love him." She raised her eyes. "They are not alike, Charles and Adam, but they do have in common their foolish, unyielding pride. Between them they broke my heart, for when I tried to heal their quarrels, each thought I was taking the side of the other."

Her eyes swam, and my heart went out to her. I remembered the pride and arrogance I had seen in Mister. It had been there in the very way he sat his great black horse.

Lady Gascoyne lifted her cupped hand and looked at the medallion. "I gave this to him the day he came to me. He said he realized that he and his father made me constantly unhappy, and so he was going away. You remember that the poem says, *'Here is a token to remind you of a friend . . .'* I prayed that in spite of everything he would always feel I was his friend."

Her mouth twisted and she brushed away a tear with the back of her hand. I took her hand and held it, trying to think what to say and feeling very inadequate. "He wore your keepsake," I said at last. "And there is great kindness in him. I wish I could help, but I don't know how."

"I'm clutching at straws, Jani. Let me explain. You see, a few weeks ago my husband's doctor informed him that he has a diabetic condition which will prove fatal within the next two years."

I drew in a deep breath. "Oh. Oh dear, I don't know what to say, Lady Gascoyne. I'm sorry, so very sorry."

"Thank you, Jani. I think, with death so close, Charles realizes how much has been wasted in his life, and in mine, because of a needless quarrel and foolish pride."

I said, "And now he wants to find Adam? To ask him to come home?"

"Yes. So that I shall not be . . . quite alone when the time comes. But for his own sake, too. He wants to make his peace with Adam.

182

From Adam's few letters we know that he bought himself out of the army in June 1899 and went to South America to breed horses. Then, three years ago, he moved to the Caribbean, and that's the last we heard of him. We have had inquiry agents at work both in the Caribbean and in America, but there has been no result. He just seems to have . . . disappeared."

She took a small handkerchief from her pocket and dabbed her eyes. "As I told you, I'm clutching at straws. When we heard of you, Jani, when we heard your story, Charles felt that during those long days of travel, Adam might have talked to you about his plans for the future."

I shook my head slowly. "No, I'm afraid he didn't tell me anything about himself."

"Nevertheless, will you do something for me?"

"Anything I can, Lady Gascoyne."

"Please spend a little time thinking back, remembering your journey with Adam, then if anything comes to mind, please write to me at our home in London." She handed me her visiting card. "Perhaps you could come and stay for a few days . . ." Her voice faltered. "I have the strangest feeling, Jani, that in some way you are still linked with my Adam. It's just foolish hope, I expect, but I shall cling to it."

She stood up, and I rose with her. Sir Charles stood by the low hedge at the side of my garden, hat in hand, idly watching the bees moving busily around the hive of straw which stood just on the other side of the hedge. We walked together to the gate and out into the lane where the carriage was waiting just off the road. As the coachman held the door open, Lady Gascoyne said, "Turn round for a moment, Jani."

Wonderingly I turned my back. Her hands came over my head holding the medallion suspended on its chain, and then she was fastening the clasp at the back of my neck.

I said, "Oh please, no! You must keep it, Lady Gascoyne."

She turned me towards her, put her hands on my shoulders and smiled.

"I have already given it, for remembrance, as it was given

to you by Adam, and as you will give it to a friend when the moment comes. Goodbye till we hear from you again, my dear."

I watched the carriage go, holding the medallion, glad to be still wearing it, my mind whirling with a dozen different memories.

ON THE NIGHT after Sir Charles and Lady Gascoyne's visit I dreamt I was riding slowly across a broad plain under a sky without moon or stars. I could see nothing but a silver ribbon of jagged peaks on the horizon, marking the division between earth and sky. I was searching for Mister, and I was listening for his voice. As I rode on, I began to hear a sound, a whisper at first but growing gradually louder. It was a voice which droned the same meaningless syllables over and over again, but to my sorrow it was not Mister's voice. Yet it was a voice I knew, and struggled to recognize.

Then I began to hear the mantra-like chant in a slowly changing way . . . *napoten-talisma . . . apoten-talisman . . . a-potent-talisman . . . a potent talisman . . .*

Vernon Quayle's voice, mellow and beautiful.

I woke with a start, my heart thundering. What had he said that day as I was leaving Merlin's Keep?

I was sitting up in bed now, fists clenched and pressed to temples, a furious urgency rising within me. Then it came. The medallion. "*A potent talisman. When you wish to find one who is lost, you may come to me with it.*"

Chapter Twelve

At dawn I was still awake, my mind in confusion. How could Vernon Quayle possibly find Mister? Only a credulous fool would believe such nonsense. Yet only a credulous fool would have believed that the Oracle in Galdong could foresee the coming of the foreign demon in search of Sembur, or that Rild could tell me of the woman in red who would be my friend, and of the Silver Man who would be my enemy.

At four o'clock that afternoon, driving Mr. Stafford's borrowed

184

dog-cart, I returned to Merlin's Keep, handed one of my recently printed cards to Thorpe, the surly man who had replaced Mayes, and asked if Mr. and Mrs. Quayle were at home. The man returned after less than a minute and showed me into the familiar drawing room. Vernon Quayle rose to his feet and greeted me with a slight inclination of the head. "So you remembered," he said.

I had been determined to remain cool, but those first words startled me. "Were you expecting me, Mr. Quayle?"

He made a movement of his lips which I had learned to recognize as a smile. "In a general sense, yes. You have had a visit from the Gascoynes, and they seek a lost son, the man who brought you out of Smon T'ang. It was logical to suppose that this was the moment for you to remember what I had said."

"How did you know about Sir Charles and Lady Gascoyne?"

"There is no mystery. Major Elliot talks to Mrs. Elliot as they dine together. The servants at table gossip with servants of other households, and Thorpe conveys that gossip to me. You have come to ask me to find Adam Gascoyne?"

"Yes." My tone was as brusque as the single word was terse. Between Vernon Quayle and myself there was no call for politeness. I had not come to beg. He would do as he pleased, to suit himself, and my greatest doubt in coming here had been exactly that. Why might it suit Vernon Quayle to find Mister?

He said, "Very well, let us make the attempt. We will go to the Round Room now, if you please."

I preceded him from the room and up to the floors above, my nerves taut. The Round Room was full of sunlight, so that the immediate impression was pleasant. It was only as the eye picked up the small disproportions in everything that the ugliness broke through and the room seemed to become cold. Vernon Quayle waved me to the chair where I had sat before, and moved to the shelf of many bottles. He took down several of them and unstoppered each in turn, taking out a tiny portion of the powdery contents and dropping it in a mortar of black marble. When he had accumulated a pinch from each of ten bottles he began to grind the mixture to a still finer powder with a pestle, and the sound grated so horribly on my taut nerves that I had to speak to break the tension, and said the first thing to come into my mind. "Pray excuse my ignorance. May I ask what you are going to do?"

He stopped using the pestle and tipped the little pinch of greyish powder onto a small flat piece of glass. Suddenly he glanced at me from those ashen eyes with heavy-lidded contempt. "I suggest you contain both your fears and your curiosity. There will be no summoning of spirits, I assure you. Let me tell you something very simple. There are no spirits, no demons, no angels, no elementals, nothing in the whole universe which is supernatural. There are only energies and forces, neither good nor bad, which may be employed by those with the knowledge to harness them."

He carried the small plate of glass to his desk and sat down with it, touched a finger to the little pinch of grey dust. As I watched, he sniffed some of it first at one nostril and then the other.

I felt nausea touch my stomach, and the room seemed to grow darker, even though sunlight still streamed through the high windows. He put the glass plate aside, folded his hands on the desk, and said, "Eleanor will assist me now."

He sat gazing before him with blank eyes. There was a remoteness about him which made me think of Rild, when I had stood before him in the great monastery of Galdong, waiting. . . .

At last the door of the Round Room opened and Eleanor came in. "Why, Jani, it's you," she said in a faraway voice.

I rose, smiling, and started to move towards her to kiss her. She wore a dress of white linen with a pouched bodice, trimmed with strips of pale brown velvet. Her face was pallid, and her hair lacklustre. Vernon Quayle's voice halted me. "No contact or emotional disturbance, if you please," he said sharply. "Take your seat, Jani. And Eleanor, kindly occupy your usual chair."

I obeyed resentfully. Eleanor did not even show resignation as she took the largest of three black lacquered armchairs, her back to the western quadrant of the Round Room.

Vernon Quayle moved to one of the cabinets and took out the tray, bowl, and flask of inky liquid. I twisted my fingers together to prevent my hands shaking, and watched as he poured the fluid into

186

the crystal bowl and carried it to Eleanor. Without a word spoken, she took it between her hands and stared down at the inky surface. Vernon Quayle stood before her, hands in front of him, fingers interlocked, palms pressed together. Her breathing became slower, and her eyelids fell, half closing. A few seconds later she gave a long sigh, and her eyes closed completely.

Vernon Quayle removed the bowl from her hands, which fell very slowly to her lap. "She will require the medallion now," he said. I unfastened the clasp at the back of my neck, and hesitated. "Is it all right for me to move?" I whispered.

"Certainly. She is far beyond being disturbed."

I went to him and held out the medallion. "Give it directly to her," he said. I held it close to her limp hands, and he said, "Eleanor, you will take this medallion." Her hands lifted and she took it without groping. Vernon Quayle said, "This object was for a long time in the possession of a man I wish to find. You will need to go back six years or more to know him. Do you understand?"

"Yes." Her voice was flat, lifeless.

There was a seemingly endless silence, then she said, "Young. Dark. He wears uniform, and—"

Vernon Quayle interrupted her quite brusquely. "You have the man. Now give yourself to knowing him."

For a full five minutes no word was spoken. I saw Eleanor's hands clutching, squeezing the medallion. At last Vernon Quayle said, "Now you must move forward to this day."

After another few minutes she said, "Yes."

"He lives?"

"Yes." She answered in the same dull voice.

In spite of the awed horror which lay upon me, I felt my heart lift at that single word. Vernon Quayle said, "Do you see him?"

A long pause, then. "No."

"Why not?"

"There is a barrier. Dark. Potent."

"Rest."

Eleanor's taut body relaxed. "Most interesting," Vernon Quayle said. "We have encountered an unexpected energy which resists

Eleanor's penetration." He moved to a chart on the wall which seemed to show a night sky with various constellations of stars. "Be so good as to draw all four blinds, please," he said, "we must gather more strength."

I moved round the room, pulling on the cords which controlled the blinds of the high windows. When I had finished there was still some light in the room, a little from a spirit lamp which Vernon Quayle had lighted and the rest from some luminous lines now showing on the tiled floor, forming a large circle with spokes radiating from the centre to the circumference. The chair on which Eleanor sat moved easily on castors as Vernon Quayle drew it to the centre of the circle and then began to turn it an inch at a time, watching the luminous lines. There was a similar circle on the star-chart, and I realized that he was using this design on the floor to position Eleanor precisely. He gave her back the bowl.

"Sit down," he said to me, "and kindly do not speak until I say you may." As I obeyed he moved behind Eleanor and placed the palms of his hands against her temples. In the eerie luminosity, I saw his eyes open wide, and those eyes were no longer dull but suddenly like two huge glowing embers. His mellow voice said,

"Now, Eleanor. We seek the man."

For what seemed an age there was no sound in the room. I could not even hear their breathing above my own. Then Eleanor, peering into the bowl, said, "I have his surroundings."

Vernon Quayle said, "Does any sea lie between us?"

A long pause, then, "No. No sea."

"Describe."

"A wide river. Much smoke. Much traffic. Cranes."

"A port." It was a statement rather than a question.

"Ye-e-es . . ." The word came slowly, doubtfully. "But I cannot find the sea. Not close."

"A river port, then. Can you see him now?"

"No. There is a darkness." Her voice slowed. "But he is there . . . above the place underground with the great casks . . . and in his hand is the tusk from which the warriors spring . . ." The last words were slurred, as if her strength had drained away.

Vernon Quayle said, "Go on."

"I have no more." It was a whisper.

"Go on."

After a long silence she said quaveringly, "The river . . . a place where long ago the bodies lay in chains for three tides."

"*Enough!*" Vernon Quayle snatched the bowl from her hands and caught her by the shoulders as she swayed in the chair. In the spectral blue-green glow I saw triumph in the face he turned towards me as he snapped, "The blinds."

By the time I had raised them, he was seated at his desk again. Eleanor sat slumped in the chair, but her eyes were open now. I ran to kneel beside her and began chafing her icy hands. She gave a weak smile and whispered, "I'm all right, Jani. Don't worry."

"You're *not* all right!" Distressed and unnerved, I angrily turned my head to Vernon Quayle. He raised one silvery eyebrow, "I trust you are pleased with this experiment," he said.

I stared, "I beg your pardon?"

"We set out to discover your friend, if you recall."

Eleanor suddenly pressed my hand and stood up. As I rose with her she closed my fingers about the medallion and chain, and said, "I shall go and rest for a little while now. Goodbye, Jani."

"Oh, please let me help you to your room, please, Eleanor."

She shook her head. "No. No, Jani. Goodbye." She turned and went slowly from the Round Room, closing the door behind her. Vernon Quayle said, "You should have very little difficulty now, I think."

With a great effort I dragged my thoughts from Eleanor and tried to understand him. "I'm afraid I—"

"The deduction is very simple, surely." He gazed through me with remote disdain. "It was established that no sea lay between your friend and us, therefore he is in this country. Perhaps you did not know this, but on the north bank of the Thames, by Wapping Wall, there once stood Execution Dock, where pirates and any others who fell foul of Hanging Judge Jeffreys, were executed. It was his pleasure to sit drinking in a riverside tavern and watch the hangings. The bodies were afterwards cut down, weighted with

190

chains, and placed on the foreshore until they had been covered by
three tides, and could therefore be considered satisfactorily dead.
Where the bodies lay must be very close to wherever your friend
is at this moment."

"Are you saying that Adam Gascoyne may be found in Wapping?"
It almost frightened me to think that Mister could be so near. "But
surely that is in the East End of London?"

"Perhaps he has taken up missionary work," Vernon Quayle said
dryly. "However, I do not propose to waste time in idle speculation.
It occurs to me that an underground place with great casks might
well describe the cellars of a tavern." He rose to his feet, moved to
the door and held it open for me. "If my memory serves, the name
of the tavern where Judge Jeffreys took his pleasure was The Red
Cow, though there are several others along the riverside there. I
offer no interpretation of the reference to 'the tusk from which the
warriors spring' but perhaps the significance will shortly be revealed
to you. And now I will see you out."

TWO DAYS LATER I arrived at Waterloo Station with a suitcase, and
took a hansom cab to an address in Grays Inn Road, given to me by
David Hayward. This was a shop which sold tobacco and sweets,
run by an ex-soldier and his wife, Mr. and Mrs. Bailey. Until her
husband's retirement five years before, Mrs. Bailey had been cook
at the home of David's parents. He had known her from his childhood, and she still sent him a homemade birthday cake each year.

After I had told David what I intended to do, he had sent a telegram to Mrs. Bailey. When I arrived in the late afternoon a small
spare room had been prepared for me, the furniture polished till it
shone, the linen crisp and snowy.

Mrs. Bailey was plump and motherly, and fussed over me as if I
were a child of ten. Ex-Sergeant Bailey had a forbidding air, but
after the first five minutes in his company I could have hugged him,
for his way of speaking and his mannerisms were so like Sembur's.

They were both kind, warm people, and were clearly startled
when I said I intended to visit The Red Cow, in Wapping, in search
of somebody who was an old friend, but they asked no questions.

Tamping his pipe, Mr. Bailey said, "She can't go alone, Harriet. I mean, Wapping. Full of rogues."

I said quickly, "Oh, please don't worry, I'll take a cab right to the door."

"You'll go with her, Albert Bailey," Mrs. Bailey said firmly. "I could never face Master David if anything happened."

"Right, my dear. That's settled." Mr. Bailey glowered at me in the way Sembur had so often done when he anticipated an argument and was trying to prevent it by pretending to be very stern. I did not intend to argue, for I would be a stranger in that part of London, and glad to have him.

If I had not been so keyed up, I would have been fascinated by the cab journey next morning, for all the way along Mr. Bailey kept pointing out whatever he felt might interest me. Near the Bank of England we were held up for a while in a great cluster of cabs, carts, drays and carriages, then our cabbie turned down towards the Monument. Less than ten minutes later I saw Tower Bridge, and the Tower of London itself. Almost at once we plunged into another world, a place of narrow, grimy streets, smoke-blackened warehouses, and mean dwellings.

Stray dogs foraged for scraps. Groups of children played in the rubbish-littered streets. The cab drew many stares, and soon the cabbie was using his whip to keep the children from trying to hang on behind. At last he came to a halt and refused to go farther.

"Eh?" cried Mr. Bailey, outraged. "Stoppin' 'ere, you say?"

"I'm not just stopping, guv. I'm goin' back, that's what," the cabbie said firmly. "These little beggars'll 'ave my wheels orf, given 'alf a chance. They'll 'ave the legs orf me 'orse I wouldn't wonder!"

Mr. Bailey was threatening to pull him off his box and teach him a lesson when I intervened. "Please Mr. Bailey, let's walk. This street is called Wapping Wall, so we can't be far away."

Watched by a dozen curious children we alighted from the cab. Mr. Bailey paid the cabbie for me, told him to whistle for a tip, then offered me his arm with a flourish. We walked away, an escort of the children skipping along beside us.

192

Two minutes later, our escort left behind, we came to a corner where a public house called The Red Cow stood. A fat man wearing a grubby apron was outside using a hook to lift a stout wooden trap set in the cobbles against the wall. A thin youth with bare feet black as mud stood watching, holding a coil of heavy rope.

Mr. Bailey said briskly, "'Scuse me," and continued as the fat man straightened up, "I'm acting on be'alf of this young lady. She's inquiring after a gentleman who might be staying at this establishment or 'ereabouts."

The fat man said suspiciously. "What's 'is name, then?"

Mr. Bailey looked at me. I said, "Adam Gascoyne. He's dark, with blue—"

"Never 'eard of 'im." The fat man grinned. "What's 'e done, then? Put you in the family way an' run orf?"

Mr. Bailey said softly, "Come round the corner and we'll see 'ow you look with no teeth."

Just as I was taking Mr. Bailey's arm to draw him away, the scrawny youth said, "P'raps she means Molly's feller. Is 'e a toff, this bloke?"

I nodded. "About thirty, with dark hair."

"Ah, that's 'im. Took the back room at The Grapes, 'bout two years ago. On'y five minutes down the road." He pointed. "Everyone calls 'im Buff."

"Buff?"

The fat man said irritably, "Come on, 'Arold," and the youth turned away.

The Grapes was a dingy tavern backing onto a slipway where a skin of litter and scum had gathered on the edge of the water.

I realized that Mr. Bailey did not want me to go in but was equally reluctant to leave me alone outside. He stood on the threshold, holding the door open, and called to a man in a dirty apron behind. the counter. "You got a toff lodging 'ere, friend? Name of Buff, some kid said."

The man jerked his head sideways. "Along the path, round the back, up the stairs, first door on the right."

"Ta."Mr. Bailey stepped back, and the door swung to.

As we walked along the narrow path at the side of the tavern Mr. Bailey stopped suddenly, frowning.

"'Scuse me asking, but d'you want me to come up with you, Miss Jani?"

"Oh, no thank you." The answer was automatic. If I had found Mister, which I still could not believe, then I wanted to be alone when we came face to face.

"It's not proper, Miss, going to a gentleman's room alone."

"I'll be quite safe, Mr. Bailey. This gentleman and I travelled hundreds of miles alone together, sharing a tent, so you could scarcely call us strangers."

"Gawd 'elp us!" said Mr. Bailey, and shook his head resignedly.

We moved on to the end of the path and turned left onto a broad terrace from which weed-covered stone steps ran down to the slip-way. When we turned our backs to the river we faced a half open door in the rear wall of the tavern, a door from which every scrap of paint had peeled. To our right, a large bay window looked out upon the river. Above the window was a narrow balcony, and there a man in shirt-sleeves sat at a small table, his back towards me, his hands busy with something on the table I could not see.

My heart gave a huge leaping thump of fearful delight, and for long seconds my mind stood completely still. It did not matter that I could not see his face. I knew the shape of the head and the way that black hair curled. It was Mister.

Chapter Thirteen

I turned to Mr. Bailey and nodded wordlessly. He smiled and raised his thumb in the air. Then he moved to sit down on a small cask in one corner of the grimy terrace, and took out his pipe and tobacco pouch.

I drew in a deep breath, moved to the half open door, and began to climb the dingy staircase. When I reached the door at the top, I stopped, felt my hat to make sure it was on straight, clutched my handbag in a shaking hand, and knocked.

His voice called: "Hallo? Come in, come in whoever you are."
He continued to speak as I entered, but my mind was too full to
hear what he said. The room was small, but in contrast to all else I
had seen it was very clean. A faint smell of carbolic hung in the air.
An iron bedstead stood in one corner. It sagged a little in the middle,
and on it was spread a very faded pink counterpane. There were
two wooden chairs, a table, a wash-stand with a big china basin and
jug, and a curtain across an alcove. The curtain was partly drawn,
and I saw that the alcove was used as a wardrobe. One or two shirts,
a jacket, topcoat and trousers hung there, all of which had seen far
better days. There was also a hanger with a well-patched, but
clean blue cotton frock on it. That would be Molly's, I thought
vaguely.

He sat framed in the window, the grey river beyond him, his
hands busy. On the table were several small white objects. I moved
forward, and saw that they were ivory chessmen, all roughly shaped.
I remembered Eleanor's words . . . *the tusk from which the warriors
spring*. He was carving warriors of the chess board. He held a king
in one hand, a steel tool in the other, and was turning the piece
deftly, paring away tiny scraps of ivory, constantly running the ball
of his thumb over the area he was carving.

He was speaking with a lilt of cheerful humour I had not heard
in his voice before, never taking his eyes from the chess piece in his
hand. ". . . And are you over your bad temper yet, Molly? If so,
then feel in the pocket of my jacket, and you'll find enough coppers
to buy us a jug of ale and some pease pudding."

I moved another pace forward, trying to speak, and as I did so his
head turned and he looked at me, still smiling, his hands not ceasing
to work. "Well, say something, girl." His head tilted, and now his
hands were still as he stared at me. "Molly? Is that you?" He put
down the chess piece and tool, and stood up. "Molly?"

They came to me together, the understanding and the pain, and
it was as if a spear had been driven through me. The deep blue eyes
were looking not at me but past me, and there was no sight in them.

"Molly?" he said again.

At last words broke from my throat in a protesting cry.

"Oh, no! Not you, Mister, not you!"

Slowly he pushed back his chair and moved a pace to stand in the window, facing me, head tilted back a little now, eyes half closed as if in puzzlement. His lips shaped the word "Mister . . . ?" slowly, thoughtfully. Then he said, "Nobody ever called me that except . . ." His blank eyes opened wide, and his face, paler than I remembered it, was suddenly alight with pleasure. He gave an incredulous laugh. "Jani! By all that's wonderful, little Jani Burr!"

He reached out both hands, and I ran to him without a moment's hesitation, throwing my arms round his neck, pressing my cheek against his chest. His hands touched my waist, then he laughed again, as if taken aback, and his arms moved up to embrace me. I was crying, struggling not to, my whole body shaking. I heard him say, "Lord, what a fool I am, Jani. I was expecting to scoop up the skinny little creature you were . . . But you've grown up!"

I said in a muffled wail, "I'm making your shirt all wet."

"It's just an old shirt. That's the only kind I have." He laughed yet again. One of his hands moved, lightly touching my arm and shoulder, my cheek, my hat, which was knocked askew now, and my hair. "Yes," he said, "you've grown up, Jani."

Reluctantly I stepped back, found a handkerchief in my handbag, and began to dry my eyes. He stood very quietly, listening as if following my movements. When I could speak without my voice shaking too much I said, "Oh, I'm so glad I've found you, Mister. I mean, Mr. Gascoyne. I'm sorry, I'm all confused. . . ."

He smiled. "How on earth *did* you manage to find me? And what's been happening to you all these years. You're different. What happened to that funny Cockney voice?"

I put my hand to my head. "Oh, dear. There's so much to tell, and so much I want to hear. You're different, too. Not so . . ." I hesitated.

"Arrogant? Conceited?" He chuckled. "Yes, I think I've mellowed a little, maybe even improved." He paused, then: "You called me by my surname just now. Do you think you could call me Adam?"

"I'll try." I found myself smiling. "It may be a little difficult. I've been thinking of you as Mister for six years now."

196

His sightless eyes gazed past me for long seconds, then he said quietly, "I'm very flattered that you should have thought of me at all, Jani Burr." He grinned. "Come on, we'll go onto the balcony. Then I can carry on working while you tell me all about yourself, and we'll be chaperoned by the river traffic."

I took off my hat and followed him onto the balcony. He moved with great certainty, placing a chair opposite his own so that we would face each other across the table. Before I sat down I said, "Until you knew who it was, you were saying something about pease pudding and ale. Are you hungry?"

"Well, there has been a slight hitch in the commissariat arrangements this morning."

"Molly went off in a temper?"

He looked rueful. "Well, yes. I'd go out and get something for us, Jani, but I couldn't offer you a decent meal." He waved at the ivory pieces. "I'm short of money until I've completed this set."

"Well, I happen to be rich today, Mister. I mean, Adam. Just let me talk to the friend who brought me here." I leaned over the rusty balustrade and called softly, "Mr. Bailey."

He jumped to his feet. "Miss Jani?"

"Would you be very kind and try to find some food for us? A cold chicken, perhaps, and some cheese. I leave it to you. Also a jug of ale, please. Oh, and fetch enough for yourself, Mr. Bailey. I shall be here for quite a long time. You have some money?"

"I've got 'eaps out of what you gave me for cab fares. Just leave it to me, Miss Jani." He marched off briskly.

Adam said, "Well . . . thank you kindly for your hospitality, Jani." He waited, listening while I sat down, then picked up the chess piece and carving tool. His hands became busy. "You first, Jani. Right from the beginning."

Without haste, I began to tell my story. He went on working, stopping me with a question from time to time, listening intently, his face showing a whole range of emotions as I unfolded my tale.

After half an hour Mr. Bailey returned, bringing us a basket of cold food and a quart jug with a lid, together with some cheap plates and mugs and cutlery.

"Borrowed 'em," he explained. "Nice little shop up near the Tower."

I said, "Mr. Bailey, you're wonderful."

"My pleasure, Miss." He stared fiercely at the sky to make it quite plain that he was not being inquisitive, and did not lower his eyes until I introduced him to Captain Gascoyne, when he sprang to attention, held his hat over his heart, gave a slight bow, and barked, "Sir! Sarn't Bailey."

Adam said, "Have you secured your own rations, Sergeant? Miss Jani has been well-trained, and she won't sit down to eat until all men and horses under her command have been catered for."

"I 'ave the honour to report, sir, as 'ow I 'ope to partake of me own rations on the terrace below."

"Very good, Sergeant."

"Sir!" Mr. Bailey made a smart about-turn, stamped his feet together, and strode out.

I set the food out on plates, then continued my story. When I had told him of Sembur's letter, and read out my copy which I had brought with me, Adam put aside his work.

"So that was the truth of it," he said quietly. "What a truly hideous business. But I'm very glad for Sembur. I always found it hard to believe his confession."

We had long finished eating when I came to tell of my leaving Merlin's Keep for the cottage on Stafford's Farm, and there I left a gap in my story, saying nothing of Sir Charles and Lady Gascoyne, but going on to tell how I had followed up Vernon Quayle's claim that he could find "one who was lost" through the medallion I wore.

"I've left out one piece of my story," I ended, "but please let me keep that until you've told me your story, Adam. It's . . . something separate, really."

"All right, but first you have to make me a promise, Jani." His face was hard and serious. He reached across to find my hand. "You must have nothing more to do with this man Quayle. Ever."

"I can't promise that. You see, there's Eleanor, and I have to go to her if ever she needs me."

"But you can't *do* anything for her, Jani." He was squeezing my

198

hand hard now. "I'm afraid Eleanor is lost. Unless Quayle decides to let her go."

I shook my head stubbornly. "I won't give up hope for Eleanor."

"All right, Jani," he said at last, very quietly. "I suppose you can't be other than the way you were made."

With relief that the argument was over, I said, "Well that's settled, and now it's your turn."

"My story?" He laughed and picked up the bishop he had been working on since lunch. "It's very dull compared with yours. I hoped to stay in Gorakhpur till you'd recovered a little, but I was summoned to Calcutta, fell out with a brigadier, was posted to Cairo, fell out with a major-general, and decided to let the army get on without me."

He frowned and held out the bishop. "Can you see a flaw there, Jani? I can feel something here, on the cope."

I looked closely. "Yes, but it's only a speck."

"Ah, they can use it for one of the black pieces, then. Where was I, Jani?"

"You'd just left the army."

"Well, let me see . . . then I went to Santa Fé in Argentina, to breed horses. Bought a share in a promising stud farm, two South American partners and I. But then Ramon's sister conceived a passion for me, and when I didn't return it she accused me of dishonouring her." Adam threw back his head, laughing without restraint. "It being Argentina, her brothers had to take it up, of course, whether they believed her or not, but I jumped a train for Buenos Aires and managed to get out with a whole skin."

Chuckling, he picked out a three-cornered file from a box at his elbow. "Then I wandered up through the Caribbean for a while, looking for something to do. In the end I settled in Haiti and started exporting mahogany and rosewood. There were all sorts of problems, but Haiti's a fascinating place and I was rather enjoying myself there." He shrugged. "Then I went blind."

My voice was unsteady as I said, "How did it happen?"

"Lord knows, Jani. I picked up a fever and it laid me low for three or four days. When I came out of it, I was blind. I saw a French doctor in Cap-Haitien and an American doctor in Port-au-Prince, then I came back to England where I have seen three or four more doctors. The only thing they all agree on is that they can't cure me."

"How long have you been in England, Adam?"

"Oh, about eighteen months. After four or five I was running out of money, so I went to old Cheng Wu in Limehouse. He sells antiques and oriental objects of all kinds. I'd often bought from him in the old days. Anyway, he found lodgings for me here and said I could learn to carve ivory. It seems his grandfather had been blind, and he'd become a master at it. Well, I'm afraid I'll never be that, but I can make very reasonable chess sets which Cheng Wu sells to people who think they were carved in China." Again he gave that whole-hearted laugh which stirred a strange blend of happiness and sorrow in me. He said, "I've been very lucky. After about a month here, Molly took me under her wing. She's an Irish girl who goes totting for junk with her own donkey and cart. She keeps this place clean, sees to my clothes, quarrels with me, and won't take a penny for her pains."

"Does she live here with you?" I asked, remembering the blue cotton frock that hung with his own clothes. "Will she be cross if she finds me here?"

"Truth to tell, I never quite know what Molly will be cross about." He began to use a slim round file very delicately. "She has a junk shop up near the Mint, with a room above it, but she stays here off and on. She's very generous, very good to me."

I hesitated, then took the plunge. "Adam, your mother and father want you to come home."

His hands became still, his face a mask. After a moment he said, "What do you know of my parents, Jani?"

"Somebody in the Foreign Office told your father about Sembur's letter, and he already knew through army reports that you were the one sent to arrest Sembur. They came to see me at my cottage. Oh Adam, I know you quarrelled with your father all those years ago, but did you never think of all the pain and anxiety you've caused your mother?"

He put down the file. "This isn't your business, Jani."

I caught his hand and said hotly, "Oh, yes it is! Stop scraping at that thing and listen to me, Adam! You saved my life and you gave me your medallion, your mother's gift to you, *for remembrance, as a friend.* So if you meant it, if we're really friends, then what you do *is* my business. Your father's asking you to come home." I still held his hand tightly. "He's dying."

There was a long silence. At last his free hand moved to cover mine and he said thoughtfully, "I do wish I could see you."

My eyes filled suddenly. "Please, Adam. Will you do it?"

"I didn't mean to be cruel, Jani. When I lost my sight I felt it was better for my mother to think me dead than to discover I was blind and useless."

"Oh, Adam, you're such a fool," I whispered, and bent to put my cheek on the hand that covered mine. "Don't you understand anything about a mother's heart? Did you really imagine she would rather you were dead than blind?"

He did not speak for a while, then gave a long sigh. "First you soak my shirt front, now my cuff. I don't know what's happened to you, Jani. In all the weeks we were together, and with all that you went through, I never heard you weep once."

I lifted my head, wiped my eyes again, gave a quavery laugh, and spoke a few halting words of apology. Adam did not know what had happened to me, but suddenly I knew very well. I was in love with Mister, and I had been since long before David Hayward had jokingly suggested it. If I wept, it might be for happiness, sorrow, yearning, despair, jealousy, or all of these together.

We sat in silence for a time, and at last he said, "Very well, Jani. I'll come home if you'll come with me. I shall need you there, especially at first, to . . . to help bring us together."

"Adam, I can't thrust myself on your parents like that."

"You won't be. I'm the one who's insisting, and if they really want me it's a very easy condition to meet. Don't you agree?"

"Yes. Yes, I do, Adam. But I must see your mother and father first. I'll go this afternoon and break all the news to them, and I'll say you're coming home when, Adam?"

He gave a wry grimace and seemed to brace himself.

"Let's get it over. Tomorrow morning? Will you call for me?"

"Yes." I felt suddenly as if every ounce of strength had drained out of me.

He stood up. "Come along now, I'll walk with you and Mr. Bailey to the Tower."

"Oh, but who'll see you back?"

"I don't need a guide, I walk miles on my own."

I moved into the room, carrying the basket which had held our food. "I must wash up the crockery for Mr. Bailey to give back as we go."

"All right, there's some soda on the dresser."

It was quickly done, for the plates were barely greasy. I packed everything in the basket, and moved to a cracked looking-glass which hung near the bed, about to pin my hat on. Molly's looking-glass, I realized with a pang; Adam had no use for it.

Even as the thought came, the door opened and a girl of about twenty-two stepped into the room. Her face was plain and red, her eyes beautiful. Her hair was gathered in a bun at the back of her head, beneath a tilted-forward hat with some rather battered imitation grapes and cherries on the brim.

Adam, leaning against the wall by the window, said, "Ah, you've forgiven me, Molly. When I can smell the lavender water on you I know I'm forgiven, Jani, I present Molly. Molly . . . Jani."

She pushed the door to behind her and stood looking at me, hands on hips.

"So you're the one, then." She said it with a toss of her head.

Adam said, "None of your Irish riddles, Molly, me dear. She's what one?"

Molly gave him a glance of pitying contempt. "It's as well you have the education, Buff, for you're stupid as any man." She moved to stand in front of me. "Have you come to take him away, then?"

I said. "He's going home to his family. His father is dying."

She shrugged. "Well, there's an end of it." Tears shone in her eyes and she rubbed them angrily away. "I've had him a year an' more, an' there's none to take that from me. But I'm glad for him to go back to his own now. When will you be taking him?"

"I'll come tomorrow morning, about ten o'clock."

"Then I'll have him ready an' neat."

"Thank you, Molly."

Adam said stiffly, "I'd be glad if you'd both stop talking of me as if I weren't here."

Molly laughed, and moved towards him till she stood very close, looking up at him. "You know what, Buff? I'll marry Sid, like he's always askin' and like you're always tellin' me." She put up her arms and clasped her hands at the back of his neck. "But you'll be the one, Buff, you'll be the one, damn you."

She stretched up, pulled his head down, kissed him hard on the lips, then swung round and went out of the room with her head in the air. Adam ran long fingers through his thick black hair. I turned back to the looking-glass and tried to concentrate on arranging my hat. Adam was putting on a threadbare jacket. He buttoned it, moved to the door, and held it open for me. A question came to my mind, and I said, "Adam, why do they call you Buff?"

He gave a little laugh. "The children dubbed me that after that game they play, Blind Man's Buff."

THREE HOURS LATER, in the lovely drawing room of a house which looked out over Regent's Park, a white-faced Lady Gascoyne said, "But may I not go to him now, and bring him home?"

"Please don't, Lady Gascoyne." I said. "I'm sure it's best for him to come here in his own time."

Standing by a window, staring out over the park, Sir Charles said, "Pay heed to the child, Mary. She has talked with him."

"But Charles, *blind!* And living in such an awful place."

"An hour ago you would have thanked God that Jani found him alive, in whatever condition. Pull yourself together, my dear." Sir Charles came to where I sat beside his wife on a deep-buttoned sofa, and looked at me anxiously. "And we can really count on you coming to stay here indefinitely?"

I put my fingertips to my brow, trying to rub a nagging headache away. "Well, for a little while, Sir Charles, if you'll have me. I can't really say for how long."

Chapter Fourteen

The first week in Chester Gardens was a nightmare for everybody. We all struggled to be completely natural, and only succeeded in being stilted, awkward and forced. It was nobody's fault. A gulf of many years lay between Adam and his parents. He had gone away from them as a boy and returned as a man nearing thirty.

The fourth day, to Adam's evident relief, he and I spent alone together, for we went to Larkfield, so that I could fetch a trunk of clothes and personal belongings from Withy Cottage. He wore a new suit and I was able to tell him truthfully that he looked most elegant and handsome, which made him laugh.

I was thankful that something which might have become an enormous problem had already disappeared. I had dreaded that Adam's pride would not permit him to live on his parents' bounty. On the morning after his arrival at Chester Gardens, however, I was summoned by Sir Charles to read out and confirm to Adam a portion of the Will of Adam's maternal grandfather, who had died two years before. A rich man, he had left a third of his fortune to Adam.

On the day of our visit to Larkfield Mr. and Mrs. Stafford were at home and gave us a splendid luncheon, during which they brought me up to date with local gossip. I asked after Eleanor, but there was no fresh news of her. "Not at 'ome to anyone nowadays, Miss Eleanor isn't," said Mrs. Stafford, "not even when the vicar's wife called to see 'er."

Next day I wrote to Eleanor, saying I had found Mister and that he was reunited with his family. I should have written to Vernon Quayle, since it was he who had really enabled me to find my friend, but I could not bring myself to do so, and in any event I was bitterly sure that he would see any letter Eleanor received. I also wrote to Major Elliot, telling him that I had been able to help Sir Charles and Lady Gascoyne to find their lost son, and that I was now staying with them at their London home for a time.

David Hayward had been away when we went to Larkfield, so I wrote to him too. I told him I felt guilty at being so far from

204

Eleanor, but that Adam needed my help to settle down with his mother and father. This was not the whole truth, for I did not say I had fallen in love with Adam and never wanted to be away from him.

David replied promptly, saying that there was nothing I could do for Eleanor and I must stop feeling guilty. He was sorry to have missed us but hoped we would come down again soon.

By the end of the first ten days at Chester Gardens things had become a little better and I realized that time was the only answer to our problem. If Adam was to settle down happily here then we all needed to build up a background of day-to-day experience, to give us a sense of belonging to one another.

Soon I had arranged for Sir Charles to accompany us when we went riding in the park for an hour every morning. During that time I contrived to let him be responsible for guiding Adam, and I was tremendously glad when I saw that they were beginning to chat more easily together as they rode side by side.

As week succeeded week, a true family atmosphere slowly burgeoned in the household. We began to receive and pay calls, and if Adam found this boring he concealed it splendidly. At night, I would lie awake, dreaming about how wonderful it would be if Adam were to fall in love with me and ask me to marry him. I knew it would not happen, and in a way I was glad, for if it did I knew I might be tempted beyond endurance, tempted to turn my back on Eleanor and try to forget what had befallen her. And if I abandoned Eleanor I would never forgive myself.

In November, protesting that it was a waste of time, Adam went into a nursing home for two days so that his eyes could be thoroughly examined by specialists. The essence of their medical report was that the optic nerves had atrophied due to unknown causes. When I read it to Adam he laughed, shrugged, and said it was medical language for, "We haven't the slightest idea."

In December I had a very official letter from a Mr. R. G. Milner, a Parliamentary Under-Secretary of State at the Foreign Office. In it he said that certain matters concerning myself and the State of Jahanapur had been brought to his attention, and he would be grateful if I would find it convenient to call on him at his Whitehall office at eleven o'clock on the morning of Friday 11th December.

I read it out to Adam as we took a short stroll in the park before breakfast, and he said, "Show it to my father and take his advice, Jani. He's been a diplomat all his life, and he knows exactly how to deal with this sort of thing."

Sir Charles read the letter at breakfast, then looked up with a gleam in his eye. "So that's their little game, eh? Well, let's teach them a lesson. First, however, confirm to me now that you have no wish whatsoever to assert your rights as Maharani of Jahanapur."

"No wish at all, truly."

"Very well. But please do not say that, or anything else on this matter, to anyone at all without first consulting me."

I agreed wonderingly. Lady Gascoyne said, "You look as if you are girding yourself for battle, Charles."

"I am, my dear, I am." He gave a rather menacing chuckle, drained his coffee cup, excused himself, and departed briskly.

Half an hour later Sir Charles came to the balcony overlooking Regent's Park, where I was reading to Adam. In his hand was a sheet of writing paper. "Would you cast your eye over that, Jani, my dear?" He sat down beside me, smiling.

I said, "Adam, it's a letter addressed to Mr. Milner, I'll read it out.

"Dear Sir,

I am in receipt of your letter offensively addressed to Miss Jani Saxon, instead of to Her Highness the Maharani of Jahanapur, whose private secretary I have the honour to be.

I now inform you that Her Highness will not attend upon you at your office on the day suggested or indeed at any other time. If you have matters to discuss with her you may call upon her at this address at half-past four o'clock on Tuesday 15th December.

I have the honour to remain, Sir,
Your obedient servant,
Charles Gascoyne, Bart. KCVO, CBE.
Private Secretary to Her Highness the Maharani of Jahanapur."

I looked up from the letter. Adam gave a shout of laughter and said, "Splendid, Father! But do please explain."

"Certainly, my dear boy. It's quite clear from Milner's letter that the India Office or Foreign Office or both simply don't want all the upheaval of Jani making a claim to Jahanapur. So they're trying to bluff her out of making it. That's why Milner asked her to go trotting along to see him. What I've done is to give the blighter something to think about. They'll know now they have a fight on their hands, and they'll have to start thinking of some sort of offer."

I said, "Perhaps they'll just . . . well, ignore me."

"Oh no." He smiled, and his eyes narrowed. "They're worried, Jani. Now we'll wait and see what happens next. We shan't have to wait long, I promise you."

He was right, for his letter was answered by return of post. The new letter said that Mr. Milner had received the communication from my private secretary and would be happy to oblige me by calling at the suggested time. Adam said, "Father, do please allow me to be present with you and Jani when you deal with this fellow. Oh, wait though—might it weaken your position?"

"Not at all, my boy." Sir Charles rubbed his hands briskly. "You could help by disconcerting him. Would it trouble you to wear dark spectacles? No? Then we'll place you a little to one side of him, so that you can simply appear to be gazing at him in silence. A mystery man. We won't even introduce you."

Adam grinned. "Father, you're an old fox. Jani shall take me out to buy some dark spectacles today, the most sinister pair we can find."

Mr. Milner proved to be a man in his early forties, very soberly dressed, and carrying a black briefcase which he rested on his knees and seemed about to open at any minute, though he never did so. His manner was pleasant but rather languid, as if this whole matter was a trivial affair and hardly worth troubling about.

The "audience", as Sir Charles insisted on calling it, was held in the drawing room. Mr. Milner was invited to sit on a rather low chair in the middle of the room. Sir Charles and I sat one on each side of the big fireplace, our chairs half turned so that our gazes converged on Mr. Milner. Adam sat unmoving with his back to the window, so that he was on the edge of Mr. Milner's vision, an ominous figure in wire-framed dark blue spectacles.

Mr. Milner spoke rather vaguely for a few minutes, saying that His Majesty's Government had studied a certain letter alleged to have been written by an alleged criminal, an ex-soldier by the name of RSM George Burr. Often he paused as if expecting some comment, but we gave him no help whatever. When he finally came to a halt, we sat looking at him and said nothing.

After a long pause Mr. Milner gave me a wintry smile and said, "I am authorized to give consideration to any comment you may wish to make, Miss Saxon."

As instructed, I gazed stonily over the top of Mr. Milner's head. Sir Charles said, "Comment on what, sir? You have wasted ten minutes saying that the Government may deny the claim of Her Highness to be the issue of Colonel Saxon and his wife, the Maharani of Jahanapur, and therefore may deny that she is now herself the rightful Maharani. If that is the Government's view, then let us proceed to test it in the courts, as we have been preparing to do." He rose to his feet and made a slight bow in my direction. "I see no purpose in prolonging this audience, Your Highness."

I inclined my head. Mr. Milner said, "Ah, now, one moment please, Sir Charles. I was about to inform Miss Saxon that the prime concern of the Government is to avoid possible dissension in Jahanapur. We have therefore discussed Miss Saxon's pretensions to the throne of Jahanapur with the present ruler—"

"The present illegal ruler," said Sir Charles, "but pray continue."

"With Prince Mohan Sudraka," said Mr. Milner. "He is a good ruler, and also a generous one. In fact he is willing to make substantial recognition of Miss Saxon's services, if she will use her good offices to avoid creating a dispute over the throne. This offer is made without prejudice, of course."

Sir Charles said stiffly, "Are you being deliberately insulting, sir?"

"Not at all." Mr. Milner was beginning to glance ever more often and with growing unease at the grim, silent figure of Adam. "I would hardly feel that recognition in the sum of fifty thousand pounds could be deemed an insult."

I smothered a gulp of alarm, did my best to look haughty and keep a straight face. Sir Charles's face grew red. I learned later that he achieved this by holding his breath and contracting his stomach muscles. "Fifty thousand?" he echoed incredulously. "My dear sir, as you and I are both well aware, the annual income of the ruler of Jahanapur is in the order of one and one-quarter million pounds. Is he seriously attempting to—to *buy* Her Highness off with two week's wages?"

For a while I lost track of the conversation. I could hear the words spoken, but could not make sense of them, and felt the dreamlike sensation which I had sometimes known in the thin air of the high mountain passes. When I collected my wits again Sir Charles was saying, "Very well, sir. It may be that for the sake of her people in Jahanapur, and to avoid dissension, Her Highness will make this great sacrifice which is now being asked of her, and renounce her rights on the terms we have just agreed. Permit me, however, to recapitulate what those terms are. First, that the sum of two hundred thousand pounds sterling be paid to the order of Her Highness, for her absolute benefit, payment to be guaranteed by the ruler of Jahanapur. Second, that the British Government recognizes the legitimacy of Her Highness's claim. Third, that the Government shall ensure that the innocence of Regimental Sergeant-Major George Burr be officially declared in the *London Gazette*, that a suitable posthumous award be made for his devotion to duty, and that his remains be brought to such military cemetery as the Colonel of the regiment shall approve, there to be interred with military honours. Fourth, that in renouncing all rights and authority in and over the State of Jahanapur, Her Highness shall retain her title, Princess Jani of Jahanapur."

Mr. Milner suppressed a sigh and stood up. "You have put it very succinctly, Sir Charles. I have little doubt you shall hear from us again within the next day or two."

Sir Charles permitted himself a tigerish smile. "I have little doubt of that myself, sir."

When Mr. Milner had said goodbye and been shown from the room, I ran to Sir Charles in panic. "Oh, I can't I can't! All that money—I wouldn't know what to do. I had no idea you were going to say all those things . . ." Quite suddenly I began to weep.

Sir Charles put his arms round me, patting my shoulder as he held me. "Now, now, child, there's nothing to be afraid of. Having a great deal of money won't change you. Not you, Jani. All I have done is to ensure that you receive a little of what is your due." He paused. "Now Adam, for heaven's sake take those dreadful spectacles off, my boy. I don't know what effect they had on Milner, but by God they terrify me."

CHRISTMAS WAS A TIME of sunshine and shadow for me. I had no greeting from Eleanor, and thought about her with aching heart, but was happy almost beyond words to sit at table with the Gascoynes now, and hear them talk easily and affectionately together. Of late Adam had been going out with his father more often, sometimes to a club in Pall Mall, sometimes to the City on business. This especially pleased me, partly because it showed how truly they had both buried the past, and partly because it gave me more time to spend with Lady Gascoyne.

One day, just before Christmas, I was in her room, hastily stitching the gown she was wearing, where a few inches of the hem had come loose, when suddenly she turned to me and asked, "Are you in love with Adam, dear?"

Though the question came unexpectedly it did not take me completely by surprise, for Lady Gascoyne must often have noticed the way I looked at Adam. I said, "Yes. Yes, I am in love with him. I think I may have been for a long time." I bit the end of the cotton and stood up.

She hugged me for a moment, then stood back with tears shining in her eyes. "Oh, I'm so glad, darling. And is Adam in love with you? Will he ask you to marry him?"

I smiled a rather forced smile. "I think he's quite fond of me, but no more than that. Anyway, it wouldn't do, Lady Gascoyne, I'm not really free."

"Not free?" She gazed at me incredulously.

"Because of Eleanor. I know it's hard for you to understand, but she *must* come first. She gave me everything. Oh please, please don't say anything of this to Adam."

She shook her head. "Of course not. But Jani, don't spoil your life to no purpose, child. Be a little selfish."

I busied myself putting away the needle, cotton and thimble, almost angry with her in that moment, for I was only too ready to be selfish and needed no encouragement. I said, "You must be thinking that one day Adam will want me, Lady Gascoyne, but he won't. He'll always see me as a rather ugly little girl with chopped off hair, and ribs like a washboard."

There was a little silence, then Lady Gascoyne said, "I know one thing. I want you for my daughter, Jani, so please don't forbid me to hope."

CHRISTMAS DAY was on a Friday. On the following Sunday evening, by arrangement, Adam and I drove down to Wapping. There we met Molly and her fiancé of recent date, a cheerful giant called Sid, and took them to a nearby shop which served eel-pie suppers. As a wedding gift, Adam presented them with fifty sovereigns neatly fitted round a horseshoe of gold-painted wood.

The occasion was not a success. We were quite out of place. Molly called over several people to greet their old friend Buff, but they were ill at ease and did not linger. When we parted Molly said, "Well, ta very much for everythin', an' God bless all here, but don't be comin' again, Buff." She gave me a friendly wink. "Not without you're flat broke like before, an' even so you'd not be needing me now."

Three days later, in the big drawing room of the house in Chester Gardens, in the presence of Sir Charles, Mr. Milner, a government lawyer, Sir Charles's solicitor, and a legal representative of His Highness Prince Mohan Sudraka, I signed an impressive legal document renouncing all claim to the State of Jahanapur. In the same moment I became possessed of a huge fortune.

Next day, the last day of the year, the whole family drove with me to the Adelaide Crocker Home for Orphan Girls. There we saw Miss Callender, who recognized me at once, somewhat to my astonishment. She showed us round the home. As we returned to her office I told her that I had arranged to endow the home with the sum of one thousand pounds a year. To my alarm she put her hands over her face and began to weep. I quickly shooed Sir Charles and Adam away, then helped Lady Gascoyne soothe and cheer her.

When we left she was full of gratitude, but I felt a great humbug. After all, what I had done was costing me nothing at all, far less than it had cost me, on a summer's day in the New Forest long ago, to offer a bacon sandwich to a fainting man.

That night, at midnight, we saw the New Year in, standing on the balcony which looked out over Regent's Park, well wrapped against the cold, straining to hear the distant chimes of Big Ben at Westminster. As we embraced one another, I had the joy of being held in Adam's arms for a moment, the first since that day in the back room of The Grapes, at Wapping. It did not occur to me then that we were entering the year spoken of by the Oracle, the Year of the Wood-Dragon. I was soon to have cause to remember it.

Chapter Fifteen

In the second week of January, by David Hayward's invitation, Adam and I took the train to Bournemouth to spend a few days in Larkfield. It was arranged that I should stay in the Stafford farmhouse, as my cottage was cold and unaired, and Adam would stay with David. The two men had not met before, but from the moment they greeted each other I sensed an immediate harmony. They were of very different natures, yet each seemed to take to the other in an easy, unforced way which did my heart good to see.

One of our first duties was to pay a call on Major Elliot, so I could tell him all that had passed between me and the Foreign Office, and thank him for the great help he had given me in the beginning. We also visited several other old friends of mine, but on David's advice we did not attempt to call upon Eleanor. "Eleanor has received no callers for months, and hasn't been out of the house for months," he said bleakly. "If it wasn't for Mrs. Burke, I'd almost wonder if she's still alive."

On most days of our visit Adam and I accompanied David on his rounds. Soon I was helping him as before. Adam would stand in cowshed or stable, waiting and listening. He never seemed to grow bored.

When added muscle was required, he could not be prevented from taking part, and on one such occasion a strange incident occurred. We were working on a small farm belonging to Mrs. Fennel, a widow who was trying to run it almost single-handed since the death of her husband. Several of her cows had eaten some wet turnips, and were suffering from bloat, their left flanks distended. It was necessary to keep them on the move and prevent them lying down while David contrived to get a tube down each in turn to vent the gas. Mrs. Fennel and her one farmhand were pushing and pulling the creatures about when we arrived, and I at once joined in, tugging at one of the cows by its nose, using my most flattering persuasion in honorific Tibetan.

Adam stood by the gate wearing old flannel trousers and a tweed jacket beneath a short covert-coat. He was about to light one of the cigars he occasionally smoked, when he took it unlit from his mouth and called, "Anything I can do, Jani?"

"Yes," I called back a little breathlessly, "you can keep this one on her feet while I give Mrs. Fennel a hand. But you'd better take your coat off. It's a long hot job."

He laid the cigar down carefully on top of the gatepost, quickly removed his coat, cap and jacket, placed them on the top rail, then came over to help.

We had to haul the reluctant cows about for an hour before David had dealt with them all and was satisfied. I took Adam's arm and walked across the pasture with him to recover his clothes, only to find that the cigar and his cap had vanished. When I told him, he thought at first that I was joking, and then that some animal had made off with them. "We'll have to look out for a dog or a horse wearing a cap and smoking a cigar," he said, highly amused.

I was holding his jacket, staring at it. "Adam, a little triangle of cloth has been torn from the lining, just inside the collar! Who on earth could have done such a thing?"

"Perhaps it was already torn."

"No, before I packed them I went over all your clothes to see if anything needed mending. I suppose you must have caught it on a nail, or something like that, since we've been here."

"It's not important, anyway." He laughed as he pulled on his topcoat. "Come on, I can hear David yelling for you."

We returned to London in the last week of January, and a cold black shadow fell swiftly upon me. At first Adam seemed a little withdrawn from me, then there were times when I felt he was hard put to suppress his irritation, and finally he began to avoid me. I was hurt, and increasingly bewildered, for I had no idea what I was doing to upset him. With his father and mother he was as amiable as before, and for this I was thankful, but the easy friendship which had grown between the two of us seemed no more than a memory now. He took to staying late at his club. Very politely he made it clear that he did not wish me to read to him any more, and I think this politeness was the worst thing of all, for suddenly it was as if we were strangers.

The end came one evening as I was making my way downstairs to the drawing room, where the family always met and chatted until the butler announced dinner. On this occasion the door was half open, and as I was coming to the foot of the stairs I suddenly heard Adam's voice, speaking rather tautly and as if in answer to something said by his mother or father: "I am not being unkind or ungrateful. I have spent the last few months being as pleasant and amiable as possible to Jani, but I've quite run out of steam. Oh, she's good-hearted, no doubt, but hardly my choice for a daily companion. I'm sorry if my boredom shows, but I really can't help it."

I had stopped at the bottom of the stairs. Now I turned and went up again as quietly as I could, my face hot with shame. What a conceited fool I had been to imagine he enjoyed my company. In all we had done together over the past weeks he had seemed amused and interested. But now I saw clearly that he had simply been humouring me.

214

By the time I reached my room my face was pale. I slapped and pinched my cheeks to bring some colour to them, held a damp handkerchief over my eyelids for a few moments, then drew a deep breath and went downstairs again. Sir Charles and Lady Gascoyne greeted me perhaps a little too warmly, while Adam said politely, "Good evening, Jani. I hope the day has been enjoyable for you."

The last thing I wanted was for anyone to guess that I had overheard what Adam had said about me, so I waited until we had almost finished dinner before I said apologetically, "You know, since visiting Larkfield I've felt rather guilty about being away for so long. I really think I must go back soon."

Sir Charles and his wife exchanged a troubled glance, then Lady Gascoyne said rather uncertainly, being careful not to look at Adam, "Oh, we hadn't thought about your leaving us, Jani. We felt you were one of the family."

"You have certainly made me feel like one of the family," I said, smiling from one to the other, "that's why I've stayed longer than I should have." I managed a little laugh. "It was Adam who foisted me on you to begin with, because he wanted a nursemaid, but he certainly doesn't need one any longer, and now I feel I must begin to put some of my plans into practice."

Sir Charles said, "What plans, my dear?"

"Well, David Hayward told me that Catling's Farm, adjoining the grounds of Merlin's Keep on the southern side, is coming up for sale later this year. It's a mixed farm of about seventy acres, and there's a very nice house as well as three cottages."

There was a silence. Adam concentrated on stirring his coffee. Sir Charles, looking very miserable, said, "But Jani—"

His wife interrupted, and as she looked at me I saw in her eyes that she had understood.

"Yes, you've been unselfish for far too long, Jani," she said gently. "We shall miss you dreadfully, but it's high time you thought about your own future."

Three days later Sir Charles and Lady Gascoyne drove with me in their carriage to Waterloo Station, to see me off. We were all very miserable while pretending to be jolly. Adam did not come. I had last seen him soon after breakfast, when he had shaken hands with me, wished me well, and then sent for a cab to take him to his club.

BY THE TIME I had been back in Larkfield for two weeks it was almost as if I had never been away, except that I had for ever to keep myself busy, to prevent the aching emptiness I felt within me whenever I thought of Adam. I spent more time than ever helping David. Mr. Stafford came with me to see Mr. Catling about the farm I planned to buy, and after some slow Hampshire bargaining between the two men it was agreed that when the farm was put up for sale I would be offered first refusal at twenty pounds an acre.

It was a week later that I woke suddenly in the night, roused by an urgent banging on the door of Withy Cottage. I struck a match, lit my bedside candle, and looked at the small clock on the cabinet. It was half past midnight. I pulled on a dressing gown and went sleepily to the window. David had never called me out in the night before, but I supposed he might do so if he had an emergency involving a very difficult animal.

Drawing back the curtain I opened the window a few inches, shivering at the touch of cold air. There had been a thin fall of snow. "Who is it?" I called.

"Me. David." His voice was strained. "I'm hurt, Jani."

"I'm coming down." By the time I reached the front door I was wide awake with alarm. I dragged the bolts back, and as I threw open the door David stumbled against me. I glimpsed his gig on the verge close to the cottage. "Sorry," he mumbled. "Sorry, Jani."

"It's all right," I gasped, bracing myself. "Now, lean on me and let's get you to a chair." As he slumped in an armchair I saw there was a cut and a swelling bruise on his temple, while blood was seeping through a gash in the side of his left Wellington boot.

I ran out to the gig and snatched the bag of vet's instruments from the seat, for I knew there would be disinfectant and bandages in it. Inside the room again I paused only to throw a log on the dying fire, then brought a bowl from the kitchen, put it on the floor,

216

and carefully eased David's boot off his blood-soaked trouser leg.

"David dear, what on earth have you done?"

"Tried to shoot Quayle," he said thickly. "Didn't work . . . he just laughed . . . devil looks after his own."

"Never mind." I turned back his trouser leg to find the wound. There was a gouge several inches long in his calf, the flesh torn rather than cut, but providing it was prevented from turning septic it was not dangerous.

For the next twenty minutes I was busy cleaning the wound thoroughly with antiseptic lotion, packing it with gauze, and making a neat bandage. I bathed the bruise on David's head, washed the cut with the same antiseptic solution, then cleared everything away and made a jug of coffee, lacing it with brandy. Then I settled myself in the armchair opposite him and said, "Do you feel up to telling me what happened?"

He sipped the coffee and nodded. "Beginning to feel . . . almost human again." He looked at me, his eyes dark and distressed. "That man Quayle. He's . . . protected in some way, Jani. He must be."

"Oh David, please don't just ramble when I'm sick with worry. *Tell* me."

"Sorry. Well, Major Elliot sent a boy round at about half past eleven. He said one of his horses was in agony, would I come along and put it down. So I drove over and helped the poor creature out of its pain with a bullet from my Webley. Then . . ." He looked at me a little awkwardly. "Then I . . . well, I came back by the track behind Merlin's Keep. I know it's a longer way round, but it's the nearest I can ever be to Eleanor these days." He stared into the fire, and I saw his face grow taut. "You can see over the wall at one point, and look along that broad path through the fruit trees to the house. And that's when I saw Eleanor."

"Eleanor? In the garden at midnight?"

He nodded, his hands shaking as they cradled the cup of coffee. "There's almost no moon tonight, but a light was blazing from that one big window of the Round Room. It seemed to be shining down on the lawn, and the window must have been masked in a special

way, because the patch of light thrown on the grass made the out-
line of a huge five-pointed star." He stared into the fire. "Eleanor
was kneeling there in the middle of it, Jani, with her arms lifted,
and her hair loose, and she was naked . . ."

"*What?*" I started up, feeling a murderous rage sweep through
me. "Eleanor . . . ? Out there on a freezing night, *naked?*"

David nodded wearily. "I know what you're feeling, Jani, because
it was just the same for me. I wanted to get my hands on Quayle's
throat. . . . Then I saw him. He was standing at the other end of the
path, with his back towards me, watching her. One point of the star
was almost touching his feet. He seemed to be wearing a short,
silvery cloak, and in each hand he had something like a wand. One
was pointing to the sky, the other towards Eleanor." David looked
at me from a drawn face. "Jani, I could swear I saw a kind of . . .
black light streaming from the tip of the thing he was pointing at
Eleanor."

My heart was still pounding, and it was an effort to make myself
sit down. I whispered, "What did you do?"

He shrugged. "I don't remember scrambling over the wall, I just
remember storming up that path towards Quayle. Then I must have
run into a tree branch in the dark, and I fell. Well, I was dazed for
a few moments, then I got to my knees. Quayle still had his back to
me. I got the Webley out of the little knapsack I carry it in, and put
a cartridge in the chamber. I was ice-cold."

He shivered as if with a fever, then took a long drink of the coffee
and brandy before going on rapidly. "I got up. I started walking
towards him, with the gun in my hand, the trigger cocked. I was no
more than four or five paces away when it . . . seemed to go off of its
own accord. I'll swear I didn't fire it. I must have just taken a pace
forward with my left foot, and the bullet seemed to rip down my
calf. I fell again. Just as I passed out, I realized that Quayle was
laughing."

David put down the mug and rubbed his eyes. "When I came
round I was lying in the darkness with the Webley beside me. No
sign of Quayle, no sign of Eleanor, no light from the Round Room."
He leaned back and closed his eyes. "So I came here."

218

Despite the warmth of the room I was cold inside, and I hugged myself, feeling close to tears as I said, "Oh David, how can we stop him doing these dreadful things with Eleanor?"

David looked at me heavy-eyed. "I'm too tired to think, Jani." He stared blankly at the clock on the mantelpiece for a few seconds, then gave a start of alarm. "Oh my God, it's the early hours, and I've left the gig outside your cottage. Whatever will people think!" He struggled to pull on his sock and the torn Wellington. "Give me a hand to get me on my feet."

"No, David, don't be silly. I'll get dressed and fetch the doctor."

"No, no, Jani!" He broke in angrily. "I've caused you enough trouble, and I don't need a doctor." He took my arm, tried his injured leg cautiously, and limped to the door. There he pressed my hand, looking at me with a rather feverish smile.

"Bless you, Jani. We'll talk about Eleanor again when I can think of her without wanting to do murder."

When I returned to my bed at last I lay awake for a long time, my mind in tumbling confusion.

For all that, the night was short. I woke at six and was making myself breakfast in the kitchen when the postman brought me a letter from Lady Gascoyne. She had written to me twice since my return. I scarcely knew whether I was pleased to have her warm and friendly letters or not, for though I treasured any scrap of news about Adam, I knew it would be far better for me to let my friendship with the family fade quietly away. The very first words of this latest letter startled me.

Dearest Jani,

That dreadful man you told us about, Mr. Vernon Quayle, actually called here yesterday. Ugh! He made my flesh creep. Charles and I received him, and then he asked if he might speak with Adam.

My dear, from the moment Adam came in I could almost see his hackles rise in the presence of this man, even though he could not see him. Adam asked him his business, but the unhealthy-looking wretch simply stared at him. At last he murmured: "So my wife's perception was quite correct. You made an enemy in Haiti, Mr. Gascoyne."

Wasn't that an extraordinary thing to say? I felt sure the fellow must be quite mad. After a moment or two Adam snapped: "What do you want, Quayle?" The man smiled and answered: "Why, to restore your sight, Mr. Gascoyne. The moon is new now. You will see before it is full." Then he wished us all good day, and walked from the room without waiting to be shown out.

Adam and Charles dismissed the whole thing as nonsense. But, oh Jani, is it wrong of me to cling to a tiny hope that Adam's blindness might be cured? Even if it were brought about by a creature who makes my blood run cold? Do please forgive my silly ramblings . . .

The rest of the letter was made up of comment on my own letter of the week before, and general gossip.

Later that day, when David called to see me, I said nothing to him about Lady Gascoyne's letter. The truth was that I felt a thread of guilt. The previous night, I could have wished for a thunderbolt to strike Vernon Quayle down. Now I still hated him, but tiny and tempting hopes kept nibbling like mice at my mind. Perhaps, with his strange arts, he could give back to Adam the blessing of sight.

David, for his part, thanked me for helping him, but said little more about what had happened to him at Merlin's Keep. It was as if he wanted to pretend that nothing had happened, perhaps because he could not bear to dwell upon Eleanor's degradation.

Next day, at about five o'clock in the afternoon, a boy came to the cottage with a note for me. My throat turned dry as I saw Eleanor's handwriting:

Dear Jani,

I should be grateful if you would call to see me at half-past eight o'clock this evening.

Eleanor.

The writing was Eleanor's, but the words were those of her husband, Vernon Quayle. I scribbled a hasty line saying I would be there, and sent the boy off with it. Then I decided that I must keep my mind occupied for the next three hours, for if I began to wonder and speculate I would be as jumpy as a grasshopper by the time I left for Merlin's Keep.

I took out writing paper and pen and wrote a long letter to Miss Callender at the Adelaide Crocker Home, putting forward various suggestions based on my own experience as a girl there. Then I wrote a chatty letter to Sir Charles and Lady Gascoyne.

At twenty past eight, after I had had supper, I was jogging along the lane in Mr. Stafford's dog-cart, a waxing moon glinting on the well-polished harness. A few minutes later, as I mounted the familiar steps to the porch of Merlin's Keep, I found that without knowing it I had taken off my glove, drawn out Adam's medallion from beneath the bodice of my dress, and was clutching it tightly in my hand, just as I had clutched it for comfort years ago as I lay in the Gorakhpur Mission Hospital.

It was then I knew I was afraid.

Chapter Sixteen

It was very quiet in the Round Room. Vernon Quayle had received me and conducted me there at once. Eleanor, in a plain white dress and sitting in the same chair as before, had given me a small, tentative smile and whispered, "Hello, Jani." She looked pale, almost waxen.

I sat watching Vernon Quayle, trying to contain the hatred which had flared up anew as he injected a colourless liquid into Eleanor's forearm. Her eyes closed as if in sleep, and Vernon Quayle started weighing and mixing small amounts of what looked like dried herbs, then putting a little of the mixture in each of five small copper bowls standing on tripods above unlit spirit lamps.

I said huskily from a dry throat, "Will you please tell me why Eleanor asked me to come here?"

"Certainly. I required her to do so because your presence will be of help to us in the exacting operation I am about to perform to restore Adam Gascoyne's sight."

My heart lurched. "An operation? I . . . I don't understand."

"It is very simple. My wife is an instrument of remarkable penetration. Through her, I have traced back certain intangible lines

221

and discovered how Adam Gascoyne's blindness was caused."
Vernon Quayle consulted a scroll but continued without pausing.
"There are primitive peoples who have faculties which they are
able to exert even though they have little or no understanding of
the laws and principles they are using. Gascoyne offended one such
person, an *obeah* in Haiti, who then performed an ancient West
African ritual of which at least half is mere mumbo-jumbo. However, the rest encompassed the use of the Law of Correspondence,
which applies to interaction between the material and non-material
planes of being, and which same law we shall call upon this evening
in order to reverse the process which made Adam Gascoyne blind.

"The spell of the Haitian *obeah* produced an effect upon Gascoyne's etheric body, and this was mirrored in due time by the
physical body. The operation that I am about to perform will itself
take place on the etheric plane where distance does not exist as we
know it. I do not expect you to understand this. I know of no more
than a dozen men in the world today who could fully comprehend
the operation I shall perform. Of these twelve, only two would dare
to perform it."

He put aside the scroll, positioned the five small tripods with
their spirit lamps and copper bowls very carefully around a slender,
ornately carved pillar of black wood. This pillar stood on three
splayed feet. Its top was a round brass disc with something en-
graved on it in a script unknown to me. Next Vernon Quayle began
to light the spirit lamps with a black taper. Threads of heavy smoke
rose lazily from the copper bowls.

He was wearing white gloves now, and held something in his
hands. It was a small doll, very crudely carved from soft wood. He
opened a little round casket on his desk, picked up a pair of tweezers,
and lifted from the casket a scrap of black cloth which he deftly
twisted about the doll's neck. Again he probed in the casket with
the tweezers. When he lifted them up to the light I glimpsed a long
curly black hair. This he pressed into a split in the softwood head
of the doll. When he brought a third item from the casket I caught
my breath, for I saw that the tweezers held a piece cut from a cigar,
the kind I had seen Adam smoke.

As Vernon Quayle teased a few shreds from the cigar, and pressed them into the tiny hole representing the doll's mouth, he said, "The Law of Correspondence. For the operation I shall perform, this doll corresponds to Adam Gascoyne."

I remembered the winter's day when David and Adam and I had been dealing with Mrs. Fennel's cows. Adam's cigar and cap had vanished, and a scrap of cloth had been ripped from inside the collar of his coat. No doubt a black curly hair could later have been found in the cap.

Vernon Quayle was doing something I could not see to the doll's face. He said musingly, "A hair, a scrap of cloth with body perspiration, a shred of tobacco touched with saliva. Few items of correspondence, but each one very potent. And I will have the medallion now, if you please."

My mind seemed to have stopped working and I felt sick. As I took off the medallion and handed it to Vernon Quayle I saw that the two places where the doll's eyes should have been were covered with blobs of what looked like black wax. He wound the chain round and round the neck until the medallion rested on the chest, then laid the doll down on the brass-topped pedestal of black wood.

"Listen to me carefully," he said. "Gascoyne nursed you when you were a child coming to maturity, the time of life in a female when certain energies are at their strongest. The correspondence between you is therefore very powerful." He pointed. "Stand here, please, facing Eleanor across the pedestal. So. And now place the middle finger of your right hand on the body of the doll."

I obeyed. He moved to stand behind Eleanor, took off his gloves, placed his fingertips on her temples, and said to me, "You will not speak or move again until I say that you may do so. To the best of your ability, simply direct your thoughts towards remembering occasions when Adam Gascoyne was kind to you. Intense concentration is not called for. Simply hold the memory in your mind, as in a day-dream."

I thought my mind would be too busy and distracted to do as he had bidden me, but I was wrong. I stood there remembering, gazing down at the ugly little doll beneath my finger yet not seeing it. I was a child again. Adam knelt over me, sheltering me from the icy wind that skimmed the deep snow and blew it into drifts. The medallion hung from his neck.

From time to time I drifted back to the Round Room. The powders burned in the copper bowls. Eleanor sat like a statue. Beads of sweat had gathered on her brow. Vernon Quayle stood with palms on her temples as before, motionless, his gaze upon the doll beneath my finger. Nothing seemed to happen, but the air in the room felt heavy as the air feels before a great thunderstorm.

I do not know how long it lasted. I only know there came a time when I was distantly aware that the blobs of black wax covering the eyes of the doll were melting, becoming liquid, running down the coarse wooden cheeks to spatter drip by tiny drip on the brass disc where the doll lay. Then Vernon Quayle broke the silence, saying, "It is finished now."

I know that I tried to say goodbye to Eleanor, but she looked at me from a totally drained face, with eyes that did not recognize me. I know that Vernon Quayle put the medallion in my hands and walked with me down from the Round Room and out to where the dog-cart stood. No word was spoken between us.

I do not recall driving home. I know that Mr. Stafford came out of the farmhouse and insisted that he would see to the horses and put the dog-cart away. And I know that when I took off my hat and coat, and sat down limply in front of the glowing fire in my little room, the clock on the mantelpiece told me that I had left the room no more than seventy minutes ago.

I fell asleep in the chair and woke much later to find the fire almost dead. With a great effort I made my way up to my bedroom. There I undressed, fell into bed, and slept heavily.

In daylight the events of the night before seemed more like an unpleasant dream, and one I did not wish to dwell upon. I told myself that if I believed Adam would suddenly be able to see again, I was a fool. But when a letter from Lady Gascoyne came for me by the morning post two days later, I found my hands were trembling as I opened it, and my heart grew heavy with disappointment as I discovered that it was her usual letter, with no startling news.

224

The only thing she said about Adam was that he had fallen downstairs and half-stunned himself the day before, much to her alarm. Over his protests she had insisted on fetching the doctor to him, and was happy to say that there was no damage. He was up and about again today.

So much for Vernon Quayle's boasts. Adam was still blind.

Two days later, on an afternoon surprisingly mild and sunny for late February, I rode up to Goose Hill and turned my horse loose while I wandered slowly about the grassy crest, trying to decide where my future lay.

My eye was caught by a horse and rider coming down the far slope across the valley at a gallop, and going much too fast I thought with a touch of annoyance. Only the Lo-bas could safely ride like that. Then, with a little start of surprise, I recognized the horse. It was Bruno, the red roan belonging to Major Elliot. But he was not carrying the Major.

For a few moments horse and rider were lost behind a line of chestnuts, then they came into view again, starting up Goose Hill. I narrowed my eyes. A man with black hair, hatless, not in riding clothes but wearing a dark grey suit. What on earth . . . ? He rode as one with the horse, body moving to the stride of his mount with a kind of careless arrogance . . .

Mister! My mind shrieked the name, and it was the old name that came to me first.

Adam? Adam riding up Goose Hill towards me? As if . . . as if he could *see?* It could not be. Yet no blind man could have ridden as he was riding.

I stood rooted. He came to the crest and was swinging down from the saddle even as Bruno slowed to a canter and then a walk. The dark hair was tousled by wind, the deep blue eyes ablaze with a kind of wild joy. He ran towards me with great strides, both hands outstretched. "Jani!"

Tears blurred my eyes, and began to trickle down my cheeks. To speak was impossible, for my throat was numb.

"Oh, Jani!" His hands gripped my shoulders so tightly it hurt, and I revelled in the good pain of it. Holding me at arm's length he

225

looked me up and down, his face full of wonder. His hands moved, and he touched my brow, my hair, a tear-drop on my cheek, my lips and my neck. It was the gentle touch of a blind man, but he was now no longer blind. His eager gaze was almost devouring as he stood there, words tumbling from him.

"I went to your cottage, and the Staffords sent me to David's place, and the housekeeper there said he was up at Major Elliot's stables, but she didn't know if you were with him, Jani, and when I got there, you weren't and I thought I'd go mad if I didn't find you soon, and David said he thought you might be up here, and the Major said, 'Here boy, take Bruno.' So here I am, and—oh Jani, is this really you? Really that funny little girl I found in Smon T'ang and could never get out of my mind? But of course it is, I can see her in you. Oh yes, by God, I can *see* you, Jani! I fell downstairs a few days ago and got a touch of concussion. Last night I went to bed blind and woke up able to see!"

His hands slid down to grip my own and hold them tightly. "Jani. Beautiful Jani. Why did I call you a funny little girl? You were beautiful then, if I'd had eyes to see. I've been blind for longer than I knew. Lord, but it's good to look at you, Jani. Did you know I lost my heart to you from the moment you came to me out of the past, and put your arms round my neck, and wept because you found me blind? Or perhaps it was longer ago I lost my heart to you, as Molly thought. She said you were the one, didn't she? And during all these past months together, I've dared to hope that you felt something more than pity for me. Do you, Jani? Will you marry me? Please?"

I knew that if I tried to speak I would only weep more tears of happiness. I looked up at Adam, remembering the many times during his blindness when I had been close to him, as I was now, and had longed to put my arms about his neck and draw his head down and press my lips against his in a long wonderful kiss. Now I did it, standing there with him on the crest of Goose Hill where we could be seen for half a mile around. But I did not care about that.

After a little while, when I was getting my breath back and he was holding me with my cheek against his chest, I said in a wobbly

226

voice, "I thought you didn't much like me. I heard you say to your parents that I . . . bored you."

I felt him give a great sigh. "Jani, sweetheart, I meant you to hear. I knew exactly where you were on the stairs when I said those words. I have a blind man's hearing, and I spent most of my time listening for your footstep about the house."

I lifted my head, "But why did you say it, Adam?"

"Because I wanted you to be happy, and knew that if you and I were together much longer I'd break down and tell you I loved you. And I was afraid you'd take pity on me and marry me. Me, a blind man. I couldn't have that, Jani."

I stood on tiptoe to kiss him again, then said in the old Cockney accent I had spoken in Smon T'ang, "Sometimes you don't 'alf say daft things, Mister."

DAVID HAYWARD leaned back in his chair and looked at us as we sat side by side on the couch in his small living room, holding hands. An hour had gone by since Adam held me in his arms on Goose Hill. David had congratulated Adam, kissed me heartily, and claimed that he must either be best man or give the bride away.

For a little while there had been much excitement, but now we were quiet and serious, for I had just finished telling them all that had happened in the Round Room on the night before Adam had taken the fall which brought back his sight.

David had gone pale when I told how Eleanor had been injected with what could only be some kind of drug to aid her trance. Now he said, "It makes me shudder to think of you going to see Quayle on your own. You might have been trapped, as my poor Eleanor was. I'd have stopped her if I'd known, Adam."

I shook my head. "Nobody could have stopped me. Eleanor asked me to see her, and I shall always answer a call from Eleanor." I looked at Adam anxiously. "You do understand that, my dearest?"

He touched his fingers to my brow, then to his own, in a strange little gesture of belonging. "We're as one now, Jani. Your debt to Eleanor is mine, and somehow we'll pay it."

David got up, paced across to the window, and gazed out on the garden with a troubled air. "I thought Quayle a charlatan once, but now I'm far from sure. Is it a coincidence that he conducted his operation shortly before the fall which apparently brought back your sight? Or did his operation cause you to fall?"

Adam said quietly, "Ever since Jani first told me of Quayle I've been finding out as much as I could about him, and also learning a little about his strange occupation from a friend of my father's, a Professor Manson who is very knowledgeable about such matters. Perhaps Quayle's science, as he calls it, consists of causing coincidences to happen."

I pressed Adam's hand and said, "I can't help wondering why he should want to give you back your sight."

Adam lifted my hand and kissed the fingers. "Because, my darling," he said slowly, "Quayle needs me for a purpose of his own, and all the threads of the past and present, mine and yours, his and Eleanor's, are converging towards that future purpose. At least, that's the view of my knowledgeable friend, Professor Manson."

Faintly in the depths of my mind I heard the voice of the Oracle at Galdong as she gazed into the bowl of liquid jet: ". . . *The foreign demon's pride will be broken . . . he will go down into blackness, and then will come the bloodless one, the Silver Man, the Eater of Souls . . . and there is the debt to pay, and in the Year of the Wood-Dragon they will come to the Land of Bod, to seize the tear-drop that fell from the Eye of the Enlightened One . . .*"

I came back to reality to hear Adam saying, "I propose to see Quayle today. I intend to find out exactly what he wants of me."

I said in a small voice which did not sound like my own, "I know what he wants, Adam. I didn't know till just now when I suddenly remembered the words of the Oracle of Galdong. She said you would go to the Land of Bod with him, Adam. And I shall be there, too. It was to happen this year. And Quayle will want you to seize the tear-drop that fell from the Eye of the Enlightened One."

There was a long silence, both men staring at me in wonder, and at last Adam said, "The tear-drop of the Buddha? Do you know what it is, Jani?"

"I'm not sure, but I think it's something to do with the Great

228

Monastery at Choma La. We used to pass the monastery on our trade route to Magyari. Vernon Quayle asked me a lot of questions about it one day, but I didn't know what he was driving at."

Adam stood up and drew me to my feet. "Let's not stand on ceremony. We'll go to see Quayle at once, just as we are. The sooner we know where we stand, the better. All right, Jani?"

I nodded, forcing a smile, but I was suddenly very frightened of all that lay ahead, frightened that the Silver Man would destroy our newfound happiness. That I would lose Adam, lose myself, lose everything. . . .

THE SURLY MANSERVANT showed us into the drawing room of Merlin's Keep. Vernon Quayle stood with his back to the fire, lifeless grey eyes looking upon us without interest as we entered.

"Good afternoon, Jani. Good afternoon, Mr. Gascoyne." The shadow of a wintry smile touched his mouth. "I do not imagine, Mr. Gascoyne, that you have come to thank me for restoring your sight?"

Adam said curtly, "That's a large claim you make, Quayle."

The man shrugged. "Will you be seated?"

"I think not. We've come to ask your price."

"Price for what, pray?"

"Eleanor's freedom. Her freedom from you, Quayle."

I was shaken by the savage bluntness of Adam's words, and for a fraction of a second I saw something I had never seen before— Vernon Quayle taken aback. He recovered in an instant and said, "Do you know what you are saying, Mr. Gascoyne?"

"I've talked a great deal with Professor Manson over the past months, if that means anything to you."

Vernon Quayle's eyes narrowed. "I have his books on my shelves. He is a competent practitioner, no more."

Adam smiled, and said, "The inquiry agents I employed many weeks ago now were also competent practitioners, Quayle. You had three wives before Eleanor. The first, a young English widow living in Hong Kong, was married to you for five years before she went into a decline and died in hospital. The Italian lady and the Belgian lady both died by suicide. All three became recluses after marriage, as Eleanor has. All three were believed by their friends to have been human tools, used by you in your occult practices. You're a spiritual vampire, Quayle, you live on the life-forces of others. You're doing that with Eleanor. I'll ask you again—what's your price for her freedom?"

"What do you mean by freedom, Mr. Gascoyne?"

Adam's answer was immediate. "Annulment of the marriage. Manson tells me it will not have been consummated, so there will be no problem. Then you clear off, and never communicate with Eleanor again."

"On what grounds does Professor Manson assert that the marriage will not have been consummated?"

"On the grounds that if it were, you would be unable to use the poor woman in the way you have done. It would infringe the Third Law of the Etheric, whatever that may mean."

Vernon Quayle's eyes stared fixedly. "Manson is cleverer than I thought," he said at last. "However, that is neither here nor there. You have asked me to name a price for Eleanor's freedom. Suppose I decline to make any kind of bargain?"

Adam said very softly, "In that event, Quayle, I shall kill you, with no more scruple than I would have in killing a rabid dog."

I knew Adam had not spoken empty words, yet I felt no shock, for now I saw clearly what I should have seen long ago. Vernon Quayle was killing Eleanor as surely as if his hands were about her neck and he were slowly strangling her.

I heard the horrid hiccuping sound which was Vernon Quayle's laughter. He said, "I have lived a long time, Mr. Gascoyne, and more than one person has attempted what you now threaten, much to their subsequent distress. Mr. David Hayward might have some advice to offer you in this matter."

"I am someone else, Quayle." Adam stared unblinkingly at him with a curious intensity. "You cannot turn my own hand against me, for I am a man who has lived in the long darkness, and my senses are too keen for you to play your games with them."

Vernon Quayle half closed his eyes. "Your friend Professor Man-

230

son has given you a little learning, which is notoriously dangerous."

Adam gave a small shrug and took my arm as if preparing to go. "You will not bargain, then?"

"I did not say that, Mr. Gascoyne."

There was a silence, then Vernon Quayle spoke in a voice that was slightly sing-song, as if he were chanting. "The Great Monastery of Choma La is built against the mountain whose name is never spoken. Seven times seven times seven steps rise to the Temple of Prayer, which lies beneath the topmost spire. Within the temple stands an altar of white marble. Upon the altar, a Buddha of gold. In the cupped hand of the Buddha lies the tear-drop that was shed in the moment when the Enlightened One turned back from the peace of Nirvana to teach mankind the True Way."

Vernon Quayle's voice changed. He said in a matter-of-fact manner, "The story is rubbish, of course, and I think it likely that the tear-drop is a semi-precious stone, perhaps only a pretty pebble. But if you will bring it to me, Mr. Gascoyne, I will meet your terms regarding Eleanor."

I felt Adam's hand tighten on my arm as he said, "What you ask is not entirely unexpected." Quayle's eyes widened for a moment, then he gave a shrug. Adam went on, "How many monks occupy the monastery?"

"Nine times nine times nine, plus those who serve them in menial duties."

"You cannot imagine that they will permit me to penetrate to the heart of their monastery and take the tear-drop?"

"On the contrary, Mr. Gascoyne. It is their belief that in the Year of the Wood-Dragon two *trulku* will come to take the tear-drop and restore it to the Buddha."

"*Trulku?*"

"In crude terms, spirits in human form. The two expected *trulku* are a male and a female. The female will have the tongue of Bod and will chant the seven times seven mantras of Galdong. I believe you will find that Jani knows them."

Adam looked at me. I nodded and said, "We used to chant them on the trail."

Vernon Quayle went on, "The *trulku* may be true or false. If they are the true envoys of the Buddha, they will come on one particular day which is known only to the High Lama of Choma La and his Council of Nine. And to me."

"You?"

"Yes, Mr. Gascoyne. I secured that piece of knowledge only a few days ago, with Mr. Hayward as an uninvited witness, I believe. It was a considerable feat, I assure you. Eleanor is quite the most remarkable source of energy I have ever used."

I think I would have flung myself at the hideous man if Adam had not held me back. Vernon Quayle gazed distantly through us and said, "I shall require you and Jani to meet me in the village of Shekhar, north of the Chak Pass, on the thirty-first day of May. Jani will know the place."

I knew it only from a distance. It lay a mile from the trail and some five miles north of the pass, a huddle of tiny hovels occupied by the dangerous Khamba tribesmen.

I heard the tinge of surprise in Adam's voice as he said, "You intend to make the journey yourself, Quayle?"

"Certainly. You need have no concern as to my physical capabilities, Mr. Gascoyne. I do not propose to travel in your company, however, for I have come to the conclusion that you may be a more dangerous enemy than most. I shall travel on the *Calabria*, which leaves Southampton on the fifth of April. You will make whatever other arrangements you please, providing that you leave England before me. Agreed?"

"Agreed."

"I think there is no more to be said until we meet in Shekhar, Mr. Gascoyne."

"Will you answer one question?"

"You are curious to know why I seek to possess this bauble from the Great Monastery of Choma La. I will tell you. For three hundred and forty-three years, seven times seven times seven years, the prayer wheels of seven lamas have spun as the lamas chanted prayers before the tear-drop of the Buddha, continuously, without ceasing, night and day alike. The potency of that jewel in the

232

Buddha's cupped hand is therefore enormous. That is why I will have it."

There was a heavy silence in the room, then Adam said slowly, "What will you do with it?"

"That is a second question, but I will answer you." Vernon Quayle's mouth stretched in a smile which showed very small white teeth. "When the tear-drop is mine, then with due ceremony and full ritual I shall proceed to destroy it. Good day to you, Mr. Gascoyne."

I scarcely remember leaving Merlin's Keep, and only came to myself as Adam and I rode side by side down the long curving drive towards the gates.

"Destroy the tear-drop?" I said. "Why on earth would he do that?"

Adam said, "According to Manson, Quayle believes that by destroying something potent, like the tear-drop, he can use the forces in it for his own purposes."

We rode on in silence for a while, and I saw that he was lost in thought. At last he roused himself and said quietly, "I wish to God I could go alone, but that won't do."

"I wouldn't let you go alone, Adam. I couldn't bear it."

He put out his hand and took mine. "Now, let's think," he said. "We have to leave England before Quayle, but since *Calabria* is the fastest ship, he'll probably arrive before us." He drew a long breath. "Marry me before we go, Jani, my love. Please. Whatever lies ahead, I want us to face it completely together, joined as one."

FOUR WEEKS LATER I became Adam Gascoyne's wife in the church of St. Mark, on the northern edge of Regent's Park. I was married in the name of Her Highness Princess Jani of Jahanapur. David Hayward was best man. Major Elliot, enormously proud that I had asked him to do so, escorted me to the church and gave me away.

There was a reception at Chester Gardens. Before we left it, I brought David Hayward to the library for a final word with Adam, who took him by the shoulders and said forcefully, "Now listen,

David. As soon as Quayle leaves Larkfield, you must get Eleanor out of Merlin's Keep. You may have trouble with Quayle's man-servant, but don't let that stop you. Enlist Major Elliot's help, and the squire's if need be. Jani says there's not a soul in Larkfield who wouldn't back you up. So . . . get her out!"

David nodded. "Right. And then what?"

"Bring her here to my parents. Get hold of Professor Manson, and he can start to free Eleanor from Quayle's influence. You must stay here with her, David. Talk to her, talk of Jani, and the good times before Quayle came, and tell her a hundred times a day that you love her and that she's going to be herself again. Manson says that will be the biggest factor in her cure." Adam smiled, and punched David gently on the shoulder. "Just one more thing. Jani has something for you."

I went to David, put the silver medallion in his hand, and kissed his cheek. "When the moment's right, give it to Eleanor with my love, David. I know she'll wear it, once Quayle has gone. And ask her to say a little prayer for us."

AFTER THE WEDDING Adam and I spent a three-day honeymoon at a small hotel in the Surrey countryside. I had been a little afraid that what lay ahead might spoil these few precious days for us, but it was not so. We were truly and gloriously happy, and perhaps our joy was the more intense because we both realized in our hearts that it might be short-lived. We were going into danger.

We sailed from the Royal Albert Docks on a ship named *Satara* and our joy in each other grew during the twenty-seven-day voyage to Bombay. By night we lay in each other's arms, often laughing together like mischievous children, the future forgotten.

At Bombay, we braced ourselves for a thousand-mile train journey in relentless heat. For three days and nights we moved steadily northeast, across the Ganges to Lucknow, then turned east to come at last to Gorakhpur.

During the third day our train spent two hours passing through the southeastern corner of Jahanapur. Once, in the distance, we glimpsed the spires of the palace which stood in the capital town, also called Jahanapur. This was where I had been born, yet I had no feeling of belonging, no wish to stay and explore the past. I was a stranger here, and content to remain so.

In Gorakhpur we bought horses, panniers, supplies and clothing. Much time was spent selecting our horses. Mine was a grey, Adam's a dark bay. They had Indian names, but I renamed the grey Nimrod, after my favourite horse at Merlin's Keep, and Adam called his Preacher, because it had a curious white band across the throat, like a vicar's collar. Twenty-four hours after reaching Gorakhpur we set off north, retracing the long journey we had made together as man and child just under seven years ago.

Twenty days brought us into Smon T'ang, and again I had no sense of homecoming. I saw the country now for what it was, bleak and poor, its people bowed under centuries of superstition, fearful of a thousand demons. We skirted Galdong by night, for I had no wish to renew acquaintance with any I had known in the old days. We could have nothing to say to one another now.

There was a little time in hand, and as we did not propose arriving at Shekhar until the appointed day, we camped for three nights in the high valley which lay halfway up the Chak Pass. Here we cached most of our supplies and equipment, before riding on very lightly laden towards the summit of the pass.

We were now in the season of summer, and though the nights were cold it was warm by day, even at this altitude. The cairn where Sembur lay buried was untouched, as I had guessed it would be. I felt no sadness as we walked our horses up the slope to it, only a warm gratitude. I said a prayer, laid on the cairn a posy of wild flowers I had picked in the valley below, and then we mounted again for the last few miles of our long journey to Shekhar.

Chapter Seventeen

A mile from the village a dozen Khambas came riding down upon us, sweeping round to form a close horseshoe about us and herd us on our way into Shekhar. Most of them carried muzzle-loading guns, the rest were armed with clubs and long-bladed knives.

I gave them a formal greeting in Tibetan, but they did not respond, only stared with hostile and envious eyes at the rifle in Adam's saddle-holster. We continued at an easy trot, and in a few minutes we came to a cluster of stone dwellings, where I was engulfed in the old familar smells of *tsampa*, rancid butter, greasy smoke, sweat-soaked leather and unwashed bodies.

Vernon Quayle emerged from a doorway and came walking towards us, hatless, his silver hair stirring in the light breeze. Incredibly, he wore collar and tie and the same tweed clothes I had seen him wear when riding out on his expeditions to collect herbs and insects. To come to this place he must have travelled as we had, living in the open for days on end, exposed to sun and weather, yet that heavy face was as white as ever.

He looked from one to the other of us with empty grey eyes. The silence grew, and at last he said, "I have perceived of recent days that my wife is hedged by an etheric barrier which only a handful of men in the world would have the knowledge to establish, your friend Manson among them. At present I require all my resources for the matter in hand, but you may be sure I shall deal with Professor Manson in due course."

Adam said, "Since Eleanor's freedom is part of the bargain, why should you still seek to control her?"

"You have yet to complete your own side of the bargain, Mr. Gascoyne."

"We're here to do so, and the sooner the better."

"Tomorrow is the thirty-first of May. We shall leave here at dawn, and reach the Great Monastery of Choma La by noon." He looked at Adam's saddle-holster. "When you approach Choma La, it is essential that neither you nor Jani carry any weapon with you. You may not take your rifle, nor the sheath-knife which you wear strapped to your calf beneath your breeches, Mr. Gascoyne."

Adam rubbed his chin. "I see no hurry about handing them over until tomorrow."

"As you please. I will instruct you fully before departure."

236

We slept in our clothes in a tiny room of one of the hovels that night, eating and drinking from our own supplies, for as Adam said grimly, "I've no fancy to be drugged by Quayle before we go walking into that monastery tomorrow." Later, as we lay side by side in our sleeping-bags, holding hands, he said softly, "Are you frightened, Jani darling?"

"No . . . not really. I think I'll be all right as long as we're together, Adam."

He pressed my hand. "We'll be together all the way."

A MILE OR SO beyond Shekhar the trail split three ways, only to converge some ten miles farther north, where the Magyari trade-route passed along the ridge from which the Great Monastery could be seen on the far side of a shallow valley.

Where the trail divided, the centre way was the shortest but most difficult. The left-hand fork swung to the west, and was a mile or so longer but much easier going. The remaining fork was known as the Way of the Pilgrim, for legend held that in the distant past a very holy man had travelled this way to found the Great Monastery at Choma La. The route he had taken was broken by a ravine, some forty paces wide, and of measureless depth. According to legend, the holy man had crossed the ravine by floating through the air. A wooden bridge had been built at the crossing-place, and this third trail had ever since been used mainly by men making a pilgrimage to Choma La. Most ordinary travellers avoided it.

We took the easy left-hand trail. Two Khambas were acting as guides. Vernon Quayle rode immediately behind them. Adam and I followed, and ten Khambas brought up the rear. As the sun rose higher, the air grew warm, the Khambas took off their leather coats. Adam and I stripped off our jackets and tied them to our saddle-rolls. Vernon Quayle ignored the change of temperature and rode steadily on, a grotesque yet frightening figure.

We came in sight of the Great Monastery half an hour before noon. As we halted, looking across the valley, I caught my breath in amazement. The sun was at its peak, and the spires were like great halberds of gold pointing to the sky. Prayer flags fluttered in rows on every terrace. A murmurous chanting filled the broad shallow valley which lay between the rocky trail and the monastery a thousand paces away. The monks were awaiting the coming of the *trulku*. Some seven hundred of them, red-robed and in tall red hats, each spinning a prayer wheel, stood little more than an arm's length apart, forming two inward-facing lines, and these lines extended right across the valley in a broad corridor leading to the massive red and gold gates which stood open on the far side.

We had halted by a crag at a turn of the trail a long stone's throw from the place where the red corridor began. Quayle said very quietly in his beautiful voice, "The rest of us must go no closer. I have given you full instructions, Mr. Gascoyne. Proceed now according to my instructions, and be sure you bear no weapons upon you. Neither may Jani take the silver medallion."

"I'm not wearing it." I twisted my head to glare at him, and said through my teeth, "But Eleanor is!"

His eyes flickered. He said, "The rifle and knife if you please, Mr. Gascoyne."

Adam drew the rifle from its holster, passed it to Quayle, then reached down and pulled up his trouser leg to reach the knife. Two minutes later we were riding at a walk, knee to knee, along the trail to the place where the twin lines of monks began. We were both hatless, both wearing shirts of khaki drill, trousers of cavalry twill with leather thigh-patches, and stout boots. Turning together between the first two monks we halted for a moment, looking down the two red lines which sloped down and then up, narrowing in perspective towards the monastery. As we paused, the soft chanting which had filled the air like the sound of distant thunder ceased abruptly, and a huge silence pressed down upon the valley.

Adam murmured, "Now, Jani, my love."

I lifted my voice, and began to chant the seven times seven mantras of Galdong which I had so often chanted with my companions of the caravans. A nudge of our heels, and together we began to pass slowly between the living red lines.

For a time it seemed I was dreaming, and that the red lines grew longer as we progressed, so that though we rode for ever we should

238

never reach the distant red and gold gates. I snatched a brief glance at Adam. He was looking straight ahead, his face unreadable.

We came to the gates at last, and as we passed through I saw that the human corridor continued across the courtyard to seven stone steps beneath great iron-bound doors which stood open, but the men were no longer monks. These were the lowest of the monastery servants, the smiths, butchers and cleaners, who had resigned themselves to little hope of progress in their present incarnation. Every man wore black, and every man carried a drawn sword. If the monks had decided that we were false *trulku*, then this was the moment when we would die.

We reached the monastery steps as I completed the last of the forty-nine mantras. Two white-robed novices moved to hold our horses as we dismounted. A narrow carpet, dull gold in colour, ran up the steps and disappeared into the gloom of the lamplit hall beyond the doors.

Side by side we mounted the steps. In the lofty hall, a hundred butter-lamps flickered, and the smell of incense hung heavily in the air. Beyond the hall, the carpet ended at a stairway of stone which rose and turned. I began to count for I knew that we must now have reached the seven times seven times seven steps which would bring us to the Temple of Prayer beneath the topmost spire.

I felt Adam's hand take mine. For what must have been almost six minutes we climbed and turned, climbed and turned. In my mind I was counting, ". . . three hundred and thirty-four . . . thirty-five . . . thirty-six . . ."

There came the murmur of chanting voices. Seven more steps and we stood in an archway looking directly into the Temple of Prayer. It was a small temple, no more than a dozen paces square. We were standing behind a row of seven lamas who knelt before the Buddha. From their robes, I took the one in the middle to be the High Lama of Choma La. Each man seemed to be kneeling in a hollow of the broad stone step before the dais bearing the Buddha. The golden effigy was of life-size, the left hand held close to the body, just below the heart, and cupped with palm upwards.

Still softly chanting, the High Lama shuffled back on his knees, stood up, and moved to one side, hands pressed together as he turned to bow towards us. Then I saw that what I had taken to be hollows in the stone were not simple hollows but twin grooves, six inches deep and more, worn in the rock by the knees of the thousands of monks who had prayed before the Buddha for centuries past. Adam pressed my hand and we moved forward, stepping up to the dais.

In the golden palm lay a milky white stone, slightly pear-shaped and about the size of my little finger-tip. To make myself reach out and pick it up was one of the hardest things I have ever done. No doubt my nerves were stretched and my imagination was running wild, but as my fingers closed upon it, I felt a shock that tingled like fire throughout every part of my body.

Adam put out his hand. I placed the tear-drop in his palm, and saw his eyes narrow suddenly. His fingers closed, and together we turned away.

The chanting ceased. The High Lama bowed again as we moved past. Then with Adam holding his tightly-closed hand in front of him, we were on the steps once more, beginning the long journey down. I knew that we were fulfilling an ancient prophecy, and yet I felt that he and I were mere common thieves.

It was a relief to emerge at last into a dazzle of sunlight, where the white-robed novices held Nimrod and Preacher for us to mount. The servants in black had disappeared. When we rode out of the great gates, the valley was again filled with chanting. It continued as we rode slowly down between the red lines of monks, then up the slope of the valley-side to the Magyari trail. As we emerged from the human corridor, all the red-clad figures suddenly turned and began to move back towards the monastery in two snake-like files, chanting to the rhythm of their slow pacing.

We turned and began to ride south at a steady walk, towards the low crag where Vernon Quayle waited. "Jani," Adam said softly, "if anything goes wrong and we're separated, make for Sembur's cave. We'll meet there."

Minutes later, we halted facing Vernon Quayle, his band of Khambas behind him. For the first time I saw two spots of high colour in

240

his dough-like cheeks, and the normally expressionless eyes were alive with yearning. He said, "Show me, Gascoyne."

There was a silence, then Adam said in a curiously strained voice, "I can't open my hand."

Quayle's face clenched with fury. "It is unwise to play games with me!"

Adam gave a short hard laugh. "Don't be a damn fool. Look at my hand." He held out his fist, and it was like white marble, with the veins standing out in cords.

Quayle drew a deep breath. His normal pallor returned, and with it his grey dispassion. He said, "Proximity to the Temple of Prayer may be exerting some influence. We will ride a little way." He spoke a word to the Khambas, who turned their horses to take up the same positions they had occupied on the ride from Shekhar, with two Khambas leading and the rest behind us. But now Vernon Quayle had fallen back to ride level with us, on Adam's other side.

A mile passed, then another, and I saw the colour coming slowly back into Adam's tightly clenched fist. After an hour, at the point where the three trails separated, Vernon Quayle gave the order to halt. "Are you able to open your hand now, Mr. Gascoyne?"

Adam stretched out his arm. Slowly, quivering a little, his fingers uncurled. Sunlight glinted from the milky white tear-drop in his palm. I heard Quayle draw a hissing breath, but he made no attempt to touch the stone. Fumbling inside his jacket he brought out a small box, about as big as the palm of my hand. It appeared to be made of stiff black leather, and was in the shape of a star with five points. On the ten vertical sides there were hieroglyphs in silver. Quayle snapped open the lid and held the box out towards Adam. "Place the stone inside, if you please."

Adam tilted his palm, the tear-drop fell with a tiny sound, and the box snapped shut. Adam let out a long breath and said, "That concludes our agreement, Quayle. My rifle and knife, please. Jani and I will make our own way back from here."

Vernon Quayle, his eyes on the small black box he held, scarcely moved his lips as he said, "I have no further use for you or your wife, Mr. Gascoyne, and no intention of permitting two such potent

241

enemies to disturb my future." For a moment, still bemused by the dreamlike happenings, I did not grasp the import of his words. He went on, "I have caused these gullible Khambas to believe that the two *trulku* who carry away the tear-drop from the Temple of Prayer are merely minions of the *silver trulku*, who is myself. It is he who will restore the tear-drop to the Buddha in the halls of Nirvana, while his minions will put off the bodies in which they have clad themselves, and return to their home in the sky."

Vernon Quayle took his eyes from the black star-shaped box and glanced at the Khambas. "That is what these men believe, Mr. Gascoyne. As the *silver trulku*, I have warned them that my minions may need persuasion to divest themselves of their earthly bodies."

In the instant I realized Vernon Quayle intended us to die I acted by instinct rather than thought. Nimrod felt my heels and responded in a flash, muscles bunching as he lunged forward. I snatched the box from Quayle's hand, spun Nimrod round, sent him forward again, then spun once more so that his hindquarters hit the shoulder of one of the two horses ridden by the leading Khambas, knocking it into the other.

I saw one of the other Khambas, the first to gather his wits, lift Adam's carbine from under the blanket draped over his saddle, where it had been hidden. Even as he did so, Preacher surged across the trail with Adam freeing a foot from the stirrup and smashing a boot into the man's chest.

I had Nimrod rearing on his hind legs now, hooves pawing the air, threatening a Khamba who had drawn a long knife. I saw Adam swerve, but he could not get to me for there were men and horses between us. Quayle was shouting orders. Adam pointed to the middle and shortest of the three trails. "*Go, Jani, go!*" and in the same moment swung Preacher towards the eastern trail, the Way of the Pilgrim.

I turned Nimrod, and he went as if flung from a catapult. For a moment I saw Adam's head and shoulders over a rounded hump of rock as our ways diverged, then he was gone.

In Gorakhpur we had spent hours selecting the finest horses to

242

be found. We were far better mounted than Quayle or any of his followers, and they would not catch us now. For this I sent up a. fervent prayer of thankfulness, tucked the small black box inside my shirt, low down near my waist for safety, and settled down to ride, putting everything else from my mind. For this was no easy trail, and if I took a tumble now it would mean disaster.

Time passed, and an hour or more later I came to the junction where the three trails merged, and moved steadily on past the track which led off to Shekhar. Some time later Nimrod went lame. I found a small sharp stone in his foot, but had nothing with which to get it out. An icy spear of terror pierced my heart. The Khambas, I felt sure, could be no more than a quarter of an hour behind me.

The cave. Adam had said that if we were separated we should meet at the cave. . . . Leading Nimrod, I plodded steadily on.

We were nearing the crest of the Chak Pass now, the point where the walls fell back, with the cave a little way up the eastern slope. I realized that Nimrod had been pricking up his ears, and I halted for a moment to listen. From behind me the sound of hooves echoed along the walls of the pass, and they were not far distant.

I turned Nimrod, bade him farewell, and gave him a little slap to send him limping back down the trail towards the Khambas. I hoped that when they came upon him they would stop for a few precious seconds to secure him and to debate what might have occurred.

I broke into a run, knowing I would need every moment if I were to reach the cave by the time the Khambas came into view. My legs were leaden, and the breath rasped in my throat as I went on at a stumbling run. I heard myself sob despairingly, "I'm trying, Adam, I'm trying . . ." and then I heard the thud of hooves, much closer now.

I looked back over my shoulder to see two Khambas come round a twist in the pass only a hundred yards behind me. Both had drawn the long-bladed knives they carried, and were holding them high as they rode. I drove my weary legs to carry me up the slope towards the cave, but the horsemen continued to close behind me. The flesh of my back crawled in anticipation of their knives, and I realized I would never gain the cave.

243

Something cracked in the air like a whip, the sharp sound of a rifle shot, and I heard a cry from behind. Then, from above me, a voice roared, "Jani!"

Through blurred eyes I saw the head and shoulders of Adam kneeling behind Sembur's cairn, rifle to shoulder in the aiming position. I flung a glance behind me as the weapon cracked again, and saw the Khamba only twenty paces behind me suddenly knocked from his horse as if struck by an invisible giant. His companion had turned and was riding for the safety of the pass, a hand clutched to his shoulder where the first shot had struck.

Then my knees gave way, and I felt Adam pick me up in his arms as a great blackness swept down upon me.

Chapter Eighteen

I was looking at Adam's boot. I was lying by Sembur's cairn and Adam sat crouched against it, gazing over the top towards the pass. As I stirred he looked down and said, "What happened, Jani? I thought you'd be here before me, and I was worried out of my mind."

I stared at his upside-down face and whispered, "Nimrod . . . went lame . . . I—I couldn't . . ." Tears came then, and my whole body shook. Adam drew me up with one arm to hold me close against his chest. Suddenly he stiffened and said, "Steady, Jani."

I pulled myself together, and kneeled to peer over the top of the cairn. Two Khambas had emerged from the pass on foot. As I watched they dropped out of sight behind a fold of rock, then appeared briefly again as they began to crawl up the slope, carrying their rifles before them. I asked Adam, "Is that rifle you used Sembur's?"

"Yes. I buried it beside him, well greased and in its case. I thought of it as soon as I got here. Luckily I only had to move a few of the rocks."

I looked down the slope, measuring distances with my eye. "How close will you let them get, Adam?"

246

"Until I have a sure target. There's a problem of ammunition. I found four rounds in the magazine, but only two are left."

Another pair of Khambas darted from the shelter of the pass and vanished amid the ridges and hollows of the rocky slope. One was carrying Adam's rifle. Then two more ran from the pass and took cover.

Adam said, "I can't afford to waste bullets on snap shots. Now listen, Jani. Preacher is in the cave, I haven't unsaddled him. Go in and get mounted. When I give the word, start down the slope, angling away from the Khambas. They can't get a shot at you without showing themselves, and I'll be ready to pick off anyone who tries. You just keep going on the Galdong trail."

I put my hand on his arm, and heard the faltering of my voice as I said, "Please don't make me, Adam. I've lost you once. I . . . I simply haven't the courage to bear losing you again."

He sighted his weapon on a fold of rock which hid the Khamba with the rifle. "All right, my sweetheart. Let's see if Preacher can carry the two of us."

I began to crawl back into the cave, but even as I moved there came a shrill whistle from somewhere on the slope. Six Khambas rose from hiding, well spread out, and began to run at us. At the same moment four more appeared from the pass, each man dropping to one knee and lifting his gun. Some shots passed above our heads. Adam fired once . . . twice. Two charging Khambas went down, one of them the man with Adam's rifle. The other four came on. Adam spun his rifle, to hold the barrel and use the butt like a club. As he did so a third Khamba dropped, and began to roll limply down the slope.

For a moment I thought the Khambas below had shot one of their own men by accident, but then came a rattle of fire from our left, from the Smon T'ang side of the crest. Two Khambas firing from below went down, the other two darted back out of sight into the pass. Only three now remained on the slope, and they turned to run. I heard an English voice shout "Cease fire!" Silence fell upon the pass. Adam stood up and drew a bare forearm across his brow, staring down the slope. I rose beside him.

247

Small dark men on ponies were pursuing the fleeing Khambas. They wore dark green uniforms with round pill-box caps. In their hands swung great curved knives. The Gurkhas, the British army soldiers from Nepal, were here with their *kukris*. Thirty men, I judged. A white officer, looking as if he had just stepped onto a parade ground, began to move up the slope towards us on a beautiful grey horse. A little to his rear came a Gurkha wearing the three stripes of a havildar and mounted on a sturdy pony.

The officer halted a few paces from the cairn, and gazed down at us with a puzzled air. He was very fair, with blue eyes and a small moustache, wearing on his shoulder the three pips of a captain. "Hello, old man," he said in a drawling voice. "Gascoyne, isn't it? Third Battalion? Remember you in Peshawar, back in ninety-six. What on earth are you doing up here, old man?"

"Well . . . that's a long story." Adam tucked Sembur's rifle under his arm, squinting up at the newcomer in the sunlight. "You're George Plunkett. I won five pounds from you in the mess one night, jumping Flint over the long table."

"Absolutely right, old man." George Plunkett studied me with a baffled expression. "Who is the young lady?"

Adam turned to me, his face very straight, and made a slight bow. "Your Highness, please allow me to present to you Captain George Plunkett." Then Adam turned to the captain and said formally, "Captain Plunkett, I have the honour to present my wife, Her Highness the Princess Jani of Jahanapur."

"Her—? Oh, I *say!*" Captain Plunkett swung down from his horse. "Then your wife's the lady who—? But that's why we're here, of course! The whole regiment knows the story. Oh, I say, ma'am, Your Highness, I'm vastly honoured." He took my grimy hand and bowed over it. "My felicitations on your marriage, ma'am. And my congratulations to you, Gascoyne, my dear chap."

I smiled at the Captain and said, "We're very grateful for your appearing at such an opportune moment. Is it in order to ask what brings you to the Chak Pass?"

"Oh, beg pardon, ma'am, I thought you'd guessed. I'm in charge of the party sent to bring back the remains of RSM Burr, for burial

248

with military honours in the regimental cemetery at Gorakhpur, do you see."

I took hold of Adam's arm and held it tightly. A few seconds passed before I could speak, and then I said, "Thank you, Captain Plunkett. Of course I should have guessed, since I was responsible for your mission, but . . . my husband and I have suffered a number of distractions today, and perhaps we are a little slow of wit."

"Not at all, ma'am, not at all," Captain Plunkett protested.

He spent the next ten minutes ensuring that I would be as comfortable as possible during the hour or so that we expected to remain here on the crest of the pass. His Gurkhas made a kind of armchair for me from boxes which had contained food supplies, and padded the seat with blankets. His batman brought me fruit, cheese, bread, and even wine. I made myself eat a few mouthfuls and drink a little wine, but could manage no more.

Six men were sent north along the pass for half a mile, to keep watch and make sure no Khambas approached. Others were detailed to remove the dead Khambas and give first aid to one who was wounded. When Captain Plunkett was giving orders for men to be posted down the pass, Adam said, "If they find an Englishman dressed in tweeds, please have your men arrest him. When we reach Gorakhpur he can be charged with the attempted murder of Her Highness and myself."

As a small group of Gurkhas began to take apart the cairn, preparing to move Sembur into the plain coffin they had brought with them, Adam said to me, "Go and wait down below, my darling."

"All right." I rested my cheek against his shoulder for a moment. "And thank you, Adam dear. I'll go down and try to find Nimrod. Perhaps he's somewhere in the pass."

"Don't go beyond the Gurkha sentries."

"I promise."

They had set up a temporary post half a mile along the pass. I found six stocky dark men with white teeth and big smiles . . . and with them was Nimrod. One of them had prised the stone from his hoof and was giving him water to drink from a mess-tin when I arrived. I made much of Nimrod, then said a few words to the

249

Gurkhas in their own tongue, thanking them warmly for all they had done.

As I walked back along the pass, leading Nimrod, I thought about Vernon Quayle, and felt a stab of satisfaction at his downfall. . . .

Suddenly the sky seemed to splinter, and I was lying face down on the ground, sick and dizzy, feeling the tremor of Nimrod's hooves through the rock as he skittered nervously away. A hand gripped my collar, and I was dragged along with my toes trailing on the ground. Now I was in shadow. I was dropped, and a foot turned me on my back. I tried to move, but the blow to my head from behind had left me half stunned, and my limbs would not respond.

I lay dazed and frightened, my cheek on cold rock, slowly working out that I had been dragged into one of the short blind crevices in the broken walls of the pass. With a painful effort I turned my head a little and lifted my eyes.

Vernon Quayle stood astride me, bending to stare down, jowls streaked with dust, grey eyes devoid of passion. He said in a musing whisper, "You and Gascoyne have seriously endangered the most important operation I have yet undertaken. You must both be destroyed, of course. Without you, there can be no witness to accuse me."

He bent his legs and sank down, straddling me, his knees pinning my arms. I tried to scream, but he jabbed a thumb into the hollow of my throat, and I was voiceless.

"To deal with Gascoyne," he remarked in a dispassionate tone, "I shall require a substantial renewal of energies. It is most fitting that the destruction of your life should provide it."

He drew from under his jacket a red cord, curiously plaited, about the thickness of a finger, and less than a yard in length. Again I tried to scream as I felt his dreadful hands at my neck, passing the cord beneath the nape, but I seemed unable to draw breath, and only the tiniest sound came from my open mouth. He made a single knot in the cord across my throat, took an end in each hand, and began to pull steadily.

Only a little time ago I had thought myself to have passed beyond fear, but now it leapt within me, raw and burning and terrible.

250

The cord about my neck was like a hot tentacle with a life of its own. I knew I was dying. My neck arched in a spasm of agony, and my blurring vision glimpsed what could not be real . . . a yellow-eyed mountain demon, crouched above us on the crag which hid the sun.

Then darkness seized me, bearing me down into an abyss where no agony could follow.

I WAS FLOATING face down, being borne up through a dark sea to a world of pain. My neck burned as if ringed with fire. Somebody was pressing on my back, crushing me. The pressure was released, and air rushed into my lungs. The pressure came again, forcing it out.

A distant, plummy voice said, "I think she's breathing better now, old man."

Then Adam's voice, closer to me. "What in the name of God were your men doing to let it happen?"

I tried to lift my head, anything to make him stop pumping at my lungs. He called out my name, and snatched me up in his arms, turning me to lie face up, holding me close, staring down into my face with ravaged eyes.

I managed a croaky whisper. "It . . . wasn't their fault . . . he was hiding . . . but you came in time."

Adam shook his head. "We didn't. Oh dear God, I thought you were gone. All the blood . . ."

I looked down and saw the great dark patches on my shirt. Adam said quickly, "It's not yours, Jani."

I swallowed to ease my aching throat. "What happened?"

He glanced away and I followed his gaze. Three Gurkhas stood by a blanket which had been thrown over a shapeless something on the ground. A smeared trail of blood led from the shadowy crevice to the thing which lay beneath the blanket.

"Quayle," said Adam. "It must have been a snow-leopard, though I never heard of one attacking a man before. Half his skull was ripped away by the blow of its taloned paw."

I closed my eyes and whispered, "I saw what I thought was a mountain demon. . . ."

Adam wiped my face gently with a wet handkerchief. "I knew something must have happened when Nimrod came out of the pass at such a pace," he said in a voice not quite steady. "We found Quayle lying dead and you, Jani, with that loathsome . . . thing tied round your neck."

I croaked, "He was going to kill us both, Adam. He . . . he needed more energies to destroy you, and he was going to get them . . . by killing me first with that crimson cord."

Captain Plunkett said in a loud whisper, "She's a bit delirious, what? Not to be wondered at, actually."

"My wife is not delirious," Adam said quietly.

I felt under my shirt, and found the box with the tear-drop in it. A little strength was seeping back into my body. I whispered, "Help me stand, Adam. I'll be all right now."

He lifted me to my feet, steadying me with my back to Captain Plunkett and the soldiers, then fastened the buttons of my shirt. On the ground nearby lay the length of curiously plaited cord. I pointed with my foot and said huskily, "Burn it, Adam, burn it where it lies."

Nobody asked any questions. Captain Plunkett gave an order, and a soldier ran off to return with a small container of paraffin. He soaked the cord where it lay, then dropped a lighted match on it. The cord writhed and twisted like a live thing as it burned, and when the flame died at last there was no ash.

Captain Plunkett said, "Extraordinary. In point of fact, this whole business is pretty strange, wouldn't you say?"

Adam, his arm about my waist to support me, did not reply. Looking at the blanket-covered shape on the ground he said in a voice of granite, "I will not have that carrion travel in the same company as my wife. Let's have him buried somewhere here."

"Quite agree, old man." Captain Plunkett turned away, lifting his voice. "Havildar!"

IN SEVEN YEARS Rild seemed not to have changed in the slightest degree. I stood in the high, sunlit chamber with Adam beside me.

Rild the High Lama said, "Destiny is wiser than man. You would have made a poor nun, had you remained as I suggested, child."

"I think it was not the way for me, High-born."

"Truly." He looked down at the milky white stone which lay on a small cushion of red silk before him. Then his gaze turned upon Adam, and became blank, unseeing. After a long silence he continued in a sing-song voice, "The Old One has passed, and in the moment of passing there came a reaching out of his inner flame, to touch the spirit of one who alone could destroy the Silver Man without penalty of heavy karma."

When I was sure Rild had finished speaking I said, "I have not understood, High-born."

His half-closed eyes opened, "Nor I, child. I speak only as I must. Dwell on my words, and understanding will come." He looked down at the jewel again, and lifted a hand in blessing. "For seven times seven years, and beyond, your names will be spoken daily in the prayers that rise from Choma La. Go now with my blessing."

"We shall remember and be grateful," I said.

Later, as we rode from the courtyard to rejoin the platoon of Gurkhas awaiting us on the outskirts of Galdong, Adam asked, "What was he saying, Jani?"

"Oh . . . well, the tear-drop will go back to Choma La, and they're very grateful. The lamas there are going to pray for us for the next fifty-odd years, so I suppose that means we'll live to be quite old. And he said it's just as well I didn't stay here to become a nun, because I wouldn't have made a very good one."

Adam chuckled. "I'm sure you wouldn't."

A pattern fell into place in my mind, and I reached out to hold his hand as I said, "Adam, there was something else. I didn't understand at first, but . . . I think Rild said your father died."

Adam stared. "It's what we've expected," he said slowly, "but why would Rild see such a thing? It's surely of no interest to him?"

"He said . . . no, wait while I try to translate it properly." I thought for a while, then went on, "He said that the Old One had passed, and that when it happened there was a reaching out of his inner flame to touch . . . well, to touch the spirit of the snow-leopard, I think. To save me. Rild was looking at you all the time, so I think he must have meant your father when he said 'the Old One'. Oh, I know it sounds silly."

Adam shook his head.

"If father has died, Jani, I'd be glad to think he had something to do with saving you and finishing off Quayle. There's nothing would have pleased him more."

ON OUR SECOND DAY out from Galdong, the monsoon came, blocking the trail with small landslides, and making every mile of our journey a punishing struggle. Adam and I did not care. After all, compared with our recent deadly struggles, the harshest of journeys was a joy to us, for we were alive, and full of love for each other.

Because of the weather, however, our journey to Gorakhpur took four and a half weeks. There we found awaiting us a telegram and a letter, both from David Hayward and both dated June 22nd, the day after Adam and I had ridden out of Choma La with the teardrop. The telegram said: *Sir Charles died while in a coma yesterday. Deepest sympathy. Letter follows. Hayward.*

The letter was several pages long. In the first part David spoke more fully about the death of Adam's father, repeating his condolences and saying that Lady Gascoyne had asked him to tell us that we were not to be worried about her, and that her love and prayers were with us. David went on to say that he had watched the *Calabria* depart from London with Quayle aboard, then had gone immediately to Merlin's Keep where, despite the protestations of the manservant Thorpe, he had virtually carried Eleanor off. He had taken her to Chester Gardens, where they had been staying with Adam's parents ever since. Professor Manson had attended her daily.

At first Eleanor had been like a sleepwalker, but as the days passed she had gradually awakened from the trance-like condition which gripped her. A marked change had come about after three weeks, when Professor Manson decided that she had roused sufficiently for David to tell her all that was happening, and to give her the silver medallion I had left for her.

Then she became distraught, weeping, crying out my name,

praying for my safety. And she began to talk at last, never speaking Quayle's name, but saying that *he* had wanted to trap me as she had been trapped, and that in all those months of horror she had used the tiny scrap of will left in her to withstand *him* in this one thing.

David's letter ended:

> . . . Over the past two weeks, however, Eleanor has steadily improved, and with our help she has begun to have faith that you will return safely. This small spark of hope and confidence flared up in a most astonishing way only today, for she took me aside and with great composure told me she was certain Vernon Quayle was dead. "His hand has been lifted from me, David," she said. "Pray God Jani will be safe now, and her dear husband also."
>
> In closing this letter I echo those words of Eleanor's. I realize, as I write, that if you read this you will indeed have returned safely to Gorakhpur. Please send a telegram at once to relieve our anxieties.
>
> Your ever-grateful friend,
David.

Within an hour we had sent a telegram, and when the train for Bombay left later that day it carried a letter addressed to David, with the full story of all that had happened to us.

TEN DAYS AFTER our return to Gorakhpur, and two days after the arrival from England of Lord Kearsey, the Colonel of the regiment, I stood watching a battalion of Gurkhas as they formed up on the great parade ground.

Adam stood beside me on a large dais at one end of the parade ground. With us were the Commanding Officer of the battalion, his senior officers, and Lord Kearsey, a small man with a face like a gnome and an amazingly loud voice. When the parade was ready he made a short speech, and then Adam led me forward to receive the Distinguished Conduct Medal which had been awarded to Sembur.

Later, in the military cemetery, we saw Sembur's coffin brought on a gun-carriage, with an escort of a hundred men slow-marching to the sound of a single measured drumbeat. Beneath his name and rank on the headstone was the Gurkha motto, *I will keep faith.*

I was very tired by the time it was all over, and thankful to be alone with Adam in the bungalow which had been provided for us in the married quarters. A little before dusk, as we sat quietly on the verandah, a servant came to say that Lord Kearsey had called and would be grateful if we could spare him a few moments. We went to the drawing room to greet him, and when he had bowed over my hand he produced a small flat box of sandalwood, intricately carved.

"I stopped in Jahanapur on my way here, and talked with Prince Mohan Sudraka, who readily saw the justice of my suggestion." He placed the box in my hands.

I lifted the carved lid. The interior was lined with black velvet, and I looked down upon an emerald ring, two gold-set ruby earrings, and a peacock-tail gold brooch with two of its diamonds missing.

My mother's jewels.

Adam said softly, "What a fool I am to have forgotten. I delivered everything of Sembur's to Colonel Hanley in Calcutta. Eventually the jewels must have been returned to Jahanapur."

Lord Kearsey nodded. "I thought it proper to restore them to your wife."

I said, "Thank you, my lord. I wish I could find words to tell you how much this means to me."

"I forbid you to try, my dear," he said sternly. He turned to Adam. "Take very good care of her, young fellow. She's battle-weary. I've seen that look in men's eyes, and I know it."

When we had left Lord Kearsey, Adam held my face gently between his hands and studied me. "I know that look, too, my little love," he said. "We're going home."

BY THE TIME our ship entered the Mediterranean I was myself again, and our happiness was even greater than we had known on the outward journey, for now the long black shadow of Vernon Quayle no longer fell across our path. When we reached Malta, and anchored for a day in Grand Harbour to refuel and take on fresh stores, a letter from David Hayward was delivered aboard with the mail.

Dear Jani and Adam,

We received your telegram from Gorakhpur three weeks ago, to our infinite joy and relief. Early last week your telegram from Bombay arrived, giving details of your sailing for home, and this morning came the long letter you posted in Gorakhpur. What you have endured is horrifying beyond words, and we can only thank God that you have come through safely.

First, Adam, your mother is well and in good heart. She is now staying with Eleanor—at Merlin's Keep! I am in my cottage again. Every trace of Quayle's existence has been removed from Merlin's Keep, and from this you will guess that Eleanor is very much her old self again, for it must have called for great courage to return as she has done. You'll be glad to know, Jani, that her lovely grey-green eyes are once more full of life and feeling. Indeed, it is my great happiness to tell you both that she has agreed to marry me in September. We hope very much that you two will take the Catling farm, so that our lands adjoin and we can farm together.

Now Jani, please know that Eleanor has tried to write you a letter to enclose with this, but finds it impossible. She says words are not enough, and is sure you will understand. She longs to see you, and to meet Adam, of course. We have the date of your ship's arrival, and we shall look forward to meeting you.

Until the joyous moment of our reunion, we send you both our full-hearted love.

Ever,
David

We were standing on deck under the golden ramparts of Grand Harbour as I read the letter, and for me this was a golden moment indeed. I could not speak for happiness as I passed the letter to Adam.

He read it through, folded it, then said quietly, "Come down to the cabin, Jani."

257

I took his arm, a little puzzled. When the cabin door had closed behind us I said, "What is it, Adam dear?"

"Three things," he said. "First, I was watching your face while you read that letter, and I'm sure you get more beautiful all the time."

"Oh my darling, I do love your nonsense."

"Second, I'm much in favour of us taking the Catling farm."

"That's wonderful. But couldn't you have said all this on deck?"

"Ah. But the third thing is that it's at least two hours since you last kissed me, Jani Gascoyne."

I reached out, and he gathered me into his arms.

Madeleine Brent is a pen-name, one of the best kept publishing secrets of the decade. Here, this highly successful author, who is known to be well established in at least one other field of literary endeavour, tells how she came to write her latest novel of romance and high adventure.

When I was a small girl, my brothers and I occasionally saw a great-uncle who had been a soldier for more than twenty years. He was particularly proud that he had been one of the small force which marched into Tibet under Colonel Young-husband in 1903, and was therefore among the very few in the world to have penetrated that mysterious country.

He had many enthralling tales to tell of his service in garrison and on campaign, but the one I liked best of all was of a young Tibetan girl on a skinny pony who hovered around the encampment at Lhasa, evidently lost in wonder. She kept talking earnestly to her pony, pointing out to it all the strange men, objects and happenings. A cart with wheels, for instance, was clearly a great marvel, and so was the sight of soldiers drilling.

The girl was of course timid, and would make off if approached, until one day a soldier overcame her fears by displaying a small shaving mirror. This amazing device entranced her. She showed it to her pony, chattering excitedly and trying to make him look at his reflection. When she understood that she could keep the mirror, she gave the soldier in return an object a few inches long of leather thongs intricately plaited and with an ornamental knot at each end. Probably it was a charm to ward off demons and bring good fortune.

I never forgot this story, and some years ago, when I felt I wanted to write a tale of romance, adventure and suspense (a new field for me), I decided to begin it in Tibet, with a young girl and a soldier, and to introduce an element of magic into what happened subsequently. After quite a lot of thought and research I found to my chagrin that the story refused to develop the way I wanted. Eventually I left it to mature in the cask of the subconscious, and wrote an entirely different story. Indeed, I wrote three books in this new genre before all the ingredients for the Tibet book came together satisfactorily, and I was at last able to begin writing the story of Jani and Sembur in the book I have called *Merlin's Keep*.

The House of Christina

A condensation of the book by

Ben Haas

Illustrated by Brian Sanders   Published by Peter Davies

"Once we buy this place, we're committed once and for all to Austria. And that frightens me."

Thus Christina Helmer voiced her forebodings when, one spring morning in 1923, she first viewed the great manor house and vineyards in the heart of the Vienna Woods. Her husband, General Kurt Helmer, confidently dismissed such fears, arranged for the house to be bought and named in Christina's honour.

Just thirteen years later, when Ben Haas's powerful new story begins to unfold, Christina is dead but all she once feared has now become very much alive. Adolf Hitler rules Germany and now threatens Austria. At the great house, the widowed general is looked after by his beautiful daughter Christa who is a superb hostess to their many friends and visitors. Prominent among these are three suitors—an American novelist and two Austrians, one a Jewish banker and the other a rising Nazi. During the terrifying years that follow, these three very different men find that their destinies are inextricably linked to that of the House of Christina.

Ben Haas has written an epic novel of love and war that brilliantly recreates one of the most fascinating and dramatic periods of modern history.

PROLOGUE: 1923

"Well," Kurt Helmer asked Christina, "what do you think?"

His wife hesitated, and he watched her closely. God, he thought, how beautiful she still is! They had been married ten years, and they had one child, Christa, who now stood beside her; yet she could leave him breathless with the same delicious emotion he had felt at first sight of her in the ballroom of the royal palace in Bucharest. At forty-five, he knew that every year of war and exile had laid its mark on him; she had suffered, too, but, sixteen years his junior, showed no sign of it. With pale gold hair glinting in the morning sun, the bone structure of her face exquisite, she might have been Christa's older sister.

The breeze riffled the rich fur of the silver fox draped lavishly around her, setting off the fairness of her skin. "Well?" Helmer repeated. "After all, it's your money."

"No, ours. And Kurt, the house is fine, it's lovely. Only—" She broke off, blue eyes cloudy. "Once we buy this place, we're committed once and for all to Austria. And . . . that frightens me."

Helmer swallowed disappointment. "Well, I can't blame you, my dear. If things go wrong, we could lose everything. On the other hand, though, this is *our one chance* to build an estate. With the inflation here, our pounds will purchase a thousand times more than they ever will again."

"I know." Christina bit her red underlip; her teeth were very white. "And Austria is your homeland. . . ." She paused, looking at him. He was not quite six feet tall, only a trace of grey showing in hair the colour of a crow's wing. His figure made the most of his beautifully cut English suit: wide shoulders, flat stomach, the erect posture of a soldier. Slowly, she smiled. "You love this place, don't you? Owning it would make you happy."

"Yes," he answered simply after a moment.

"Then the decision is up to you. Because I know that whatever you decide will be the right thing for all of us." She took her daughter's hand. "Christa and I will leave while you make up your mind. Come, darling. Let's pick some of the lovely flowers."

Helmer watched his womenfolk go down the terrace steps and cross the wide lawn of the *Schloss* park, beneath huge old linden trees. Christina had been right; he had fallen in love with this place. It had everything he had always dreamed of—three hundred hectares of rich land in the Vienna Woods, wholly rural, yet only an hour from the city itself. By the standards of the times, the *Schloss* was, perhaps, rather plain, not so much a palace as the word implied, but rather a substantial country house, painted the imperial yellow of nobility, its steeply pitched roofs of tile, its walls fortress thick to withstand brutal winter winds. There were sturdy matching outbuildings connected with it to enclose a court-yard, deep wine cellars, all the appurtenances of a working farm, yet within there was space and luxury enough to satisfy a woman of Christina's tastes: a nice balance of the functional and elegant that had struck a chord within him immediately.

Not as strongly, though, as the land itself, for he himself had been born and raised in the Wienerwald. This was the country of his childhood, and his return was like a homecoming. Below, the mountainside fell away in a long, gentle sweep to the valley of the Fernbach, a small clear stream foaming down out of the far hills to join the Danube a few miles away. Beyond the park's walls, the orchards—plum, pear, cherry, and apple—made a frothing sea of white and pink blossom. Lush green meadows blazed with the bright yellow of enormous dandelions. And beyond the meadows, row on row of staked vines marched in for-mation towards the valley floor—the vineyards, the heart of the whole estate.

The lifeblood of eastern Austria was wine; and the success or failure of the Helmer family would hang on these vineyards. With hard work and close attention, he intended to make them the foundation of a fortune.

He looked up the valley, and within him his heart lifted. The rugged, seamed hills rolled away as far as the eye could see. All was as it had been in his childhood and for centuries before. The Wienerwald, at least, Helmer thought, had survived the end of the rest of his world—the end that had begun in 1914.

Only nine years ago, Austria sprawled across central Europe— a great power with fifty million subjects. Then, incomprehensibly, what should have been a quickly won war against a tiny country had been taken over by the Germans, Russians, French and English. And Austria had lost. Generalmajor Kurt Helmer, once a fêted hero, had returned to Vienna and become a target for the vengeance of the masses. Catching wind of trumped-up charges being drawn against him, he had fled.

Christina was Rumanian, and they found asylum in her homeland. From there Helmer watched with sinking heart, while poor, shattered Austria was torn to bits. When the reckoning of the Western Allies was done, there was almost nothing left—only a tiny rump of six million German-speaking people, burdened by the great city of Vienna, an imperial capital without an empire. Slowly, painfully, an uneasy order emerged. Yet much as he yearned for home, Kurt Helmer still could not return. The Helmers had no money.

Suddenly that last had changed. Christina's maternal grandmother was English; she died, and the Helmers received a substantial share of her estate. Only a modest fortune in British pounds, it was enormous in the devalued currency of central Europe. Kurt Helmer had come home, and now he had to decide whether to stay. Everything in him cried out to purchase this place, put down roots at last, and use all his energy not only for his family but also for Austria. . . .

Christina and his daughter reappeared through the gate, clutching bunches of the yellow flowers called keys of heaven. The girl laughed, looking up at her mother, and Christina laughed, too. A cloud passed across the sun, muting the colours of the distant hills. Then the bell of the parish church in the village of Ferndorf farther up the valley began to ring. It was exactly noon.

Helmer watched them there, against the dappled pattern of the lawn beneath the lindens, and his decision was made. He belonged here; *they* belonged here. From now on this house would be named the Christinahof.

BOOK ONE: 1936–1938

1

It was an absurd thing to have done, but Lan Condon had got himself lost here in the Vienna Woods. Stupidly, he'd taken a wrong turn; and now he had no idea what direction to travel towards the car. Not to worry. There was brandy left in the rucksack and he was in no hurry to go anywhere. He had, in fact, nowhere to go, except back to the hotel room in Vienna, or the hotel bar. So the hell with it. He strode on through the beech forest, following a winding track. Where it would take him, he had no idea. All he knew was that he was somewhere in Austria, for no particular reason except that Willi Orlik had suggested it.

"You need a hiding place," the little film director had said, looking around the bungalow in Los Angeles—a hog wallow of books, scripts, empty bottles, and soiled clothes—out of which Condon had barely stirred since Ross O'Donnell's funeral. "A place to recover from the shock. So . . . why not Vienna?"

Condon had only grunted.

"Of course Austria's Fascist, now. But it's a typically Austrian kind of Fascism, more a defence against Hitler by cuddling up to Mussolini than an ideology. And I'll guarantee this: Austria's totally unlike any place you have ever been before. Wine, Lan, women and song. All the ingredients for forgetting."

"If it's such a paradise, why did you leave it?"

"Two reasons. Who in Austria's going to pay me sixty thousand dollars to direct a picture? And I'm a Jew. In Vienna a Jew, no matter how successful, must take a lot of crap." He went to the door.

"But that has nothing to do with Vienna from your standpoint. So?"

"I don't know," Condon had muttered.

"Go to Vienna, Lan. Stay a while. Write when you can. Not scripts, but another novel, a good one. Then you will see a lot of things in a different light. *Wiederseh'n.*"

After Willi had gone, Lan had poured himself another drink and looked around the stinking little room. Why not? he found himself thinking. Why the hell not?

BELOW HIM the path dropped steeply down the hillside into a deep ravine through which ran a trickle of muddy water. It looked forbidding, but it was the only path he had, so he skittered down the slope. Just as he reached the bottom, something large burst through the woods. One moment he was alone, the next a man blocked the path. Lan jumped back, stared, short hair prickling on his neck. The man was out of a nightmare or a childhood book of fable—short, with iron-grey hair, a frowzy grey beard hanging matted to his chest, square, leathery face contorted in a snarl. He wore a low-cut leather shirt and shapeless leather breeches, bound around the calves with thongs, vanishing into leather boots, obviously homemade. In his right hand was a sword, bronze blade glinting in the soft afternoon light. Either Lan had gone mad or he was confronted with a primitive Teutonic warrior.

The man stepped forward, brandishing the sword, rolling out a string of guttural words, of which Condon recognized a single one: *Verboten.* Then the wild man gestured with the sword, unmistakably ordering Lan back the way he'd come.

"All right." Lan backed away. "All right." The man stood there scowling, sword upraised. Lan turned around and hurried back up the hill. Presently, breathing hard, he reached the level again. He looked back. The creature in leather had vanished. Lan went on again, retracing his steps, often turning to look behind him.

Eventually he reached the edge of a kind of glade, and there he halted. A few yards away, where a shaft of blue-gold light splayed down through a foliage rift, he saw another man, this time dressed in sombre black, sitting on a log, his back to Lan, a curl of cigarette smoke wreathing itself around his head. Cautiously Lan moved forward. The man heard him and stood up, turning. Not tall, he had a thin face nearly as white as the clerical collar at his throat. Lan relaxed. Priests he could cope with.

The man smiled. He was younger than Lan, perhaps in his late twenties. "*Grüss Gott*," he said, voice unexpectedly deep and mellow.

"*Grüss Gott.*" Lan groped for German. "*Ich bin Amerikaner . . .*"

"Oh, an American! Well, how do you do?" the priest said in perfect English, coming forward with hand outstretched.

"Oh, good." Lan felt sanity returning. "You speak English."

"Of course. As a matter of fact, I teach it. I am Doktor Martinus from the monastery of Altkreuzburg. At your service."

"Well, Father, I can use some service. My name's Condon, Lanier Condon, and I'm lost. I left my car at a little place called Oberfelsdorf, to take a walk, and I got turned around somehow—"

"Oberfelsdorf? Oh dear, you *are* turned around. It's nearly ten kilometres. Ah, well, don't worry, Mr. Condon. I'll be glad to show you a well-marked path that will take you there."

"Thanks. I hate to put you to so much trouble."

"No trouble at all. I'm just strolling in the woods, and one direction's as good as another. . . . Lanier Condon, did you say? Do you write, Mr. Condon?"

"Yes," Lan said. "Yes, I write—a little."

The young priest stared at him. "Perhaps more than a little?" He tapped his temple with a slender forefinger. "Somehow, I think . . . Ah. Ah, yes! You wrote *Sup With the Devil!*"

Lan Condon's mouth dropped open.

Dr. Martinus looked shy. "Well, as I said, I teach English. And I have a friend in London who sends me new books of consequence as they are published." He put out his hand again. "This is indeed an honour." He shook Lan's hand vigorously. "Well, we'd best be getting on. Perhaps I'll walk all the way to Oberfelsdorf with you." He gestured towards the ravine. "This way is shortest."

"Wait a minute," Lan said, and when the priest looked at him inquiringly, Lan told him about the apparition with the sword.

268

"Anyhow, that's what I *think* I saw," he said.

"Professor Busch." Martinus smiled, a little sadly. "He was brilliant once, a leading authority on old Germanic tribes."

"A *professor?*"

"These things happen. A few years ago he suddenly resigned his chair. Civilization, he proclaimed, was doomed; the only salvation was to revert to the old pure Germanic way of life. Up there on that hill—" Martinus pointed "—he built a wattled hut, authentic pre-Christian construction, right down to the last twig, and settled there as nearly like an ancient Teuton as is possible these days." Martinus shrugged. "Really, he's quite harmless."

"You wouldn't have thought so if you'd seen him wave that sword."

"Odd. Usually he has no objection to visitors." Martinus rubbed his chin. "Maybe it's better if we don't go that way after all." Suddenly he smiled, pale face lighting. "Never mind, Mr. Condon. I have a better solution. Don't know why I didn't think of it at first, but I've a friend living not far away who has a motor car. A General Helmer. He'll be happy to have you driven to pick up your own." He pointed up the track, away from the ravine. "It's only a few kilometres to the Christinahof, and the walk's a scenic one. We can be there in less than an hour."

2

As usual on a Sunday afternoon, visitors came in droves—the invited and the uninvited. Christa was nearly exhausted from playing hostess, while frail old Aunt Alma kept the servants busy replenishing food and drink on the tables on the terrace.

Well, Christa did not mind, really, the poor old things. Some of them were aristocracy and some were military and some were simply middle class. But they all had one thing in common: the world they had lived in no longer existed. And for many of them, what they would eat here would be the only square meal of the week.

Somewhere in the house a bell rang. Christa dodged back to the entrance hall, prepared to receive the newcomers; there would be a time lag, for the bell was wired to the gate. Out there on the terrace, she thought, many would be talking about her picture.

Of course, she had been the first to show the magazine to her father, realizing that things would be much simpler that way; for there, the largest picture in the spread, in the two-piece bathing suit she had bought without his knowledge, was "Fräulein Christa Helmer, daughter of Generalmajor Helmer. . . . One of the beach nymphs at Baden . . . modelling the latest bathing dress."

For a moment he had stared at it. Slowly his face turned brick red. "Christa," he finally managed: "How could you? What would your mother have said?"

"Papa, Papa." She smoothed the hair along his temples. "You always said yourself, Mama was the most fashionable woman in Vienna. Don't you think she would have worn it at my age?"

She felt his body relax. "Yes," he said. "Yes, she would have worn it if it were the fashion." He closed the magazine. "So . . . it will be a minor scandal, a tempest in a teapot, and next week there'll be something else in this rag and it'll be forgotten."

"Of course it will." She kissed him. "Thank you, Papa, for not being angry." She threw him another kiss and went out.

Now this afternoon she'd heard enough conversation to know that the older people indeed were shocked, the younger ones admiring. The degree of scandal was absolutely perfect. After all, a Viennese who had reached the age of twenty-one without creating *some* sort of sensation, well, what a poor dull creature she would be!

Christa smoothed her silk summer dress. Then Traudi, one of the servant girls, opened the door and Christa gasped, feeling her heart kick beneath her breasts with shock and excitement. The man in the doorway was Josef Steiner.

Entering, he handed his hat to Traudi, strode forward, a tall, angular man in a black suit, his face pale and very handsome. As she stood motionless, he came to her. Automatically she raised her hand and he bent gracefully, touched his lips to it. "Your servant, *gnädiges Fräulein*." Straightening, he handed her a bouquet—a dozen roses, velvety black.

Christa swallowed hard. "Herr Doktor Steiner." She wondered

if Traudi caught the tremor in her voice. Josef Steiner stood motionless, as did Christa, until the girl disappeared. His eyes darted around the hall. Then he said, "*Du*", and embraced her.

For one second something dissolved within her, and she returned the kiss. Then she broke away, appalled at the risk she'd taken.

"Josef!" she whispered. "Have you gone mad?"

He smiled, in that weary, wholly confident way that made her feel as if he could read everything inside her. "Of course. Ask my brothers. They'll all testify that I am mad."

"But to come here—"

"Your father banks with my family. If we are good enough to handle his money, are we not good enough to drink his wine?" Then, earnestly, "Listen, don't worry. I won't embarrass you. But I couldn't stay away. So, now, I will greet your father, your aunt, stay only a little while. But at least I can look at you for a few moments and. . . ." His voice dropped to a whisper. "I shall be in Vienna all this week. Please. Monday afternoon, at my flat?"

"Josef, I don't *know*."

"I shall wait. Monday, Tuesday, the whole week if necessary."

Frightened, yet profoundly excited, Christa pushed his hands away. She had not bargained for this at all. It was one thing to meet Josef Steiner in some secluded coffeehouse, to ride with him in his roadster along back roads where they would not be seen. It was quite another to have this Jew show up bold as brass at the Christinahof; it was embarrassing and downright dangerous.

"Come," she said firmly and led him through the house to the crowded terrace, where the young people she'd invited from Vienna were foxtrotting to music from the gramophone, while the older women sat gossiping on the wicker outdoor furniture, and their husbands stood talking politics or hunting. Thank God, Christa thought, their neighbours, Robert Schellhammer and his father, whom she knew as Uncle Max, were not among those present this afternoon.

Her own father was in a group of men at the far corner of the terrace, avidly discussing stalking methods. They did not look up as Steiner entered, but others did; and, like an infection, a diminution of the chatter spread. Then her father raised his head and saw Josef Steiner. The instant surprise in his eyes was immediately masked by hospitality. Excusing himself, he strode across the flagstones. "Good day, Herr Doktor Steiner," he said in a loud, clear voice. "This is an unexpected pleasure."

"Herr Generalmajor. I hope you will forgive the intrusion. I was on my way to Vienna from my estate in the Wachau and I thought I would call and pay my respects."

"You are most welcome." Kurt Helmer's voice was, if not warm, courteous. But what else could he say? Christa thought. Next to the Rothschilds, the Steiners were perhaps the most important family banking firm in Vienna, and the Helmer accounts had been with them for years. A financial connection with the Steiners was too important to be damaged by discourtesy to any member of the family, even a black sheep like Josef. "Come," said the General smoothly, "and try my latest bottlings. . . ."

Christa drew in breath, her cheeks hot, her palms moist. Papa was not stupid, and he must be wondering why Josef had stopped by. If Steiner paid her any undue attention, the game was up, and then there would be an explosion that would make the scandal of the magazine a bagatelle. And yet, she told herself, it was Papa's own fault that she had got mixed up with Josef. The increasing pressure he had put on her, subtle yet unrelenting, about marrying Robert Schellhammer, had upset and dismayed her. Her father's obvious approval of the son of a farmer—even as rich a farmer as Uncle Max—had puzzled and embarrassed her. Not that Robert was a clodhopper; he had his degree and was a graduate of the Wine School at Klosterneuburg and she had known him all her life. But when she married, finally, she knew how she wanted it to be, and she had no intention of some flat, dull, earthbound union with poor earnest Robert. She had been already rebellious and vulnerable that night Josef had approached her at the Opera.

Alone briefly in the buffet, the tall, pale young man in faultless evening dress had strode towards her, a glass of champagne in each hand. "Allow me," he said, smiling. There was something strange about his eyes, large, absolutely black, unreadable. When he introduced himself, Christa barely suppressed a gasp of shock and excitement, for Josef Steiner was legendary. The Viennese were dedicated gossips, and his affairs with women high and low had provided grist for their mill. Yet, somehow, not knowing how it happened, never remembering afterwards any conscious decision, she had agreed to meet him the next day for lunch. And she had met him many, many times since then.

3

Slight as he was, Martinus seemed totally indefatigable; and Condon was hard put to match his pace through the woods. The priest explained that he was a member of the Augustinian order resident at the monastery at Altkreuzburg.

"We are a community whose duty is to go out into the parishes and serve the people as ministers or teachers. I teach English at the *Gymnasium* in the town. The restrictions on us are considerably less onerous than those of other orders, and we are, perhaps, a bit more worldly."

Condon nodded. A little farther on they saw a crone, bent almost double under an enormous bundle of sticks, a scarf around her head, a basket on her arm. She shuffled with tiny crippled steps through a glade, never seeing them, eyes riveted on the ground. "Gathering firewood and mushrooms," Martinus said quietly. "Poor creature. Times are very hard here for many people, Mr. Condon."

"Not only here. In America as well. Better now than four, five years ago, but bad enough."

"A judgment," Martinus said. "Perhaps a judgment on us all." They emerged from the woods, into a meadow. Vast deep valleys fell away on either side, gilded by the special light of late afternoon. Martinus raised his arm and pointed. Ahead, a big yellow house towered on the crest of an even higher hill.

"There," Martinus said. "That's where we'll get a car. The residence of General Helmer: the Christinahof.

"I'll tell you, Mr. Condon," said Martinus, as they walked on

273

towards the big house on the hill, "the General would be a good subject for any novelist. His father was an obscure gamekeeper of a royal hunting lodge. The boy came to the attention of a colonel in the Imperial Army who was shooting with the Archduke Rudolf. The Army was always alert for promising material, and Helmer, at the age of twelve, must have been very promising. The colonel sponsored him at cadet school, and at the military academy in Wiener Neustadt. He must have had a natural talent for soldiering, for he rose very quickly to become the youngest colonel in the Imperial and Royal Army."

He paused to accept a cigarette from Condon, then went on. "Later, Helmer was sent to Rumania as a military attaché. There he married Frau Helmer, a Rumanian by birth but of German stock. When the war began, he was sent off to command a regiment against the Russians. In 1915 the Czarist army mounted a tremendous attack against the Austrian line. The old generals lost their heads, but Helmer kept cool. He flagrantly disobeyed orders to retreat, and his regiment attacked instead. The story is that soon, more or less by default, he was the real commander of the Austrian forces in the field. At any rate, he smashed the Russians, turned defeat into victory.

"Helmer was promoted. But after the war he was forced to take refuge in Rumania. Anyhow, he and his wife came back several years later, bought this place—and named it after Frau Helmer. She died several years ago. The General took it hard, of course, but he's himself again now, and you'll find him a most hospitable and likeable man. He and his family all speak fluent English, incidentally."

The path circled, brought them to a steep, broad drive. Before Martinus could ring the bell, an attendant opened one leaf of the high wrought-iron gate. From the way he and Martinus greeted each other by name, Lan could tell that the priest had been a frequent and welcome visitor. Then they passed through, following the drive across a wide grassy park shaded by giant trees, studded with statuary, dimpled with pools. In its centre was the house itself. They went through a lofty arch in a wall into a courtyard. Lan halted, impressed.

He was no stranger to manor houses: he had seen the great old plantations of Louisiana, and had been a guest in the big pseudo-Spanish houses of Beverly Hills. But the Christinahof was of a style new to him. Seldom had he seen a place so welcoming.

Dr. Martinus led him up the steps to the front door and rang a bell. Dressed in old-fashioned black, a plump servant girl opened the door, smiled, curtseyed, and to Lan's amusement, kissed the priest's hand. Then, after a few words in German, she scurried off.

The hall in which they waited had a parquet floor and walls hung with paintings. The ceiling was high, wreathed with plaster ornamentation. Then the terrace doors opened, and a girl came through them smiling. Lan Condon tensed, suddenly aware of his rumpled hiking clothes.

"Dr. Martinus." Her voice was a little husky. They spoke briefly in German. Her smile, her whole face, was open, undevious. Her hair was blonde, gently waved, her blue eyes large, direct, and clear, lashes very long. Her skin was flawless, with an outdoor cast of tawniness; her body, in its silken summer dress, slender, long-legged, athletic, yet well rounded. She bore herself with grace, energy, and pride. She was, Condon guessed, hardly out of her teens, and yet one sensed immediately a vast realm of possibilities within her. Then he became aware that she had turned to him, was speaking to him in English.

"Mr. Condon." She put out her hand. "How do you do? I am Christa Helmer. Welcome to the Christinahof." Her hand in Condon's was slim, and strong, her handshake straightforward. "We shall be glad to help you. But first you must come and meet my father and have something to eat and drink."

She led them through the drawing room, and out onto the terrace. She gestured. "There's Papa over there."

Helmer was a man better than medium height, body somewhat thickened but still ramrod straight. His grey suit trimmed with velvet and with silver buttons seemed half uniform, half folk dress. His English was more heavily accented than his daughter's, which was nearly flawless. He greeted Lan, then turned to the tall, dark young man in black with whom he had been conversing. "Mr. Condon, Dr. Martinus, may I present Dr. Josef Steiner?"

"Mr. Condon." Steiner bowed slightly. There was something complex, mysterious, Lan thought, behind Steiner's pale and saturnine good looks. Then a servant appeared with a tray of glasses.

"Some wine, Mr. Condon," the General said. They all took glasses and Helmer raised his. "*Pros't.*" The wine was dry, tangy with earth, sun, and grape. Over his glass's rim Lan saw a glance as if of complicity pass between the girl and Steiner.

"Do you like it?" Helmer asked.

"I'm no expert, but I think it's fine."

"Every man should be his own expert." The General smiled. "Tastes are as various in wine as in women, and it's unreasonable to expect everyone to agree. But—" He turned as a short man with a bearded face like that of a mournful goat touched his elbow. They spoke in German. Then Helmer said, "Please excuse me, gentlemen. . . ." He drifted away with the old man at his elbow.

For a moment, silence. Then Josef Steiner said, "Mr. Condon, I would be most interested to know what do your people think of Herr Hitler and events in Germany?"

Lan hesitated. The Americans for whom he'd written filmscripts were not supposed to think. They were supposed to have the minds of children, wanting everything made simple, and always with a happy ending. He shook his head. "It's hard to say. Most Americans are too busy to think about things over here. Hitler's just not our problem."

"Oh," said Steiner, and he drank. Then, lowering his voice, he said almost angrily, "Mr. Condon, I assure you, Hitler is very much your problem. Believe me, unless we get help—help from England, France, or America—there will be another war, and you may count on its making the last one look like a children's party."

"I don't follow you." But Lan was interested.

"All right. After the Great War, your country and its allies broke up our empire. Now what's left is a clutch of separate little countries, all quarrelling, all suffering from economic chaos. This power vacuum must be filled. The Germans and Russians will obviously fight to fill it. Already Adolf Hitler has proclaimed he'll not rest until Austria's part of Germany."

"I had the vague impression that Austria was under Italy's protection," mused Lan.

Steiner's mouth twisted. "A flimsy shield. Yes, to some extent we are. In fact, to gain it was one reason our Chancellor set up a Fascist state in 1933. That was the price for Mussolini's aid. But things have changed since then. Hitler's manoeuvring Italy into a position where she must choose between Germany and Austria. And I hardly think she will choose Austria." He shrugged. "I'm sorry if I've bored you. I tend to get carried away. Now I'm afraid I must run; I have an appointment in Vienna. Awfully nice to have met you, Mr. Condon. Dr. Martinus."

"Dr. Steiner." There was hostility in the priest's voice.

"So. *Wiederseh'n.* Fräulein Helmer—"

"I'll see you to the door, Doctor. If you gentlemen will excuse me. . . ."

Condon watched the two of them move off across the terrace. Again he had a sense of complicity between them.

"I shouldn't pay too much attention to Steiner's diatribe," Martinus said, turning towards a long table laden with food. "He has an axe to grind, you know. After all, he's Jewish. His family is one of the old, powerful Jewish banking families of Austria. Josef himself, however, takes no part in the family business."

Lan joined Martinus at the table.

"My preference, Mr. Condon, is for the present régime. But suppose the worst does happen? Given a choice between the Nazis, who at least arrange an accommodation with the Church, and the Reds, who would stamp it out altogether, what is a clergyman to do?"

He stacked pickles on his plate. "Austria is poor; out of six million people, nearly half a million are jobless. People are literally starving. Meanwhile, Germany prospers. If we become part of Germany, maybe we could share that prosperity. In any event, one comforting fact is clear. The Church can live with Hitler."

"Which is all-important," Lan said tonelessly.

Martinus looked at him keenly. "You are not a Catholic?"

"I'm not an anything." Cutting off the conversation, Lan turned to the table. "Just hungry."

277

After all the others had drifted off into the woods, bound for home, Robert Schellhammer remained behind inside the smoky dimness of Busch's wattled hut, sharing his pocket flask of schnapps with the man from Munich.

"Forty," Gustav Holz said, jotting something in a little notebook. "Forty Party members in a place so small. Herr Ortsgruppenleiter Schellhammer, I congratulate you."

"Thank you. Remember, these are only the *active* members. We have as many sympathizers again who don't dare to join the Party yet, including all three policemen in Ferndorf."

"A most remarkable performance. I'll see that it's included, with special mention of you by name, in a report that will come to the attention of the Führer himself."

Robert nodded modestly, accepting the praise as his due. Still, he could not suppress an inner glow, a quick vision of the Führer in the Chancellery in Berlin poring over the report.

"This place stinks."

Robert laughed. Busch's hut, as always, reeked of woodsmoke, and the goats that wandered in and out. "That's part of the reason we meet here. It's a lot more secure than meeting out in the open. All the locals avoid Professor Busch. Besides, he's like a Red Indian in the woods; nobody's going to sneak up on us while he's on guard." He gestured to a wooden box in one corner. "I even keep the records here, what few I have."

"God grant the goats don't eat them," said Holz, stowing his notebook in his rucksack. "Well, Herr Ortsgruppenleiter, I must be on my way."

"Thank you for coming, Herr Holz. You explained a lot of things, answered a lot of questions for the boys."

"That's my business. I'm sorry some of them were disappointed. But, as I explained, for the time being you people here must lie low. The Führer has certain important negotiations under way which must not be hampered by any major incident. Do you understand?"

"Perfectly." Robert pocketed the flask and rose, a man of medium height, in his early twenties, with a big head, broad sloping shoulders, his muscles tempered by hard work. His hair was blond, his eyes the steel blue of a razor blade, his face square and handsome. "We'll be careful in every respect."

"Good. So . . ." Holz's right arm shot up. "Heil Hitler!"

"Heil Hitler!" They shook hands and Holz went out.

Robert sat down again, lighting a cigarette. *Absolutely the best local organization I've seen so far in Austria.* High praise from a man like Special Party Representative Gustav Holz. But, then, he'd earned it. And, if the truth be known, not for his own glory—though that was important—but for his country. *Ein Reich, ein Volk, ein Führer!* A goal worth any risk.

Most men were manipulated by events; Robert had long ago decided to shape events to suit his dreams, and so far he had succeeded. Take the matter of his education. Though academic subjects came hard to him, he had studied and striven, so that he had received his *Matura.* And meanwhile he had found the cause to which he would dedicate his life, the lever he would use to change the world.

That it needed changing, he had long realized. When his father Max had come home from the war, he had been loud and articulate on the betrayal of Austria: by the stupid generals, the corrupt politicians, and, of course, the moneymen, the Jews. As a child Robert had listened and absorbed. The traitors were in the saddle —the godless Socialists, the kikes, the Communists. They had robbed him and every Austrian of his rightful heritage. Something must be done, revenge taken, things somehow set to rights. And somehow, he knew, he would do it—or play his part in doing it.

Then, when he was sixteen, he was out skiing one day, and had worked up a high bleak slope to a stout Alpine shelter hut. By chance there were two other youths already there, blue-eyed, blond, and handsome.

He skied and talked with them all day, and by late afternoon they were like the brothers he had never had. One of them, Moritz, had taken a book from his rucksack. "Here. Read this."

"*Mein Kampf.* Yes, I've heard of it, but I've never read it."

"This book will change your life," said Moritz. "It has changed ours. We're organizing the National Socialist Youth Movement. If we young people don't take the lead, who will? Read the book, Robert. And if you have questions, write to us in Munich. Now, let's have one more run before the snow crusts."

It had taken Robert five days to read it, slowly, thoroughly, as was his wont. Then, more swiftly, he read it again. By then he knew Moritz had been right: the answers he'd been seeking were all there; and his life *was* changed.

At first he recruited farm and village youths his own age. Bored, restless, penniless, they were ripe for anything. Galvanizing them to action, he was so successful that soon older men were drawn in. As Hitler rose in Germany, so did the Nazi Party in Austria. When the Führer became Chancellor, Robert scented victory. Germany put on pressure, imposing surcharges that nearly destroyed Austria's tourism. It restricted imports; and as the Austrian people suffered, the power of the Nazis grew. The Austrian Chancellor tried to dissolve all rival political parties, both Socialists and Nazis. Robert's group retaliated by showing their teeth. They travelled up the Danube to another district, blew railway lines there with dynamite supplied by Germany, firebombed a Jewish store, and burned the barn of a vocal anti-Nazi farmer. Simultaneously, another group hit targets in the Ferntal. It was happening all across the country—a campaign of sabotage and terror.

Robert was now known in the inner councils as a young man to watch. When the new Austria was built, part of Germany, yet ruled by Austrians, Robert Schellhammer would become a man of power.

And then, Robert thought, he would need a wife. Not just any woman, but the one he had to have—Christa Helmer. He had loved her from first sight, when she was eight and he eleven. But there was an enormous gulf between them. Her mother had been a baroness, her father was a famous general; Bertha Schellhammer was the daughter of the village butcher, and Max a farmer. Still, as Robert knew, these were no ordinary times, and hard economic necessities levelled barriers. General Helmer was no fool. He must have already imagined what a magnificent thing it

would be if someday the Schellhammer and the Helmer holdings
were merged under the management of a man like Robert.

More than that. Helmer kept his ear to the ground. So far, he
had expressed neither approval of nor opposition to the Nazis. But
he must have appraised the situation and himself come to the
conclusion that the New Order was inevitable. And when it came,
he would not be caught short; he knew Robert was a Nazi, and he
would take out insurance. There could be none better than his
daughter's marriage to a man of power in the Party.

5

Steiner was leaving the Christinahof.

"Monday," he said firmly. "I shall await you on Monday
afternoon."

"I—" Then Christa heard herself say, "Yes. Yes, I'll be there
on Monday."

"Time will crawl," he whispered. He smiled and then was gone.

Feeling frightened yet exhilarated, she returned to the terrace.
Martinus had been captured by three dowdy old women, and the
American was leaning against the balustrade sipping wine, looking
out at the valley.

"I'm so sorry you were left alone, Mr. Condon."

"It's all right." He smiled faintly. "Just admiring the view."
He looked haggard, she thought; and there was something in his
manner that put a distance between them, as if he did not want
anyone to come too close.

Suddenly she was intensely curious. "Dr. Martinus says you're
a writer. Would you mind if I asked you about your books? Papa
and I both read in English."

He hesitated. Then shyly he told her that he'd written two
novels. "I'll ask my publisher to send you a copy of each."

"Oh, that's too much trouble, surely."

"Not as much as your father sending a car to Oberfelsdorf.
Where should I have them sent? You write it out for me." He
handed her his pen and a small notepad that he always carried in
his shirt pocket.

She did. He slipped the piece of paper in his pocket. "Now," she said, "may I ask what they're about?"

"Well, the first one, *Sup With the Devil*—it's about Louisiana. That's a state in the South—"

"I know. New Orleans. It must be fascinating."

His brows lifted, surprised at her knowledge; she was flattered. "Right. Well, my father owned a little country newspaper in Louisiana. Then a man named Huey Long took over the state, almost the way Hitler took over Germany; he got elected governor, then senator . . . Well, *Devil*'s mostly based on the Long régime."

"I see. And the other?"

"*Road to Nowhere*? That's about the Depression. About people with no jobs, no money, riding freight trains back and forth across the country, desperate, living any way they could. The first boxcar I was ever in, there was a bank president who'd lost his bank—"

"The first one *you* rode in? You mean you—?" The idea startled her, a writer reduced to such expedients.

"I sure did. For about a year." His voice was grimly wry. "You see, my first book was a mistake. I thought it would make me rich, but it didn't. What it did do was turn the Long régime against our newspaper. They broke us, just wiped us out. Took everything we had. My father died soon after. So—" He shrugged. "Finally *Devil* was reprinted in England. I got some money from that, which bought me time to write *Road to Nowhere*. After that things went better. For the last two years I've been writing scripts in Hollywood."

"Oh! How marvellous! I'm mad about Garbo! And Charlie Chaplin. Have you ever met them?"

"I'm afraid I've only seen them at a distance. Writers don't move in those circles very often. But—" His eyes shadowed suddenly. "You know, it's getting pretty late."

"Oh, do please stay for dinner."

He shook his head. "Thanks, but I'd better pick up that rented car and get back to Vienna."

"Then maybe you'll come back again. Will you be in Vienna long?"

"I don't know. My plans are . . . uncertain. But—" his smile was

282

strangely mechanical "—thanks anyhow for this afternoon. It's been most enjoyable. Now, do you suppose your father. . . ."

"Of course. He'll have the car sent around right away." She was both disappointed and a little angry at the easy way he'd detached himself. A Hollywood film writer! Well, glamorous as his occupation was, there was certainly nothing sparkling about him. Compared to Josef. . . .

HER TAXI turned off into side streets where, without trees or gardens, people lived like wasps in nest-cells. Rain was falling as the vehicle entered the cul-de-sac that was her destination. Christa's throat was dry, her heart pounding. Why was she doing it? Why was she in this cab riding towards a rendezvous with Josef Steiner? Now was the moment of decision, a last chance to change her mind, tell the driver to take her home.

Instead, she paid, opened her umbrella, got out in the rain. On the pavement she halted before two big wooden doors, iron-strapped, set in the blank front of a grimy building. The right one was unlocked and she pushed through, into a grubby entrance hall, as stony, dim, and chill as a cave, with stairs running up to right and left. Here again she halted. Suppose . . . suppose today. . . .

She was like a woman with a single coin: to spend it wisely or to squander it on a single whim? Once gone, it could never be retrieved. Something rebelled in her, and her knees were weak with fear. Nevertheless she climbed the stairs.

The door was one flight up, in a narrow paint-peeling corridor. The handwritten name above the bell was Schmidt: J. Schmidt. Christa stood before it folding her umbrella. How many women, she wondered, had delivered themselves to him in secret in this place, just as she was doing now? She hated to be like those others. But with a gloved finger she pushed the bell.

Instantly the door swung open and he was there, in black cardigan, the rest of his clothing just as black, only the shirt crisply white. His eyes lit up the paleness of his face. "Ah," he said, "you did come," and he stepped quickly aside to let her in. Closing the door, he took her hand, pressed his lips lightly to it. No more than that, which surprised her. "Let me take your coat," he said.

He helped her out of it, bending forward to touch his lips to the place behind her ear as he did so. A shiver rippled down her spine. She peeled off gloves as he hung the coat on a hook in the small tiled entry. "Come in," he said.

The sitting room was large, the walls done in a filigreed damask pattern of black predominating over scarlet, the furniture upholstered to match the walls, and rows of bookshelves lacquered glistening black. The carpets on the floor matched. One lamp in a corner provided soft indirect light; a blue flame hissed beneath a samovar on the table before the divan.

"Incredible weather," Josef said. "What about hot tea with rum to warm you?"

"Thank you." The steadiness of her voice surprised her; she sounded as if she were quite accustomed to coming secretly to men's apartments.

"There are no servants here," he said, pouring out the tea. "A man in my position needs total privacy. I purchased this building through an agent and have three rooms incognito."

The Josef Steiner touch, she thought with mingled admiration and revulsion; needing a love nest, he'd bought an entire building. He looked up, appreciation gleaming in his dark eyes. "Lovely," he said quietly. "You're absolutely lovely, did you know that?" He motioned to the divan. "Sit here."

He had been liberal with the rum; she felt its warmth spreading through her, melting apprehension. To her surprise, though, he did not sit down beside her, but stood, cup and saucer in his hand. For a moment he did not speak. On the wall a clock ticked loudly; rain hissed against the windowpanes.

"I hope," he said at last, "my visit did not embarrass you."

"It was . . . a surprise."

He smiled. "Your father was very—gracious."

"He always is. But he wondered. He didn't say anything, but I caught him looking at me strangely several times last night."

Josef nodded. Then, suddenly: "And if he knew about us, what would happen?"

Christa stared at him, surprised, searching for words. "He would be most unhappy," she said finally.

284

"Yes, I suppose so. Josef Steiner, the roué, seeing his daughter. Even worse than that, Steiner, the Jew." His voice was bitter.

Christa looked down at her cup. Somehow it had never occurred to her that he, too, could be hurt. "Josef," she began. Then from the next room came the buzzing of the telephone.

Steiner frowned. "Excuse me." He rose and went out. She heard the door close, but not tightly, for Josef's voice came to her: "Schmidt here." Then his voice became a murmur.

Christa set down her cup, rose and wandered around the room. Inevitably she was drawn by the shelved books. One could read another's personality from his books, almost like a glimpse into his soul. To her surprise, most were thick, forbidding volumes on science—biology, genetics. Her hand slipped down to a row bound uniformly in black calf, no titles, only volume numbers. She pulled one out, opened it—and gasped.

It was an album containing photographs, two to a page, each large, brilliantly clear, and totally obscene. Revolted and aroused simultaneously, she stared in fascination.

"Oh," Josef said behind her. "So you've found those, have you?"

Christa jumped, slammed the book shut, turned with flaming face. Josef smiled, took it gently from her hand. "You see? I *am* a monster. I'm sorry if they have shocked you."

He slid the book back on the shelf. Then he led her to the sofa. "Sit down, Christa," he said. "Forget the pictures. I need them neither to increase my potency nor to aid in the seduction of the innocent. They have quite another purpose, which I am not at liberty to explain. They're a kind of . . . business investment." He stood over her, looking down. In the oyster-coloured light from the lamp his face was tense. "So," he said. "General Helmer wondered why I came to Christinahof. What would he say if you and I got married? I want to marry you."

She stared at him, dumbfounded.

"I know." He smiled faintly. "This is not precisely why you thought the spider had enticed you to its web. And I must confess that I am as surprised as you—my original intention was . . . what you thought it was. But along the way something has changed.

286

I want more of you than I could get that way. And so, I'm gambling. All or—nothing."

"Josef, I don't know what to say." This was more than she could grasp; a trick, a tactic, or did he really mean it? And if he did, what did she feel, what should she answer?

"Say nothing until you've heard me out. There is much about me you don't know, much I must explain, but this you must believe—I love you. And I do not say it lightly.

"Now," he went on crisply, "I am aware that there are objections that must be dealt with. I am a Jew. Even though I don't pursue the ritual of it, my Jewishness is a fundamental part of me." His expression turned sardonic. "However, it's mitigated by two factors. First, my family's old and, Jewish or not, thoroughly Viennese. The Steiners have been here nearly as long as the Habsburgs and have played almost as important a role. The second factor's even more important: I'm a *rich* Jew. Extremely rich. And almost—not quite—that erases class distinctions. You would find few doors closed to you that are now open and many open that may now be closed." He went on, eyes meeting hers. "As I say, I'm rich. So much so that even I sometimes am startled."

"Josef—"

"I know. You can't be bought. But it's a fact of the life you—we—would have, just as if I had to confess to you that we were poor and would have to live in a garret. It's part of what you should know about me. And there is more."

He sat down in a chair across the room, leaned forward, elbows on knees, pale hands twining. "I also have the reputation of being an idler. That's absolutely false, a rumour that began when I did indeed withdraw from any active part in the family business. I had no intention of wasting my life in the dreariness of the counting house. But believe me, I run my estate at Schloss Schwarzgipfel just as industriously as your father runs his." He paused. Then he said, "There are, beyond that, other activities crucially important to a lot of people. But those I can't discuss until we're married."

Married. That word sounding again dispelled some of the numbness; she looked at Josef with new eyes, and now he no longer frightened her. She felt a strange sense of power. It was a heady feeling, and yet somehow disappointing. She had expected more strength from him. For all his poise, he was no stronger than any other man in love. When she had come here, her life had been in his hands; now his was in hers. She liked him better; but his magnetic attraction had quite dissolved.

"Well?" he said. "I am finished. What will be your answer?"

Christa stared at him. "Josef, I don't know what to say," she answered finally. "I am . . . flattered, complimented. But maybe you've seen things in me that aren't there."

"No. I know what I see: so many possibilities waiting to be discovered. Maybe you yourself don't even know they're there. But they are, challenges and riches enough to occupy a man a lifetime in exploring." He took a deep breath. "Christa, I know you must feel something for me or you wouldn't be here. Whatever you feel now, time will increase and deepen it, I promise you."

As he got up and moved towards her, she raised a hand; he stopped. "Josef, of course I feel something. But there's so much to think about before I could give you an answer. Papa. . . ."

"Is it your intention to let him arrange a match in the old way and meekly marry whoever he says, with or without love?"

She thought of the union her father was trying to push her into with Robert. "No. No, I'll never marry any man I don't choose."

"And if you chose me?"

"Then I'd marry you, regardless."

He drew in breath. "Ah. Then it must be my business to make you choose me. Will you come tomorrow?"

"No, not tomorrow."

"Then the day after."

She stared at him a moment. "Yes. Yes, I'll come then. After I've had time to think." She rose and turned towards the door. "I'd better go, now. My mind's all mixed up."

"Very well. My car is in the courtyard. You wouldn't want me driving you, so I'll have the building superintendent do it. Put on your things while I ring him. He'll meet you at the entry."

Numbly she put on her things, Josef kissed her hand, then she hurried down the steps.

288

By seven that evening the sky above Vienna had not only cleared but was tinged with a lavish glow of pink and pearl which, washing over the city, transformed its stony greyness into muted lambent radiance. Lan Condon, sipping a Scotch and soda at the Hotel Sacher's pavement café, watched the streams of well-dressed people flowing towards the Opera across the way and felt a touch of awe at the sudden beauty surrounding him. He could see now why Willi had said there was something magical about this place. Nothing in it had ever been planned for efficiency, only aesthetic pleasure.

He leaned back in his chair and reread the cable. His contract with the studio still had a year to run; now they wanted him back or there would be trouble. His agent wanted to know what he intended to do so he could negotiate.

Lan signalled for the white-jacketed waiter, and folded the cable. No hiding place, he thought. Still, maybe this was a jolt he needed; decisions must be made. He had a life to get through somehow, and it could not be spent hiding in a hotel or a bottle.

But the thought of going back to the studio filled him with nausea. He could do the scripts easily. But they were not why he called himself a writer. The novels were the real reason for his existence, and he had been away from them too long. . . .

"Will you have another, sir?" The waiter made to pick up the empty glass. His voice brought Lan back into the present.

"No. No, nothing else. My bill, please."

"Of course." The man hastened off. While Lan waited, he shifted restlessly, drummed his fingers on the table. He could sit no longer; he needed action. No more drinking, get out and walk, as he had done on Sunday, only this time around the city. Wear himself down, clear his head—and make a decision. The head-waiter came; he paid and left the Sacher.

Lan crossed the street. He could stay here in Vienna, transfer his money to Switzerland and let the studio sue and be damned. Learn enough of the language to get along, find a decent place to stay, give his emotions a chance to sort themselves out—and maybe even write another novel. If he could forget.

Los Angeles . . . Phyll. No matter how far he ran, it seemed, he could not outrun that, the memory of catastrophe. Guilt was a hound that could trail even across an ocean. Violently he shook his head, but the image was already there: Ross standing in the doorway of the bedroom, round face as pale as tallow, eyes wide with shock, mouth gaping. And his wife, naked, bent over Lanier Condon's body, also naked. And then that strange, incoherent cry breaking from Ross's throat, raw agony and. . . . He could have come on in, Lan thought; he should have! He could have beat hell out of both of us; I would never have raised a finger! Instead. . . .

He remembered shoving Phyllis sprawling off the bed, springing up. "Ross!" he'd yelled, but there were already footsteps on the stairs, the slam of the outer door.

Phyll pulled a robe about her, poured two drinks, hands trembling, gave one to him. "Damn him," she said with husky fury. "How dare he do that to me! He was supposed to be in New York until Monday! He didn't even wire." She turned on Lan. "It was a trap!"

Lan's first impulse had been to hit her. He could not imagine how desire and revulsion could so intermingle. Well, he could not lay the blame on her; it had been his fault as much as hers. "No," he said dully, "it wasn't any trap. It was the oldest dirty joke in the world. Husband comes home to find his best friend and his wife—God damn it!" he roared and began to pull on his clothes.

"Where're you going?"

"To find him," Lan had rasped.

"Find him?" She laughed harshly. "What then?"

"How the hell do I know? All I know is I've got to find him."

But he had not found Ross. Not at the studio, not in any of the usual bars. And finally, exhausted, he had driven back to the O'Donnell house, and got out of his car.

Then he heard it, the steady sound, very muffled, of a car's engine running, idling. Had Ross come back unheard, was he—?

Then he understood. The sound came from the closed garage.

Worst of all was the recollection of how he had rolled open the

290

door of the garage, pulled Ross's huge, inert figure from the front seat of the car. "Call an ambulance!" he screamed to Phyll, and then, there on the asphalt of the drive, began to give Ross artificial respiration. He was still at it, begging, pleading, crying out to the unresponsive body to awaken enough to hear contrition, when the ambulance screamed up. They dragged him off, clamped on the respirator, but it did not help. The police were there, too, by then. They questioned Phyll first, and he heard her coolly tell the story that he had not even known she had devised. It was all neat and logical: she had been alone when Ross had returned unexpectedly from a visit to New York, where his mother had been ill. He had been depressed from the trip, had acted even more strangely than he had been acting lately. They had quarrelled. He had, she thought, driven away. For a long time she had been afraid of suicide. Upset, she had called his best friend, Lan Condon, and Lan had searched for him, ineffectually. Had returned to the house on Camden Drive to comfort Phyllis. Had heard the motor running in the garage. Ross hadn't driven away at all. He had driven into the garage, left the engine idling, closed the door, and. . . . They knew the rest. Mr. Condon had worked tirelessly to save him, but hours had passed and it was too late. She did it marvellously, every nuance exactly right; but, then, she had been a damned fine actress until she'd married Ross and he'd taken her out of circulation.

The detective turned to Condon. "Is that right, Mr. Condon?"

"Yes," he heard himself say. "Yes, that's how it happened. . . ."

It was all like some dimly-remembered nightmare, and the thought of returning to California now filled him with a kind of sickness. He would have deliberately to kill something within himself, like a doctor destroying a nerve that carried pain. With the nerve gone, you could do anything and it would not matter.

By now he had roamed deep into a section of Vienna neither particularly picturesque nor lively. Something small, a cat, or maybe a cat-sized rat, scrabbled away in darkness. A blob that was a human figure straightened up from its delving in a box: a scavenger in garbage. Lan moved on, warily, and finally he reached a well-lit street. Light spilled from the plate-glass window of a tavern; opening the door, he went in. The room was large, its peeling walls brightened by signs and calendars. There was a bar, some tables, warmth, the air thick with taints of stale alcohol, harsh tobacco smoke, and garlic-flavoured grease.

He took the only vacant table, and managed to make the paunchy waiter in a dirty apron understand his order for white wine. Then he lit a cigarette and scrutinized the other patrons.

Working men mostly, in shabby clothes or blue overalls, drinking steadily to ease the aches of the day's labour or the worse pain of having none, arguing in hoarse gutturals or staring morosely into their glasses. Only three customers were of a different pattern. Sitting at a table before the bar, they were younger, cleaner, better dressed than the others, wearing what he took to be a folk costume of some kind—cocky little narrow-brimmed hats with small colourful feathers in the bands, sweaters over white ties, leather knickers, white knee stockings, and heavy walking shoes. He supposed they'd stopped in on their way home from a club meeting of some kind. One met his appraising gaze, raised his beer mug, smiled and nodded. Lan nodded back.

Then the door opened and a small man entered, wearing a heavy frowzy overcoat despite the evening's mildness. He paused, looked round, saw no vacant place except at Condon's table, and came over. He spoke in German and Lan nodded somewhat grudgingly. The man hung up his hat and overcoat, sat down, shooting frayed cuffs from the sleeves of a shabby suit jacket. Taking out a little purse, he squinted in it judiciously, then signalled for the waiter, ordering a glass of wine.

When the waiter shambled off the small man groped in his pocket with unmistakable purpose and, finding nothing, sighed. Automatically Lan shoved his own packet of Lucky Strikes across the table. "Have one," he said.

To his surprise, the reply was also in English. "Oh, thank you very much. But, no, I couldn't." Nevertheless, longing for the good tobacco trembled in the thin voice.

"I've got plenty. Go ahead."

Now the man accepted, inhaling sensually. "American cigarettes. The best in the world. Are you American?"

292

"Yes, sir. Condon. Lan Condon."

"Ah, so! I have a cousin in Milwaukee." He put out a hand. "Berger. At your service, sir. My card." His hand flashed into his pocket, brought out a worn leather case.

"Julius Berger. *Briefmarken für Sammler*," Lan read. "*Briefmarken?*"

"Postage stamps, for collectors. I've a little shop in the market." Berger's wine came then. "*Pros't*, Mr. Condon."

Suddenly one of the three young men at the table near the bar raised his glass. Grinning, he shouted, "Heil Hitler!"

His companions and half a dozen others echoed the words. Lan stared, a chill creeping down his back. "Nazis?" he whispered.

"Yes," Berger muttered. "I'm afraid so."

"I thought they were illegal here."

"Yes, supposed to be. But still very bold, many of them, and many sympathizers. You see, they wear white stockings, a sign they use sometimes since the swastika and the brown shirts are forbidden. One feels danger in the air all the time. Especially if one is Jewish." The last sentence was barely audible. "I must go."

Lan looked at the young Nazis with new eyes. They seemed absolutely commonplace: only jovial young men with lots of beer in them. But Lan remembered Louisiana. The crowd that had destroyed his father had been jovial too. One of the Nazis was certainly a joker, with dark hair and a mercurial face; his sallies sent the others into repeated laughter. Another was big, with the clean look of an athlete. The third was skinny, with lank blond hair. His face was pale; he looked a brooder.

Now the joker said something and the blond man smiled and the big one stared with opaque eyes at Berger. "Hello, little Jew," the joker shouted. "Would you like us to walk you home?"

Once, hunting, Lan had chanced upon a baby rabbit, immobile beside a bush with fear. He had picked it up and felt its body vibrate with the thudding of its frightened heart. Berger was now shaking with the same palpitant fear as he fumbled with his coat. Suddenly Lan was angry. He drew himself up and deliberately let his eyes meet those of the three men at the table, in defiance. "Don't worry," he said. "I'll go out with you."

293

"No, no." Berger's terror grew instead of lessening. "Please. Please, I shall be quite all right. Thank you, but please don't." He touched Lan's palm, then scuttled out.

All three men were staring back at Condon now, their whole manner changed, the good humour drained, their eyes hard. As he sat down again, they rose. The dark one pressed a note into the waiter's hand, then they came towards Lan.

He sat tensely, looking at them. They returned his stare, trying deliberately to intimidate him. He waited.

They passed on by him, each looking at him carefully. "*Wiederseh'n,*" each said, not to him but to the room at large. Behind them came a chorus of answers.

The door swung shut behind them. Condon sat there looking at it, indecisive. Then he dropped some money on the table, followed, knowing it was crazy; yet all the accumulated tensions of the past weeks were rolling up in him so that he could not help himself.

Outside there was no trace of either Berger or the Nazis. He drew in a long breath of clean, cool air, looking to his right and left. As his eyes grew accustomed to the darkness, the shapes of three men resolved themselves. Then, like a hound's bay, a loud voice rang out in mockery.

"*Hallloooooo . . . . . lieber Abraham. . . .*"

No answer, and the three spread out, moving forward across the square. Condon then saw the short figure, too old or dignified to run, making for distant streetlights that threw it into silhouette.

"*Ooooh, Abraham!*" They increased their pace. Lan cursed softly. He ran across the street behind them. The taunting cries, edged with menace, rang out eerily from everywhere.

Berger halted, confused. He changed direction, stopped after a few uncertain paces, turned again. "Berger!" Lan roared, dismayed by this paralysis of terror. "Run! Run, you idiot!"

Berger came to life. Suddenly he was dashing, coat streaming. The three Nazis made no effort to pursue, only stood and watched. Lan halted, breathing hard, as Berger disappeared. And then the Nazis turned and, almost casually, moved towards Lan.

For an instant he stood there indecisively, with half a mind to face them down. Then rationality returned. Now it was he who turned and ran, rushing for the sanctuary of the tavern. If he could make that, he'd be safe; surely they'd attempt no violence in front of witnesses.

They were clattering after him. With every ounce of speed he had, he fled ahead of them. Now, the tavern doorway. His arm was outstretched to seize its handle when the fat waiter's figure loomed behind the glass. He heard something click and then a blind came down. He slammed against the door, but it was locked. Panting, he turned. Fanned out, they came off the square up onto the pavement, closing in. Lan straightened up. They would hurt him; but, he thought grimly, by damn, he would hurt them back. His heart was full of hatred then for them and all they represented.

They were smiling. Their kind always smiled when they had you trapped. They ringed him in, up close, the big one's eyes level with his own. The big one's teeth were very white. "*Grüss Gott*," he said almost pleasantly.

"*Bin Amerikaner*," Lan said.

"*Amerikaner? So?*" For an instant, he thought that had its effect; they looked curious and interested. Then the joker said something terse, and the big man moved. Lan turned to meet him, and the little blond one hit him hard above the kidneys. He rocked off balance, and the big one caught his outflung arm, twisted with tremendous strength, pivoting. Then he was in a hammerlock, arm twisted up behind his back, the cartilage in its joints almost on the verge of ripping. "Now," the big one said in his ear in English. "We go, *ja?*" His grip merciless, he frog-marched Lan down the deserted pavement and into a narrow alley.

"God damn you," Lan grunted. "Damn you, all you bastards."

7

Christa had hardly slept at all, dropping off finally around two in the morning, and even that rest was troubled. Now she awakened unrefreshed. It was a fine morning, but she took no pleasure in it. Ever since leaving Josef yesterday, she had been excited and confused. The prospect of marriage with Josef Steiner was not something to be dismissed out of hand. It had forced her to look hard at herself. What she had seen had not pleased her. She could see no special virtues to recommend her to anyone. But Josef had seen something in her—challenges, riches, he had said—which he yearned to develop. Was it possible he could hand her the key to unlock herself and set free the things she had always felt within her, but which, when she looked for them, she had never found? Or did he mean it simply in a sexual sense—to teach her his own voluptuous sensuality? That, too, had its own attractiveness.

She brought herself up short. *Hold on. You're forgetting one thing—love.* Love. Drawn as she was to him, excited as she was, did she love him? Slowly she shook her head.

No, there was the rub. Love was what she had seen between her parents—a continuing happiness enduring through even the excruciating pain of illness, a marvellous and magnificent emotion. But she was not Mama. A great love demanded greatness in the lovers, and she lacked Mama's greatness and surely would never find a man like Papa. Most people she knew seemed simply to have made do with what they could get in the way of love. And when what you could get was a man like Josef Steiner and a life of the sort he offered. . . . She did not know. All she knew was that she needed to confide in someone, and there was no one. Well, she would think about it later. Hoping it would clear her mind, she went to bathe and dress. At half past six she joined her father on the terrace. The General had long since had his breakfast, been about his work, but he always came to drink another cup of coffee with his daughter. Traudi brought her breakfast, and as she ate, she could feel his eyes, warm with affection, on her. And suddenly she made her decision. She had to tell him everything. Only he could help her reach a decision.

But even as she sought an opening, he said: "Christa, would you like to go to the wine fair this Friday? The Schellhammers and I are entered. We thought you might want to go too."

Christa was half amused, half angry. Poor Papa, so transparent.

296

He and Uncle Max would tend the exhibition booths, leave her fair game for Robert. Well, at least she had her opening now.

Before she could speak, though, there was another presence on the terrace. "Excuse me, Herr General," Traudi said, voice flustered. "There are gentlemen here to see Miss Christa. Police."

"At this time of the morning?" Helmer was astonished. "Please show them in."

"Yes, sir." Traudi disappeared.

Helmer stared at Christa, a frown ploughing his face. "Daughter, have you had an accident with your car?"

"Papa, I swear to you—" Then they were there, and Helmer rose to meet them: the local inspector in his iron-grey uniform, a Viennese officer in dark green.

"Sit down, gentlemen, have some coffee and some breakfast," Helmer said. "To what do we owe the honour of this visit?"

"No need to be alarmed," said the Viennese officer, dropping into a chair. "We seek your help. Early this morning a young man was found unconscious in an alley near the Naschmarkt. He had been badly beaten—several cracked ribs, a skull concussion, so the doctors say. He apparently will not recover consciousness for some time. He had also been robbed; his wallet and all identification were missing. However—" he looked at Christa "—the malefactors overlooked a slip of paper in his coat pocket. Perhaps you recognize this, Miss Helmer?" From his wallet he took out a sheet from a small notepad, handed it to her.

She stared at it, her name and address in her own handwriting. For a moment her mind was frozen. Then she remembered. "My God," she heard herself say. "It's the American."

For a long time Lan floated in darkness, aware occasionally of intense pain when he breathed in, but then someone would come with a needle and that would cease, yielding to dreams. Gradually, however, the confusion and darkness receded, and he awakened to find himself in a small tan-painted room, lying between crisp sheets, his head and torso wrapped with stiff bandages.

Policemen came, asked questions, went away. A gentle nun with a face like an aged chipmunk's fed him porridge. She spoke only

297

German, patted his hand reassuringly and left. He found himself strangely content. All power of decision had been taken from him. . . .

There was a discreet knock at the door, and then the chipmunk-nun ushered in another woman. She wore a huge-brimmed straw summer hat with flowers on it, and a sleek blue summer dress; she was young, blonde, very beautiful. He immediately knew her: Christa Helmer. "I'm sorry," he said. "I haven't got around to sending for your books."

She smiled. "Good morning, Mr. Condon. Never mind the books. How are you feeling?"

"Fair, all things considered."

The blue-grey eyes were concerned. "You're very lucky. You had a bad concussion of the brain and some cracked ribs. But Dr. Kleinmann says you will be perfectly all right."

"Good. Maybe you could tell me where I am?"

"Of course. You're in the Altkreuzburg hospital. You were first taken to hospital in Vienna. Your attackers took your wallet and passport and all identification. But the slip of paper I gave you with my address was in your jacket pocket, and so the police came to us." The late afternoon sunlight struck her face, bringing out its high-cheekboned elegance, the sensuality of her mouth. "The Vienna General Hospital is crowded, so Papa and I decided you would be much better off here in Altkreuzburg. Dr. Kleinmann is a dear friend of ours and a fine doctor. You're in good hands, so you needn't worry about anything but getting well."

Devoid now of the tension that had gripped him on that Sunday, Lan thought he had never in his life seen a girl more lovely. Yet, strangely, she had none of the hard arrogance of a great beauty.

"That," he said, "is a lot of trouble to go to for a stranger."

"Well, I suppose that's just the point. We are Austrians and proud of our country. Now truly, could we let you, a visitor from a great country like America, go home and say all Austrians are Nazis, brutes and thieves? And it was really no trouble. Dr. Martinus said you were staying at the Sacher. We had them store your baggage—" She broke off. "Papa said not to count on your attackers being caught. Nobody in the tavern will have seen a thing. Nobody wants trouble. Besides, he says, many Vienna police are Party members."

They were all the same, Lan thought, cops, Viennese or American.

She said, "You must be very tired. I should leave now."

"No. No, please stay, if you can. I want to thank you for all you've done. You and your father. And I owe you money."

She shrugged. "Such matters can be settled later, Papa says. Now—" He was surprised when she touched his hand briefly, reassuringly. "You are not to worry about anything. There are two visiting times a day, but I imagine Dr. Kleinmann will let me see you more often. You will be here perhaps ten more days, he says. After that, for perhaps three more weeks, you must rest and live very quietly." She paused. "Really. It was a brave thing you did."

Lan grinned wryly. "It was a stupid thing."

"I think it was admirable. Here everyone minds his own business very, very closely. There are not many who would have done what you did." She opened her handbag and took out a notebook and fountain pen. "It occurred to me that there must be people in the United States you'd want to notify. If you'll speak very slowly, I'll try to write any letters you wish to send. But you must help me. My English spelling is absolutely dreadful."

"There's only my agent in California."

Her brows went up. "No other people? No wife?"

"My parents are dead, and I was an only child. And I've never been married. A cable to the agent will do."

"Very well." He dictated it and she read it back. "I'll send it right away. Mr. Condon."

"Lan," he said. "It's my first name. Or what everybody calls me. In California everybody calls everybody by first names."

"Really? So soon after meeting? Here one has to know someone for a very long time before one uses a given name. But—" her forehead wrinkled slightly, charmingly, as she considered. "But I rather think I like the California way, Lan. So you must call me Christa." She giggled slightly, then was serious. "When you're stronger, I hope you will tell me all about America."

"Sure," he said. "I—" But then the nurse stuck her head in and said something cautionary, and Christa rose.

"Oh, dear. Now I must leave. May I come tomorrow?"

"You'd better. You're my only link with the outside world. Without you, I'm stranded."

"Then I shall be here." She took his hand, shook it gently.

AT THIS TIME of year it was not dark until nearly nine, and there was still daylight left as Christa drove slowly home. "Lan," she said aloud, aware of pleasure and excitement within her. Something was happening to her, something nice. She did not dare try to analyse it, but she thought she discerned the outlines of a miracle. Why else should he have had that slip of paper in his pocket, why else should the police have come just minutes before she was going to tell Papa about Josef Steiner? Why else had she conceived the idea, persuaded Papa to have him moved to Altkreuzburg, and so excused her from going to the wine fair? She had not at that time even known that he was single, or that he was so nice.

Now she had something else in mind; and that might take more cleverness on her part, for Papa might offer more resistance. Still, it shouldn't be too difficult, especially if. . . . Yes, that's it. She must be very nice to Robert. Divert attention until. . . . But, she thought, that still left Josef Steiner. What about Josef? She decided, she did not want to think about Josef right now. She would think about him later. Right now what she wanted was to cherish this strange excitement. . . .

As Christa entered the hall, she heard the sound of voices from her father's study and knocked on the door. "Come in," the General said. All three men stood up as she entered: Max Schellhammer, Robert, and her father.

"Uncle Max." She went to him first. He was short, hard as a chunk of oak, in sweater, short lederhosen, and knee socks. As always, he smelled of schnapps, tobacco.

"Christa, *Schatzi!*" He patted her back uncle-fashion. His hair was short, salt-and-pepper, his face seemingly covered with old wrinkled leather, his eyes bright blue, lively.

She patted his cheek. "I guess you won all the prizes at the wine fair!"

"Not I," his voice was resonant with pride. "The expert there." He jerked his thumb towards Robert. "There must be something to his newfangled ways after all."

Christa turned to Robert. The adoration in his eyes made her uncomfortable, but she masked that. "My congratulations," she said and went to him and kissed him briefly on the lips.

"Now, that's the real prize!" Uncle Max exclaimed.

Robert glowed. "Thank you very much. I really was quite pleased." Dressed like his father in leather, and with his strong bare legs, he was almost breathtakingly masculine; that she had to acknowledge. She turned away from him, kissed her father. "May I join you for a glass of wine, or is this business?"

"Nothing special." He found a glass for her and poured.

"By the way, how's the American?" said Uncle Max.

"Improving," she said. "Did you know he's a *writer?*"

"Not a very smart one, or he wouldn't be so crazy about Jews. But I suppose that's the way the Americans are. After all, they've got a Jewish president, that Rosenfeld." Uncle Max belched loudly and took another drink of wine. Then his face went hard. "It was the Americans, don't forget, *Schatzi*, who destroyed Austria. They could have stopped Clemenceau and Lloyd George from tearing us apart in 1919."

"Well, you can't make one American responsible for his government's mistakes," Robert said, surprising her. "The real Americans—the ones of English or German or Scandinavian heritage—are on our side." He put down his glass. "Incidentally, Christa, it couldn't possibly have been Party members who did that to him. He just got mixed up with some of those thugs who hang around the Naschmarkt. He should have used better judgment."

Christa thought, I must not lose sight of my objective, and she nodded. "The whole thing is rather hazy. Anyway, he's coming along nicely. Papa, I think in a day or two you should drop in on him. He'll want to talk about the expenses of all this with you."

"Yes. I'll find the time," the General said in a neutral voice.

"Good." Christa stood up. "It's an absolutely lovely night and I'm going out to walk in the park." She glanced at Robert. "Maybe someone would come along and tell me about the wine fair."

Max Schellhammer grinned. "It was your show, boy, not mine. I don't think she means me."

Robert stood up, pleased. "No, *Vati*, I don't think she means you. General, you will excuse us?"

DARKNESS had settled over the Vienna Woods; a crescent moon rode high above a distant ridge. The air was perfumed with the smell of forests, meadows, grass, and flowers. Robert and Christa walked under the old lindens on the dew-wet lawn.

"I'm very pleased about your prizes," she said. "And sorry this thing about the American came up. But what's one to do?"

"You're too softhearted for your own good," Robert said, but his voice was easy, loving. "Still, I guess you did the right thing. Only . . . it was all a little spoiled because you weren't there."

She found that touching, and she wondered, Why can't I just be friends with Robert? Why does he have to fall in love with me? She steeled herself for what she had to do, because it was going to be fairly ugly.

She took his hand in hers. "Let's walk," she said.

They walked to the wall, climbed up on a step, and looked out at the sparse lights twinkling in the Ferntal. Robert put his arm around her. "There's a Garbo film coming to the cinema in Altkreuzburg on Monday," he said quietly. "Will you go with me? I know you worship Garbo."

"But you said she bores you."

"I can stand her if it will make you happy."

"Thank you," she said. "I'd love to go."

Emboldened, he suddenly bent and kissed her on the mouth and she sensed the hunger and yearning in him, felt pity and affection and she gave a little of herself.

When he raised his head, however, she tried not to look at his eyes. Instead, she deliberately shivered. "Let's go in, it's getting chilly."

"Here, take my sweater, Christa."

He draped the sweater, warm with his body heat, about her shoulders. "I don't want you catching cold," he said. Then putting his arm around her, he led her into the house.

8

By the end of the first week in the hospital at Altkreuzburg, Lan had begun to realize what was happening to him, but he did not know what to do. At first he was amused. After all, for two years he had devoted every working day to plotting love stories by formulae as well-established as Newton's laws of motion. But what was happening between himself and Christa bore no relation to any of that, and cynicism was no armour against it. She came to see him at least twice a day, and for him those hours were so full of a strange tension it nearly crackled as they talked.

It was refreshing to find a woman who matter-of-factly betrayed a sense of values without embarrassment, even if the values were not always his. He was dumbfounded, too, by her range of knowledge—of literature and music and art and the world—which, he supposed, was what was meant by a European education. Above all she was young and lovely and desirable, and he wanted her, wanted possession in every possible way, and could not now imagine, if he had her, ever wanting anybody else.

She was sitting now on the chair in the room as he lay on the bed. As always, the door was discreetly left slightly open, a precaution insisted upon by the nursing sisters. She laughed in a deep husky way that moved something inside him. "What a strange people you are, with your cowboys and gangsters and your Wall Street."

"No stranger than you and your wine and music and dancing."

"We are not like that at all," she said stiffly. "We are very serious and industrious."

"Then how come Willi Orlik told me that the philosophy of Austria is 'Elsewhere the situation may be serious, but it is not hopeless. In Austria it is hopeless, but it is never serious'?" She laughed. "The impression I got from him, is that you're living in a Germanic fairyland."

"Not a fairyland," she said. "And you must understand that we are not Germans, either. I have German, Austrian, Rumanian, English, Hungarian, Serbian, and Italian blood in my veins. So I think you could hardly call me German." She shrugged. "I am what I am."

"And I," said Lan, "am pure Anglo-Saxon, both sides." And then he heard himself say, "What extraordinary children we'll have with all those strains."

"I—" She sat up straight, and he was as unprepared for the change in her face as he had been for his own statement. Her eyes widened, and her lower lip trembled as she stared at him. "I beg your pardon?" she whispered.

"I said, what extraordinary children we'll produce." Clad in his dressing gown, he swung off the bed, stood up. Her eyes followed him as if she were hypnotized. He went to the door, closed it.

"That is not allowed," she whispered. "The sisters—"

"Damn the sisters. Christa, I love you and I intend to marry you." And he came to her and took her hand.

She dropped her cigarette case. It clattered on the floor.

"And we *will* produce some extraordinary children," he said, and pulled her to her feet and kissed her.

He felt the slenderness of her against him, and smelled her perfume and found her lips to be very soft. And for just one instant her body was rigid. Then it pressed against him, and her arms went about him, and he felt a great surge of triumph and happiness. When finally they broke apart, she moved only a little distance away, keeping her hands on him. Her eyes were shining. "How did you *know?*" she whispered.

"I don't know. I just knew."

"So did I. Oh, Lan—"

"God, I love you," he said, and they kissed again.

Just after they broke apart that time, the door opened, and a young nun said something threatening. Christa replied, and the sister went away, lips pursed.

Christa turned back to him.

"Oh," she said, "I wish you understood German. It would be so much easier to say it now."

"I understand *Ich liebe dich.*"

She shook her head wonderingly. "Then I'll say *Ich liebe dich.*"

He let go her hands, turned towards the table, picked up an envelope. "I've already written my agent. I'm not going back to Hollywood. I'm going to stay here. For a while, anyhow. Write another book. The studio can sue me if they want to, but I don't think they will. It won't be worth their while, really." He grinned. "You see, I plan ahead. I even asked Dr. Martinus when he visited me yesterday, about joining the Church, in case your father made an issue of it. It would take about two months, Martinus said."

Christa laughed, then came to him, pressed her head against his chest, regardless of the open door. "You planned. . . . How delightful." She drew back. Her smile was wicked. "Because I have also planned. After all, you must have three weeks to regain your health somewhere. And where else but the Christinahof? There was Papa to deal with. . . . But I have everything in *Ordnung.* Now, you must not be jealous if . . ." and then she told him about Robert Schellhammer.

"Poor Robert," she finished. "I feel badly about it, but I simply don't love him. Papa thinks it would be a good marriage, and if he thought you would spoil it, he would not consent to your coming to our house. So for the last few days, I have given Robert—and Papa—much encouragement. Now you will come to the Christinahof for three weeks to rest. Papa will come to know you and fall in love with you like I did, and after that it will be easy. Except," she said, a little sadly, "for Robert."

"Christa, I don't *need* to come there. I have money enough to take an apartment in Vienna."

"But then I could only see you two or three times a week. At the Christinahof we could be together every day."

"Sold," he said.

"I am a terrible woman," she said. "I know it. But I love you, and I will do anything for you. You are the first man I ever loved so much that I didn't care what I did to anybody else."

"I'd better be the last one, too."

"Listen," she said. "All my life I've dreamed of finding someone to love as my mother loved my father. Now I have him. And please—" she gripped his hand, as if in sudden fear "—you must not ever leave me."

"Never," he said, and took her in his arms. "Never, never."

"Then," she murmured, "everything will be all right."

Much later the nurse came again to push the door wider. "And now," Christa whispered, "I must go." In defiance of the watching nun, she kissed him briefly on the lips. "Tonight I shall finish all the arrangements with Papa. And in only a few more days you'll be at the Christinahof."

"I don't care where," he said. "Just where you are."

They looked at each other, and laughed; then she went out.

CLIMBING THE STAIRS of Josef's building Christa felt armoured against anything that could happen. She would have preferred not to be here at all, but there was no way she could snap her fingers and make Josef Steiner vanish. She had been lax. Instead of making constant excuses on the telephone, she should have seen him and put an end to all of it long before now. Well, today she would do that.

In the corridor, she rang the bell beneath the nameplate SCHMIDT. Almost at once Josef himself opened the door. "You! Thank God you've finally come! I've been going mad, brain cell by brain cell!"

He pulled her in and closed the door. Then he tried to kiss her. She moved away. He stared at her, stricken. "So," he said. Then. "Let's go into the living room."

"Yes," Christa said, and went ahead of him.

"Please sit down," Josef said, motioning her to the sofa. He stood above her like a desperate waiter, long fingers intertwined. "What would you like to drink?"

"Nothing, thank you."

There was silence in the room. Then he said, "Before you say anything, I want you to know that I have handled all this very badly. From the very beginning. I have repeated in my mind every word that I said last time, and . . . I must have sounded like an idiot, and looked like one, too, here in this place." He turned, gestured. "This—" his lip curling "—absurd den of iniquity."

He turned to face her. "I did nothing right—nothing. First, my talk of money, as if I'd tried to buy you. How you must have laughed at that! And then explaining how industrious I am! But I withheld from you the one thing that *is* important to me. And I see now that if I cannot trust you—" his face darkened "—and I mean with my very life, then you would be right to reject me for lack of faith in you."

Christa stared at him.

"I am many things," Josef said. "And one of them is a Jew. And because of that, I am a member, a leader, of an organization with two purposes to which I have dedicated my life and fortune. The first is to rescue as many Jews from Germany as possible. The second is to overthrow Adolf Hitler."

Whatever she had expected, it was not this. The two of them were silent for half a minute, frozen in a tableau, staring at each other. Then Josef went to the cabinet, took out brandy and a glass, poured himself a drink. He took a swallow of the brandy, faced her, his eyes lambent above the dark circles beneath them.

"It all began with pleas for help; letters that would break your heart. We were Jews and we were rich and powerful and, best of all, outside the Third Reich. And where else should the poor Jews inside Germany turn but to us? So, I begged my brothers to throw the whole weight of the firm behind helping those poor people. But they refused. Business is business, and the German government's bonds were a substantial part of our investments." His voice went harsh. "That is why I finally broke with them. My reputation as a dissolute rogue fortunately gave us a good reason for the break and gives me a fair disguise."

"Josef, this is incredible," Christa whispered.

"But true. Through certain channels, I pay passage—or ransom —for as many as possible. But there are hundreds of thousands, and the number I can help is only a drop in the bucket. There really is only one way to save them all—change Germany. And the only way to change Germany is to destroy Adolf Hitler. In the long run, that's my aim."

307

Christa stood up. "Josef, please don't tell me any more. Such talk is dangerous. Even here in Austria, if it got out—"

"My darling," Josef said, "I know all that. If you speak a word outside these walls, I am destroyed. But the truth about myself is my gift of love to you."

"Josef, I think I'd better go."

"No." He interposed himself between her and the door. "Not until I finish. Please."

Resignedly she nodded.

"What I'm saying may sound mad. I assure you it is not. To the outside world, Christa, Hitler looks to be all-powerful. But he's not. Right now his throne is shaky. There is a chance, given cleverness or luck, of disposing of him and his gang. I can't tell you how or when, but while the chance exists, it *must* be taken." He spread his hands. "So there you have it. The secret life of Josef Steiner. I lay it at your feet."

Christa swallowed hard. If two weeks ago he had told her this, laid himself bare like this, she might well have said yes on the spot. But not now. The thought of Lan possessed her wholly. "Josef," she heard herself say in a tone that left no room for doubt. "There is someone else."

For a moment he was silent. Then he dragged the back of his hand across his mouth wearily. "Not the American?"

"How did you know about him?"

His smile was weary. "I know almost everything that goes on. Far more than I should like to. Christa, his need for you is temporary, mine is deep, and—"

"Josef, stop it, please."

"But it's not fair. You've only known him a few days—"

"I know," she answered. "But it's happened, and there's nothing I can do about it. Just like it happened to Mama, she said, when she first saw Papa." She raised a hand, dropped it.

"So," Josef's mouth twisted. "Well, thank God it's not that Schellhammer."

Her brows went up. "You know about him too?"

"Yes. He's a Nazi, of small consequence right now, but likely to be of much more later on, if there's *Anschluss*. It's necessary for me

308

to know about all such; they are my enemies." His eyes met hers. "You need repeat only a fraction of what I've told you to Robert Schellhammer and I'm a dead man."

She stared at him, touched by a chill. "Robert wouldn't—"

"Robert would—and leap at the chance. He's a fanatic, and as dangerous as a loaded pistol. Don't ever deceive yourself about him. You've seen what his comrades did to the American. He's not one jot different from them."

Suddenly she could not bear being here and subject to his intensity any longer. "I shall do my best to guard your secret, Josef," she said levelly. "But remember, I didn't ask to know it, and—"

"And if you slip. . . . Yes, that's a risk I've made up my mind to take. I know you, Christa, and I don't think you will slip."

"I want to go."

He moved to the door. "Surely. For your sake, Christa, I hope it may work out for you and the American. If not, I'll be waiting." Then, very formally, he kissed her hand and said *auf Wiedersehen*.

9

Through the freshness of early summer morning, Helmer walked across the courtyard, passed through the arch in its wall and, a couple of hundred yards farther on, entered the heart of the Christinahof—the pressing house and bottling works. He strode past the machinery, unlocked a massive door, switched on a light. He descended ancient steps of stone into the labyrinth of cellars honeycombing the interior of the mountain.

The only ranks he commanded now, the General thought, were these ranks of oaken casks, cradled in lines along each wall, with choice vintages maturing in them. He walked down the aisle between them slowly, pausing here and there to stare at the head of one or another. These were the ones whose ends bore intricate carved bas-reliefs, some decades, even centuries old, which would have done credit to any museum. There was one to commemorate his purchase of the Christinahof, with Christina's name and a view of the house itself wrought in the dark wood. And a row of others, one for each wedding anniversary, until—

Until, he thought, and braced himself against the remembered horror. Cancer, and a long courageous time in dying, and no way he could end her misery. But he knew one thing for certain: she had been his woman, and there would never be another one. How he missed her! And, God knows, just now, because of Christa, he missed her more than ever.

He could, he thought, manoeuvre a regiment, command a division, manage an estate; but his inability to handle one young girl seemed total. It was as if they spoke two languages that sounded exactly the same but in which each word had contrary meaning. His sister Alma was no help, and he was worried.

More and more it appeared to him that Christa was tending to skate on thin ice. That minor scandal, the picture in the magazine, had been a symptom; soon something must be done, a choice made. If necessary, for her own good, he would make the choice for her: Robert Schellhammer.

If Christina were alive, she'd have put an end to that at once. To her it would have been unthinkable, marriage of Christa to a farmer's son. But in this era no rules held—and Robert was no ordinary farmer. He was educated, would someday inherit a fortune at least as large as Helmer's own. Until this spring, Helmer's only objection to him had been his politics. But now these had become an advantage. The handwriting was on the wall. Helmer knew the Nazis. If you were not with them, you were against them. He had not been with them. But if he had a son-in-law, one destined to rise when the Nazis gained control, he would have perfect protection for his dangerously exposed flank.

And then Christa had suddenly kicked all his careful plans to flinders! Helmer grimaced, but the grimace changed to a smile of almost fond admiration. If nothing else, she had at any rate inherited his genius for strategy; and the way she had outmanoeuvred him in the matter of the American had been smooth and expert.

Still, there was no way he could have known that morning when the police came what would happen. And Christa had been right —it was something that, as Austrians, they owed the man. And arranging to have him moved to Altkreuzburg had been simple.

Nor had there been anything untoward about Christa seeing

him every day—he did need a translator. He simply could not be left there in isolation. For that matter, Helmer had dropped in on him twice himself, had found him likeable, and interesting. Martinus had been there during one of his visits and they had left together. Helmer had asked, "What do you think of Condon?"

"A very decent chap," Martinus said, "in my estimation, extremely talented. And it's really amazing how his brush with death has turned his mind towards spiritual matters. He wants to receive instruction for conversion to the Holy Mother Church."

And that, Helmer thought now, was when he should have smelled a rat. A bell had rung in the back of his head, but, at the moment, not quite loud enough. And it was true, a narrow escape did make men consider the condition of their souls.

The bell had sounded louder as he watched Christa. He thought he saw something in her eyes after each visit to the hospital. His misgivings grew—until she disarmed them. Her visits tapered off and suddenly she was paying attention to Robert. Several nights in a row she'd gone out with him. By the time her real assault was mounted, he had been distracted by the diversion that she'd created. Otherwise he would under no circumstances have agreed to Lan Condon coming to the Christinahof to recuperate. And even now, to Helmer, much of how she'd managed it remained a mystery. Somehow she'd overcome his reservations, obtained his consent, and set to work arranging a room for Condon on the ground floor, so he'd have as few stairs to climb as possible.

The day after that she brought him home to the Christinahof. Two days later, when he noticed that Robert had not appeared or called, he asked her about it. "Robert?" she replied off-handedly. "Oh, we had a quarrel. Really, Papa, he can be so stupid—"

"A quarrel about what?"

"Oh, just things." She shrugged, and, seeing her complete indifference, the General sighed. There was nothing he could do.

And now Condon had been here for nearly three weeks, and even a blind man could have seen it. Max Schellhammer was not blind. Together, walking over their hunting grounds one afternoon, they had paused to rest on a fallen log. Max tamped his pipe. "Well, Kurt, we have trouble."

Helmer looked at him keenly. "What kind of trouble?"

"Girl trouble, boy trouble. Christa and Robert. She's hurt the boy, hurt him as bad as anything I've ever seen."

"Max, I'm sorry. What—?"

"She led him on, built up his hopes; then she threw him over. Now he's angry at the whole damn world." Max shook his head. "Oh, I don't blame you. But that American, he's a mistake." Max turned, fixed Helmer with keen blue eyes. "What'll you do if he marries her and takes her off across the ocean?"

"Max—"

"It could happen. For Robert's sake, I hope you're firm with her."

Helmer then was suddenly rankled. As if, he thought, Robert were all that counted. He stood up. "Max, in the long run the main thing is for her to be happy. What *she* wants must be considered."

"Excuse me," said Max, "but what she wants and what is good for her may be two different things."

"Yes, but that's something that only she and I together can decide." There was an edge to Helmer's voice. It was one thing for him to dictate his daughter's future, quite another for an outsider to attempt that.

Max looked at him obliquely, then took the schnapps flask and cup from his rucksack and poured a drink. Tossing it off, noisily smacking his lips, he rose. "Excuse me, Kurt, but what she did to Robert was not nice."

"No," Helmer said. "I'm sorry."

"And when you think," Max said, "what it could be here in the Ferntal someday if those two got together. . . . You and I could sit back and take it easy then."

"Yes, we could take it easy," Helmer said. Greed, he thought, that was what he heard in Schellhammer's voice; and suddenly he looked at the stumpy farmer with new eyes. Something within him rebelled. He could hear Christina saying *No. Absolutely not.* And he saw himself, too, in a new light. But his voice was mild when he said, "Well, we'll see how it all works out. . . ."

The fact was, the more he'd seen of Condon, the more he liked him. The man was well-spoken and had a quick, clear mind; he was learning German with amazing speed. And as for money— people who wrote motion pictures raked it in. He had courage, too, and a quality of gallantry rare nowadays, or he would not have tried to help that Jew against the Nazis.

And he was no indoor man, no hothouse flower. He had talked with fair knowledge of guns and hunting. But—in God's name, what was he trying to do? Make a case for Condon as a son-in-law? A foreigner, a man whose family and origins were still unknown, uncheckable? A writer, a breed notoriously unstable? One who might take Christa thousands of miles away, leaving an emptiness in his life he was not sure that he could bear?

And yet. . . . Helmer remembered a girl in white across a seething ballroom, a girl so young, so lovely in the muted light; and he remembered, too, a soldier already in his middle thirties, from a foreign land and his parents simple people of the back country. What if he had not been able to convince Christina's parents? Suppose she had not used all her wiles, played merciless-ly on their love for her?

Max was wrong, he thought. Happiness must come first. They would, he was sure, present him with the necessity of decision soon. But he knew the decision was already made, not by him, not even by Condon and his daughter, but by Christina.

WHEN THEY HAD FINISHED, silence hung thickly in General Helmer's study. He had listened carefully for fifteen minutes, as first Lan had spoken and then Christa. Lan had kept his voice steady, confident, displaying neither arrogance nor humility; Christa's had trembled with passion. And now there was nothing more for them to say until the General spoke.

Which he did not do. Instead, his eyes went from one of them to the other, probingly, and he ground out his cigarette in the ashtray and rose, neat, imposing in his grey suit; and he stood there wordlessly looking through the window. Christa and Lan stared at his back and then at each other. She opened her mouth, but Lan gestured her to silence.

313

After a pair of minutes stretching to infinity, the General turned. "I give my consent," he said. "With conditions."

"Oh, Papa!" Christa stood up, voice full of relief and tears.

Helmer smiled at her a little wanly. "These conditions. The marriage will take place within the Church. And in not less than sixty days. During that time, Mr. Condon, I shall ask you to remain as our guest here at the Christinahof. I think the sixty-day limit is fair. The two of you have not known each other very long—"

"You and Mama hadn't either," Christa said, but she was laughing.

"No. But her family certainly saw to it that the wedding was postponed until we did." He turned to Lan. "You will also give your word that you and Christa will remain in Austria for at least a year after the wedding. Partly because it will take some time to become accustomed to . . . the prospect that you might take her away. That is wholly selfish on my part. But also . . . it is necessary for a man to understand his wife. You will never understand Christa without understanding Austria, and a year will hardly be time enough for that. You will be happier for it. Mr. Condon, do you agree?"

Lan stood up jubilantly, admiration for Helmer's insight swirling in him. "Yes, sir; you're being very fair."

"Then good. I congratulate you on your choice of a woman and on being chosen by such a woman, and I hope the two of you will be entirely happy." And as Christa cried out and ran to him, he put out his hand to Lan.

WHEN, MUCH LATER, the two of them were gone, Helmer went once more to the window. Suddenly he felt old. "I think I did the right thing," he said aloud, not addressing himself. "They were so much like the two of us." He sighed faintly. Well, her happiness came first, but now the fat was in the fire. No more Robert Schellhammer, and Max would be unhappy; he wondered if even his diplomacy could smooth it over. His flank was still exposed, and he must move swiftly, rearrange his affairs to cover it. Well, he could do that somehow. He could manage. He always had.

314

They were married in August 1936 in the ancient Baroque parish church attached to the monastery of Altkreuzburg. Christa, sitting, kneeling, standing beside Lan during the various phases of the ceremony, had seemed to float in a mist of white, the veiled pearl-seeded dress that had belonged to her mother. Afterwards there had been a reception where wine flowed freely at the largest tavern in the town. Lan knew enough German by then to understand the congratulations and make the responses, but not much more. Finally, heads buzzing, they had escaped in the General's ribbon-decked Mercedes, leaving the party to roar on without them. Christa leaned against him as he drove, and Lan held her tightly. His wife, he thought, with disbelief. He was amazed to find himself so full of primitive emotions at the age of thirty-three.

Those sixty days had sped by. With Christa as guide and interpreter, they had roamed Vienna, attending concerts and the Opera and a few private parties, had explored the Wienerwald, swum at Baden, and listened to music in the park. Martinus conducted them on a tour of the monastery at Altkreuzburg, a vast, cold labyrinth full of treasures and the relics of saints. To Lan the countryside had seemed a kind of jewel box, packed with unexpected pleasures. But Christa was the real treasure trove, the unending source of surprise and delight to him.

Now, the marriage was accomplished and they drove up the Danube to Krems. At an inn perched on a cliff above the river in this wild, romantic mountain valley they spent their first night.

For Lan that night was a revelation. It seemed they could never get enough of each other. Christa was not, of course, experienced but she was full of natural passion that made everything exquisite.

The next day they drove on up the river, where each rocky peak was crowned with a castle's remnants, like grim, tattered skeletal eagles on their perches. In Spitz, a town at a valley's mouth, they paused for lunch in a restaurant's garden on the riverbank. There they watched strings of barges pushing up and down the stream. A white passenger ship, a stately sidewheeler, passed them. Lan was about to comment on it when Christa raised her head, eyes widening, and laid down her fork. "Josef," she said.

"Frau Condon," a quiet voice said. "Herr Condon." The tall lean form in the black suit moved around the table, coming into Lan's vision. "I congratulate you on your happiness. Mr. Condon, perhaps you don't remember me, but we met once at the Christinahof."

"I remember you," Lan said. Christa had told him something of what had gone on between her and Josef Steiner. *But he is not at all what he seems,* she had said. She had volunteered no more than that. Steiner had not been invited to the wedding.

"May I join you for a moment?" He sat down without waiting for assent, ordered a glass of wine. Lan watched him suspiciously. "So. Beautiful weather for a honeymoon. How nice you're passing through the Wachau and I have this chance to see you."

"Yes," answered Christa quickly. "We're driving on to Melk after lunch and then to Salzburg. I'm showing Austria to my husband. After the Tyrol we'll come back through Carinthia."

"And you will live in Vienna?"

"Yes," Lan said. "We've sublet an apartment there."

"Delightful. But please, before you move on, can't you let me show you Schloss Schwarzgipfel? It's only twenty minutes in that direction." He gestured up the valley.

"That's very kind of you," Christa said at once, "but I'm afraid we simply haven't time today. Another time, perhaps. We'll be coming to the Wachau often."

Steiner nodded. "Yes, of course. Another time." For only an instant a shadow of melancholy crossed his face. His wine came, and he raised his glass. "To your happiness."

"Thanks," Lan said, sensing in the man a curious vulnerability.

"I was just passing, saw you sitting in the garden, couldn't resist intruding. Now. . . ." He took another swallow of wine and rose. "I shall be getting along. Again, Mr. Condon, my best wishes. And to you, Christa, my dear." He kissed her hand. "Perhaps I may call on you in Vienna when you are settled? I should very much like to talk to you some more about the United States, Mr. Condon."

Lan felt as if he were being appraised, and not necessarily as the victorious rival. Was there something Steiner wanted of him, a proposition to be broached at a later date? Curiosity aroused, he said, "Sure. We'd be glad to see you." And he gave Steiner the address of the apartment.

When Josef was gone, Christa looked at Lan oddly. "I'm not sure I want—"

"Don't worry. I'll protect your honour. But there's something about him that makes me want to know him better. He's up to something, and I'm wondering what." Then, at the expression on her face, he broke off. "You already know."

Christa licked her lips. "I promised not to tell. Not to anyone."

He stared at her, felt a sudden stab of jealousy, forced himself to say, "Well, if you're honour-bound not to tell me. . . ."

But when she saw that he would not press her, she reversed herself. "On the other hand, I don't know why I couldn't tell *you*. But not here. Wait until we're in the car."

Driving on up the river, she told him. "I don't know whether it's true or only to impress me."

Lan considered. "I'm pretty sure it's true. Well, at least he's doing *something*, which is more than a hell of a lot of other people can say. But—overthrow Hitler! He's sure playing in the big league." He said no more, but was doubly intrigued now and hoped the man had meant it about seeing them in Vienna. Then, he and Christa travelled deeper into Austria and he forgot Steiner.

As THEY SWUNG through Carinthia, Lan began to see there were a great many things the Austrians accepted that few Americans would tolerate. Having to turn over their passports for registration with the police at every overnight stop, for instance. And the endless forms and stamps necessary for even the slightest official transaction. Then when they moved into their apartment on the Argentinierstrasse, almost in the heart of the city, what shocked him most was going to the news kiosk to buy a paper, only to find that the government had confiscated the entire edition or that great white spaces were left where stories had been censored. Still, he had to remind himself that this was, as Willi Orlik had

317

warned him, a Fascist dictatorship for all the courtesy and smoothness, the gaiety and cultivation of the flow of everyday life. And most of the opposition against it came not from rebels seeking the return of a democracy, but simply from opposing factions like the Austrian Nazis, and Reds, who sought to install their own system of totalitarianism.

Even in Christa he saw it: not so much an indifference to political freedom as an ignorance of it. This acceptance, this passivity before authority, sometimes infuriated Lan and always made him uncomfortable. But for the moment it was an almost imperceptible taint of uneasiness in what was otherwise sheer happiness.

11

Rocketing out of the brush, the cock pheasant climbed straight up, wings blurring, long tail streaming. For half a second before it levelled off, it seemed to hang, pasted, against the cold grey sky. Lan's shotgun roared, the spread wings folded, and heavily it plummeted to earth.

"Good shot!" Robert exclaimed, lowering his own weapon.

Lan broke the gun, replaced the spent shell, and then descended into the wooded gully to help the dog find the bird.

Standing there in the beet field at the gully's edge, Robert Schellhammer watched Lan's back, clad in green loden-cloth, disappear among the trees; when it vanished, he consciously relaxed the clamped grip of his hands on the gun. How easy it would have been, he thought, how simple, at that moment of the bird's rising. An accident, of course. . . . But who could dispute that he had become confused, fired prematurely as Lan moved in front of him? His father and General Helmer were down inside the gully, and they could not have seen.

Schellhammer shook his head, lit a cigarette with hands that trembled slightly. I must be going mad, he thought. And yet, in that moment, when Lan, wholly absorbed, had raised his gun to aim at the upward spiralling bird, the temptation had been nearly irresistible.

The cold wind blew across the field; the sky darkened. For eighteen months, he thought, he had lived with his hatred for Lanier Condon, and it had never lessened, indeed had become more intense with every passing day. Beginning on that summer morning when Christa's Steyr had pulled into the driveway of the Schellhammerhof.

He had been supervising the loading of a lorry when he had seen the car stop and Christa get out, lovely in a summer dirndl. Something leaped within him; he felt a glow of satisfaction. She was coming back to him. He strode across the courtyard to her. Then, as he took her hand, reached to give her a brief kiss of greeting, he sensed something wrong. Her body was stiff; she did not respond. "Robert," she said. "I must talk to you."

"Surely. Come into the house." But already a knot was forming in his belly.

"No. Over there will be all right." She gestured to a table with wooden benches near the back door, where his family ate its midday meal on pretty days. He tried to smile as she sat down.

But her eyes were grave. "Robert—" And then she told him.

A chicken, dust-bathing, clucked somewhere. Pigeons on the cowstall roof cooed softly. Robert felt as if the ground had simply fallen away beneath his feet. "You must be joking," he said.

"No, I am not. Oh, Robert!" She jumped up and embraced him, laying her head against his chest. He raised his arms to embrace her, then let them drop. "Oh, Robert," and her voice was strangled. "I do so hate hurting you. I am so sorry, but. . . ."

I will not permit it! he wanted to bellow. He wanted to seize and shake her. I will not permit it! He mastered that impulse. Instead, he stood there motionless until pride came in a saving surge. By the time she had backed away, staring at him white-faced, he was in possession of himself again. "I'm sorry," she whispered once more.

"Sorry?" His voice was steady. "Why should you be sorry?" He managed the mixture of indifference and curiosity nicely, he thought.

"Because . . . I know it hurts you."

"Hurts me? Why should it hurt me? I'd think it's the General who'd be hurt. Your choosing to marry a foreigner, a stranger. But if you have his consent, you certainly don't need mine."

"You don't mind?" she asked wonderingly.

"Of course I mind. I don't want to see you throw yourself away on some . . . some mongrel foreigner. Still, if that's what it takes to make you happy. . . ." He looked at her opaquely. "My congratulations," he heard himself say, putting out his hand. Numbly she took it. Then he let hers drop. "Now, if you will excuse me, the driver is waiting for instructions. This business is quite important." He turned away. He could not face her for another instant. It was with relief that he heard the Steyr come to life, its engine's sound fading down the mountain.

At lunch that day he told his parents in an almost offhand way. Max, mouth full of black bread, sat up straight, jaws ceasing to work. Beneath his tan, he was pale, then red. "Are you serious?"

"I tell you what she told me." Robert went on eating; although he had no appetite, it was important to show that he did.

His father swallowed audibly. He struck the table so the dishes rattled. "Helmer must have lost his senses! He's a great man, but when it comes to her he's absolutely blind." He stood up. "I think I'd better go straight over and have a word with him!"

"No!" Robert almost roared. "It's none of our affair!"

Max stood there. "It is," he said at last, quietly. "It truly is. It changes everything we'd planned for the Ferntal. But. . . ." He came around the table and—it was not with him a usual gesture —laid one rough hand on Robert's shoulder. "All right."

Robert's mother said stoutly, "Frankly, I'm relieved. That girl's useless, she can't cook, can't clean, all she knows how to do is drive around in that car of hers with her fancy clothes and her nose up in the air. There are plenty of nice girls in Ferndorf and Altkreuzburg. Just the other day I met Charlotte Richter on the Hauptstrasse, and there's a fine young miss! And she asked about you and—"

"Bertha," Max growled.

"It's all right," Robert said. "It's nothing." He got up and, on impulse, kissed his mother on the temple. "Now, I'm going over to Professor Busch's. I've got some paper work to do."

THEY ALL CAME UP out of the gully: Lan, the General and Robert's father. the light was fading fast now, and Max, the appointed leader of the hunt, gave the command to unload guns. It had not been a formal affair, but still the rules had to be observed, and now there was the time-honoured ceremony of laying out the cumulative bag of pheasants and hares. Helmer's pride in Lan's marksmanship was obvious: six shots—four pheasants, two hares. "They teach them to shoot out there in the Wild West!"

Robert dropped the butt of his cigarette, ground it out. Lugging the game, they walked towards the car parked on a nearby farm road. Lan fell in beside him. "I enjoyed this," he said. "It was a fine day. I don't get out of the city often enough."

"You must come for the Big Hunt at the end of the season," Robert said, with automatic courtesy. He envisioned it, then: the great circle of guns and beaters; there would be a lot of shooting, and. . . . No, he thought. No. And yet, the thought that he would never have Christa now, never make her yield to him, was intolerable. Some day, he thought, I will have her, and I will make a cuckold of him. After we have won.

He took consolation in that thought. When they had won, he would be a man of power. Once the Party ruled and ruled completely, he could do anything he wanted, to anyone he wanted; and she would feel his power then. And that day was coming soon, he could feel it in his bones.

How masterly, he thought, the Führer had played his cards! His stroke last year had helped, to some extent, offset the shock of Christa's betrayal. In that month Hitler and von Schuschnigg had signed a treaty. In the clauses first made public, Germany had promised to respect Austria's sovereignty, not interfere in its internal affairs. In return, von Schuschnigg had promised to conduct Austrian policy with the full recognition that a special bond existed between the countries.

Secretly, however, von Schuschnigg had agreed that Nazi organizations could exist in Austria provided they did not propagandize. More important, the Austrian government had agreed to allow five German newspapers to circulate—including one that was the mouth-piece of Hermann Göring. And then the greatest coup of all. Von Schuschnigg had agreed to take Nazis into his cabinet. Oh, they were not overt National Socialists. "Pronounced Nationalists", they called themselves, but they were staunch adherents of the Führer.

So, almost immediately, though still officially illegal, the Party had surfaced. And from then on they were on the streets, demonstrating, fighting the counter-demonstrators of the Schuschnigg government. The police cracked down halfheartedly, but it was too late anyway. The great wave was towering now, about to break, destroying an old world, washing in a new one.

His men could hardly wait. Robert felt sympathy for them. They lived for the day when they could get their hands on wealth, the day when all the money of the Jews was forfeit to the Party; and they were the Party and they would get their share. Let them have the loot. He would take the power. He was already high in the province's shadow council: the Gauleiter knew him. Power, and then. . . . He looked at Lan beside him. And then he would decide. Maybe he would not even want her. But he knew he would. As they walked on through gathering darkness, he knew there would never be a time when he did not want her.

LAN, DRIVING home from the Schellhammers' shoot, passed Franz Josef Bahnhof, the grey pile of railway station named after the old Emperor, headed towards the city's centre and his home. Vienna, he thought, as the Steyr rattled over trolley tracks, was perhaps the only place where two such different people as Christa and himself could have so truly mingled. He loved the magnificent city, as he loved Christa, for its fascinating variousness and its grace.

The Helmer connections had gained him entrée into many levels of society. Fluent now in German, every day he came in contact with the ordinary people of the city; and, high and low, they all seemed friendly, warmhearted, easygoing. Yet the twin wolves, Depression and Germany, would not go away. And then the demonstrations, the near riots. The Nazis demonstrated at the slightest pretext, showing their massive muscle. And the same smiling taxi driver who bowed and called you Herr Baron one day would be there the next in a brown shirt or white stockings, cursing the Jews; for anti-Semitism was another ancient omnipresence in the city, as solid, central, and typical as the Opera.

All of that could be ignored, of course, if one chose to. Christa ignored it because it was something that had never impinged upon her own existence. Lan tried, too, because it was not really his business; as a foreigner, it was obvious that he had no right to have opinions. Besides, he was busy working on his novel. Anyhow, maybe, just maybe, all the problems would go away if properly ignored. That was, after all, the sovereign Viennese remedy—ignore, keep up appearances.

He turned into the Argentinierstrasse, then swung through the gates of the courtyard of his apartment building. Parking the Steyr, he was surprised to see Josef Steiner's black car also there. Usually Josef was meticulous about not calling unless certain he was home. Lan grinned faintly. It didn't matter; he supposed he trusted Josef. The main thing was he trusted Christa.

Josef, true to his request, had called, directly after they returned from their honeymoon. Lan found he enjoyed his company. Partly that was because he would have welcomed any man his age who spoke fluent English; but as time passed, he discovered that he and Josef had a great deal in common. Now Josef came often, or entertained them at his own luxurious house, and the friendship between the two men had ripened.

Their closeness, however, was intermittent. Steiner was gone from Vienna for long periods, sequestered at his *Schloss* in the Wachau. They too had other friends, and Lan had discovered the Café Louvre.

It was a coffeehouse, that uniquely Viennese institution of which there were hundreds in the city. Less café than club, each catered to its own specialized clientele—jewellers, perhaps, or politicians—who could, for the price of a single coffee prepared in any of the countless Viennese ways, linger all day without disturbance. The Louvre, because of its nearness to the National Telegraph Office, was the choice of foreign newspapermen in Vienna, among them several Americans and Englishmen who had formed a loose trade association; Lan, as a writer and former newspaperman, had found prompt acceptance among them. Now the Condons spent one or two evenings a week at the Louvre. Christa enjoyed them and the resulting friendships as much as Lan did.

With his gun and gamebag, and two hares dangling from his hand, Lan entered the building, took the antiquated lift to the third floor. He reached his apartment and, too heavily burdened to find his key, rang the bell, and Christa let him in.

"Oh, you had a good hunt!" she exclaimed and kissed him.

"Careful, I'm all bloody." He returned the kiss. "*Grüss di*, Josef. Rezi!" But the maid was already there, exclaiming over the game and taking it away to hang in the pantry.

"Home is the hunter," Josef said, grinning.

"Yeah, and glad to be here. Look, let mè wash and change. Good wife, what about a whisky with ice."

Everyone thought Lan mad for drinking iced drinks at all, much less at this season, but it was an Americanism he would not give up. She brought the drink, refilled Josef's wine glass and her own. Lan went off to the bedroom.

Josef sipped his wine. "It's wonderful the way you light up when he enters a room."

"Really? It's something I can't help."

"I know. And I know something else now. We would have been wrong for one another." It was the first time he'd mentioned that old relationship. "While I still feel a twinge of envy, it gives me a certain aesthetic pleasure to see such perfection of happiness. I only hope—" He broke off. "Christa, you and Lan should seriously consider going to America soon. Very soon."

"We've talked about it," she said, startled by his gravity. "And, of course, I'm dying to see the United States. But Lan doesn't want to go until the book's finished."

Steiner shifted restlessly. "Look, Christa, may I ask a favour? Could you hold dinner for perhaps half an hour? And make sure your girl doesn't disturb us. I need to talk to you and Lan. It's . . . important."

"Josef. What's wrong?"

"Christa, if it's not too much trouble—"

"Well, of course. I'll see to it right away." Puzzled, she went to the kitchen, gave instructions to Rezi, who was not pleased.

When Christa returned to the living room, Lan was there, in slacks, soft shirt, and cardigan. He shot her a puzzled glance as she went to the big wooden doors of the dining room and closed them, sealing off the area from Rezi's ears.

"Thank you." Steiner stood by the radiator, looking tensely from one of them to the other. "Christa, perhaps you remember one day long ago when I told you a secret about certain of my activities?"

"I . . . Yes. I remember."

"I asked you not to tell anyone. But, of course, that was before you married. Have you told Lan?"

"I . . ." Her face began to burn. "Josef—"

"She told me," Condon said. "She told me briefly, not in detail. She's told no one else, and neither have I."

"Then good," Josef said. "I'm glad she told you. It will save me some time." He paused. "I must ask if you will do me the favour of hearing more. You see Lan, I need—Austria needs—help which you can give without undue risk to Christa or yourself, and with very little effort. But I do not want you to agree to anything blind, and so first I must tell you the whole story, with only the condition that you will never repeat it."

Christa looked at Lan. He was frowning. Then he sat down on the sofa, motioned Josef to a chair. "All right," he said. "Sure. You have our promises. Nothing you say will go beyond this room."

"So—" Josef took a gold-tipped cigarette from his case, lit it. "As I recall, Christa, what I told you was this, that I had broken with my brothers and gone on my own to do something for the Jews in Germany. I also told you that I could aid only a fraction of those who needed help, and that the only way to help all of them was to get rid of Hitler." He turned to Lan. "Really, we're not mad, my associates and I. And instead of diminishing, we feel our chances are improving. Oh, I know Hitler's wiped out nearly every vestige of opposition in his Reich. But there's one force in Germany too powerful for even Hitler to destroy or bring to heel. I mean the German Army—the General Staff and the Officer Corps."

Lan sat up straight. "You think the German Army might turn against him?"

326

"I think there's that strong possibility," Josef said. "I'm connected with certain people in Germany—non-Jewish—who are connected with people in the German Army in a most influential way. My function is to provide certain financing. Beyond that, I can't go into detail. And—" Suddenly his face went hard and he looked drawn and tired. "Last summer, as you know, Hitler signed an agreement respecting Austrian independence. Now, so my sources tell me, there has been a meeting in Berlin—most secret. Only Hitler and his chief commanders. And he has laid it to them flatly: they must prepare for war. Because he intends to take Austria and Czechoslovakia, by force if it comes to that. And if France and England fight, then so be it."

Christa stared at him. Suddenly she felt a coldness in her stomach. "War," she whispered. "No. Surely he wouldn't dare."

"He's mad," Steiner said. "He's a genius, but he's also mad as a hatter. He would dare anything."

Lan stood up. "And what do your German generals think about that?" he asked, voice strained.

Josef smiled bitterly. "They're outraged. Which is our only hope." The smile went away. "They know Germany isn't ready. And my hope is that if their hands are forced they'll act. And . . . there must be pressure on them to act. Which is where you come in, Lan. You can help to build those pressures."

"Me?"

"You." Steiner took from his coat pocket a folded sheet of paper. "This is an account in general terms of the meeting I've just described. There can't be many specifics for fear of betraying the source of my information. I would be very grateful if you would turn it over to your friends of the foreign press at the Café Louvre. I realize that it's little more than a rumour, but all the German Army needs is a reasonable intimation that Herr Hitler's ambitions will indeed bring on war with France and England— a war that will surely ruin them—and there will be a confrontation with him. Once it comes to a test of strength between the National Socialists and the generals, the Nazis will surely lose. Can you get this information to the American, French, and British correspondents? You know them all, the right ones, which ones to trust, the ones who'll make best use of it." He paused, eyes glowing. "If you love Austria, it would be the greatest service you could render her."

Lan unfolded the sheet, read it swiftly. "You're right; it's more a rumour than anything else. Not much for them to go on. But—" he grinned "—it'll start some of them checking, asking questions. It might create excitement." Then he was completely grave. "Look, Josef, why don't I put you in touch with these people myself? They're good men, and they know what's going on, too. If you all worked together—"

"We shall work together," Josef said. "But only through you, Lan, if you are willing. I was coming to that. This—" he gestured "—is only the beginning. I can provide a constant stream of stories that give the lie to Herr Goebbels's propaganda. But I cannot do it directly. The Café Louvre is out of my usual circle, and it would be noted if I began to frequent it more than I do."

Something about the way he said that chilled Christa.

Lan toyed with the paper. "So you're being watched," he said harshly. "That means they'll be watching us, too. God knows you come here often enough."

"Yes," Steiner said. "That's true. But I have a good reason for that, which has nothing to do with what they're interested in. Everybody knows that Josef Steiner never gives up, and never lets a marriage stand in his way. So any contact with you would be presumed to be. . . ." He glanced at Christa.

Lan smiled. "God damn you," he said. "You're clever, aren't you?" He put the paper in his sweater pocket. "I know now why you looked at me that way the first time in the Wachau. You were already figuring out how you could use me."

Josef nodded, his own smile crooked. "Of course. I had no idea then exactly how, but I knew this: as an American, you'd have access to channels I couldn't reach, a freedom of movement I couldn't achieve. And I knew you already had reason to hate the Nazis. But now you are a friend, I would not use you as an instrument without your consent."

Lan looked at him a moment, then turned away. He went to the table and poured himself another glass of whisky. "Look," he said,

328

"let's get down to business. Josef, I'll do what I can. I'll pass this along, and anything else you send me; and, of course, I'll keep you out of it. It's little enough for me to do, if you're right about what's happening. Myself, I doubt it'll have any effect. Outsiders always overestimate what a newspaper can do. Generally, I suggest you mail to me whatever you want me to have. And—" his face shadowed "—I think that had better be the extent of our contact from now on. I don't think you should come here any more and I don't think we should go to you."

"Lan," Christa said.

"He's right," Josef cut in. "There's no reason to draw any more attention to you two than necessary, or to take the slightest risk of exposing you to danger. So, we will appear simply to cut each other off. Perhaps—" he smiled "—I became a bit too affectionate towards Christa. So the thing between us is over."

Christa's eyes stung. Her voice was choked, angry. "Damn them! Why can't they leave us alone?"

"Because Hitler needs the Austrian economy to arm for war. And because—" Josef's mouth thinned "—he wants his revenge on Austria, Vienna."

"Revenge?"

"Yes. He's from the Innviertel, you know, out in the backwoods, but as a young man he came to Vienna, afire to be a great painter. But they rejected him at the Academy—God, how I wish they'd accepted him! Anyhow, after that he became a drifter, a vagrant. He just sank into the lower depths of Vienna. I have taken the trouble to do some research on his activities during that period, and by and large he lived like a pariah dog. He has never lost his hatred of those who abused him in those days. It is a period of his life he would like to obliterate—along with all those who figured in it." He paused.

"Lan, I don't know how long Austria has if he isn't stopped— a few months, maybe a year. Anyhow, I think it would be prudent for you and Christa to be prepared. I'd certainly keep a reserve of money in Switzerland. And, frankly, if you and Christa plan to go to America, you'd best watch things carefully and get out of Austria in time. Otherwise, even though you're an American citizen and she's your wife, you're likely to have some trouble with red tape. And, without revealing from whom you heard it, you might pass along what I've told you to the General."

"Yes," Lan said. "I'll do that. Now I think we'd better eat."

THAT NIGHT, warm though the bedroom was, Christa shivered. Lan was already in the bed beneath the thick down comforters. Hastily she slid in beside him, seeking his warmth, and he put his arms around her, held her closely. "Oh," she said fiercely, "it's rotten, isn't it? Why don't the Germans let us alone?"

His arms tightened. "Don't worry. Maybe it will never happen. And if it does, I'll look after you. I'll see that nothing ever harms you."

But later, when he was asleep, still holding her, despite his closeness and his warmth, she grew cold again.

13

In well-drilled ranks, they marched past the café windows, booted feet clumping on the icy cobblestones. Their banners, with their awkward barred-end crosses, neither Maltese nor swastika, but something halfway in between, were damp and limp, and their bearers had to swirl them to give them any bravery. The air was icy, with drifting flakes of snow adding a new layer to ·the six sooty inches already blanketing the Burg Garden. "It's those damned silly crosses that bother me," Lan said. "It's almost as if von Schuschnigg were trying to give these Austrians their own version of the swastika. Competing with Hitler."

"Precisely," Mark Gorton said. In his early forties, short, with a red weathered face, Mark was one of the most brilliant newspapermen Lan had ever met; and, having lived in Austria almost uninterruptedly since 1919, he was in many respects more Austrian than the natives. He had come here with a British military mission, and ever since had felt more at home in Vienna than in his native London. "It's something in their soul that must be appealed to—the love of militarism, and all its trappings. They're not much good at fighting, but they do love to put up a fierce show. And Schuschnigg gives them the chance, hoping to keep them loyal."

Lan nodded. "All I know is that every time you turn around somebody's marching."

"Schuschnigg's committing suicide, of course. That's all it comes to. He tries to out-Herod Herod with all this pseudo-Nazi militarism, and that turns the stomach of liberal elements in France and England. Why should their young men die to save one Fascist state from another one?"

"The stuff I've been feeding you isn't helping?"

"It's good. Keep it coming. It's raw meat, and it's creating discussion. But I'm afraid it's too late to save the Austrian government from its own stupidity." He sipped his coffee, shook his head. "Not a very pleasant subject for Christmas Eve, is it?" Then he glanced at his watch. "Blast, I've got to run. Marietta's waiting for me." Mark's English wife, far less fascinated with Vienna than he, had divorced him and gone back to London years before; now he lived with a music student less than half his age. "*Wiederseh'n*. Greetings to Christa. And a merry Christmas."

"The same to you." They shook hands and went their separate ways into the snow-swirling afternoon.

There was, Lan thought, walking towards the Argentinierstrasse, something almost magnificent about the monumental bleakness of Vienna on a winter day. After the first of November there was rarely sunshine until March, and the city was a stony massiveness of unrelieved grey narrow streets. The warmth of home was good.

Christa was packing; they were spending tonight and tomorrow at the Christinahof. Lan embraced her; she was as excited by the season as a child. "Your nose is cold." She laughed.

He kissed her again, poured himself a brandy. "Get to work. It's getting late, and I want to leave in a little while." Then he went into his study.

There he lit a cigarette, sat down behind his typewriter, sipped the brandy, stared sourly at the page in the machine. It was slow, tortuous going, this book, and it got harder every day. Besides, he was caught up in events more urgent than any fiction.

For six weeks now the envelopes had come from Josef Steiner.

They were full of dynamite, documenting the ugly brutalities that had become routine in the Third Reich. Lan read them with horror and disgust, and then took them to the Café Louvre.

He was, he thought, in a sense drifting, waiting for something to happen, some climax which he could not predict. But he had taken Josef Steiner's warning and had put five thousand dollars in a Swiss bank. If something sudden, shocking, and unexpected happened; if overnight the Nazis came, there would be no way they could tie that money up.

He finished the brandy, shook his head. Well, let it ride. This was Christmas Eve. For thirty-six hours, anyway, they could all pretend that there were such things as peace on earth and good will towards men.

THAT CHRISTMAS EVE Helmer drove them to midnight mass himself, down the steep icy way to the valley floor, the Mercedes's low gear growling, its chains gripping. They passed a number of people on foot or travelling in sleighs, bells jingling, all bound for church in Ferndorf. For Helmer, appearance at mass was not only piety but politics, binding him that much closer to the people of the valley.

He parked the car beside the church, and carefully he and Christa helped his sister Alma across the ice. Inside, the organ was murmuring softly—it was very old, he and Max had just donated considerable sums for its repair—the wooden benches and prayer rails had been polished to dark gleams by generations of rough cloth. Everyone was bundled to the eyes in heavy clothing against the dank chill. As his family settled down in its accustomed spot, Helmer saw that, as usual, the Schellhammers sat just in front of them. Max turned, and so did Robert and his mother, and they all shook hands; then the Schellhammers turned forward again. Helmer thoughtfully rubbed his chin.

Well, there was no help for it; Max and Robert were both entitled to feel as if somehow he had double-crossed them, but in retrospect he was glad it had worked out as it did; one Lan Condon, he now believed, was worth a handful of Robert Schellhammers. And Christa's marriage was not the only thing that had driven a wedge between him and the Schellhammers. He was disappointed, too, in their readiness to yield Austria to the Germans. The cleft between the older men was now so deep that they no longer even debated the future with each other.

Then the organ pealed, and the service began. In the candle-light, Martinus's face was a sharp blur. His slender form was lent size, dignity, authority by the religious ritual and its trappings; his sermon, though brief, was truly poetic. But Helmer did not like its theme: Peace, all right. Reconciliation, yes. Brotherhood, certainly. But not the thinly veiled references to pan-Germanism, to the oneness of Austria and Germany. He meant to speak to that young man about it. Meanwhile, with the fine old hymns lingering in his ears, the General led his family from the church.

The parishioners had gathered, breaths white fluffs in the still, bitter cold, to exchange Christmas greetings, and to wait. It was five minutes until midnight, and the service would not be complete until a custom old here in Ferndorf had been observed.

Minutes ticked away, and then it was time. Down the street, the lights in the wing of the tailor shop in which Birnbaum and his family lived went out, as if the Jew somehow felt it not fitting to be in evidence at this moment.

Then, from the belltower of the church sounded a trumpet's notes, clear and sweet in the icy darkness: "Silent Night, Holy Night." The old carol rang out across the town, across the snow-clad sleeping valley. Helmer could imagine the deer in the coverts on the hills raising their heads, wondering. The trumpet sound finally died, only the last notes echoing, along with the final words of the refrain, softly sung by a few people in the crowd: ". . . Sleep in heavenly peace."

Helmer put his arm around Alma, whose thin frame was shivering with cold. "Sister, you're about to freeze. Come."

Then even before he heard the sound he saw it from the corner of his eye: a giant explosion of orange, like a miraculous flower in the darkness. The following thunder was like a fist against his ear. Helmer whirled instinctively, shielding Alma with his body. Women screamed. Then, from somewhere in the alleys a jeering voice: *Merry Christmas to the kikes!* The patter of falling stone

333

fragments, a cloud of dust. Raising his head, Helmer saw what had happened; the corner of Birnbaum's shop had been blown away.

"Christa! Mind your aunt!" he shouted.

"Papa!" She was there at once. Helmer turned, strode across the street, not daring to run because of ice on the cobbles. Lan was behind him; so were others, now that he'd taken the lead.

"General," Lan said hoarsely. "Careful."

"Only the one bomb," Helmer snapped. "Small, controlled. They knew what they were doing."

They circled the house. One corner of the one-storey shop had collapsed. Helmer picked his way to the door leading to the living quarters. "Herr Birnbaum! General Helmer here! Are you safe?"

A half minute passed. The village policeman, plus half a dozen others crowded up behind. Then a key turned and Birnbaum was in the doorway in his nightshirt, a short, dark man with powerful arms and hands. He stared past Helmer into the wreck of the shop, which the policeman was sweeping with a torch. "No," he whispered. "Oh, no . . ." Somewhere in the house a child was screaming.

"Your family, man! Are they all right?"

Birnbaum shook his head dazedly. "Yes. *Gott sei dank*, we are all right. But look. Look what they have done."

"Yes," the General said and raised and dropped a hand. "I am sorry. We'll catch them," he lied. He patted Birnbaum's shoulder. "Don't worry. Look I'll get a car brought up. Get your family together and you can come to the Christinahof for tonight."

"Please, no. Thank you, no. We must not leave here. Not now."

Undoubtedly the tailor had valuables in the house, and he would not leave them.

"Very well," the General said, and he turned to the policeman. "A guard must be kept over this house," he ordered. "There must be no harm to these people."

"Nobody's going to hurt 'em," the policeman answered, almost sullenly; and immediately Helmer knew that the officer had probably been involved in the planning, and this whole affair had been designed not to injure, but to warn and frighten.

"See to it," the General repeated and waited until an obedient, respectful "*Jawohl*" finally came.

"Very well. You will be safe, Herr Birnbaum. I personally guarantee it."

"Thank you. Thank you." The man's teeth chattered with cold. "Now I must get dressed. Excuse me." He closed the door.

Someone plucked at Helmer's sleeve. It was Dr. Martinus, his face pale. "General Helmer, this is terrible. This is . . . ." He groped for a word. "Absurd."

"No," Helmer said. "It is normal. Perfectly normal for our brothers in the Third Reich with whom you said tonight we should join hands. We have our culture and they have theirs. As you see, the two are already mingling. This is your brotherhood, Dr. Martinus. Now that you have seen it, perhaps you should go home and prepare another sermon."

Martinus stepped back, and Helmer regretted having flung it at him that way and in public. Then, angrily, he told himself it didn't matter. There were such things as decency, honour, and an end to patience.

"I'll . . . I'll get the sexton," Martinus said, "and we'll help Herr Birnbaum clean this up."

"Good." Helmer's tone was more gentle. But he was still seized by fury as he said, "Come, Lan." They left the shop and walked across the street. Robert and Max stood before their car, with Frau Schellhammer huddled in her coat inside.

Helmer stopped before them. Max's eyes shifted away and he bit on his pipe. But Robert's gaze met the General's. Helmer did his best to keep his anger from shaking his voice. "I will not," he said, "tolerate this. Do you understand? This will not be tolerated in the Ferntal."

After a few seconds Robert answered very slowly, "I agree, Herr General. It is regrettable. If those who are responsible are found, we must see that they are severely punished. I cannot imagine that any of our people did this." Each word was distinct, so weighted as not only to be devoid of regret, but faintly mocking. Helmer knew that in a way Robert was right; no one from the Ferntal had done this. Someone from a different district would

335

have been brought in. Then Robert said, "Merry Christmas, General Helmer," and turned away and got in the car.

Max took his pipe from his mouth. "Kurt," he said hoarsely, "I agree. There were children and a woman in there. Anyhow, why pick on some helpless little yid like Birnbaum when the big-wigs still run loose? The wrong time, the wrong man. Don't worry. I'm going to look into this." He was abashed, and put out his hand. "Merry Christmas, Kurt."

Helmer hesitated, then took it. "Max—"

"Now let's all get home before we freeze." And Schellhammer turned away.

<h2 style="text-align:center">14</h2>

For Christa, now, there was a sense of time running out. It was a sensation she had never known before, and one she hated.

In early February news seeped out of a shake-up in the German Army. The two most powerful generals, von Blomberg and von Fritsch, were dismissed—the very men, Lan told her, that Josef was counting on. The Brownshirt legions marched in the streets of Vienna. Nazi propaganda blossomed in the Nazi-supported papers, and every day there was violence of some kind in the capital and in the provinces.

Once she would have been unable to follow all this. Now she knew all too well what it meant. And she knew what the Nazis were as well—the men who'd kicked her husband when he was down, had blown up Birnbaum's tailor shop. They were beasts, she thought. And remembering Robert, who was not a beast, she could make no sense of it at all.

Dr. Martinus was convinced that Robert was innocent. On their last weekend visit at the Christinahof, he had been there at dinner. "Arrangements have been made for the damage to be repaired," he said over coffee. "Surely you must understand that it was some rowdies from Tulln. No one in Ferndorf would do such a thing to the Birnbaums."

"Rubbish," Lan said crassly in English.

"I beg your pardon?"

"I said rubbish." There was a tone in Lan's voice that Christa recognized. He had been pushed too far. "Martinus, why don't you come out with it? You're a goddamned Nazi."

The priest rose, trembling, lean face pale, eyes wide behind his glasses.

"Lan," General Helmer said.

"No. It's time Martinus heard some facts." Lan's voice crackled. "The fact is that the Catholic Church and the Nazis are a lot alike. Everybody who isn't for them is against them. All right, I'm a Catholic too. But I'm fed up. I'm fed up with Catholics rolling over and playing dead in Germany, and the Lutherans forming the only real opposition. I'm fed up with the hammering of acceptance of authority and infallibility into the heads of all these people. Authority, infallibility, that's the Nazi gambit—"

"Sir," Martinus said, and spots of red blazed on his cheekbones. "You are an outsider, and you don't know what you are talking about."

"I know about dictatorships. I've lived in Louisiana and been kicked in the head in the Naschmarkt."

Martinus drew in a breath that made his thin chest swell beneath his black clothing. "Yes. Yes, perhaps you know these things. Now, suppose I tell you some of the things I know."

"Do that," Lan said harshly.

"Yes. Well, now, some of the things I know are these." Martinus met his gaze unashamedly. "Because I am privileged, and I hear confessions, and I know secrets you will never hear. What I know—" he rubbed his mouth "—I know about despair," he said. "About husbands who can't feed their wives and children because they have no jobs. Men who contemplate suicide because of their shame in such a situation. Girls going into prostitution. You," he said bitterly, "you are an American and rich. You can afford the luxury of ideology. The people I must deal with every day cannot. I cannot. What do you tell a woman who says, 'I slept with him because he gave me twenty schillings, and my kids were hungry!' What, may I ask you, is the answer? It is not a matter of the Pope or authority or anything. It is a matter of people! Germany was like that, too, before Hitler—and now it is not! There men have

337

work, and children have food! And if that is what it takes here to rid me of my burden, then I am for it."

Again he drew in breath. "I think there are some evil aspects to Nazism, but one must weigh the good against the bad. I think the good overbalances the bad. I think we can take the German drive and the Austrian compassion and combine them into a New Order that is really new!" His face was hard. "I can stand here before you and say that in good conscience. I say to you that there must be some way to let every man live as a human being. Marxism is no answer, because it denies God, and man cannot live without God. The Nazis offer both God and bread in sufficient amounts."

"Martinus—" Lan said.

Martinus shook his head violently. "I seek answers," he said heavily. "You only ask questions. Good day." Then he rose and took his leave.

There was a long silence. Lan said, "I'm sorry, General Helmer."

"No." Christa's father stood up. "No, there is right on both sides. But Martinus is correct in this: You are from another world. You must not judge us by the standards of America. America is so big, there is always somewhere you can go. But in Austria there is no place to run. So, we compromise." He raised his glass, tossed off his wine. "I've lived a long time, and this I've learned: that nothing is ever quite as bad as one expects. And we Austrians can always wriggle out."

BUT LATER that night, Christa remembered, her father and Lan had sat up talking; and she had been excluded.

Papa was right, though: Austrians could always wriggle out somehow. And now it seemed that Schuschnigg might have found the answer. On the ninth of March, he made a fiery speech in Innsbruck. There would be a plebiscite on the thirteenth of the month. A vote of the people, long demanded by Hitler, to determine whether Austria would remain free or voluntarily become subject to Germany. She and Lan had heard the speech on the radio.

338

Lan listened to the end and then clicked off the radio. "Well," he said, "at least he's found one way of fighting. If he can get a whopping majority for an independent Austria, against a German takeover, he will have something to use to face down Hitler, and Britain and France might even stir their stumps. *If he can bring it off. . . .*" Lan paced their living room. "Christa, we've got to make some decisions. How long would it take for you to get ready to go to America?"

"To America? But your book's not finished."

"Christa." His voice was crisp. "I don't think Hitler can any longer let this plebiscite take place. I think he'll move in and try to break it up. If he does, that may mean war between now and the thirteenth of the month—five days. If there's war, the best thing is to get you out of the combat zone."

Christa sat there numbly. What he was describing was the end of her world. But she met his eyes with courage. "All right," she said. "We don't really need to take a lot. But Papa—"

"The General and I have already talked. He'll stay here and do whatever he thinks he has to. Meanwhile, I'll take you away, and then we'll wait and see what happens."

Christa swallowed hard. "Very well."

Then, next morning, Josef Steiner telephoned.

THEY GOT OFF the train at a small town called Braunkirchen, where Josef's driver met them. Lan had tried on the telephone to beg off, but Steiner had phrased his summons in terms he could not refuse: *Absolutely imperative. If you have any friendship for me, I implore you.* The car wound through the village and up a narrow valley. It was unseasonably warm for the second week of March, and the road they travelled was deep in mud. Presently on a squat peak ahead they saw Schloss Schwarzgipfel, dead white walls and dead white towers, with tile roofs black as anthracite against the sky.

Reaching the entrance of the palace's enclosing wall, they passed beneath a raised portcullis and entered the main courtyard. The car stopped, and they got out and looked around at the complex of window-ranked walls and soaring towers and turrets.

"This makes the Christinahof look like a shanty," Lan said. "Josef must—" He broke off as a grating, ear-splitting scream from above and behind made them whirl. It came again, high-pitched, squawking, a nightmare sound going straight to the nerves. And then they saw the bird, large and lustrous, on a low roof across the court. Extending its long neck, snakelike head weaving, it screamed again and spread its tail into a luxurious fan. "Peacock," Lan said. "I understand they make good watchdogs."

They were led up high steps through a door into the *Schloss*. Josef came to meet them, his face drawn, his mouth grim and weary. "Thank you for coming," he said. "I know it was an inconvenience. But it is a matter of utmost urgency, and it's impossible for me to get to Vienna." He smiled faintly. "Anyhow, I've at last succeeded in enticing you to Schwarzgipfel. Now, something to drink?"

"Thanks," Lan said. "But, Josef, we can only stay the one night. We need to get back; we're packing to go."

"Yes, you told me. And a wise move." Steiner went to a table, poured schnapps, handed glasses to the Condons. "I'll get directly to the point. *Pros't.*" He drank. "Please. If you will bring your glasses and come with me to the library. . . ."

Christa and Lan followed Josef through double doors into a vast book-lined room with a big table in its centre. There was an open fire, and he motioned them to the sofa before it. Then he went to a shelf and pulled down a pair of outsized volumes bound in black leather. Christa sat up straight. She had seen those before—or their like.

Face expressionless, Josef laid them in Lan's lap. Lan opened the topmost one and stared at the vivid mounted photographs. He raised his head. "What the hell," he asked harshly, "has this got to do with anything? Dirty pictures!"

"Dirty pictures are important," Josef said. "As a matter of fact, pornography and vice may have settled Austria's fate. Hitler has just used them to dispose of his two most powerful generals. When von Blomberg married his secretary, the Gestapo learned that her mother had once run a Berlin brothel and that she had posed for pornographic pictures. Hitler used this to break him. Then

340

von Fritsch, von Blomberg's most likely successor—and even more opposed to the Führer's war plans. They trumped up charges of homosexuality against him . . . and now he's gone, too."

Lan stared at him a moment, nodded. "Go ahead."

Josef looked at them strangely. "What," he asked, "do you know about the early life of Adolf Hitler?"

"Not much," Lan said. "Only what's in *Mein Kampf.*"

"Deceptive and self-serving. There's more, much more."

"Suppose you tell us," Lan said quietly.

Josef relaxed. "Very well. He's Austrian, of course, from a small town on the German border. His father was a customs official and a holy terror at home, it seems; he and his father didn't get along, the home was full of tensions, and as soon as possible he left to study in Linz. There, apparently, he was an indifferent student— not stupid, just idle, dreamy, lazy. He had some talent for art and conceived the idea that he'd be a great painter; and, truth to tell, I've seen some of his early work and it wasn't bad. Be that as it may, when he was not yet twenty, he came to Vienna to apply at the Academy of Arts and . . . they turned him down."

Now Steiner's manner was that of a classroom lecturer. "Even Hitler in *Mein Kampf* admits that his next four years in Vienna were dreadfully unhappy. Anyhow," he continued, "after four years he went to Germany and when war broke out joined the German Army. After the defeat he fell in with the National Socialist Movement, took it over, and made it his, having discovered his talent as an orator. You know the rest—his manipulations, rabble-rousing, his rise to power—"

"Yes," Lan said.

"Now, for a moment, I want to talk about sex again. As the Führer, Hitler poses as an ascetic, a man wedded only to the German people, far too busy to have time for sex. But my associates and I have done a great deal of digging and we have unearthed information as to his real tendencies." His face grim, he picked up a volume from the table, thumbed through it, found a place, and passed the book to Lan.

"Judas Priest," Lan whispered.

"Not pretty, is it? Never mind. The pictures make clear what

I'm driving at. An ultimate, grovelling subjugation: that's his fulfilment." He shut the album.

"If you could document that—" Lan began.

"If I could have, I'd have done so long ago. But he's had years to cleanse Germany of incriminating evidence. At least one girl involved with him has killed herself—or been murdered—and a couple more have tried suicide and failed. Apparently they fall in love with the great leader, the ultimate in masculine power, and then find out that *this* is what he wants. No, Lan. He has purged Germany of all proof. But—" Josef paused and looked at them "—he has not been able to do the same with Austria."

Slowly Lan Condon stood up. "Go on," he said.

"Four years in Vienna. Four lost years. By his own admission, Hitler was a drifter, barely staying alive. And, of course, in such a situation, absolutely at the bottom, one does what one has to in order to survive."

"If I get you right," Lan murmured, "you're trying to say—"

"A rumour reached me a couple of years ago. Incredible on the face of it, and yet it had a real kernel of possibility. Since that time I've become a valued customer of the makers of pornography in Vienna. Known—" he smiled coolly "—as a man with extremely special tastes who will pay premium prices for merchandise that suits him. I have, consequently, first refusal of almost everything that turns up, particularly photographs made before the war."

"Which would cover the period Hitler spent in Vienna."

"Yes. And eventually I was rewarded. At last I found a single photograph—obviously one of a broken set—and I felt at once there was little doubt of the identity of the young male participant. Here." He unlocked a drawer in the table, took out a postcard-size photograph and a number of clippings from magazines and newspapers. He spread them on the table, and Christa rose to look.

One glance was enough; she turned away, but Lan and Steiner bent over them. "You see," Josef said, "the face shows quite clearly. And here are photographs, official ones, from his younger days for comparison. In my opinion, there can be no doubt. What do you think, Lan?"

342

Lan straightened up, drawing in a breath. "It may be," he said. "It sure as hell looks like him. But it wouldn't be enough."

"Of course not. But when the picture fell into my hands, I pretended to be enraptured by the woman in it. She's quite ordinary, but—" He shrugged, smiling ironically. "Anyhow, I let it be known that I would pay fantastic prices for more pictures featuring her, and, more than that, if she were still alive—though obviously she'd be quite old now—I'd pay even more handsomely for the privilege of meeting her. I set a trap baited with financial incentives." He paused; his eyes met Lan's. "A week ago it sprang."

Carefully he restored the picture and the clippings to the drawer. "She's still alive," he said. "She lives in Vienna's Second District in poverty. And . . . she has a complete set of these photographs. And she remembered well the young man who posed for them; his name was Adolf."

Lan Condon made a sound in his throat. Christa said, "Josef, you can't mean—"

"I told you it was incredible. At first even I wondered if I were the victim of some elaborate plot. Especially when I learned that he had written her letters, warped love letters, if you will, the outpourings of a young, deranged, and desperate mind. Signed with a simple *A*."

Christa shook her head. "Only *A*? Not his whole name?"

"He was not that demented. But handwriting experts could make confirmation. I am sure others would be as quick to see the resemblance, and that there is too much here to be sheer coincidence."

After a second, Lan said, "Where are the pictures and letters?"

"She still has them. Two days ago I had a letter from her naming a staggering sum for immediate delivery. Even so I am sure that never once in all these years has she made the connection between *that* Adolf and the other one. I sent an acceptance, but, naturally, considering the gravity of the matter, I would trust no one but myself to pay and take possession of those pictures.

"And I set out to do that, but I was followed and I couldn't lose them. And my associates in Vienna I know are in the same

343

boat. So, Lan, I was stuck, and I tried hard to think what to do. And I kept coming up with only one answer." He paused. "An American with the proper documents would have nothing to fear from either the mob or the police. An American could pick up those pictures and deliver them to me. Now do you see why I insisted that you come to Schwarzgipfel? And do you see the magnitude of the favour?"

Once more there was silence as he and Lan looked at each other. Then Lan said. "Josef, this is the damnedest thing I've ever heard. To try to blackmail Adolf Hitler—"

"Not myself. I would get those pictures to certain people. I am convinced that within twenty-four hours of their receipt and a full explanation of their significance, the leading officers of the German Army and Navy would confront Hitler with them."

"And the outcome?"

"I can't guarantee anything. But I think it would be fair to say that he who lived by the sword would die by it. His use of pornography against von Fritsch and von Blomberg has made him vulnerable. The ideal would be the usual Prussian procedure: they would lock him in a room with a pistol with a single bullet and expect him to do the rest; if he did not, somebody would do it for him."

Lan stood up. "You think the pictures would do all that?"

"We shall never know until they reach the proper hands."

Lan turned towards the fire. "This," he said, "is a hell of a thing to throw at a man."

Josef said quietly, "I know. But I and my friends have gone as far as we can. Now we need your help."

Lan stared into the flames. "You say you're watched. Suppose they're watching *her*? After all, Hitler, if it is he, can't have forgotten those pictures, and he knows a set of them can ruin him. I'd think, if he has undercover agents here, they'd be looking high and low for her."

"Put yourself in his place," Josef replied. "Given the shifting loyalties in his régime, whom would he dare tell? Whoever got his hands on them—Himmler, Göring—might seize the opportunity to use them against him. Would he risk that? If I were he,

344

I would tell myself that after twenty years they were bound to have disappeared."

Lan was silent. Then: "How would I get the pictures to you?"

"Once you have them, take the train from the Franz Josef Bahnhof to Horn in the Waldviertel. From three o'clock tomorrow on, my black Mercedes—I'll give you the plate number and the keys—will be parked near the Bahnhof in Horn. Anyone watching me will naturally follow me and ignore the car. You merely unlock it, get in as if it belonged to you, slide the pictures behind the seat, get out, and lock it again. After which you catch the next train to Vienna."

"You make it sound like buying candy," Lan said acidly.

"For you it should be no more difficult. What do you say?"

"I say nothing. Not yet. I need to think about it."

"Certainly. I realize that. You and Christa will want to talk. But please, Lan, take everything I have said with the utmost seriousness. And you, my dear—" turning to Christa "—it is your country as well as mine."

15

Arriving back in Vienna next morning they found the Franz Josef Bahnhof crowded with people. Some wore the uniforms of units of the government's private army; others flaunted swastikas and white stockings. As they jostled through the crowd and left the station to find a taxi, a plane flew low overhead, unloosing a snowstorm of propaganda pamphlets. Lan caught one out of the air: *JA! With Schuschnigg on Sunday for a Free Austria!* But the grey walls of the Bahnhof were smeared with huge red swastikas and Nazi slogans.

They caught a taxi, told the driver to take them to their apartment. Vienna seemed different. Yesterday there had been activity in the streets, but nothing like today's. Police and soldiers were everywhere, and the streets were clogged with marchers. A steady stream, many of schoolboy age, headed towards the Inner City wearing Nazi armbands. Even the hammer and sickle had come out of hiding to join the other symbols.

Christa's misgivings grew. Today was no time for anyone to be on the streets. She clutched Lan's thigh. "Lan. Look at it. I don't want you to go ahead with this thing for Josef! We didn't know it would be like this when we said—"

The driver's head was cocked. "Hush," Lan said.

"Ho," said the driver in thick Viennese dialect as he waited for a channel through the square. "A big mess, hah? You can bet all the dirty kikes are hidin' under their beds today!" Then the taxi crept on, halting once more for a howling, shrieking platoon of teenage girls, each wearing a swastika.

In the Argentinierstrasse Lan told the driver to wait and carried their luggage upstairs himself. Outside the door, he took Christa's hands. "Now, do *not* worry. Just get the packing finished and plan on a late supper tonight. O.K.?" He pulled her to him, kissed her. "*Wiederseh'n.* I love you."

She watched him start down the stairs. She stood as motionless as if paralyzed. Then her numbness broke and she rang the bell. Rezi could bring in the bags. And then she was running.

"Lan!" she called as she made the stairs. Below at the main entrance, he halted. "Lan," she said, reaching the bottom. "I'm going with you."

"The hell you are."

"Yes. I insist. We're in this together."

He looked down at her, and she braced herself for more argument, which she was determined not to lose. But, after a moment, he smiled faintly and nodded. "O.K. Come along. Maybe I can use an extra pair of eyes. I don't much trust that driver; he's a Nazi bastard if I ever saw one. I think we'll let him take us to the Praterstrasse and walk from there." He took her hand. "Let's go."

IT TOOK the taxi half an hour to reach the Schwedenbrücke over the Danube Canal, and each time they halted for a group of marching Nazis the driver chortled. Once, unabashed, he leaned out the window, arm raised, and shouted, "Heil Hitler! Good luck, comrades!"

"You're for *Anschluss,* eh?" Lan asked in a carefully neutral voice as the man settled back.

"Absolutely, Herr Baron. Things have got to change, and the Führer is the man to change 'em! Look, I've got a wife and three kids and I was out of work for two years before I got this job. How we lived? Don't ask me! My wife scrubbed floors for a rich lady; I pinched a schilling here, a schilling there."

Anger vibrated in his voice. "I got debts you wouldn't believe! Had to borrow—and from a dirty Jew! Nobody else may ever have any, but they're always *stuffed* with money! You look at the banks and stock markets. Who runs 'em? People like the Rothschilds and the Steiners—lousy Jews! They got all the strings in their hands, and honest Christians got no chance at all!"

Lan had known it for a long time. When a man was desperate enough, especially if he had a family, he would steal and even kill to survive. It was hope that made all the difference. Roosevelt had offered it in America, Hitler offered it here; and desperate men would seize any hope.

"Here," Lan said. "We'll get out here." They were across the Danube Canal in the Praterstrasse. After the driver had pulled away, they stood on the kerb warily looking around. Strangely there were no demonstrators and very little traffic.

"Well, let's go," Lan said. "We're just going to wander until we make sure the coast is clear. Stop and look in windows from time to time, but don't turn and look behind you."

Ten minutes later, in an alley so narrow Christa could almost have spanned it with her outstretched arms, Lan halted and lit a cigarette, his eyes moving covertly. "I've seen nobody, have you?"

"Only those policemen at the bridge."

"They were just guards on duty there. Well, I think we can get down to business now. It should be up this next street. Let's go."

In a moment Lan halted before a three-storey house, its plastered walls peeling. He checked the number, nodded. "This is it."

The entrance hall was small and dank. Stairs, worn concave by generations of shuffling feet, led upwards on their right. "Second floor, room seven," Lan said, and they began to climb. It was even colder here than outside. They found a plain wooden door with a seven on it. There was no bell. Lan knocked.

No one answered. He knocked again. Christa held her breath,

hoping there would be no response and they could go home to safety. But then she heard the sound of footsteps within.

The door opened, and not a woman but a man stood there, in a neat blue suit, his eyes small jet dots, his face broad and Slavic.

"Yes?"

"I—" Lan broke off. "I'm sorry. I have made a mistake."

"You're looking for Frau Charim?" The man's face relaxed. "I'm her brother. I think she's expecting you. Please come in."

"Expecting me?"

"If you are from a certain gentleman in the Wachau." He stood aside, his voice urgent. "Please. Quickly. Before someone—"

"All right," Lan said and entered; Christa followed. They were in a tiny room curtained off from a larger one by dingy patterned fabric.

The man closed the door, turned a key in the lock. "Now," he said loudly, and through the curtain came two more men.

Christa stifled a cry of surprise, and Lan said harshly, "Oh, hell."

"Don't move," the man with the dark eyes said. "You are both under investigatory arrest: Vienna Security Police." With one hand he drew a revolver and with the other brought out identification, holding it before their eyes.

Lan asked sharply, "What's going on here? Where's Frau Charim?"

"She is . . . unavailable. What do you want with her?"

"I came to pay a debt."

"On whose behalf?"

"A friend who's an American newspaperman. He bought some merchandise from Frau Charim." Lan licked his lips. "Pictures of a certain sort. He collects them."

"His name?"

"I'll not tell you that. Now, look here, I'm an American citizen and my wife's an Austrian citizen and we'll not have—"

The dark-eyed man's voice snipped off his words coldly. "Your papers, please. Yours, too, *gnädige Frau.*"

Christa found her courage. "First, I want an explanation—"

"Your papers," he said in a metallic voice.

"Give them to him," Lan said quietly, taking out his own.

"Search them, please," the dark-eyed man said to another, who was blond and lean. He did so, whistling softly as he pulled Josef's three thousand schillings from Lan's wallet, then put it back. He touched Christa respectfully, and emptied the contents of her handbag, then replaced them and returned it to her.

"Come in now," the dark-eyed man said. He pushed them through the curtain.

They were in a squalid room containing a bed, a dressing table, and several large photographs on the wall of a young dark girl in old-fashioned deep décolletage. The room smelled faintly of perfume, but there was no sign of any woman.

"Where is Frau Charim?" Lan demanded.

"She is away," the dark-eyed man said. "Please. Make yourself comfortable. Would you like some tea?"

"To hell with tea! I demand to be allowed to call my legation!"

"In due time," the man said. "Now," his voice roughened. "Sit down and be quiet. Wolf, turn on the radio again."

Rage welled up in Christa, generated by fear, not so much for herself as for Lan. "Now listen here, I insist—"

"Madam, you may insist on nothing," said the man. "*Sit down!*"

"Christa," Lan said, "do as he says."

Furious and frightened, she dropped into the single chair by the bed. Her hands were cold as ice. The radio was on now, spilling music. She took out cigarettes, lit one. She smiled at Lan. It was important to reassure him, to show him she was not afraid. "You gentlemen have certainly made a mistake you'll regret," she said quietly. "I hope you realize that."

Nobody answered. The dark-eyed man went out and a door closed behind him. The blond man and the other sat on the bed opposite Lan, watching him. The blond man had a revolver in his hand, though he did not point it at either of them. The news came on the radio: first an optimistic outburst about the prospects of an overwhelming government victory in the vote on Sunday, then other items completely ordinary and reassuring.

"Lan," Christa said, "you understand that if we're not home tonight, my father will take drastic measures—"

350

"You will not talk with one another," the blond man said.

"You can't stop me," Christa said. "If I want to talk to my—"

"My dear lady, we can't stop you. But we can take your husband elsewhere."

"Be quiet, Christa," Lan said heavily. "It's better if you're quiet."

The radio droned on. Cheerful voices sang old songs: "Vienna Is Always Vienna", "My Mother Was A Viennese". . .

Time crawled by. The dark-eyed man returned, bringing with him a huge bag of sausage rolls, some pickles, and cheap wine. The room was full of the odour of the cheap cigarettes the men smoked. No one asked them even a single question. Later Christa and Lan were taken, separately and under guard, down the hall to the toilet. There was nothing but music on the radio. The dark-eyed man came in and out repeatedly, as if he were very busy.

And now it was dark outside. Another couple of hours crawled by. Twice Christa tried to speak to Lan, each time she was cut off. Then the dark-eyed man ran back into the little room. He was grinning broadly, eyes shining, as he went to the radio, turned it up. "Listen!" he said.

The radio was silent. Then a voice said, shakily, "Please stand by. Please stand by." Another silence. Then: "Chancellor Dr. Kurt von Schuschnigg."

A pause. Then the voice that came from the speaker was one she recognized, though it trembled slightly now, lacking its former authoritarian certainty. She leaned forward, straining to catch every syllable.

"The German government has today handed to President Miklas an ultimatum with a time limit, requiring him to designate as chancellor a person designated by the German government. Otherwise German troops will invade Austria. . . ."

"Hell," Lan whispered.

"I deny before the world," von Schuschnigg said, "the reports from Germany that the workers are in disorder, that the government has shed Austrian blood, that we are no longer in control of the situation. But at the request of President Miklas, I now tell the people of Austria that we have yielded to force, since we are

not prepared even in this awful hour to shed German blood. We
have ordered our troops to withdraw without resistance.

"And so—" he drew in a long, audible breath "—I take leave of
the Austrian people with a German word of farewell and the single
wish from the depths of my heart: *God save Austria!*"

For a moment the radio buzzed with a silence. Suddenly it was
broken by a ghostly voice remote from the microphone: "Long
live Austria! Today I am ashamed to be a German!" Then there
was an audible click as something was disconnected.

Christa wrestled with what she had heard. "Lan—"

"It's over," he said harshly. "The Germans are coming in."

"Yes!" the dark-eyed man snapped. "That's absolutely right.
It is settled now, after all these years." He raised his arm. Almost
reverently he shouted, "Heil Hitler!"

"*Heil!*" his companions shouted back. "*Sieg Heil!*" Then, faces
glowing, they shook hands among themselves.

Lan got stiffly to his feet. "All right," he said. "It's settled now.
There'll be no war, right? You've won, you have nothing to fear
from us. Will you please take us to the American Legation at
once."

The dark-eyed man nodded. "Yes," he said. "It's time for all of
us to go now. Please, madam—" He took Christa's hand and helped
her up.

Outside on the deserted street a black Mercedes was parked.
They were shoved into the rear, and the dark-eyed man got in
beside them. Lan put his arm around Christa.

"Don't worry," he said.

She leaned against him, desperately, not only seeking
reassurance, but also giving it. Together they were strong.
Divided, anything could happen.

The streets reeled by. Lan said, "This isn't the way—"

"Be quiet, Mr. Condon," the dark-eyed man said.

They rolled on through streets suddenly packed with jubilant
people, past windows hung with swastikas. They turned into a car
park. Christa sat up straight, recognizing the massive bulk of the
East Station. "What—?"

"Get out," the dark-eyed man ordered. The blond man seized

Christa, and the dark-eyed man locked his hand around Lan's arm. His other hand was in his pocket.

"Come with us."

They entered the great echoing station. It was bedlam, jammed with people. The man shoved ruthlessly through the crowds, dragging Lan and Christa. Somebody shrieked, "But I must get to Prague! Don't you understand? Who has a ticket? I'll pay any price."

They were dragged through to a platform where a train waited. They reached a third-class carriage. Lan jerked his arm free. "I demand—!" he roared. The dark-eyed man seized him, pulled out his gun and shoved it in his belly. In spite of the uproar, Christa heard every word.

He spoke in English. "You demand nothing, Mr. Condon. You have been declared *persona non grata* by the new Austrian government, by the new chancellor himself. If you do not resist, you will not be harmed. If you have representations to make to your government, they can be made in Prague."

"Prague?" Lan flared.

"You are being expelled, Mr. Condon, to Czechoslovakia. You . . ."

The train whistle, a blast of steam, drowned the rest.

Christa saw Lan tense, go pale. She fought the blond man, but he locked an arm around her neck. The dark-eyed man shoved Lan into the carriage and followed.

"Lan!" she screamed. She kicked the blond man in the shins, but he might as well have been made of marble. The train whistled again. People clung to the side, then fell away as it picked up speed and rushed into the night. A great collective sigh of disappointment filled the huge hall.

"Lan," Christa whispered, sagging back against the man.

"He is gone," he said. "It will do you no good to create a disturbance. You belong here. He is American but you are not. Come with me."

She hardly heard. She only stared into darkness, head craning at the emptiness along the track, as he led her roughly back towards the car.

1

He did not even have a chance to kiss her, touch her. He could still see her standing there, face pale, stricken, as the man with the gun shoved him towards the train. He heard her scream. Then they were in the carriage, and suddenly the train began to roll.

Despite the mob, they had a compartment to themselves, blinds drawn, door locked. The man with the gun sat across from him, refusing to speak or let Lan speak. Totally alert, he gave Lan no chance to jump him. In a couple of hours they reached the Czech border. The man rose, handed Lan his passport. "Goodbye, Mr. Condon. For your sake and your wife's, do not try to enter Austria again, ever." He went out, leaving Lan to the Czech officials. Shortly, the train rolled on towards Prague.

By now Lan knew what he would do. He would work from Prague, turn the American Legation upside down to get Christa out. But, in the meantime, what would they do with her? A concentration camp? God damn Josef Steiner! God damn himself for playing cat's paw in such a hare-brained scheme. . . .

After two hours of competing with other desperate people at the great grey railway station in Prague, he found a taxi to take him to the American Legation. It was a madhouse, swarming with Austrians with American relatives or connections. A weary clerk listened to him for thirty seconds, checked his documents, told him to find a hotel and come back tomorrow.

Mercifully, his memory of the next two weeks was fragmentary. He got an interview at the legation; they promised to do whatever was possible. He haunted the place every day, but nothing was ever done.

Frantically Lan tried to get through by telephone to the Christinahof or their apartment in Vienna; it was hopeless. But finally the operator reached the Café Louvre, and something unclenched within him as he heard Mark Gorton's voice: "Yes, I heard about it. Christa seems to be all right for now. She's safe

354

at her father's house in the country. Look, where are you staying?"

Lan gave him the name and address of his hotel.

"Don't leave for another two weeks at least. That's all I can say just now. I'll be in touch, but I suggest you don't phone again. And for God's sake, don't phone her. Don't worry. Maybe I can do something. Goodbye, Lan."

"Mark, wait—"

"Goodbye," Mark said firmly and hung up.

TEN DAYS LATER Gorton was in Prague. They met in a coffeehouse near the old City Hall.

"First," Mark said, "here's a letter for you." He handed Lan an envelope. "Nature calls," he said and discreetly vanished. Lan's hands shook so that he could hardly get the flap unsealed.

My darling [she had written]. I love you, love you, a hundred times, a thousand, much more. I am well and so is everyone. Robert says we have nothing more to fear if we are careful and correct.

You must not write to me directly or try to phone; as things are now, it is too dangerous. When our friend told me that you were safe and well in Prague, I cried, and then I lit several candles at the monastery in gratitude.

Papa and our friend both say, please, don't do anything on our behalf just now, it could be dangerous. It is terrible, not having you here. I am lonely all the time. But we must manage somehow for a while. Poor Aunt Alma's died. I'm doing my best to take her place. I work from morning to night, and that is good because it leaves less time to think.

We must only be patient and love each other very much until we are again together. Your C.

"Mark, I don't know how to thank you," Lan said when Gorton returned.

"Don't bother. I'd do anything to confound those bastards. Now listen. My days in Austria are pretty well numbered, but as long as I can, I'll serve as go-between. I don't know why all this happened, but I suppose it had to do with the information you were feeding to the Louvre. Anyhow, here's what I can do."

He sipped his coffee. "I've good friends in the British Ministry. Here's the name and address of one in Prague. Take your letters to Christa to him, and they'll go to Vienna by diplomatic pouch, where I'll pick them up and dispatch hers to you. You can be as frank in those letters as you care to; no one else will see them. But for God's sake, don't try to write by ordinary mail. It's a damned sure bet the Helmers' mail and their phone are monitored by the Gestapo. All right?"

"All right? My God . . . Mark, you've seen her?"

"We met. She looked pale and rather thin, but fine otherwise. After they put you on the train, they took her back to the Christinahof but, at the same time, arrested General Helmer. They kept him for some time and then released him, mostly, I understand, through the intervention of a man named Schellhammer."

Mark's eyes were sad and angry. "Here's the big picture of what happened. Hitler knew the Austrians would vote overwhelmingly against him in the plebiscite, so on Friday, the day you had your troubles, he issued an ultimatum: Schuschnigg was to resign in favour of Seyss-Inquart, who was to form an Austrian Nazi government. At first Schuschnigg resisted. He sought help from France, Britain, Italy. Everybody waffled; nobody would move. So it boiled down to Austria fighting alone."

Mark's voice was bitter. "Von Schuschnigg had five thousand troops on the frontier against the whole German Army; and yet still I blame him for not fighting. They would have made a stand if he'd given them the chance. And any show of resistance might have forced France and England to act. But he simply caved in." Mark sighed. "Did you hear that strange voice after his final speech, off microphone? *Long live Austria! Today I am ashamed to be a German!* That was old Baron Hammerstein-Equord, Minister of Culture. He was there when Schuschnigg spoke; ill, on crutches. But Schuschnigg's surrender was too much for him. He staggered up and yelled his battle cry before they could turn off the microphone. I suppose it's earned him a berth in a concentration camp."

He shook his head. "To get back to the Helmers. Temporarily, they're safe, but you must be very careful not to rock their boat.

For the time being, there's no hope of getting Christa out or you back in. Maybe things will get better by and by, but if you try to force it, there could be real trouble."

Lan nodded. "Mark, thanks again—"

"*F'Gornix*," Mark said in Viennese dialect. "For nothing. Now, go and write a letter and I'll take it back with me."

LAN STAYED in Prague and traded letters for another month. Then, as predicted, Mark himself was expelled. "I'm *persona non grata*," he told Lan. "However, all is not lost. I've made inquiries and it should be fairly safe for the two of you to write to each other directly now if you keep your letters innocuous. You shouldn't— and I've told her this—put in anything that will embarrass the Helmers. Nothing about any plans to get her out, no criticism of the régime. And she must lard her letters with how well everything is going, how everyone's so happy. Understand?"

"Right. But . . ."

"See here," Mark said. "I know a little bit more about what you were up to than I did before. I had a rumour from a friend of Josef Steiner's; and, Lan, you were dealing in dynamite."

"Where is Josef?"

"Who knows? He's vanished and his property's been confiscated. Anyhow, they've expelled you, and kept Christa as hostage, insurance that you wouldn't spread any ugly rumours about their noble leader once you were in the clear. As long as they've got her, you don't dare talk. On the other hand, you're *her* insurance. If they hurt her and you find out, you *will* talk. So it's a stalemate. You can thank your American passport for saving you and Christa, but sleeping dogs must be let lie."

"You're saying I'll never get her back."

"*Never* is a long word. I'm saying that for now the two of you must play your cards very close to your chest, be discreet."

Mark and Marietta left for England. Lan remained in Prague, double-checking the possibility of getting Christa out, but with no success. Every day he wrote to her. Without the freedom of the diplomatic pouch, though, the letters were only affirmations, not communications. *I love you. The weather is good/bad/terrible.*

And from her the same, plus shameless propaganda as insurance. *Things are much better now; everybody has work. My darling, I think of you all night long. . . .*

As the summer dwindled, history began to repeat itself, inexorably. Obviously after Austria, Hitler now intended to occupy Czechoslovakia. By the time autumn turned the lovely old city of Prague into burnished bronze, Lan knew he must get out.

"*You won't,*" he wrote, "*hear from me for several weeks. I'm going back to America. Write me in care of Matthews. . . .*"

He fled from Prague only just in time, bound for California. Matthews, his agent, a tall, still-handsome man in his sixties, sympathetic, listened to Lan's story. "So the book isn't finished. And you want the studio to take you back?"

"They've got to. Matt, I've got to have some money. I left five thousand in the Swiss account in case she needs it, but otherwise I'm broke. And if I can get cash, maybe I can buy her out."

"Yeah." The agent nodded. "I'll find you something. But Lan, you've got to understand. It won't be like it was before. Hitler's not the only dictator who can make or break you."

"But the studio knows what I can do."

"You had a contract and you broke it. I had a hell of a time blocking a lawsuit. You promised them the film rights to your book, and now you have no book. So they'll make you eat a lot a crow before they take you back."

Lan stared at him. "If I can just get back to work, I'll manage."

"I'll do my best." He knuckled Lan's shoulder. Then: "Oh, yeah, Lan. Phyll O'Donnell."

It was a name he had not wanted to hear. "What about her?"

"She's still around, you know. Went East for a little while after Ross. . . . But she's back and I still hear from her. I told her you were married. It seemed to hit her pretty hard."

"Yeah," Lan said.

"She's still got the house and she's picked up a few parts here and there. And . . . she hasn't given up on you."

"That's her problem. My one concern is for my wife. Maybe it sounds like a line from a lousy script, but I happen to love her."

"Sure. Well, you're my client and you and Phyll are both my

friends." Matthews shrugged. "Never mind. You sit loose and phone me tomorrow late, after I've had time to nose around." He put out his hand. "Lan, I'm glad you've come back to the fold."

MATT GOT HIM A JOB at half his former salary: Lan had had to crawl for it, cower meekly before all the little dictators at the studio, hating it, but reminding himself that it was for Christa. He could not be living in the old way, but if he was careful he could manage and still save. That, plus the reserve in Switzerland, might do it.

Willi Orlik had been hopeful. "I've brought out three cousins already. The Nazis want hard currency. But it's a delicate business. What you need to do is put, say, twenty thousand dollars in a Swiss account over which she's got authority."

"There's one already set up."

"Fine. Anyhow, she applies for an exit visa. When she does that, she has to list all her assets, so she puts down that twenty thousand. But since it's in Switzerland, they can't touch it without a release from her. Usually, in return for signing over an account of that size, they'll issue the exit permit. It depends on how badly they want to keep her."

"Her father could put up twenty thousand right away."

"No good. They can take everything he has any time they want. No, this has to be extra. That's what makes the deal attractive to them. . . . You say the State Department won't help?"

"Got nowhere with them."

"It's the money. They won't let her go unless they make a profit. Look, you get the money, and the next time I go to Switzerland—"

"I'll have it," Lan said. "Somehow."

And he raised it in under a year—scrimping, saving, and currying favour with the studio. No more arguing in script conferences, no more foolishness about art. He knew what they wanted, and he gave it to them, grinding it out as a butcher grinds out sausage, working on scripts at night, too, alone in his apartment, to keep from going crazy. When he had the money, he gave it to Willi, and Willi went straight to Switzerland, for it was August, 1939. Both

359

France and Britain had pledged to fight for Poland, and Christa's release would have to be arranged before the inevitable war. . . .

LAN parked behind a wood-panelled station wagon in Willi's drive and got out. He strode on towards the big white house. But Willi's voice came from one side. "Hello, Lan. This way!"

Lan turned. Willi rose from a chair beside the swimming pool. Seeing weariness in his haggard eyes, Lan knew.

"I'm sorry," Willi said bluntly as they shook hands. "It's impossible."

"Willi," said Lan desperately, "you don't mean that."

"I do. Here, have a drink." He poured a martini from a shaker. "She's one of the impossibles. The kind there is no price on. Believe me, I explored every avenue, but nothing worked. You might as well face it. They are not going to let her out."

Lan drank the whole martini in two swallows. "Damn it, Willi, they can't do this! I'll go back! I'll get in somehow and I'll—"

"Get yourself killed. They'd rub you out in a minute and make it look like an accident. Besides, you couldn't get there before war breaks out. And with wartime security in force, you'd have even less of a chance."

Lan stared at the shimmering sunlight on the pool. "Oh, Christ," he said.

"I know," Willi murmured. "But look at it this way. Even if there is war, it can't last forever. Sooner or later it will end—and they can't win, not even with Italy on their side. So when it's over, maybe in a year or two—"

"A year or two," Lan said. "It's already been so long."

"But it can be borne if you stay busy. Somehow you can bear it." He gripped Lan's arm. "Yes, old friend, it's bitter medicine to swallow. And you must stay with us now, today. Lan, please. Sit down and have another drink and we will talk . . ."

HE HAD a lot of drinks with Willi, and more when he got home, sitting at the table in his apartment, the letters, every one she'd written, in an untidy pile before him. They were all cut to a pattern. A paragraph of love, a paragraph of praise for the Third

360

Reich, another one of innocuous news, and a final one of hinted private desire.

Suddenly he knocked them all fluttering to the floor. He had failed her. She had counted on him and now he had failed and what was he to tell her; how could he go on scribbling banalities, torturing himself and her, when there was no hope?

He poured another drink, then whirled as someone knocked on the apartment door. The knock came again. He cleared his throat. "Who is it?"

A woman's voice said, "Phyllis."

Heavily he lumbered to the door. As soon as it was open just enough, she pushed through. Several paces into the room she halted, facing him, a slender figure in trim black, dark hair falling to her shoulders. Uncertainly, she removed her sunglasses. She had never been a great beauty, her features too uneven for the perfection required for stardom, but she had always possessed something better than that: a magnetism that drew men.

"Hello." There was uncertainty in her voice. "It's been a long time, hasn't it?"

"Phyll—"

"I heard that Willi was back, so I called him and he told me. And I made up my mind—this didn't seem precisely the time for you to be alone. Willi thought not, too. You need someone now."

"No. Just leave me alone."

Her voice was soft. "Is there no hope, really?"

"Willi says not. It depends on if there's a war."

"Maybe there won't be a war."

He switched on the little radio on the table. A voice, strained and tense, said: "The Polish government has rejected . . ." Lan clicked it off. "There'll be a war," he said. He took a swallow from the bottle, gagged.

"I think I'd better make some coffee," Phyllis said. She put down her bag and started towards the kitchen.

"No," he grunted.

She turned. "What do you want, then?"

He shook his head. He wanted her to leave, yet now dreaded being left alone. "I don't know," he mumbled.

Phyllis shrugged. "In that case, I'll make some coffee."

He no longer protested. It was a good feeling to have someone taking care of him again—and a better one to have another person in bed with him that night.

2

War or no war, the grapes would not wait; the harvest must go on. The invasion of Poland and the declaration of war by France and England had all come so quickly that everything had been thrown into turmoil. Just when needed most, workers who were in the military reserves were called to duty. The General drove himself furiously, from first light till last. For Christa there was no rest either, with hordes of people to be fed, and some of them quartered at the *Hof* as well.

Tonight it was after nine before she had a chance to rest. Exhausted as she was, there was no possibility yet of sleep, and so she bathed, changed clothes, and savoured the luxury of being alone with a glass of wine on the terrace. Above the Wienerwald the moon was high and rich; a couple of bats swooped and darted over the lawn. In the house only Traudi was still awake. Christa sighed, leaning back in her chair, kicking off her shoes.

How, she wondered, had Aunt Alma done it, old and crippled as she was? Even after more than a year, managing the household still stretched Christa to the limit. Which was a blessing, she supposed, for it left her no time for grieving.

The recollection of that first dreadful day had softened a little. Yet still, sometimes, it rushed back unbidden. The brutal loss of Lan. Her father's arrest. The whole house seething with fear and dismay. The radio blaring Nazi bulletins. The second day, a Sunday, had been a duplicate. Aunt Alma, drained, collapsed, was put to bed. By Monday Christa's head was clearing slightly. Surely they had not dared hurt Lan, and he would find a way to get in touch with her. Surely Papa would be released before long; he had done nothing to harm them. And later she could get out to Czechoslovakia, meet Lan there. Then Robert Schellhammer had come. . . .

As Traudi showed him in, Christa stared. This was a Robert

362

she had never seen, erect and military in crisp brown uniform, shining boots, a pistol at his waist.

"Kreisleiter Schellhammer, NSDAP, at your service, Frau Condon." His smile was faint.

"Kreisleiter?"

"Yes. I'm the senior Party officer in this district. Surely that's no surprise to you."

"No," she said heavily. "No, it isn't."

"I would have been here sooner, but I've been so damned busy, Christa." Now his face was grave. "What in God's name were you and Lan mixed up in? He's been expelled, your father's been arrested, you almost were. The Gestapo tell me the entire matter is absolutely and completely secret. What kind of danger have you let Lan expose you to?"

Christa hesitated. Her mind worked swiftly, clearly. So Robert didn't know about the pictures. Of course not. The Gestapo would let no one know about the pictures. She could lie. "I don't know, really. Lan was working on a story with some foreign correspondent in Vienna, something about the reaction of Jews to the *Anschluss* or . . . I'm not sure what. All I know is we were arrested and dragged to the station and . . . and he was sent away. They brought me home and took Papa and . . . and we've heard nothing since." The tears coming then were genuine, but the move was calculated when suddenly she threw her arms around him. "Oh, Robert, you've got to help us. I'm so frightened."

As she began to sob, his arms encircled her and his hand stroked her back as if she were a frightened child. "All right, Christa," he kept whispering. "All right, now, my girl." When finally she reached the end of tears, he gently pushed her away, took out a crisp, clean handkerchief, and wiped her cheeks. "Now, steady. We must talk. Did your father know what Lan was doing?"

"No, absolutely not. I swear it."

Robert nodded. Thoughtfully he began to pace. She waited tensely, daring now to hope. Abruptly he halted, turned. "Very well. Perhaps there is something I can do. I shall certainly try. You understand, of course, there is nothing I can do about Lan's expulsion. But . . . General Helmer is a patriot, whatever our misunderstandings. It's not a simple matter for an ordinary Party man to mix in Gestapo affairs, but. . . . On your word that he's innocent of any activities against the Führer, I'll go to the limit for him."

"You have my word. Oh, thank you." And she meant it this time when she embraced him, kissed him.

She felt him draw in a deep breath, and as she moved away his eyes met hers. "One should help his friends," he said quietly, "and show no mercy to his enemies. Now, I must leave for the city." His eyes flared. "There's a chance the Führer will arrive this evening. You realize, Christa, this is the fulfillment of my dream! Not just for myself, but for Austria."

"I congratulate you." Her voice was toneless.

He picked up his hat. "Now, some advice. You should not leave the Christinahof until you hear from me. Just stay quietly here and wait." He started towards the door, halted, turned. "And Christa—"

"Yes?"

"I suggest you do not try to get in touch with Lan. And if he should communicate with you, be careful of every word. Bluntly, your mail will be read and your telephone tapped. Do you understand?"

"Yes."

He smiled. "Now don't look so glum. All will come well. *Wiederseh'n.* Heil Hitler!"

"*Wiederseh'n*, Robert," she answered numbly.

He seemed about to speak, thought better of it, and went out. When he had gone, she leaned against the door jamb, weakened by relief. Then slowly some strength ebbed back into her. She was not as powerless as she had thought; she had a certain power of her own, which she had just used to good effect.

No triumphant Caesar entering Rome could have been more jubilantly received than Adolf Hitler in Vienna. The Army that preceded him had been welcomed along its route as a band of heroes and saviours; he was greeted like a god. Tens of thousands cheered and shrieked his name, and Christa, listening to the radio, found it awesome, terrifying. None of them—not Papa, Lan, herself, or Josef—had realized how hungry the crowd was for a leader of real strength and decisiveness.

364

Robert phoned twice, reassuringly, and finally, eight days after his first visit, he reappeared, this time with General Helmer beside him in the car. Her father's eyes were deeply sunken in a haggard unshaved face, but his shoulders were straight, his voice firm and steady, his smile quick as Christa rushed to him.

"Yes. Yes, I am quite all right. No trouble at all. How is your Aunt? I must go up and see her at once." He turned. "Robert, I am deeply grateful!"

Robert glowed with pride. "Herr General, I'm glad to have been of service. Now, I know you and your family want to be alone."

Christa could not help it; she ran to him, kissed him. "Robert, thank you. Thank you so much."

He looked down at her. "I told you I would do what I could. Now—" he raised his arm "—Heil Hitler!"

Christa was startled when the General briskly returned the salute. "Heil Hitler! My greetings to your parents."

Robert got into the car, waved, and drove away. Christa stared at the General. "Papa, you—"

"Yes," Helmer sighed. "I'm afraid it's something we'll all have to do as if we meant it."

After dinner he spoke of what had happened to him. "When they took me to the Gestapo," he said, "I was questioned in a most peculiar way. There was something they wanted to know, but seemed reluctant to ask me directly for fear of revealing knowledge that I might not already have, certain activities of you and Lan and, of all people, Josef Steiner." His eyes held her, his fingers drummed on the table.

Christa felt blood mount to her face. "Papa—"

"No." He held up a hand. "I know nothing about it and I do not want to know anything about it. It is something that must be forgotten." He looked down at his plate. "Even the Gestapo seems to want it forgotten," he said. "And that perhaps is the only reason why we are still alive and free. With Robert's help, the police and I have reached the following tacit understanding."

She had never seen his face so grave. "First, Lan has been expelled and he will never be allowed to return. Second, under no circumstances will you or I be allowed outside the country.

Apparently what Lan knows is explosive; we are the insurance of his silence."

"Papa—" Christa stared at him, then turned away. "You're saying," she whispered, "that I'll never see Lan again."

His voice softened; he came to her, put a hand on her shoulder. "Things change, matters are forgotten. Perhaps one day. But I mustn't give you false hope. It will be a long time."

She raised her head, swallowed hard. "I understand."

"Good. You are your mother's daughter; I knew you would." He backed away, continued, tone more businesslike. "Beyond that, we owe a great debt to Robert Schellhammer. He went to some risk on our behalf. We must continue to have his good will. Now, let me make myself clear. You are a married woman, and all of us must understand and respect that, most especially Robert. I am sure he will. But Robert still loves you. With Lan gone, that could create an embarrassing situation. And. . . ."

Christa somehow managed a smile as she stood up. "Yes, Papa," she said. "Don't worry. I know what you mean. Robert and I will continue to be friends. I shall do nothing to damage his love for me. But beyond that, we should all be clear. I *am* a married woman. And I love my husband and I always will."

The General did not meet her eyes. "Good." After a few seconds' silence, he went on briskly. "Well, we shall dispose of your apartment in Vienna. You will live here from now on." He put his arms around her. "So," he said. "We shall do the best we can, and the main thing is that we must not, ever, despair."

"Yes, Papa," Christa said.

FIVE DAYS after her father's release, Aunt Alma had died in her sleep. Normally, hundreds would have attended her funeral; in fact there were hardly more than two dozen mourners. Word had spread: the Helmers were tainted, association with them dangerous.

Christa threw herself into managing the household. But there was no word from Lan, and she sank into deep depression.

Then, three weeks after his expulsion, the post brought a ticket to a concert in Vienna, Fräulein Marietta Duncan in a programme of Schubert Lieder. Enclosed was a terse note: "*Please* attend."

Something clicked in Christa's mind. Marietta was Mark Gorton's young American mistress.

Gorton sat in the front row; Christa's ticket was for a seat at the rear. On her left was a classmate of Marietta's, a girl her own age who chatted in abysmal German. When the lights went down and the applause began, she pressed an envelope into Christa's hand.

Marietta sang superbly, but Christa did not hear. At the interval, in the privacy of a toilet cubicle, she opened the envelope with hands that shook! *Our friend is safe and well in Prague. He misses you terribly, and sends all his love. Be in the main courtyard of the monastery at Altkreuzburg and bring a letter for him on Saturday 3 p.m. MG.*

THE MONASTERY at Altkreuzburg had been founded in the Middle Ages, and over the centuries it had amassed rich treasures of painting, sculpture, and manuscripts. On that pleasant Saturday afternoon, it swarmed with sightseers, mostly Germans, in uniform and out.

The main courtyard was dominated by a huge crucifix erected to the memory of the town citizens who had fallen in the war. Christa, at three o'clock, pretended to be preoccupied surveying this. Then Mark was there, only another tourist standing by her. He told her of Lan's phone call, took her letter, and promised to deliver it to Prague and bring one back. When she met him the next Saturday in the same place, he had one for her. And suddenly everything changed; the depression lifted.

After that she lived for Saturday afternoons; then, one day Mark told her, "I'm being kicked out, too, and Marietta's going with me." Christa's heart sank, but he went on quickly. "Listen, I've made inquiries. I think now it's safe for the two of you to write to each other directly, *if—*" And he told her what he would tell Lan: the letters would undoubtedly be opened and read. "Anyhow, just remember, nothing lasts forever and tyrants always overreach. Just hang on. Do what you Austrians always do so well: survive. And someday it will be all right."

She looked at him, this stumpy red-faced man who had selflessly run so many risks for her. She knew that he loved

Austria as much as she, maybe more. Briefly, she hugged and kissed him.

His red face turned even redder. "It will be all right," he repeated. "*Wiederseh'n*, Christa."

"*Wiederseh'n*," she whispered and watched him walk out through a vast grey arch and disappear behind a buttress.

THE GENERAL joined the Party. Wehrmacht and SS officers began to show up at the Christinahof. The word spread, not only about the food and the view but, also, no doubt, about the General's blonde daughter. Anyhow, the quarantine was lifted.

She herself performed like a monkey on a stick at those affairs, Christa thought bitterly, always careful to be charming, not quite flirtatious, still armoured by her status as a married woman but using her sex appeal to dazzle Austrians and Germans alike. And sometimes there were afternoons when some officer wittier and more cultivated than the others would seek her out, and suddenly she would realize, *I'm having a good time!* And then, full of self-reproach, she would draw back.

And there was always Robert Schellhammer to consider. She had promised Papa that she would manage him, and as time passed she realized how all-important that was. He, not General Helmer, was now the real power in the Ferntal, and their lives and property were in his hands.

They saw a great deal of each other. And yet he was always absolutely correct, careful never to go beyond the bounds of the friendly intimacy they had always shared. Underneath, she knew, he seethed, and so she herself was meticulously proper, careful neither to tantalize him nor arouse his jealousy. . . .

SUDDENLY, inside the house a bell rang. Christa put down her wine and slipped her feet back into her shoes. A moment later Traudi appeared on the terrace.

"Herr Schellhammer," she said a little shakily.

Christa turned to meet him. "Christa. I hope I'm not intruding."

She masked a frown. His uniform, usually so natty, was rumpled. There was a faint unsteadiness in his movements as he took her hand and kissed it. He had, she saw at once, drunk a lot of wine. "No, certainly not." At all costs he must be welcomed.

"Good." He stood there motionless. "May I have a little wine?"

"Of course. Traudi, bring another glass."

Robert walked across the terrace. "I am truly sorry to disturb you at this hour—"

"Don't give it a thought. Is something wrong?"

"There are things. . . ." He broke off, dropped heavily into a chair. Then Traudi came with a glass. "Thank you," he said, tersely. "We won't need you any more. Go to bed."

When she was gone, he took a long, almost savage, swallow from the glass. "They took Professor Busch today." His voice was rasping, bitter. "Without consulting me, they just came and took him. Old Busch . . . Never a man more dedicated to the German soul."

No need to ask who *they* were. She felt a pang of pity for the strange old man. "But why?"

"He wouldn't work in a factory or farm. He's nonproductive. And with a war on we can't afford to feed the nonproductive."

"And you couldn't stop them?"

"No," he said harshly. "I couldn't stop them. How could I? I'm just an Austrian." He rose, went to the parapet, stared out at the woods. "It was a blow at me, a deliberate blow at me. There was a post coming open, to a promotion. I was due for it. Of course there was somebody else who wanted it. Naturally, a German, and—"

"And he got it?"

"It's his." Robert let out a long rasping breath. "*We're* the ones who risked everything to bring Austria into the Reich, but now it seems we're not competent to manage our own country. They send people from Berlin down here to show us how—" He turned. "You know, of course, you're part of the reason."

"I?"

"If I hadn't stuck my neck out for you and the General. . . . I was taking a chance, I knew, but I hadn't expected it to be *this* costly."

Christa said nothing. She had never seen his reserve break;

what had happened must have been shattering. Then he said, commandingly, "Come here. I've got some things to say to you."

She found herself moving towards him. When she was in reach, he took her hand, pulled her very close. "Maybe it's all for the best. There's no more damage they can do to me if I marry you."

"Marry?" she whispered.

"Hell yes, why not? I love you. I always have. Lan is gone," he said thickly. "And you might as well understand that. He's gone and he's not coming back. It's as if he's dead. You're not a wife, you're a widow!"

"I am not!" she cried, pulling away from him.

"You are! You have to face it! It's over, ended, and you've got to make a new life for yourself. Well, I'll help you do that. We'll get married and—"

Christa backed away. "Robert, you're drunk. We were married in the Church. We'll always be married until—"

He took a step towards her. "Christa, I've already checked. It's dead easy! The Church is crawling to the Party! All you have to do is sign the papers and there'll be an annulment." He snorted. "Hell, he never even gave you a child. But I'll give you sons and daughters and put these two estates together and—"

"You'd better go," Christa said flatly.

But he was on her then, had locked her in his arms, his face close to hers. "Listen, you'd better see the light! You and your father both, you're not in the clear with the Gestapo by a long shot! Without me to stand between you and them. . . . But you marry me, it wipes the slate clean." His mouth came down on hers.

She jerked her face aside, began to fight. "Let me go!" she said. "I tell you, let me go!"

To her surprise he did. She dodged back as he straightened up, panting, "Christa—"

"Listen," she heard herself fling at him, "I'm sorry, I don't want to hurt you. But I'll never ask for any annulment, not for you, not for anybody! I love Lan, I—" Her voice broke. "Just leave me alone! I hate you, I hate all of you. Oh, God, you and your crooked crosses, I hate. . . ." And then no more would come and she turned to the wall, face buried in her hands.

He was still there, in silence. After a while, he said, "Christa, you didn't mean that."

Still she could not speak, just shook her head, her hands still over her face. She knew that she had destroyed too much in that outburst, that for her father's sake, the sake of both of them, she had to turn, make it right somehow. But she seemed to have no power to speak or move.

"All right," Robert said presently. "Well, I will tell you now, for your own good, I did not hear what you said. Not about the Party symbol, not. . . . You are distraught." His voice was harsh, the pleading gone. "But, thank you for being honest with me. Don't worry. I won't bother you again. I have some pride of my own."

Still she did not turn or answer.

"*Auf Wiederseh'n,* Frau Condon. Heil Hitler!"

TWO WEEKS LATER the engagement of Kreisleiter Robert Schellhammer was announced—to Charlotte Richter, the plump, blonde daughter of the owner of the largest butcher shop in Altkreuzburg. Christa's father showed her the item in the Altkreuzburg weekly paper. "Christa, I don't understand this. Do you?"

"Papa, I'm afraid I do," she said, and then she told him. Suddenly she was struck by how *old* he looked and realized with a shock that he was now past sixty. "Papa, I'm so sorry. I know it means more trouble for you, but I just couldn't."

He rose, smiling faintly, came to her, held her tightly to him. "Of course you couldn't," he said quietly. "Of course you couldn't."

He let her go, stepped back. "Look," he said quietly. "In 1914 I went off to war. I was gone for months, years, at a time. Your mother waited, never knowing from one minute to the next whether I was alive or dead, what news the post would bring. She was lonely and she was frightened, but she never faltered, never lost faith. . . . Do you expect me to criticize you for being her daughter?" He found no more words, but she knew what he meant, and she loved him fiercely and went to him again and they held each other.

Ever since *Anschluss*, Dr. Martinus had continued to serve the church in Ferndorf. It was there in that same spring of 1938 that Frau Sattler had come to him, a lean, dynamic woman in her early forties. Her husband, the town's leading livestock dealer and a member of a Monarchist organization, had been taken by the Gestapo. Now, a month later, Frau Sattler entered the church office, carrying in trembling hands a curious utilitarian ceramic canister.

"This," she said in a dull whisper, "came in the post today."

"I am afraid I don't understand."

She opened the canister. Within it was a curious grey substance. "This is my husband. His ashes. They have burnt him."

Martinus gaped.

"In the post," she repeated. "With this." She fumbled in her pocket, brought out a paper. The letterhead was that of Dachau concentration camp.

The government regrets to inform you that subject individual died on April 17 of a sudden illness. His remains have been cremated and are dispatched to you herewith. The enclosed reckoning for cremation charges must be paid within one week. Heil Hitler!

Numbly Martinus handed back the letter, looked at the urn, seeing in his mind the tall good-humoured horseman.

"They killed him," Frau Sattler rasped. "That dear good man —the strongest man in the Ferntal, never sick a day in his life, and they say. . . ." Her voice broke. "The children. What am I to tell them when they come home from school? What am I. . . . Ashes. Only ashes." Her voice was low, terrible. "Father, you must come with me, be there when the children come. I can't—"

"Yes," he said. "Yes, I will come."

MERCIFULLY, he could no longer remember how he had got through that day. If he had known how many more like it there would be, his words of comfort would have stuck in his throat. But

Sattler's death was only one of many; soon all over Austria the postmen were delivering urns.

Meanwhile, Austrians were prised from the last vestige of control over their own destinies. Nothing was as Martinus had imagined; and as the dimensions of the catastrophe became clear to him, he saw how dreadfully mistaken he had been. The disaster touched even the classes he taught at the Gymnasium. Those he conducted in English literature were virtually gutted. The classes in religion were worse; contortions were necessary to square what he believed with what was happening, to give Hitler primacy over Christ. But, as Cardinal Innitzer had said in his pastoral letter, it was the duty of the Church to pray for the objectives of the Party. All problems had been resolved by the ancient formula concerning those things which were Caesar's and those which were God's. And the Cardinal had signed his letter of capitulation "Heil Hitler!"

And then in November 1938 had come the nightmare of *Kristall-nacht*—the night of the broken glass—a poetic name for a brutality that had extended from the North Sea to the Italian border. All across the Reich, synagogues were desecrated, Jews rounded up and shipped off to concentration camps. Assuming the end had come, whole Jewish families committed suicide.

Slowly something in Martinus grew, rough and jagged as a swallowed stone—a shame that would not let him eat or drink or sleep in peace. This evil, he decided, must be fought. And he was not alone.

The brighter tenth of his classes resented what was happening —the abridgment of their academic freedom—and they had the raw courage of youth, its disdain for consequences. They assaulted Martinus with demands for explanations of what was happening to their education; and finally in self-defence he began teaching special secret classes in literature and religion. The response was startling; not only students but their parents came. He sensed in them a kinetic energy. In secret sessions after class, the Organization for Austrian Freedom was born. Hardly realizing what was happening, he found himself its leader, converted from a man of words into a man of action.

By the autumn of 1940 in and around Altkreuzburg, there were three groups of more than thirty, each ignorant of the membership of the other as a precaution, and they were in touch with similar groups that had sprung up independently. And yet, Martinus thought, there was so little that any of them could do. Only circulate newsletters compiled from listening to illegal radios, scatter anti-Nazi slogans printed on cheap paper. Now, after a wintry Sunday afternoon meeting, he waited at the bus stop at Ferndorf. As always these days, he was taut, nervous, exposed.

"Dr. Martinus!"

He looked up. From the Steyr that had just pulled over to the kerb, Christa Condon beckoned to him, smiling. "Dr. Martinus, where have you been? It's so long since we've seen you!" She patted the seat. "Get in, I'll take you wherever you are going."

"Thank you, no," Martinus said. "I'm waiting for a friend. He should be along directly."

"Oh." She looked disappointed. Martinus appraised her covertly. She was still a stunning woman, but he saw marks of strain around her eyes, and there was something mechanical in her smiling charm. "Well, if you're sure. . . ."

"I am. Again, thanks very much."

"Oh, you're welcome. You must come to see us. Papa and I often talk about you."

"I've been very busy. You know how it is."

"Oh, yes," she sighed. "everyone is always so busy. Well. . . ." Behind her a car honked. "*Auf Wiederseh'n*. Heil Hitler."

"Heil Hitler," he said automatically, attaching no importance to her use of the words than to his; really they meant nothing.

She put the car in motion and, stepping into the alcove of a shop door, he watched it go. It had been for her sake that he had refused the lift; the Helmers had troubles enough with the régime without being linked to him if anything should happen. Of course, that worked two ways. Presumably she was still under Gestapo observation and he did not want her to draw undue attention to him.

He felt depressed, helpless. Then the postbus roared up the street, and he got on board, savouring the warmth inside. It made

374

him drowsy, and for a while he hardly thought at all as it roared down the Danube valley, into Altkreuzburg. It climbed the hill to the high market square, pulled over to the kerb, and its doors cranked open. Martinus waited until two thick-ankled women got off, and then he descended, opening his umbrella as he did so, his briefcase under his arm.

He started to cross the square. Then two men who seemed to come from nowhere fell in beside him. One spoke his name.

Martinus turned, throat suddenly tight and something in his stomach fluttering like a wounded bird. He looked into the polite, grave, ruthless faces and knew it would do no good to run. He could hardly breathe and found it impossible to speak; all he could do was clutch the briefcase more fiercely to him, as if he would lock it forever with his arms.

CATASTROPHE hit the Ferntal. Like angels of death that winter weekend the Gestapo swept through the valley and the town. Nearly two hundred people, most from leading families, were taken unexpectedly, people the Helmers had known for years. Newspapers blared triumphantly the destruction of a traitorous spy ring for the British, its leader a renegade priest from Altkreuzburg.

A fear-sick tension settled over the whole area. The "Hitler Look" became a part of life—the quick, apprehensive twist of the head to see who was watching, listening, before one spoke. Now there were means at hand for the vindictive to settle old scores; even an anonymous letter was all the Gestapo needed. And, of course, already tainted, the Helmers were doubly vulnerable.

Thus, Christa knew, her father was entangled in a spiderweb of problems. Without the cachet Robert had lent them, only rarely now did Party officials appear at the Christinahof. There was even chilling gossip that Charlotte Richter Schellhammer was pressing her husband to acquire the Christinahof. And Christa and the General both knew that any time Robert wanted the Christinahof, he could have it almost for a snap of his fingers. The Party owed him that much.

There was nothing she herself could do about any of this except

manage the house as best she could and minimize the strain of petty annoyances on her father. Into that she threw herself whole-heartedly, letting it blank out everything else.

But despite her efforts, she could see as winter wore on into spring the toll all this took of General Helmer. He had begun to drink now to relieve the pressure, and not just wine, but potent brandy and slivovitz. But even that did not worry her so much as his headaches.

HELMER WASHED the three aspirins down with brandy and buried his face in his hands, waiting for the pain to go away. Sometimes it did, sometimes not; and when it did not, it took all his strength to mask it.

Outside, summer was on the land, vineyards in full June leaf, bees buzzing in the clematis around the window of his office. Slowly the headache faded. Finally Helmer took another drink of brandy, a measure of his desperation. Something, he knew, was badly wrong with him. He needed a doctor, but he dared not go to one. He would be immediately sent to a hospital; and once he was helpless, the wolves would pounce. Only he stood between the Christinahof and destruction. So the pain must be endured. If the harvest was very good this year, if England finally surrendered, it was possible that he could organize things so he could rest; until then he must hang on.

There was one thing, though, that always helped, distracting his mind from its worries: the battle map pinned on the wall. He marked it every day with crayons. Surveying it relaxed him, for the triumphs it showed made up for a great deal of what the Nazis had cost him. If one blamed Hitler for domestic difficulties, one had as well to give him credit for the victories. As a professional soldier, Helmer could feel nothing but admiration.

It had all been done so beautifully and with the fewest possible casualties. The armoured sweeps across the Low Countries, and the delightful totality of the French defeat, at which he could only gloat. All the lands of the old Empire were back under German domination. All the old shames had been erased. And, with superb cleverness, all of that had been accomplished without arousing the sullen bear of Russia. So it had to end soon, Helmer thought, feeling better. Not even Churchill, not even the help Roosevelt was giving the English, could save Britain much longer.

Now his head was clear and he could tackle the problems on his desk—the need for priorities for new stocks of bottles and new equipment. They had changed the damned rationing system again and there were new forms to be deciphered. These bureaucrats, clogging the pipelines with their papers, were worse than Jews. Maybe when the war was over, they would all be shipped east to Poland, too.

The Jews. Helmer lit a cigarette. Well, that had been pretty rough. And yet, there again, maybe the method was justified. In wartime, you could not have a nation within a nation, loyal only to itself. How else to uproot them? On the whole, they were lucky. The Russians would simply have exterminated them. As it was, they were only being relocated to where they could all live together in one vast Jewish enclave, which was what, anyhow, they seemed to prefer to do wherever they settled.

Still, it was strange not having them around. Dr. Kleinmann— there was one Jew he really missed. He could have sat down with Alex, discussed not only his symptoms but his problems, and they could have worked out something. But that stupid swine who had taken Kleinmann's place in Altkreuzburg, he knew a lot of Nazi doctrine but damned little medicine. Damn it, he did miss Alex. And he hadn't been able to find a decent tailor since the entire Birnbaum family had been resettled.

Well, let that go for now. All these papers to be filled out. . . . Start at the beginning, be methodical and orderly. He wrote in the date on a priority application, 22 June 1941, and went on from there meticulously, losing track of time. He was only vaguely aware of the ringing of the gate bell until Christa knocked on his door, then opened it.

"Papa, there is a gentleman here to see you. A writer for the Propaganda Ministry." She passed him a card.

"Dr. Abelard Hossbach," he read aloud. "What does he want?"

Christa shrugged. "An interview. Something about Russia."

Helmer frowned, but he could not help being vaguely flattered.

So they had not forgotten him. Still, they had been soft-pedalling Russia and it was certainly better that way. Probably Christa was confused; likely they wanted his views on the strategic situation in North Africa. He had been consulted several times by the press on such matters.

Anyhow, this was a vital aspect of his connections. "Show him in," he said.

Dr. Hossbach was a towering man in his late forties, with a greying beard and a substantial corporation. "Herr Generalmajor. How nice of you to receive me." His palm was soft, slightly clammy.

"Not at all."

Hossbach opened his briefcase, taking out notebook and pencils.

"What can I do for you?" the General asked.

"I am here by direct order from Berlin, at the specific request of the Propaganda Ministry. You will remember that in the First War you figured in exposing Russian atrocities. We should like you to give us your personal memories in an interview which will be widely published in the press."

Helmer stared at him. "Are you sure? We're at peace with Russia. I can't possibly see any use in—"

Hossbach sighed. "My dear Generalmajor, the Ministry has a reason for everything it does. Now with your permission, shall we get on with it? An hour should suffice."

"THANK YOU, HERR GENERAL," Hossbach said at last.

"You're welcome," Helmer managed. His face felt flushed, his spine chilled; and he knew his hands trembled and that the last quarter hour of the interview had been disjointed, partly from pain, partly from the brandy that he had used to quench it. "You will, of course, stay and eat."

"Sorry, no. I have a deadline," Hossbach said. "But thank you for your courtesy. Now perhaps I can repay it. It is exactly noon and I am now permitted to explain it all. This morning our armies invaded the Soviet Union on a tremendous front. We're smashing forward without opposition, and their air force has already been destroyed on the ground."

Helmer listened, the words blurred by a sudden veil of pain. A vein throbbed in his temple and his left eye began to water. "No," he heard himself say. "No, that is impossible."

"But true." Hossbach smiled. "The Führer is disgusted with Russian provocations and is determined to settle the problem of Russia once and for all, for a thousand years. It has all, of course, been kept very secret until now. But—" his eyes shone "—with them disposed of, we are masters of all Europe! And—"

"The fool!" Helmer roared. "The fool, the idiot!" The pain lanced through his skull and flared. "Doesn't he know? He had it won! But, my God, now—Russia? Russia? Oh, the fool!"

"General, you can't mean the Führer!"

"I—" The rage, despair, within Helmer was almost too great to contain. "Napoleon," he said huskily. "For God's sake. It was on this same date that Napoleon crossed the Niemen."

"General, you are overwrought," Hossbach said.

"War on both flanks? It's madness," Helmer said. Tears of pain ran down his cheeks. "Absolute madness. And so . . . useless."

"Herr Generalmajor—" He touched Helmer's shoulder. "I shall not report this. But please get a grip on yourself. And remember, you must have faith. The Führer knows what he is doing, and the German soldier is invincible. General—" He shook hands.

Helmer did not see him to the door. Russia: Napoleon, Moscow. A three-front war, counting the Mediterranean—and those great reaches, those limitless depths of the East, which Hitler had never seen; oh, it was madness, sheer madness.

Something must be done. He reached for the phone. There was someone he must call about it, someone who. . . . He would go straight to the Emperor if necessary. . . . No, that was not right. Whom was he to call? He could not remember, but it would come back in a minute.

There was a flare of pain in his temple, as if he had been wounded. Then it died completely and at last he was all right again. Behind him the door opened and he turned. For a moment he stared at the person standing there. Then he sighed. "Christina. Darling."

He sprawled, arm across his eyes. "Thank God. I am tired, so tired. But now. . . . Darling, we've been apart so long."

CHRISTA stroked his forehead. It was clammy to her touch. She waited a few seconds; he did not stir. Quietly, watching him, she edged from the room. In the corridor she leaned against the wall, knees suddenly weak, heart seemingly about to wrench itself from its moorings. "Oh, my God," she whispered. "*Oh, my God!*" Then she ran to the telephone.

Rather than the Party hack who had taken Dr. Kleinmann's place, she called a certain Dr. Walzer, who, while impeccably Aryan, was a strange and prickly character of independent mind. He was not a Party member, and that, combined with his personality, had reduced his practice to almost nothing. But that did not disturb him; nothing ever seemed to disturb Matthias Walzer except the stupidity of mankind.

She kept vigil over her father; in half an hour he woke. To her relief, he knew her now, but he was still far from normal. He knew Walzer, too, when the doctor finally arrived, but was puzzled. "Where is Kleinmann? If I'm ill, Alex Kleinmann should see to me."

"Dr. Kleinmann couldn't come, Papa," Christa said. "He sent Dr. Walzer." She tried not to cry as her eyes met those of the doctor. He was smooth and reassuring as they led the General to his room.

"That's right, Herr General. Alex is very busy these days. I'm helping him with his practice. Now. . . ."

Helmer obediently took the pills Walzer gave him. In the corridor the doctor said, "I think he will sleep for several hours." He sighed. "As you've probably guessed, Frau Condon, he's had a stroke, fortunately one comparatively minor. He doesn't seem impaired physically, but as to his mind . . . well, only time will tell."

"Shouldn't he be in the hospital?" Christa tried to wrestle with the implications of all this.

Walzer lit a cigarette. "Under normal circumstances, I'd say yes. But—" He looked at her through smoke. "I've known substantial businessmen to be . . . well, ruined quite needlessly because word had got about that temporarily they could not control their own affairs."

Christa saw exactly what he meant. She thought of the rumours Walzer must have heard—Charlotte Schellhammer and her longing

381

for the Christinahof; she thought of the Gestapo. The coldness within her grew. "All the same, his health is what counts. If he can get better care in the hospital—"

"He can't," Walzer said bluntly. "Not under the, ah, present administration. In fact, I think remaining in familiar surroundings would hasten his recovery."

Christa drew in a deep breath. "Then you think he'll recover?"

"To some extent. Only time will tell. These things are unpredictable. But his confusion was already lessening as I examined him and . . . I am hopeful that in a few days he'll be rational again."

"Thank God," Christa whispered. "I was afraid. . . . Then you do think he'll soon be back to normal?"

"Rational, I said. Normal—that I can't guarantee. We have to face the fact there's been some brain damage. It's unlikely that he'll ever be completely the man he was before. Even under the best circumstances, there's usually a fall-off in drive, alertness. You or someone had better be prepared to familiarize yourself with his business affairs and to help him with them. And, of course, there may be a repetition; there often is. But I'll prescribe a diet that will bring down his blood pressure. For the moment, that's all I can tell you. I'll see him again tonight and tomorrow." His grim face softened. "It could be worse, much worse. And I still recommend that you keep all this strictly within the family if possible." Then, briskly, he shook her hand and left.

Christa hurried back to Helmer's room. He slept soundly; and looking down at him, she found the courage of necessity and made her decision. The doctor had been right. Until she knew how things stood, she must not let word of this get around. Fortunately she had told the servants only that their master was not feeling well; she would pass it off as summer flu. Later she would see.

She had a bed moved into his room and remained with him day and night. In twenty-four hours he was already returning to a semblance of normality. "But I don't understand," he said. "What happened? Some journalists. Russia. And. . . why am I in bed?"

"Papa," Christa said gently, "you had a small temporary collapse. Too much work, too much strain, at your age. Nothing serious, but you need rest."

A few days before, Helmer would have snorted, *Rest? Nonsense! I've better things to do than loll in bed all day!* Now he only blinked vaguely, his face strangely wan and old. "I see," he murmured.

A few more days in bed and then he was up and around, and seemingly as physically strong as before. But to Christa, who knew him so well, what was left was only a mockery of the man he had been. All the drive, all the force, was gone; the mind once lightning swift now worked tortuously, its attention span short as a child's. Yet, an outsider meeting him only briefly would have seen no change.

Now a new weight bore down on Christa; it fell to her not only to manage the house itself but every aspect of the Christinahof and its holdings. Long into the night she pored over records and correspondence, trying to comprehend the place's finances—the entire intricate network spun by Helmer for their survival.

Nothing in her life had prepared her for this, and much was incomprehensible. Sometimes she could get clarification from Helmer and sometimes not. All she could do was blunder through, and slowly an eerie, nerve-racking pattern evolved. Like a good child, Helmer said and did what she told him to. It was desperately necessary that the world at large continue to believe in his undiminished strength and capability. She had to foster that illusion while learning to manage the Christinahof herself.

4

The massive oak stood in the centre of a clearing deep in the Wienerwald. Crude wooden cabinets encircled its thick trunk five feet above the ground, crammed with cheap pictures of the Virgin, crucifixes, and the like, and numerous little jars and vases containing fresh or artificial flowers. A *Waldandacht*—a place of devotion in the woods—and nothing in it could have been worth more than a few pfennigs; yet to Christa its surroundings and the very simplicity of its contents, placed there by devout villagers, had always transcended its essential tawdriness. Here, far more easily than in a church, she could pray, and often had. Yet today, standing alone before the oak, autumn sunlight slanting through the forest, she could find no words—not even here. All her prayers, all her faith had been used up; for Lan had ceased to love her.

At first she had blamed the disruption of transatlantic mail. Discreetly, she checked with the postal authorities, but when it became obvious that communications with the United States were only minimally disrupted, she had to face up to the realization she had tried to keep where it would touch neither mind nor heart. Lan simply was not sending any letters. He had given up, or had found someone else. Jealous rages had hit her, fierce and suffocating. Her mind filled with images of brutal, obscene clarity, leaving her physically sick. . . .

Eventually the rages became rarer. Presently they ceased altogether, to be replaced by despair, like grief at a loved one's death. With time's passage, that grew less profound; but it was always there. Sometimes she was startled to realize that she was only twenty-five; most of the time she felt like an old woman—listless, joyless, only getting from one day to another as best she could.

She crossed herself and turned away. And, she thought, walking on into the woods, it could not go on like this. But she had learned this much from all she had endured: self-pity was the most destructive enemy of all. Only yield to it for a moment and you were lost, and too much depended on her—her father, the Christinahof—for her to risk that luxury. No, she would manage somehow, she would think of something.

The path led her down into a ravine. The clean simple exercise of walking was good, restful. Nimbly she followed the track up the other side; and then, at the crest, she came into a clearing. Here she halted, looking at the curious house and its adjacent sheds, wattled structures of sticks and mud and thatch. Professor Busch, she thought, poor mad old man. And he was gone now, too. Absently, she went up to the house, still sound, undamaged by time or vandalism, and touched the rough wooden door. To her surprise it swung open. It was dim inside and musty-smelling and. . . .

She gave a startled cry as the man sitting at the table in the dirt-floored room jumped up. Then the swift beat of her heart slowed as she recognized that wide-shouldered shape. "Oh," she said. "Excuse me, Robert."

He stood there in the light streaming through the door, neatly dressed in his full regalia, his face unsmiling, something almost guilty in his bearing. Then he said hoarsely, "Come in." With one hand he closed a file that had been open on the table.

Christa hesitated, then found herself moving towards him. "I didn't know anyone was here," she said. "I was just walking and—"

"I come here sometimes. It's a good place to . . . to work and think in peace. Besides—" he gestured "—it brings back memories. This is where we started. In the old days when we were illegal."

He shoved the file to one end of the table, gestured to the bench made of a split log. "Sit down. Would you like a cigarette?" She was surprised to see his hand shake a little as he worked two from a packet. "Decent ones. Gauloises. French."

"Thank you." She took it, sat on the end of the bench. He struck a match, bent to light it for her; the flame wavered, his hand still trembling. Looking up at him, she saw the dark circles beneath his eyes, the lines at the corners of his mouth.

He lit his own cigarette. Somewhere in the clearing a woodpecker drummed. "Well," Robert said in an oddly tinny voice. "Well. Almost like old times."

She thought of what it would have been like. He would have been decent to her, probably even indulgent. There would have been no excitement, but neither would there have been the grief. She would have been cared for and protected. There was something to be said for security, comfort, shelter. As she felt now, being simply *secure* was all she would ever ask of life again. But, of course, it was too late—for both of them. Suddenly she wanted to be away from him and that new regret. She stood up. "Yes. But I must be going."

"Oh." One toneless syllable. Then, as she turned towards the door, he was across the room in a pair of strides. "Christa." His fingers bit into her arm, pulled her around.

Startled, she tried to pull away, but he had both her upper arms clamped in his big hands, and then he was kissing her. She tried to wrench her head aside; angry, frightened, not because of the assault but because control of the situation was not hers. But his mouth followed hers, and then he was dragging her across the room to the rude bed that had been Busch's. Again she tried to pull away and this time her mouth came free. "Robert, stop! Are you mad!"

"Absolutely!" he said, and he twisted her and bore her down and fell on top of her. "Absolutely!" he panted. "By God . . . have waited long enough. Now—" He had her pinned with one arm. She was wholly captive to a strength greater than her own, completely helpless, guiltless, and suddenly something flared in her, and all at once desire was there, and her mind disengaged. Now, instead of pushing him away, her arm went around him, holding him closer.

IN THE CLEARING the woodpecker kept on drumming. Bathed in sweat, they lay on the crude bed, drained, exhausted. Christa's head was on his arm, her eyes closed. She could think again! Examining her own feelings, she felt no exaltation, but no shame, no regret—only a tremendous relief, a sense of safety after fear. She hardly heard Robert's murmuring in her ear. "Waited so long. . . . Love you, you know that . . . Charlotte—she doesn't count. Oh, this is what I have wanted for so long. Darling." He turned her head to kiss her on the mouth again.

And she let him, returning the kiss, no passion in her now, and no love; but that did not matter. Because now she knew where the help she had to have would come from. She moved closer to him, glad to be no longer alone.

5

In California two years had drifted by, and with every Nazi victory Christa became less of a reality, more a dream. There was no longer any hope of reaching her, not soon, maybe not for ever.

And he could not write to her. He no longer had anything at all to say that she would understand within the limits of what she was allowed to read. In the context of things as they were, it was mockery. He could not get a letter off; and her letters came for a while, and then—by then it was a blessed surcease—they stopped. You took what you had and cut your losses; and what you dreamed at night did not matter. Christa was a dream; Phyllis was real.

By eleven, the brunch at Willi Orlik's, really only a continuation of last night's party at Lan's rented beach house, was in full swing. Lan sought Phyllis, who had been going hard at the drink; he failed to find her. It made no difference. After more than two years he'd had all of this he could take. Out on the porch, he stared at the ocean, swallowing a nausea compounded of gin and nicotine and disgust. It was a fine bright day, warm for December even in California. Beyond the Malibu strand, a great white yacht moved against the skyline like a swan. Two men emerging from the house took up station near Lan.

"They'd better look out for Japs," said one.

"Japs!" the other snorted. "The Japs ain't that stupid."

"You never can tell. The radio this morning—"

"The radio! Listen, I hate Franklin Roosevelt's guts, but he's not gonna let those Japs make a dime. The Japs!" He spat. "Listen, you seen that new broad in there? Come on, I wanta show you." They went back inside.

Lan watched gulls wheeling across the horizon. They were free to soar as high as they could; he was not. Not even in his writing. His contract gave him no choice. While the world crumbled, he wrote of puppy love. Money flowed in; he donated much of it to England, but that was painless; there was plenty left.

Mostly he followed where Phyllis led. He'd given up his apartment, moved in with her, shut out memory. Once Christa had been a woman, his wife; now she was only a symbol. . . .

He watched the bright ocean for a while, drank the clean salt air, and rebelled at the thought of going back inside. Maybe the hangover was catching up with him. He needed rest. He went down the steps, walked towards their own house next door. He climbed the outside stairs of their veranda, went through the sliding door. The living room was still a wreck from last night's party—stale drinks, overflowing ashtrays. He left the door open; the radio was on. Sunday morning: a church service, the bleating of a choir. One more drink, then he'd sleep. He went into the kitchen. He had just taken the bottle from the cupboard when he heard sounds coming from the bedroom.

He made no noise as he padded to its doorway. The door was ajar. The two figures on the bed were wholly unaware of his

387

presence. Soundlessly he turned away. It was not anything he had not seen before. In the past two years with Phyllis he had seen a lot.

Carrying his drink, he went back out to the porch. There was in him a tiredness almost lethal. Behind him the choir kept on singing. He took a swallow of his drink, rubbed his eyes. He was not immediately aware that the singing had stopped suddenly in mid-stanza. Then an excited voice brought him around to face the radio.

"We interrupt this programme for a special news bulletin. Pearl Harbour, the U.S. naval base in the Hawaiian Islands, has been attacked without warning by air and naval forces identified as Japanese. The surprise attack occurred about seven thirty a.m., local time. Some American warships have been damaged and casualties may be substantial. A number of Japanese planes have been shot down. This is an act of war by Japan against the United States. The fighting is continuing. A statement from the White House is expected momentarily. Please stand by.... We repeat...."

Lan stood there rigidly as the announcement was completed. "So," he said aloud, and he threw his glass out into the sand.

When he moved, that weary heaviness no longer weighed him down. He knew exactly what he would do now, and there was no time to lose. He went quietly down the steps, walked swiftly around the corner of the beach house. By the time he reached his parked car, he was running.

THERE WAS NOTHING the studio could do about it; he had been sworn into the U.S. Army before they knew. And because in an hour the temper of the country had wholly changed, as if a sudden thunderstorm had cleared unwholesome air, there was no way the studio could challenge him. Phyllis, of course, was almost in shock. "You could have told me." The cords in her neck stood out, as she poured herself another drink. "I feel like I've been shipwrecked."

"I'm sorry."

"That Sunday afternoon at the beach house. Why didn't you *tell* me? Why did you just run off?"

"You were . . . busy," he said.

Her face paled; then she nodded. "Touché." She tossed off her drink. "Well," she went on, wearily, "now I have to rethink my life completely. Maybe I'll prowl the waterfront and make the sailors happy. Maybe I'll scrape lint for bandages or whatever they do nowadays. But I think we ought to break clean here and now. I'm going out to have a drink at Frenchy's. When I come back, your stuff ought to be gone. O.K.?"

"O.K."

"Then so long." Picking up her bag, she started towards the door. "Oh, God damn," she said halting. Then she came to him and threw her arms around him and kissed him briefly, fiercely. "All right," she said when she broke away. "Good luck, do you hear? I hope you find her. I would like for somebody in this world to have one damned thing turn out right." She wheeled, ran out of the door.

EVEN BEFORE he had stepped forward with the others and taken his soldier's oath, his major objectives were roughed out in his mind. Though it might take years, he had to get back to Austria—and Christa—by the shortest route. It took some doing, but presently he had got where he wanted—Fort Ritchie, Maryland, attending special schools in language, prisoner-of-war interrogation, and the analysis of captured documents. His fluent German, kept fine-honed by conversations with Willi and his coterie of exiles, got him into Intelligence.

His record at Fort Ritchie earned him an almost immediate giant step towards Christa. As a second lieutenant, he went with the First Armoured Division to North Africa, and there he met war firsthand. Like scavenging ravens after the fighting had receded he and his team prowled battlefields searching the corpses of the enemy for documents, letters, diaries, anything to yield a tatter of intelligence. It was repulsive work.

Then he was mercifully transferred to the interrogation of the living. He scored coups, built a reputation, moved up in the hierarchy of Intelligence. He made connections and used them to push himself forward, ever closer to the goal which he never once lost sight of, from North Africa to Sicily, from Sicily to Italy. Promoted to major now, he was sometimes even privy to advance planning.

When he came due for rotation home, he refused it, lest he lose all the ground he'd gained. Three years slid by, and with each passing month hope rose higher in him. Until, in July, 1944, like the Allies themselves, he found himself stalled in Italy.

6

They had all eaten their last meal and taken—except for the Communist—their last communion; and now they spent the minutes remaining to them in various ways as they waited for the hand of Death to reach into the cell and pluck the first one to go. The thief, convicted of looting the window of a butcher shop, sat slumped in a corner mumbling something incoherent that might have been a prayer. At the table the Communist was scribbling furiously, producing, Martinus supposed, his own final manifesto. The lawyer who had been caught with an illegal radio paced the room chain-smoking the twelve cigarettes given him. Martinus, all letters written, all prayers said, only waited, sitting on the cell's single bed. For nearly four years he had been shuttled from court to court, prison to prison, all across the Reich. Not until now had anyone seemed able to take responsibility for the execution of a priest.

He was back where he had begun—in Vienna. The "Poor Sinners Cell" they called this cubicle. What lay beyond, down the corridor, was the guillotine. After that—he had inquired and been told—the body would be crammed into a cheap sheet-metal box and either sent to the Medical School at the University or transported to the Central Cemetery, to be buried without ceremony.

His body did not concern him; he had long since written that off. Only his soul mattered now, and it was at peace.

The thief let out a kind of sob. Martinus rose and went to the corner where he slumped. Kneeling, he put a hand on the shoulder of the man. "My son, you've made your peace with God."

"Yes." Teeth chattered in a lean face not yet thirty. "Yes, Father, but I'm still afraid. Oh, God, I'm so afraid."

"It's only a passing through a door," said Martinus gently. "On the other side Christ is waiting to take you by the hand."

Pen stilled for the moment, the Communist twisted in his chair.

390

"If he does, friend, you'd better count your fingers! Father, have you no shame? If it weren't for your kind, none of us would be here. Your Catholic Schuschnigg refused to let us fight the Nazis."

The lawyer stopped his pacing, whirled, face furious. "Now, you . . ."

Martinus raised his hand. "Here at least we have free speech." He smiled at the Communist. "I'll not quarrel with you, brother. The final answer to all our questions lies too close; debate now would be only academic. Allow us our comforts, and you take yours. We are convinced we go to meet the Almighty. If He turns out to be Lenin, the last laugh is yours." He sobered. "Yes, we have made mistakes, all of us. But only because we're human, and to be human is to be fallible. But He is infallible and all-forgiving." He turned to the thief. "Cling to that."

"Yes," the man said, but his teeth kept chattering and he dropped his head, staring at his bent knees. The Communist picked up his pen. But it never touched the paper. Outside in the hall, cadenced footsteps resounded. Two uniformed warders holding keys and handcuffs appeared outside the door. For a seemingly endless moment they stood in utter silence, eyes raking over the quartet in the cell. The thief stopped his whimpering; there was not even the sound of breathing.

"Friedrich Preisser," the taller of the guards said at last.

"Oh, sweet Jesus," moaned the thief.

"You will come with us." And the guard unlocked the cell.

After that there was no more talking, only the feverish scratching of the Communist's pen. Martinus sat on the bed, lit a cigarette, ashamed at his surge of relief that he had not been the first to go, that he still had moments more of life. He was not afraid; it had been a good life, richly textured, more perhaps than he deserved. God had been good to him. What had happened to his group had been inevitable, but it had not been futile. Hundreds of people had borne witness with their lives to their belief in Austria and the nobility of man. The record of that remained, beyond expunging, and the time was coming soon when it would count. Because now, in August 1944, the Nazi monster was doomed, and everyone could see that, even a prisoner like himself.

It was surprising how much news one could acquire in prison. He knew everything of any consequence that had happened since his arrest four years ago. Of England's determined resistance; of the invasion of Russia and the débâcle at Stalingrad; of America's entry into the war, the defeat in Italy, and the invasion of France this June. He knew, too, of the Twentieth of July—how only a month ago a group within the Army had very nearly assassinated Hitler. But the anti-Christ's luck still held; he had been only slightly injured by the bomb Colonel von Stauffenberg had planted underneath a conference table, and Hitler's vengeance had been terrible.

He ground out his cigarette and lit another. The Communist had stopped writing now, and placed his pages in an envelope. They had all been given the materials to write last letters. They would be entrusted to the Protestant pastor, Dr. Rieger, who had already become a legend for his compassion towards the condemned of every faith and for the personal risks he took on their behalf.

Now that the thief was gone, the cell was absolutely silent. For Martinus, there was nothing left but to pray. They had left him his rosary, and now he knelt.

The footsteps sounded in the hall again. His fingers froze on the beads. Then they were there once more, the guards. Still on his knees, Martinus turned.

The tall warder savoured the endless moment of suspense. Then his eyes came to rest on Martinus. "Dr. Martin Peter Fischer, known as Dr. Martinus," he said. "You will come with us."

Martinus swallowed hard, stood up on knees gone weak, and crossed himself.

The lawyer put out his hand. "We'll meet again. Soon." He smiled faintly.

Somehow Martinus managed an answering smile. "Yes. Peace to you, brother."

The Communist stood up, face dead pale, also extending his hand. "Forget what I said a while ago, Father. Good luck."

"And to you," Martinus said, and his hands were wrestled behind his back and cuffs snapped on. Holding him by each arm, they led him from the cell. Outside in the corridor waited Dr. Rieger. After the last communion and confession the Catholic chaplain considered his duties discharged; the Protestant, however, never let anyone go to the blade unaccompanied unless his presence was declined.

Earlier, before transferring him to the death cell, they had stripped Martinus naked, then given him cheap, ill-fitting prison jacket, trousers and felt slippers. The slippers made a hissing sound now on the corridor floor as he shuffled along between the guards. The pastor was on his right, his voice firm yet gentle as he said the Lord's Prayer. Martinus's own voice matched his automatically, word for word. Then they had reached a door.

The pastor touched his shoulder as the guards halted. "I may not go farther with you. But now you shall find the peace that passeth all understanding."

"I'm not afraid," Martinus said. "After all, this is the moment towards which my whole life has been pointed. Thank you, Pastor Rieger, God bless you, and *Wiederseh'n*."

"God bless you. *Auf Wiederseh'n*."

The doors were opened then and Martinus pushed through.

He found himself in a large brightly lit dingy-walled room, divided in two parts by a black curtain hanging from the ceiling. At a long table in the fore part sat three men, the one in the centre in civilian clothes, the ones on the flanks in SS uniforms. Martinus was hustled before them. The civilian glanced at his file. "You are Dr. Martin Peter Fischer?"

"I am."

"All pleas, requests for postponement and/or pardon have been denied. The death verdict of the people's court will now be carried out." He raised his arm. "Heil Hitler!"

"Long live Austria," said Martinus quietly.

The civilian jerked his head. The two warders led Martinus towards the curtain. Just this side of it they halted; his handcuffs were unlocked, the jacket thriftily stripped from him. His wrists were then quickly bound with thongs. He stared at the curtain, and it was true, he was not afraid. Indeed, he was exalted. If he believed anything, it was that this was no end, only a beginning. All that remained was to comport himself as a man.

But, oh God, there were so many memories and life here had

often been so sweet. He sucked in breath, felt tears running down his cheeks. One more defiance, and this time he tried to yell it. *"God bless Austria!"* But even as he opened his mouth, a huge piece of adhesive was clamped tightly across it, stopping his defiant cry. Then, like a carcass in a butcher shop, he was picked up and carried through the curtain.

He saw it then—the frame, the poised blade, the stack of sheet-metal coffins—had time to glimpse all that and the rolling platform, mounted on two rails, before the guillotine. Then he was thrown face-forward on that conveyor, rolled forward at frightening speed. Mary, he thought, Mother of God, pray for me now. . . .

7

The little cinema in Ferndorf was jammed. There were only a few reserved seats—wooden chairs with backs—otherwise the audience sat on benches. Naturally Kreisleiter Robert Schellhammer and Christa had the best seats in the house.

The film was a rerun of a musical confection, the era portrayed being 1940, a time as remote as the Garden of Eden, as carefree. German armies then were victorious everywhere; no Stalingrad; no El Alamein, no Normandy invasion. It had seemed impossible then that the English would come back to Europe, or the Americans. Now, in this October of 1944, everything had changed. All the victorious dreams were turned into nightmares. So one sat here in darkness watching the tender, naive love story, and for a while forgot that the Reich was encircled by its enemies in a ring of iron. One forgot the thousand-plane raids—and tried to forget that only last month the bombers had finally reached Vienna, too, and that now they came every day with brutal regularity, and there was nothing in the skies to stop them. At least, though, the Americans had shown some vestige of civilization; so far the Inner City with all its fine old buildings had been left comparatively untouched.

When the show ended, there was applause and a universal sigh of regret. Christa's hand was on Robert's arm as they filed out into the garden separating the cinema from the tavern next door. The night was crisp with autumn, the smells of farm, garden, woods and fields all mingled in the air. Most of the crowd flowed towards the inn, reluctant to go home. "A glass of wine?" Robert asked her, and they followed the throng, he accepting and answering the respectful, even fawning, greetings. Christa felt no shame ·at the general knowledge that she was his mistress. In any case, no one but Papa could have objected, and he did not even know, or at least did not comprehend. She neither knew nor cared what Charlotte Schellhammer thought about the arrangement, and it seemed to be a matter of indifference to Robert, too.

Behind the blackout curtains the tavern was dimly lit, pungent with the smoke of the dreadful home-front cigarettes. There was the clink of glasses, the chatter of voices. And there were half a dozen men in uniform, not one of them not somehow maimed— lacking hand or foot, arm or leg. The war had had its way and was finished with them. Christa could not bear to look.

The wine came, she became aware of what Robert was saying: "How do I interpret the situation, Herr Kubiak? Well, certainly not in any defeatist way. One must look beneath the surface, beyond the obvious; then all is clear. Our supply lines are shortening, those of our enemies are lengthening. They are springs stretched to weakness; we are a spring compressed, powerful, ready to explode and strike. And that we shall when the time's right! Guided by the Führer's genius, aided by the secret weapons even now in production, we'll turn the tide, never fear!"

She had heard it all before, tuned it out, though the others lapped it up. Robert himself believed it, she knew, and of course so did she; after three years of total indoctrination by Robert Schellhammer, she had become an expert at believing anything. Otherwise how could you keep going?

The door opened, a young man swung in on a crutch, the left leg of his rumpled Wehrmacht uniform cut and sewn to cover the stump that ended just above the knee. In his middle twenties, he was lean and handsome, hair blond, the eyes that he blinked against the sudden light a bright steel blue. A little awkwardly he closed the door behind himself, then hobbled across to the bar.

Robert shoved back his chair and strode across the room, booted feet thumping solidly; all eyes were fixed on him.

"Corporal Glaser, it's good to have you back with us!" Robert's voice was bluff and brisk. "I have some news for you—good news, which reflects great honour on your family!"

"Oh?" Glaser tossed off his cognac, held his glass out to be refilled. His eyes raked up and down Schellhammer's resplendent uniform. He had, Christa realized, been drinking somewhere else before coming here.

"Oh, yes. You knew, of course, that you'd been put in for the Iron Cross, First Class, for your heroism at Minsk. Well, it has come through! And I think it should be presented in an appropriate ceremony here in Ferndorf!" Robert grinned, put his hand on Glaser's shoulder. "You must be properly honoured."

The flare in Glaser's eyes was instantaneous. "Take your hand off me!" he snapped and knocked it from his shoulder. A hush fell across the room. "And," he rasped, "take your Iron Cross, Herr Kreisleiter, and shove it up your arse! That's an appropriate ceremony!"

Robert stepped back, face flaming. "Corporal, you are drunk. And your sacrifices have damaged you psychologically."

"Psychologically, hell!" Leaning on his crutch, Glaser moved away a pace from the bar. He pointed at his left leg's swinging stump. "You think this is psychological? You and your fancy words and medals and your goddamn swastika—you're finished, do you hear me? You are finished, *we* are finished! They can't be stopped! And what we'll get we'll deserve, because you've betrayed us, betrayed all of us with what you've done—and in our names!"

The young man was screaming now. "Have they ever told you about their death factories for killing Jews? Where they gas 'em by the thousands and put 'em in ovens and burn 'em up?" His head swivelled. "Women and children along with the men! Little babies! Little girls and boys—they burn 'em! You don't believe me, do you? Well, they're there, I've seen 'em." He broke off, voice choked in his throat. "War's one thing. That is another. And I'm ashamed, do you hear? I'm ashamed to be a German soldier! Anyhow, they're coming and we can't stop 'em, and what they do to us when they get here— Well, you and the Führer can thank yourselves for that! Maybe they will burn our babies, too."

396

He stood there for an instant, silent. Then he whirled on his crutch, walked towards the door.

After one frozen second, Robert instinctively started after him, face tallow-coloured. "Young man . . ."

An awkward scuffling of feet drowned the words. They were standing up, too, the other soldiers. Robert halted as a young one-armed private moved out to block his path. Then three or four others were moving in, encircling him in grey.

Robert stood, head turning, looking at the men surrounding him, enduring the contempt in their eyes. "Your friend," he said presently, "is very drunk. In this case, allowance will be made for him for that reason, for the limb he has sacrificed, for the heroism he has shown. If you are truly friends of his, you'll make sure there are no more outbursts. Otherwise, hero or no, he'll have to take the consequences. Now, if you will stand aside. . . ."

They moved. He turned, strode back towards the table where Christa sat. "Come, Christa. And you, Herr Semmler, be more careful about whom you serve. He was already intoxicated when he came in." He put on his own coat, turned. "Heil Hitler!"

The older men in the room returned the greeting in a shout. Robert and Christa went out into the night.

He was grimly silent as he drove his official Mercedes through the village, and she sensed he was shaken in a way she had never seen before. Was it the humiliation he had endured, or was it possible that even his faith had been rocked by the intensity of Glaser's jeremiad? And that business about burning babies—what nightmare madness had put that in the soldier's mind?

Robert turned up the hill towards the Christinahof, driving slowly, with utmost care, the red blackout shields cutting the reach of the headlights to almost nothing. It burst from her without her even realizing that she spoke: "Robert, what did he mean about those places—gas and ovens?"

"The man was drunk! What he has seen are simple concentration camps. There are many in the east. Naturally they are prisons, not rest homes. Sometimes prisoners die, are cremated." He paused. "There must be facilities for disposing of the bodies. He has, perhaps, seen those. But as for the rest. . . . Well, most of the Russian propaganda is created by Jews, and you know how clever they are. With his brain weakened by combat, he would be susceptible. I hope he knows how lucky he is, the young fool. If there had been any SS there tonight, I'd have had to take decisive action."

They had reached the gate now, and he got out, opened it with his key, slipped back behind the wheel, drove through, relocked it, and pulled into the courtyard. She turned towards him. "Will you stay the night?" Genuinely she hoped he would; despite the ugliness of the aftermath, the romanticism of the film had aroused her.

"Unfortunately I can't, tonight. I wish I could—" He looked down at her a moment, then pulled her to him, and they kissed. Suddenly he pushed her away, straightened up, and smoothed back his hair. "Tomorrow night," he said softly. "I'll be here and stay over." He gave her one last kiss. "Good night, my darling."

"Good night." She slid out of the car, waved briefly as he turned it. Then she let herself into the Christinahof.

As always, as soon as she had hung up her coat her first move was to check on her father. And, as always, she was apprehensive when she knocked on the door of his apartment. He answered instantly: "Come in." She entered, wondering if he would recognize her tonight. More than half the time he took her for her mother.

Helmer looked up at her, blue eyes watery in the shrunken shell of the once strong face. His mouth drooped at one side, lips slack. His hair was now silky white, and he had lost thirty pounds, which the doctor said it was unlikely he would ever regain; his pyjamas hung slackly on his gaunt and bony frame. "Why, Christa," he said, "you're home early from the ball."

"Yes, Papa."

"Aren't you enjoying Fasching? Your mother and I went out every night."

"Yes," said Christa tonelessly, "I'm sure you did. Now, Papa, you must go to bed." She took his arm and lifted. "Up. Up."

He came easily. Once he was under the covers she kissed him and went out.

Traudi was in the kitchen, sleepily waiting up. She had made a few sandwiches in case Robert came for the night. Christa sent her off to bed and, though she did not really want it, ate a sandwich, chiding herself that she would get fat. But, of course, if she put on weight, that would please Robert. "If you would just gain some weight," he said so often, "then you could conceive."

And always she told him, "No, it's quite hopeless. Dr. Walzer says so."

Charlotte had given him two daughters in four years and was pregnant once again. He loved his children, even if he did not love his wife; but, Christa knew, a child, a son, by her would be for him an absolute culmination. For her it would be a surrender to . . . what? An inevitability, a Rubicon she could not bring herself to cross. And Dr. Walzer had been very understanding. He had fitted her with a diaphragm. So, having made it through the first week safely, she was ready from then on.

She finished the sandwich, and started for the stairs. But there was no real hope of sleep. The various excitements of the film, the incident in the tavern, had wound her up like a clock. And the night outside was a fine one, though nearly moonless.

By now, of course, everyone would be asleep. She went to the cupboard, took down her coat, donned it, and tied a scarf around her head. Closing the blackout curtains carefully behind her, she went out on the terrace. Below her the whole valley lay dark, no longer a jewelled spangle. So far the bombers had not come at night, but there was no guarantee of anything.

It was amazing how the onset of the bombing had changed everybody's thinking. Many Austrians had never quite considered the Americans their enemy. The Russians, yes, everyone feared them; and there was no doubt that the British were implacable. But until recently, except in official propaganda, one heard few words of hatred for the "Amis". But now they, too, were an enemy without mercy, hated as they had never been before. Even Christa felt hatred of their strength and the brutal way they used it.

But one thing she was sure of—Lan was not up there in those planes. He might be fighting somewhere, yes, but he would never lend himself to the slaughter of helpless civilians.

Looking out at the valley, she forced the thought of Lan from her mind. Maybe he was already dead on some battlefield halfway

399

around the world. And anyway she must not think of him. Turning from the wall, she crossed the terrace, went down the steps. She crossed the parklike lawn, reached the far stone wall that encircled it, and turned to follow its length past a heavy thicket of lilac bushes. Factories for burning children! What rotten propaganda the Russians spread! She shuddered. It was too fantastic. . . . Two circuits of the wall, then to bed; and if she still could not sleep, she would take a drink of brandy. . . .

The bushes shook, leaves clashing. Christa jumped back as something rushed from the thicket, and her mouth opened in a scream. Then the man was on her. One hand seized her hair, jerking her round; the other slid between her teeth, filling her mouth, muffling her scream. She was pulled hard against a thin, bony body.

The voice in her ear was a savage whisper. "Christa! For God's sake, don't scream! I mean no harm. It's Josef Steiner!"

He released her. "If you cry out," he whispered, "I'm a dead man!"

Christa stared. "Josef Steiner, what . . . where did you . . .? I thought you were dead."

"I have been, several times. Why I keep being resurrected I don't know." His voice was a thready whisper. "All I know is that I can't go on any more. Maybe . . . maybe you can help me."

The grove was silent, save for his raspy breathing. Christa's mind struggled to comprehend. Of course, he was a fugitive, from a concentration camp or somewhere. Resentment rose in her; this man had cost her Lan, had cost her everything. What right had he now to still be alive? She shook her head. It was not fair; she should go and phone Robert this very minute, she should . . .

Murder him? It came to that. Of course, she could not. She drew in a long breath. "Josef—the Christinahof. Everyone's asleep. If I could get you to the attic. . . ."

"Yes, yes, if you could give me a little bread, that's all. Then I'll be away."

She peered round. Everything was tranquil; no reason for it not to be. "Come."

Exhausted, panting, he leaned against her as they stumbled across the lawn. It seemed to take forever to get him through the

400

house; she had visions of Mitzi or Traudi appearing suddenly: *Anything wrong, gnae' Frau?* But, of course, they were long since asleep.

They made it to the first floor. There in her own apartment she closed and locked the door, switched on the light. At her first full sight of him she let out a muffled cry. Bearded, filthy, his clothes no more than rags, this was a parody of Josef Steiner.

Yet somehow he found a smile. Two of his teeth had rotted away to jagged stubs. "Yes. You have not changed, but I have."

"Shhh. Wait." She fumbled through the key box, found the attic keys, slipped them in her pocket, got the torch she kept by her bed.

Above the ceiling of the house's highest floor, under the very eaves, there were sprawling storage rooms, packed with obsolete furniture, old books, papers, travel luggage and the like, rarely entered. Further, for every door and every cabinet, chest, or wardrobe drawer there was a lock; for every lock a key. That had always been the Austrian way: trust no one, control your property. The keys remained under the total control of Christa, and it was to her that everyone must come for access to any attic room.

This one was small, three by four metres, maybe, set under the sloping roof of the south wing, and contained a bed with three straw mattress segments in place to form a whole, a coverlet and a piece of muslin over the coverlet to catch the dust. The rest of the room was filled with junk.

Josef Steiner sank down on the bed, eyes closed, groaning softly with the pleasant pain of rest. Christa took off his shoes, stripped away foul stockings. "I'm sorry I'm so filthy," Josef whispered.

"Never mind. Drink some wine. Eat." She gave him bread and cheese that she had collected from the kitchen, telling him meanwhile something of herself and Lan, and what had happened to them. He wolfed the food, and washed it down with wine. Then, sighing, he eased back, eyes closed. His face was like a skull, skin stretched parchment yellow over bone.

"Thanks, Christa. Am I safe here?"

"Absolutely, if you make no noise."

"I'll be quiet. I know how to do it. I've been living in a room like this for years."

"All right. Sleep. I'll be back soon." She went out, locking the door behind her. In her own apartment she leaned against the wall for a moment, feeling the thudding of her heart. Now what? she thought. What do I do now?

It was after one and she was exhausted; morning would come soon and the day would be long and taxing, but for the moment she was far beyond sleeping. She rubbed her face, then poured herself a drink of brandy. Suppose police were on his trail? He must not stay here long. Tonight, tomorrow—but tomorrow night Robert would be here. That thought almost caused her to panic: Robert here, Josef just above him in the attic. Then she told herself that she must keep her head. If she stayed cool, she could manage.

Although she should have given them to the Winter-Help, all of Lan's clothes, fresh and clean, were stored in a chest; she had kept them as if they were talismans. Now she took out underwear, shirt, trousers, jacket, socks. For the next three-quarters of an hour she was furtively busy, assembling everything he would need: food, wine, cigarettes, water for washing and drinking, soap, towels, a chamberpot, a magazine to read. She was taut with excitement, feeling a burglar's guilt in her own house. He was sound asleep as she arranged things in the little room, and she left a note for him on the food: *Here are supplies for two days. You should be safe as long as you are quiet. Robert Schellhammer will be here all night long just downstairs tomorrow night. I may not see you for forty-eight hours. Then we will talk.*

When she left the attic, she locked every door behind her as she went, imprisoning him, and hid the keys in her dressing table; no one could possibly enter his hiding place without first getting her permission. Then she undressed, washed away the attic dust, fell into bed. Strangely, instead of tossing restlessly as usual, she fell asleep almost at once, her mind occupied now with something besides futility.

ALL THE NEXT DAY the attic drew her like a lodestone, and half a dozen times she almost entered it, drawing back each time at the last moment. What if one of the servants sought her out and found

402

her there? She must excite not the least suspicion; the moment she had not turned Josef over to the police, she had committed high treason.

Then Robert came and her tension grew until she was certain he would read her guilt through her skull. Yet, she must have brought it off; he seemed to suspect nothing.

In bed, though, she took no pleasure in his lovemaking; all she could think of was Josef up there in the attic. And she could feel only relief when Robert went away in the morning.

MIDNIGHT. She had the food and drink waiting for Josef when she led him down the stairs through the sleeping house to her apartment. Before daylight came, of course, she must erase all signs of this meal. But that could wait. For the time being they were utterly safe here, and they must talk.

"How did you escape them?" she asked.

His eyes were huge, haunted, in the skeletal face. "Waiting for Lan in Horn, I saw them moving in on me. Their kind is easy to spot. By then I knew what was happening, that the game was up. I ran. Somehow I dodged them, escaped. I took the train to Vienna and made it to my flat—the 'black' one." He smiled faintly. "They had not yet connected it with me. In preparation for just such an emergency I had false documents waiting for me."

His hand trembled as he lit a cigarette. "But there was no way I could get out to Switzerland or Italy. Fortunately, a Christian family, who were secretly anti-Nazi, took me in. That little room" —he gestured towards the attic—"for years I've lived in one much like it, not daring to let myself be seen, coming out only at night to join them, living off what they could share from their own rations. They were magnificent to me. But then the bombers came—and four days ago my luck ran out. The house blew up around my ears."

He closed his eyes, rubbed them hard. "By a miracle, I wasn't harmed. While everything was still in turmoil from the raid, I ran. In the confusion I caught a tram to Grinzing and then I faded into the Wienerwald. All I could think of was you, the Christinahof. I knew nowhere else to turn, though I wasn't even sure you were still here; I thought maybe Lan had taken you out."

He paused. "For four days I've been walking through the forest. At nights I almost froze. But finally I was here and with just strength enough to get over the wall. I planned to break in somehow—but then you came to me, straight to me, almost as if . . . as if you felt me there. And . . ." he stood up, Lan's clothes hanging on him like bags, "and now I've rested and eaten my fill and I shall soon be on my way."

Christina stared at him. "To where?"

"I haven't the faintest idea. And if I had, I wouldn't tell you. You've already risked enough without being involved any further. If you'll let me out, I'll be over the wall and gone. And I shall eternally be in your debt. Of course, I already am, having, from what you have told me, very thoroughly ruined your life and Lan's."

"It wasn't you. It was everything."

"You're too generous. It was I. Still, it will all soon be over, and there is no longer any chance that the Reich will win. A few more months, and then one day Lan will come and take you with him."

Suddenly she turned away. "No. No, don't say that."

"Have you had bad news of him?"

"No, I've had no news of him. But he is through with me; I know that much. We were apart too long." And she heard herself, still not looking at him, tell Josef about how the letters had stopped coming. "I couldn't expect him to wait any longer. He was right to make some kind of new life. Find someone else. And even if he hasn't, how could he want me anyhow? I have been . . . sleeping with Robert Schellhammer for three years." She drew in breath. "What a nice whore that makes me."

Josef was silent for a moment. Though her back was turned, she could feel the pressure of his eyes on her. "I think you misjudge Lan. He would know why you do what you do; he is no fool." He was silent for a moment. Then his hand touched her shoulder. "Christa, time is passing. I need as much darkness as possible in order to get as far from here as I can."

But she did not move. "Josef," she heard herself say, "why can't you stay here?"

When seconds passed and he did not answer, Christa turned. Slowly he shook his head. "I have enough on my conscience already.

With Schellhammer in and out of here every day. . . . Do you want me to give you the *coup de grâce*? Complete the destruction I began?"

But now the idea was fastened in her brain. It was almost as if his presence here offered her some kind of salvation. "There's no way Robert could know, if we're careful," she said. "You'd be locked in the room up there all day, of course, and could only come out at night, on certain nights, like this; but I have all the keys, can keep the servants out, the food's no problem. And Robert— Don't you see? He guarantees the rest of it. There'll be no surprise Gestapo search or anything like that." She gestured. "And maybe you're right. Maybe it won't be for long. A few weeks, a few months. . . ." She paused. "But, of course, if you don't trust me . . ."

"Trust you? Don't be a fool." Relief flooded Josef's face with such suddenness that only now did she realize fully how he had dreaded going. "If I could only be sure you wouldn't be hurt by it."

"I won't; we won't. And maybe even helped. If . . . if what you say comes true, if it's all over soon and we lose, then that we tried to help you may count for something."

"After what you've already suffered, you don't need more credentials. But maybe you're right." His smile suddenly had a different quality and his eyes changed, he looked younger. "If you're willing to take the risk, God knows I am. To know I'll have a roof over my head again, someone to talk to." He broke off, came to her. "Thank you, Christa," he said softly and kissed her forehead. Then quickly he stepped back. "And now," he said, "since I am staying, do you suppose. . . . May I have a real bath before daylight comes?"

"Yes." Christa laughed with real amusement for the first time in weeks. "And Lan's razor's still here, if you want to use it."

8

Lan's section was housed in a shabby Italian villa above a village that had somehow escaped destruction. Well out of reach of the enemy artillery, it was still close enough to the lines so that he could hear the sullen rumble of the guns. His office had been a library, but even with the oil burner going full blast, the cold was omnipresent, seeping constantly from the old thick walls, which for two years had never been fully warmed.

He had finished with the morning's digest of captured documents, had a few moments to himself. Going to the window, he looked out at a convoy rumbling past along the old Roman road below, headed north. The Germans were backed up hard against the River Po, and standing there, Lan's mouth twisted. They'd keep on holding that line, the only solid one left.

The master sergeant appeared in the doorway, a big blond second-generation Bavarian from Illinois. "Sir. There's a British officer outside. A brigadier. Says he's got to see you right away."

"Oh." Lan sank back in his chair. "Well, Gunther, send him in."

"Yes, sir." Gunther turned. "Sir, Major Condon is free, now. Major Condon, this is— What was that name again, sir?"

"Brigadier Mark Gorton," said the man in the doorway.

For a moment Lan only stared. Then he hurtled from behind his desk. The two men embraced. "Jesus Christ, Mark!"

"I say, Lan, I—" Mark broke away, stepped back, a squat figure muffled in a heavy overcoat. He had put on a lot of weight; his wind-reddened face was almost perfectly round.

"Hell, I thought you were dead," said Lan.

"Very nearly, several times: Greece, Crete, Malta. Lan, you have changed."

"I'm seven years older now than the last time you saw me. That's a long time, Mark. Here, let me take your coat. Some coffee?"

"Fine. And if you've got a spot of brandy. . . . I've been a long time on the road in the cold grey light of dawn." Mark said it heavily.

Almost at once the sergeant was back with two steaming canteen cups and a bottle.

When Gunther had gone and closed the door, Lan spiked the coffee, passed a cup to Mark. *"Pros't."*

"Pros't." Mark drank. He sighed, shivered, drank again, and took out cigarettes. Then, soberly: "How is she, Lan? Have you had any recent word?"

"I've had no word at all," Lan said. "Not since we lost touch in

1939." His voice thickened. "I've read a million letters, questioned a million soldiers, but I've never had news from the Ferntal."

"Well, I have," Mark said.

Lan tried to speak, but no sound came.

"Quite by accident. At present I'm on Field Marshal Alexander's staff. From time to time I visit the front line and buck them up a bit in their interrogation procedures. I happened to look in on the South Africans last week when they'd taken a nice lot of POWs and I sat in on the interrogation. Do you remember a grocer shop in Altkreuzburg run by a family named Leder?"

"No," Lan said.

"Well, apparently there is one. And the oldest Leder boy was a sergeant in a platoon making a reconnaissance. Our chaps surrounded them and he took it on himself to surrender. When I heard where he was from, I took over the interrogation personally. When he found out that I knew the Ferntal and the Helmer family . . . well, he was a veritable repository of local gossip. Lan, she is well."

"She is well. She is well?" Lan heard himself repeat the words numbly.

"Or was six months ago. Living at the Christinahof. The General is still alive, too, though not in good health. There's more, though. Do you remember a man named Schellhammer?"

Lan hardly heard him. For the moment the knowledge that she still lived, was where he had left her, was all he could absorb. "Robert Schellhammer," he said automatically.

"Yes," said Mark. "Well, it's only gossip, but you might as well know it all, the worst. Schellhammer's a Party official, a *Kreisleiter*. Leder says that he's also Christa's lover."

He had, throughout all these years, prepared himself for almost anything. Not for that specifically, but for worse than that while hoping for better. Still, something seemed to pierce him. "I see," he said almost calmly. "Thanks, Mark." He took a long swig of spiked coffee. He had, after all, long since assumed something like this. Men went off to war and the women they left behind were not made of marble.

"You're welcome," Mark said. For a while the room was silent. Then Mark said, "Lan, I should like to know—and don't ask me why—the reason you enlisted on Pearl Harbour day in 1941. Patriotism? Or Christa?"

"For God's sake, Mark. You know!" The words burst from him.

"I thought I did. But, as you said, it's been a long time."

Lan stood up, went to the window. The lorries were still rolling past down there in the village. He was aware of Mark getting to his feet behind him.

"It may be that some things are better let alone. I've been through that with two women: my wife and Marietta. There are times when it's better to let go. Why do you want to find her?"

Lan turned. "I only know that I have to try. I'm under no illusions. Maybe it will all be gone, just a dream, and none of it ever counted. Anyhow the Russians will be there first, and by the time I find her, God knows what will happen. There's no chance now."

"There may be," Mark said. "But first tell me this. What about Schellhammer? Doesn't he make a difference?"

"Sometimes people have to . . . do things," Lan said. Then the rest of it sank in. He straightened. "You said there may be a chance?"

"Yes, I rather think there is. But first I had to know how you felt about it all. If my interpretation of the file was right—"

"The file?"

"On you at Alexander's headquarters. Supreme Command, Med Theatre." Mark smiled faintly. "It's all there. To one who knows, it's plain as day. You've homed in on her like an arrow to the target. Pushed, shoved, manoeuvred, bucked, risked. . . . Well, I won't drag this out any longer. In a couple of weeks I'm going to Hungary on a liaison mission with the Russian Army—Tolbukhin's Third Ukrainian Front. Our guess is they'll be the first to reach Vienna, which is my eventual destination. If you want to come along, I'll be glad to take you with me."

Somehow the village church had escaped undamaged. Now, above the rumble of the convoy, its bells chimed nine. Lan said, "*Vienna?*"

"Right." Mark's voice was crisp. "Essentially this is something the Prime Minister has cooked up personally. He's always seen Vienna as crucial to postwar settlements. These Anglo-American liaison teams have more or less been rammed down Stalin's throat. The whole idea, essentially, is to make sure the West doesn't get screwed in Vienna; we want to know who's on our side there and who isn't."

He helped himself to more brandy, went on. "Anyhow, I'd not forgotten you. When I found your file, there was no question— except that I had to be sure you were prepared for what you might find when you got there. Apparently you are, as well as any man could be. So if you want to come along, just say so and I'll have your orders cut. Alexander will see that no one blocks you."

"Want to go—?" Lan stared at Mark, could find no other words.

Mark smiled. "I take it silence means assent," he said. And he put out his hand.

THE RUSSIANS received the Anglo-American mission with grudging correctness. Communication was no trouble. Lan had been familiarized with the language at Fort Ritchie, and had been boning up since that day with Mark. Master Sergeant Finch, his assistant, was fluent, as was Mark after years of roaming the Balkans and beyond. Also a lot of Russians had had the opportunity to learn German in the past four years.

The Russian Army was unlike any Lan had before encountered, almost medieval despite its mastery of the technology of modern warfare, lacking all the amenities modern soldiers took for granted. No frills were expected; life in Russia had been mostly devoid of frills ever since the Revolution. Morale was superb. The Russians knew why they fought; their land had been invaded, their homes burned, their families brutalized or killed; they fought for revenge. They had seen the mass graves outside every village, and if they had any illusions left, they had been dispelled by what they were now discovering as their northern wings drove into Poland.

When Lan was first shown photographs of the camp outside Lublin, he was incredulous. There had been rumours, but he had discounted them as propaganda. There was no discounting the pictures, the affidavits. Mark, he found, had already seen the data and more besides. He was sunk into a deep depression.

"I knew and yet I didn't know," Mark whispered. "I didn't

really want to believe. But, Lan, it's true. And if it's true, then I must think about the world a whole new way. Even about myself. There are so many questions I can't answer: What would *I* have done? If the papers had crossed my desk for signature and I had never had to see what they represented, would I have signed?

"When Hitler dies, as he surely will, it should be smiling. Because his legacy will live on: his concept of total war. Not just in the Germans. We're all infected with it now. If we're not careful, that little Austrian bastard will make Jesus Christ look like the village idiot when it comes to influence on civilization."

BUDAPEST FELL AT LAST. On the northern fronts the Reds drove on across Poland, hammered at East Prussia. In the west the Allies reached the Rhine. In Italy negotiations for surrender were under way. Still the Wehrmacht fought fanatically, often gallantly; and men—and boys too young to shave—kept on dying. Striving to save Vienna, Hitler threw tank divisions profligately into a counteroffensive on the Hungarian plain—Operation Spring Awakening. It was a lovely name for slaughter. For a time the Panzers even pushed the Russians back; then they ran out of fuel. The Germans fell back and at last, on March 29, 1945, Russian tanks crossed into Austria.

Lan Condon, in the wake of battle, forced himself into a strange suspension of emotion. Now, after all that effort, he stood on Austrian soil again, and Christa was somewhere over in the misty distance. Now it could not be more than a few days. But he had no illusions about war left; he knew its ghastly ironic jokes. Instinctively he tucked his thumbs into closed fists, a German gesture equivalent to crossing fingers, and looked out across the plain.

Wisps of greasy smoke fingered blackly against the grey of sky. Bodies—of animals and men—were scattered flecks against the earth, like fallen leaves on the churned fields. From the horizon came the crackle of small arms fire, interspersed with the stomping thump of tank cannons. High above the plain black dots circled: ravens, rooks, and crows, building nerve to come down and feed.

And if in days or weeks, thought Lan, they did find each other once again, what then? Seven years, and the last of his youth was

410

gone; he was forty-two now, sliding into middle age. He had changed, and, of course, it would be the same with her. She had been almost a child then, both in years and knowledge; now she would be nearing thirty. She could be ugly now, scarred inwardly or outwardly; she might hold dear all sorts of things she once had loathed. She might even be his enemy.

He drew in breath. So, he thought, he might be a fool. Anyhow, soon he would have to make a choice. It did not matter. He had come too far now to lose his nerve.

He got back into the jeep. "We might as well go on," he said, and the sergeant put the vehicle into gear.

9

They had spent almost all of that interminable March day deep in the cellars under the Christinahof. The alarm had sounded just after eleven in the morning. Christa had been walking with the General in the garden when she heard the sirens in Altkreuzburg blare, and Mitzi screamed at her, "They're coming! The Amis come!" She raised her face to the cloud-tattered sky instinctively. There was nothing to be seen up there, but the sirens went on howling, shrieking the world's end.

"Papa!" She seized his arm, pulled him around.

"Yes, Christina," he said mildly.

Heart pounding, she realized how deeply sunken he now was into the past. "Kurt," she said. "We must go to the cellars. There is a problem with the wine. Now, Kurt, come with me. Hurry!"

"All right, if it's so urgent." He came with docility, but breathing hard from the exertion. Through the pressing house, then down the cellar stairs, but before they passed through the wooden door, she turned, stared at the house across the courtyard. Josef was up there, helpless in his attic room. If a stray bomb should hit the house. . . . Two had fallen in Altkreuzburg last week, not five miles away; the lower market place had been wiped out.

But there was nothing she could do. Clinging to her father, she hurried down the mould-slicked steps, through the upper cellar, to the deepest one, its walls massive and ancient. There was food, water, and, of course, wine, cask on cask of it; they had installed chairs, beds, and wiring for a radio. Even so, for a while they had been careless about using it; they were, after all, so far from the main targets. Then one day after the siren had sounded, they had emerged to see a single American Flying Fortress circle back from the south. Like a wasp sprayed with insecticide, it wove back and forth across the sky, drunk and dying.

Around and around it lurched, trying to rise and failing. Turning northward, it came, trailing black smoke now, and, before their eyes, with terrible impact, ploughed into the hill across the Fernbach, directly below the Schellhammerhof. It did not explode, only flew apart in a shower of fragments.

"Maybe there're survivors!" Mitzi had yelled. "Get a pitchfork!" Before Christa could stop them, the servants had seized farming tools, were running down the hill. People were pouring from the Schellhammerhof as well. Christa hesitated, then ran after them.

But when she reached the road that ran beside the Fernbach, she halted, and then she turned away, vomiting. It sat there in the middle of the road looking at her—a head, undamaged, of a young man with dark brown hair and wide-open eyes, affixed to the upper half of a torso, balanced on gleaming white ribs protruding from bloody flesh. The face was not even bruised. She would never forget the staring eyes, the astonished mouth. She knew then there were no survivors, and she went no farther, only threw herself into the cold winter-killed grass and waited until she had the strength to climb the hill again.

But it had been a near miss. It could have as easily ploughed into the Christinahof. Since that day, she insisted that everyone go to the cellar the moment the alarm sounded.

Down here now, she sat by the General, his gas mask and hers on her lap. He had fallen silent, as if he vaguely understood that this was serious. There were only two men besides himself left on the place, and both were nearly seventy, too old even for the Volkssturm, which, with the Russians driving ever closer, had been mobilized to stand before Vienna. They had tapped a cask, were drinking; there was no way to stop them. Nobody cared about anything any more, it was ever harder to enforce any authority.

412

She leaned back on the bench, worrying about Josef up there in his room. . . . Maintaining him in the attic was far from simple. Food was the main problem. They were better off than people in the city, but nevertheless Robert was strict about seeing that everything above allowable rations went to market, to the war effort. Fortunately her father ate almost nothing nowadays; she herself cut back and salvaged leftovers for Josef. She stole a little, juggled supplies, and had managed so far to see that he was fed without anyone the wiser. And when she was certain that Robert would not stay the night, he would come down to her apartment.

Their second night together they talked endlessly, revelling in the chance to speak their minds. Freedom of speech! She had almost forgotten what that was like—to have a listener who would not betray you. She had been starved for mental intimacy, and obviously so had he. It was nearly daybreak before he went back to the attic; she went to bed exhilarated, totally alive.

Two days later they had another night together. Bathed, shaved, he was wearing Lan's dressing gown. It was as if Lan himself had materialized. Josef saw the expression on her face. "I feel like a usurper," he said, half smiling.

He had already changed, was filling out a little, his gaunt, haggard look diminishing. Watching him, she remembered that first afternoon in his absurd apartment, and she could not help smiling. Now he was neither frightening nor overpoweringly fascinating; they were equals now, only a pair of mortals of different sexes. Yet they still had power over each other; she felt the magnetism that he still gave off.

And he felt hers, looked at her strangely. "Well," he said, "it's taken a long time and a wide way round to come to this, hasn't it?" He smiled. "After all, it was all I ever really wanted. To be alone with you, in your bedroom."

Then he came to her, touched her cheek. "How many years? I've waited for this so absurdly long—and imagined it a million times. Christa, who knows whether we have ten thousand nights left, or only this one night? Do you understand me?"

She didn't even answer, only moved into his arms. Just before he kissed her, she thought of Lan. This was a betrayal of him—and yet

413

somehow a coming closer to him. He and Josef were all mingled in her mind. Then his mouth found hers, and she was not thinking any longer.

When Josef finally raised his head, he laughed breathily. "You may have to show me how. It's been so long, I may have forgotten."

He had forgotten nothing. But she had; she had forgotten until then what it was to make love with mind and body simultaneously. With Josef, she could give all of herself and he would do the same for her. So she had learned again what making love with someone whom you could love was like.

And so for months now they had played it out, their weird midnight drama, both of them living always on the knife-edge of discovery and danger. It was worth it. She was alive again.

But that very fact made the nights with Robert agony. She saw him now in a new light. Despite all his honesty and kindness, she knew that if he ever got the chance, he would kill Josef Steiner without compunction. Not because Josef was her lover. He would kill Josef simply for what he was—a different kind of man.

Factories for burning people! She had mentioned that to Josef, who was instantly alert and grim. "I've been locked in so long I know nothing. But who would put it past them? The people who hid me had heard rumours; that was why they took the risk for me they did. They'd heard talk of camps where there were mass executions. But only rumours, never any confirmation."

Once she was determined to know, it was fairly easy to find out. She went with Robert to all sorts of Party functions and, pretending bitter anti-Semitism herself, she learned things that chilled her blood. The brassy wife of an SS colonel made it plain one night in the ladies' room of the Hotel Sacher—in surroundings of red damask, veined marble, and crystal. "The Jews? Forget them, darling. They've all gone up the chimney."

"What?" Christa stared, then remembered and casually opened her compact. "How curious! You can't mean they burn them?"

The colonel's wife belched; she had drunk a lot. "Oh, not alive, you goose! First they're put out of their misery—quite painlessly. You see, they think they're going to the baths. But it's a shower of gas they get, and they never know what hit them. It's absolutely humane, Gotthard says. And then cremation, and hey, presto! they've vanished from the earth. So—" she belched again "—one thing you can be sure of about the postwar world: there'll be no Jews to clutter it. That's *one* problem that's been solved forever!"

"But there must be millions—"

"Oh, there *are*. But it's all so *organized*, don't you see? The SS has it all in hand! It's very efficient, and they feel absolutely nothing, no pain at all."

Christa closed her compact. In the mirror she could see the bone-whiteness of her face beneath the rouge. "But surely not the little children!"

"Nits make lice, Gotthard always says!" The woman's voice was airy. "Now, are you *almost* ready? They're waiting for us."

In the private dining room they were all more than a little drunk. "You took long enough," Robert said and grinned, putting his big hand on her wrist as she sat down beside him.

"The Frau Colonel and I were talking about the handling of the Jewish problem." She watched his face intently. "It sounds quite efficient."

"Well, that's one thing you can count on the SS for—efficiency." He took the whole matter for granted, asking her no questions about what she had heard. And she knew, with a chill around her heart, that it was true, and that Robert knew all about it and approved. She moved her hand from under his, and where he had touched her she felt as if she had come in contact with something loathsome.

When she told Josef, he nodded gravely. "In the context of their thinking, it makes perfect sense, of course."

"Josef, I can't stand it. I absolutely can't stand it. It makes me want to scream just to think about it. And when I look at Robert and I think— My God, how can I go on sleeping with him?"

"You must," said Josef. "If not for my sake, for your own. But it won't be long now. The end is in sight." He was silent for a moment. "The bastards," he said at last. "God knows when this is over what the verdict of history will be on Austria. It will have to take into account the Roberts. And it will not ignore men like Martinus. But what about all the others—people like you, who resisted, then yielded, doing what you had to do? Or like me, who perhaps should

415

have found a gun and died fighting them, but chose to hide to save our skins? And what about the couple in Vienna who risked their lives to take me in? What about those who were just deluded and those who were completely powerless? I hope when the winners come they'll make allowances. But I hope—" and his voice roughened "—they will hang every bastard like Robert Schellhammer out of hand."

IN THE CELLAR the radio buzzed and crackled as Traudi fiddled with it, but Vienna was not sending, lest it provide a beacon for the bombers. Christa glanced at her father. Slumped on his bench, he laced and unlaced his fingers, staring at nothing. Maybe his answer was the best one, she thought: find a private madness as refuge from the general one.

She felt a chill. Suppose Lan were still alive? Suppose somehow, when all this ended, he came back and she had to confront him as the mistress to two men. How could he ever understand? But, of course, he was not coming; he would never come, maybe he was not even alive, maybe he was like. . . . She remembered that torso in the road, sickness rose within her, and then the radio sputtered into life. "It's the all-clear," Mitzi said.

10

The Russians could not be held. Four days after they crossed into Burgenland, Wiener Neustadt fell. Now they bombed and shelled the outskirts of Vienna itself. The Volkssturm was called up right down to the very bottom of the barrel; the SS, the Waffen SS, and the Army braced themselves for the final shock.

In the living room of the Schellhammerhof it was very still. Early April sunlight slanting through the windows projected the pattern of the lace curtains in a shimmering dance on the wall opposite; and somehow, in this instant, Robert was acutely aware of the fall of light on all the polished, homely surfaces of the furniture and objects he had known all his life, that were almost part of him. Then his father worked the rifle bolt, and its loud significance broke the spell.

"It's a good gun," said Max Schellhammer. "It's good to hold it."

"*Vati*," Robert said. "You don't have to—"

"Yes, I do," Max said. His blue eyes glinted; he chuckled softly. "Don't worry about this old badger, boy. I know all the tricks. I learned them before you were even dreamed of. Hell, it's like being twenty-five again."

Robert stared at his father in his field-grey uniform. A surge of admiration filled him; the tough old man was actually looking forward to combat. Robert's own preference would have been to fight as well; and when in his capacity as a Party officer there was nothing constructive left for him to do, he would assert his automatic rank as colonel, join a unit in the thick of the action—and then he'd show them. He was a Schellhammer, a German, a National Socialist, and he would serve his country and his Führer to his dying breath. Meanwhile, he had never counted on this—that his father would have to leave the *Hof* to fight in the streets of Vienna. He felt a queasiness of guilt. "Damn it, I should be there with you."

His father smiled. "No. You've got your own duty. Somebody's got to keep things running. That's your department, son. This is mine."

He patted the gun. "You know, I never went overboard for Hitler the way you did. When you're my age, you know damn well no one man is God, no one man has all the answers. I guess I half expected it to work out this way. But you know what? Maybe it was worth it. Even if we are losing now, at least we have got back our pride."

He went on, "What happens to me doesn't count. Killing Russians is just unfinished business as far as I'm concerned. But, you listen. What happens to you *does* count. Whatever happens, you save yourself." His gesture encompassed the *Hof*. "And what you can of this." He paused, groping for words. "We've lived through it before. The bastards ground us down, it took twenty years for us to finally come back. Well, they'll grind us down again; and, by God, we'll come back again if it takes another twenty years. It will be up to you and your generation to see we do that—and next time we won't make the same mistakes."

417

Again silence. His father looked around the room once more with a kind of hunger, then glanced at his watch. "Time for me to go." He cradled the rifle in his arm, pulled his son to him, and they kissed. Max patted him hard on the back. "*Leb' wohl*," he said.

"*Leb' wohl*," said Robert thickly.

"So. . . ." From the doorway Robert watched the jaunty figure in its home-guard uniform saunter down the hill, rifle slung, until it was out of sight. Then he turned back inside the house.

Its emptiness made the sound of his footsteps hollow as he prowled around it. In the bedroom doorway Robert halted, staring bitterly at the bed. Charlotte had gone to safety in the Tyrol with the children, taking up transport space that Christa should have occupied. Just as she had taken up the space in his life that should never have belonged to her.

He had not realized the depths of his mother's hatred of Christa until she made it clear that unless Charlotte went, she would not go, and that if Christa went she would not go. So there'd been no way around it; his allocated space went to his rightful wife, his mother, his two children. What was worse, they had brought three tanks up the hill and dug them in only a few hundred yards from the Christinahof. He had argued bitterly with the officers. "Don't you fools understand? You put those tanks up here, they'll draw all sorts of fire. That whole *Hof* there will be smashed and all the people in it!"

The Panzer captain had looked at him with sour, weary eyes. "Herr Kreisleiter, I have my orders. Besides, even if I wanted to, I couldn't move 'em. No fuel."

So Robert was powerless—as much so with Christa as with the captain. "Don't you see?" he ranted at her. "Now that those guns are up here, they'll pound this ridge with everything they have! They'll blow the Christinahof to bits! You've got to move to the Schellhammerhof. Please. Charlotte isn't there now."

Christa merely shook her head. "No, Robert, this is our home. Look, there's no use moving. If planes come over, they'll hit the Schellhammerhof as well. It's too nice a target, all white and clean over there. And the cellars here are much deeper and safer. No."

He argued on, to no avail. Appealing to the General got him

418

nowhere; the old man only looked at him blankly. Finally he gave up. "Promise me you'll go to the deepest cellar at the first sign of danger."

"I promise," Christa said.

"Very well. I'll check in as often as I can. But I've got so much to do, I don't know. . . . And, of course, if they break through, I'll be fighting."

She was silent for a moment. Then she raised herself on tiptoe, touched his face, looked into his eyes. "Good luck," she whispered. "Be careful."

"I'll see you again," he managed. "I'll be back. I—" Everything seemed to be falling around his ears. He got a grip on himself, and his arm came up. "Heil Hitler."

"Heil Hitler," Christa answered.

Then he had left her, cursing fate savagely.

Now, standing alone in the bedroom doorway, he told himself, once he was free of his duties as *Kreisleiter,* he would force her and her father into his car, give them all sorts of passes, make her go northwest, to meet the Amis. Much as he hated them, better they than Russians.

Already the thunder in the distance was perceptibly closer, and towards the east the April morning was black with smoke. Hope rose in him. It was the one thing they all had left to cling to. Sooner or later the armies of the Allies and the Russians would collide, and when that happened there would surely be a brand new war, and the British and Americans would see the need of German help. A month from now he might find himself fighting alongside the English against the Reds. And that was all right, too. It might happen. The idea was something to sustain him.

11

In the inn Mark Gorton was conferring with Colonel Ognev, and Lan could see from Mark's face that his request had been denied. He had never thought it would be granted. Even as he watched, Mark raised his hands, dropped them, and turned away. Then, seeing Lan, he jerked his head. They went outside.

They walked up the street a distance, and then Mark halted. The little town north of Wiener Neustadt, actually on the very city limits of Vienna, had fallen without a fight; its little plastered, tile-roofed houses and cobbled pavements remained intact. In the distance, however, beneath a pall of smoke, battalions of tanks accompanied by infantry crawled towards the actual city, while lorry-mounted rocket launchers the Germans called "Stalin organs" lit the twilight as they sent hundreds of warheads arcing simultaneously towards strongpoints on high ground.

"I should have known it," Mark said bitterly. "I did the best I could with Ognev, but he wouldn't buy your proposition at all. He understands your concern for Christa, he says, but he'll not allow you to go off on your own to find her, and that's final. I agree, and I'm not going to tell you again."

"God damn it, Mark." Lan turned to stare at the humped, mist-shrouded hills, darkly wooded, in the near distance. "Only an hour in a jeep, I know every road. Just one hour, I'd be with Christa, find her, bring her out."

"Don't be a fool. You know as well as I do the German line's anchored in the Wienerwald; you wouldn't stand a chance. Damn it, Lan, this is no cinema romance; you've been around long enough to know one man can't swoop in there and knock off half the German Army and rescue the heroine." He paused. "Anyway, Schellhammer will be watching after her. Maybe he's already moved her west. After all, by all accounts, he loves her, too."

Presently Lan said, "And that's what I pin my hopes on? That Robert Schellhammer loves my wife?"

Gorton did not answer. At that instant a voice called Lan's name.

He turned. Starschii Leitenant Nechiev beckoned. The first lieutenant was the chief interrogator for Regimental Intelligence.

"We have a few more," Nechiev said. He was a genial man who had worked in a Moscow bank before the war. "Just brought in. Not too much—a couple of Wehrmacht corporals, and an SS captain. Care to join me? I could use some help with these damnable Austrian dialects."

"Go ahead," Mark said. "Let me have a report when you finish."

"All right," Lan told Nechiev. "I'll meet you." And he went to get his briefcase, moving briskly, ravenous now for every scrap of information from Vienna.

The prisoners were in the house adjoining the inn. Its furniture had been thrown into the courtyard to make room, and there a tank crew had built a fire with part of it, was cooking chicken and drinking wine. A tall private with a hatchet was chopping an ornately painted peasant chest to splinters.

In what had been the parlour, the interrogators took their seats behind a long table. "Let's bring in the big fish," Lan suggested to the Russians.

There was a report on the circumstances of the SS captain's capture, which had been peculiar. A patrol had surrounded an isolated house with a walled garden in the country. As the Reds approached, there was gunfire from the garden; they lobbed in grenades, and it soon ceased. When they attacked the black-clad SS man had surrendered, ammunition exhausted.

In the garden there were three dead Waffen SS soldiers. In the house itself the Russians found two more bodies, a well-dressed couple of elderly civilians, each shot neatly through the head. They had obviously been victims of execution, and the Russians had thought it worthwhile to search for and bring in their papers of identity. Herr Professor Adelbert Wenzmer, retired from the University of Vienna, and his wife Gerda, both on pension now. No Party membership cards were found.

The captain's name was Hofstädter, and he once must have been Hitler's very dream of the man he himself would have liked to have been: lean and muscular, blond and blue-eyed, handsome. But his captors had worked him over. His black uniform was muddy, torn, the right side of his face was one enormous swollen bruise, and his lips were puffed and cut. Yet he tried to bear himself with defiance and refused to give more than his name, rank, and serial number.

Lan Condon came around the table, perched on one corner of it, leg swinging. "I'm an American officer, but let me make this clear, I'm only an observer; I have no authority. Your final disposition is up to the lieutenant here. If you are cooperative, I might be disposed to use my good offices with him; if you aren't, to the devil with you, I'll not interfere. The choice is yours."

The Russians treated prisoners of war exactly as they pleased, unbound by any Geneva rules. The SS captain knew that—every German soldier did. Lan waited. Hofstädter's eyes flickered away. "How old are you?" Condon asked.

The man bit his lip. Lan could read his mind: That question was innocuous, why not answer it? "Twenty-five," he said at last, and Lan knew that he had won.

"Your place of birth?"

"Vienna."

Lan's mouth twisted. "You're lying to me, Hofstädter. You're from somewhere in the Waldviertel." The man had a faint accent that had rung a bell in his mind. He slid off the table, threw up his hands. "Well, if that's the way you want it—"

"I was born in Vienna. But I was raised in Raabs."

"That's better," Condon said. "Now. Your unit?"

Hofstädter hesitated. Condon gestured towards Nechiev. "The lieutenant maintains a list, Hofstädter. You have two minutes to answer. If you don't, the names of Hofstädter and the town of Raabs go on the list. At the end of this day's work that list will be turned over to the Russian secret police. When the Waldviertel falls, as it surely will any day now, any relatives you have in Raabs will pay for your refusal to cooperate. Do you understand?"

Hofstädter's mouth twitched, fearful images racing through his mind. The truth of that was something he had no reason to doubt; in his own experience that was how such matters were handled. He drew in breath; and now it was not for himself that he yielded, but for his parents. With that way out for his self-respect, and realizing anyhow that the game was up, he began to talk.

He had been a political officer with a squad of Waffen SS under him attached to a Wehrmacht battalion to watch for any sign of faltering, and to execute summarily anyone whose nerve broke. "If they do not fight," Hofstädter said, "they die."

"I see. But the old man and woman in the house. They were not soldiers, but they were executed. Why?"

Hofstädter was silent for a moment, and Lan thought at first he might rebel. Then the Nazi managed a wry smile. "They were on my list. You are not the only ones who have one." Then he

422

sobered. "Each of us was given a list of the unreliables. Of those who might conceivably be useful to the enemy. I don't know who made them up, they came from Gestapo records, I suppose. All I know is that if we found it necessary to retreat, those people must be located and disposed of."

Condon felt a strange tingling in his wrists, a knotting of the stomach. "Where is your list?"

"I threw it away. Somewhere out there."

"What kind of people were on it?"

"Everyone who might have been of any use to the occupiers. I suppose everyone who ever ran foul of the Gestapo in any way. Those two in that cottage were on my list. Naturally I had to carry out my orders."

"Naturally," Lan said. He mastered his revulsion. "How many names were on your list?"

"Twenty-five, I think."

"Can you remember them?"

Hofstädter fell silent. Nechiev, face grim, said, "We can help your memory."

The man licked his lips. "I remember some of them," he said, and concentrating, began to recite. Nechiev started writing and Lan followed suit; such people would be valuable to the British and Americans, too. But he was not concentrating. *Everyone who ever ran foul of the Gestapo. . . .* Then he could sit there no longer looking at that battered face, listening to that recital, scribbling with a pencil while. . . . He shoved back his chair, walked out.

IT WAS DARK now, the houses locked and shuttered, no lights showing. The street swarmed with drunken soldiers; some of them were singing. Not far away a woman screamed, a shrill sound of terror stifled abruptly. Lorries were still coming in, military police directing them; their engine-growl filled the night. On the horizon there were the dry-lightning flares of artillery, and star shells made magical brilliance in the sky. Every muscle in Lan's body felt as if it had turned to lead. He grappled with what he had learned. Every SS officer had such a list.

Lan walked back to the inn. Entering by the back door, he saw that Mark was still in the public room with Russian officers, and he went quietly up to the room they shared. There he picked up the Russian submachine gun he had been issued, along with several box clips of ammunition. He slung the gun, put the clips into a bag, and went quietly back down the stairs to where his jeep was parked. Its tank was full, and there was a five-gallon jerry can in addition, plenty for a round trip of less than forty miles. He fumbled for the key to the lock that chained the jeep's steering wheel. Then, from the darkness behind him, Mark's voice said, "Lan. No."

Lan started, turned. Mark's blocky figure moved towards him in the darkness, and then Mark's hand gripped his arm.

"God damn it, Mark, I've got to. You don't understand." Mark's fingers never relaxed their grip as he told Gorton about the SS man and the lists. "They'll have her on one, the General, too, and. . . ." He jerked his arm away. "Mark, I've come this far. If when I find her she's dead because I didn't make that one last try . . . I won't let you stop me."

"Lan, I know how you feel. But no. Not until tomorrow."

"Tomorrow?"

"I've been talking to Ognev. He's just got orders down from Army. Before daylight tomorrow he's to swing an armour-infantry task force out through the Wienerwald. Want to know its objective? The road junction at Altkreuzburg. If they secure it we'll have Vienna pinched off south of the Danube. When they go, you go with them."

Mark was silent for a moment; then he squeezed Lan's arm. "All right? Let's go in and fix it up with Ognev."

WHEN THE TANKS CAME, emplacing themselves in the orchard, she had been terrified. Surely their crews would demand to be billeted in the house, and undoubtedly they would find Josef's hiding place. To her relief, the captain in command of them had no such plans; they would sleep near their vehicles. "And you, *gnädige Frau*, you must not stay in the house either. They'll spot us sooner or later, and then all hell will break loose. This house hasn't got a chance."

Except for Josef, she had never seen a man with a face like his. It was so unutterably weary, devoid of hope, that it was hardly human. "I am sorry, Captain. My father is in no condition to be moved away. Besides, I will not leave my home."

He was too tired to argue. "Very well, then. Stay if you must. But for God's sake, stay where you can get to the cellar at a moment's notice. Once we start firing, the Russians will know where we are, and their Stormoviks will be down on us like hawks on mice. How much wine do you have?"

"A great deal, both in casks and bottled."

"You must give me the keys to all your storage areas. It has to be disposed of."

She stared at him. "Our *wine?* But–"

"Yes, for your protection—and the whole valley's. Look, I was in Hungary. Sober, the Russians are bad enough; drunk they are beyond belief. If you insist on staying, you mustn't have a drop of alcohol on the place. Please, your keys."

So she had given them, and save for a few bottles for themselves, a week's supply for her, they had destroyed all of it, smashing the bottled wine, staving in the casks, careful to avoid damage to their historic carved heads. Until the cask wine drained away, it flooded the cellar to a depth of two feet.

Then the captain asked her, "Do you have a pistol?"

"No," Christa said. "You've seen my father's condition. We used to have a lot of guns. But we were afraid he'd hurt himself, so we got rid of all of them."

"With my compliments," the captain said, and unsnapped his holster and handed her his revolver, a P-38. "Do you know how to use it?"

"Yes. Kreisleiter Schellhammer showed me."

"Then good. If you will not leave, keep it with you every hour of the day. Do you understand why?"

Christa stared at him a moment, then said numbly, "Yes." She thrust the gun in the waistband of her skirt. It was hard and cold against her stomach, even through her slip.

"So," the captain said, draining his glass. "For the moment, this is the front line, what there is of it. We have more guns over there, directly across the valley. But we have little ammunition. If you have the opportunity, would you send this letter to my wife in Karlsruhe?"

He bowed, kissed her hand, and left her.

"DAMN IT," Josef said fiercely, "do what he says! Get out! Don't you understand? You've got to get away from here."

They were in Christa's bedroom. She had not seen Robert in four days, and doubted whether she would ever see him again. She had sent all the servants to the village. After that she had wrestled with her conscience. Her father—she owed him safety, too. But he had solved that problem for her. When she sought to take him from the house, he not only regained a measure of rationality, he fought so violently that she feared another stroke. "I will not leave!" he roared in his old deep voice. "Do you think I'd leave you to them?" Short of binding him, there was no way she could get him out, and she ceased trying.

And now, as Josef urged her once again, she turned. "No," she said. "No. It's quite impossible. For Papa's sake and yours."

He was silent for a moment. Then he said, a little wryly, "All right, Christa, come off it."

"What do you mean?"

He sat there on the bed in Lan's pyjamas, looking at her. He had filled out, was almost the old Josef of years ago, save for the deep-etched lines in what had once been a smooth face. He puffed on a cigarette; she still had several packets left, gifts from Robert. "It's not the General," he said quietly, "and it's not me. It's just that if he comes back, this is where he'll look for you."

Christa was silent for a moment. Then she said, "Josef, he won't come back."

"You know damned well that if he's alive he will." Josef stood up. "Or else you don't know Lan the way I do."

"And if he did, what difference would it make?"

"I don't know," said Josef. "But I know how I would feel."

That night, she lay on his arm, eyes closed. Sleep eluded her; Captain Weber had given her the latest information received on his tank radios. Today, the eighth of April, Vienna was burning

426

up. The cathedral was in flames; the Russians were in the south-western districts pouring artillery fire into the Inner City; a fall-back had begun to the north bank of the Danube. . . . It could not be long now. Then she began to drift into sleep. In drowsiness her fears and doubts dissolved. Not long. Soon. Soon Lan would come again. Much as she loved Josef, he was not Lan. She dreamed of a night in the Tyrol. . . .

12

Robert Schellhammer had not taken off his clothes for four days, and his Party uniform was rumpled, stinking. The offices of his *Kreis* in Altkreuzburg had been a madhouse for forty-eight hours, and in that interval he had not even lain down to rest. Frightened citizens had besieged him, wanting everything under the sun—safe-conduct passes west, petrol, food—and there were even a pair of absolutely mad old people who wanted their dog's license renewed. Then the Gauleiter, whose offices were in Vienna, had simply disappeared. No more orders came.

It was finished now and there was nothing more he could do here. He dismissed his staff, what few of them had showed up, told them to seek what safety they could. Then he flopped on a couch, slept like a dead man. Early next morning he was awakened by the buzzing of the switchboard.

Blearily he groped his way through the deserted offices to it. He fumbled with the plugs, then had trouble with the earphones. A crisp voice said, "Kreisleiter Schellhammer, *bitte.*"

"Speaking," Robert answered.

"Lieutenant Trappner, SS, speaking here. Herr Kreisleiter, I have sad news for you. I was with your father when he died."

"My father . . . died. . . ." Robert rubbed his eyes. "Oh. . . ."

"Yes. He died in my arms. A grenade. His last request was that I notify you. Herr Kreisleiter, my sympathies. He died a hero of the Reich."

"Yes," said Robert. "Yes, of course. Where are you calling from?"

"Why, I am in—" Then the line went dead.

"Hallo?" Robert yelled. "Hallo?" But there was not even a buzz.

Groggily he shoved off the earphones. He stood up, not even aware that he was crying. He stumbled across the office, opened the windows. From this height he could look out across the whole valley of the Danube. Vienna was an inferno of flame beneath a pall of smoke. Killed in action. Well, they had both expected that. A hero of the Reich. Robert dropped onto the couch, sat there with head in hands for a long time.

Presently he rose, and in the bathroom down the hall removed his shirt, sluiced down face and torso. *The German soldier regardless of the temperature will wash in cold water to the waist every morning.* There was grey at the temples, and the eyes that looked back at him from the mirror were bloodshot, strangely dead.

It was nine o'clock when he returned to his office. Still no one had come in. Everyone had run west or gone home to shield his family. He dropped into the operator's chair at the switchboard; he felt that he should tell someone about his father. He tried the Christinahof. But no one answered. After a while he gave up and went to a cupboard. From it he took a machine pistol and a cloth bandolier of ammunition. Now, petrol for his car; he must find enough to fill it. He had no idea where. The whole country had run down like a clock. But he would get some, drive to the Christinahof, get Christa and the General on the road, and then find a unit somewhere with which he could fight. They had killed his father, his country and his dream, and he would fight them for as long as he had breath. Then he heard footsteps in the corridor.

He went into the outer office. Its double doors opened and two men entered. Robert relaxed; they both wore black, with the death's-head insignia on their caps. There was something solid and reassuring about a couple of SS officers; here were men who did not panic.

One was a colonel, the other a lieutenant. There was no doubt or faltering in their Heil Hitler salutations. Robert responded in kind, pleased at the firm timbre of his own voice.

The colonel had a knobby, reddish face with black brows like crayon marks. "Herr Kreisleiter Schellhammer?"

428

"I'm he."

The SS man put out his hand. "Colonel Mittler; this is Lieutenant Dorfmann."

They shook hands. Mittler looked around at the empty outer office; "Business is slack," he said, grinning slightly.

"Yes. What can I do for you?" It was good to hear the voices in the empty room.

"A few minutes of your time." Mittler hooked out a chair with a booted foot, sat at a desk, opened a dispatch case. "Just some information."

"Of course." Robert took a chair at the same desk. "You've come from Vienna?"

"Yes."

"What's the situation there?"

Mittler took glasses from his pocket, put them on. "The Russians have almost reached the Ring. So far we've held the highway from here to Vienna open, but they'll cut it soon. I may as well be frank. Preparations are being made to fall back to the north bank of the Danube. We'll consolidate there and then blow all the bridges."

Robert let out breath. "That bad?"

"Yes. You'll soon be cut off from the city, at least on this bank of the river. They have another wing coming through and around the Wienerwald, but the main thrust of their drive is towards Vienna; we're going to let them have this whole area. But—" he glanced at the machine pistol "—if you intend to join the fight, there'll be units farther up the valley who'll fight a rear-guard action."

Mittler laid a typewritten list of names and addresses before Robert. "Time presses. We're strangers to the area. Could you help us locate these addresses?"

"Of course." Robert went to another desk, opened a drawer, took out a map of Altkreuzburg and the area. He sat down by the colonel again, took his pencil from his pocket, stared at the list. Then he froze.

"May I ask," he said, his voice seeming to him to come from far away, "the purpose of this list?"

"All we know is that the Morzinplatz has flagged their files and they are considered hostile to our cause. Anyhow, we're taking no chances. If we should have to go underground, there's no reason to leave all these people alive, intact, for the Reds to use. So— As many of them as can be located, Lieutenant Dorfmann and I will deal with today."

"Kill them," Robert said numbly. He raised his eyes, stared at Mittler. "All these? Only the two of you?"

"Yes, we're all that could be spared to handle this immediate area. Now you see why we must hurry. If you'd just mark the map. . . ."

"But these people— I know most of them. There are some who don't belong on here. Some mistake's been made."

"Too bad for them. No time to correct it now."

"But I tell you, there are names that should be taken off that list." His voice rose. "This is my district and. . . ."

"Herr Schellhammer—" and Mittler's voice was cold "—I beg your pardon. You have no district." His eyes met Robert's. "And if you insist too much, you do so at your own risk. A name cannot be taken off the list. One can be added. Do you understand me?"

They were both looking at him now, hard: the colonel and the lieutenant. Robert swallowed a thickness in his throat. "Yes," he said. "You are right. Forgive me. I was overwrought."

He bent over the map, jotting numbers on it in a firm hand, circling each. Signing, he thought, death warrants. But his hand was steady as he shoved the map at Mittler. "There."

Mittler handed it to Dorfmann, who folded it and stood up. "Thank you, Herr Schellhammer. Now . . . until we meet again, good luck."

"The same to you," Robert said huskily. He raised his arm. "Heil Hitler."

"Heil Hitler," the two men answered. When they had closed the door behind them, Robert stood there as motionless as if carved from wood. Then he began to tremble. He did not know what to do. The list was in alphabetical order. The third name on it had been Christa's. The eighth had been her father's.

He drew a deep breath, let it out. He picked up the Schmeisser

430

and ran across his office into the hall, towards the stairs. He heard the sound of the booted feet of the two officers as they reached the bottom flight. He ran after them, making the lower landing just as they were about to open the massive door.

"Colonel Mittler!" he called, halting on the landing. "One moment. You forgot—"

They both turned. Robert had held the Schmeisser behind his back. Now he brought it out and up. Their eyes widened as they saw it; Dorfmann opened his mouth to yell.

Robert killed the two of them with two short bursts.

THERE WAS ALMOST nothing left to eat. Christa had given each servant baskets of food when they had fled to sanctuary behind the lines. Apologetically, Captain Weber had requisitioned rations for his men, and meanwhile a party of infantrymen had come through and slaughtered the pigs, driven off the cattle, and killed most of the chickens. And now, incredible as it seemed, the once endless resources of the Christinahof had dwindled down to almost nothing: only a few loaves of bread, a couple of hoarded jars of marmalade, and a sheaf of unused ration cards not worth the paper they were printed on.

With the house empty of everyone except themselves, there was no need for Josef to stay confined in the attic room. Robert had not been seen or heard from in four days, and Christa supposed that he had either gone to fight or that he was dead. The thought of Robert dead moved her more than she had expected; she felt grief not for the *Kreisleiter* who had been an accomplice in horrors she would not let her mind dwell on, but for the gold-bright young dreamer who had shared her childhood afternoons.

Anyhow, if anyone came unexpectedly, there were plenty of places Josef could quickly hide; and so they took the chance. He sat at the table with them in the dining room as they ate breakfast.

It had been his first encounter with the General, and although Christa had prepared him, Josef had been shocked. When Josef had last seen him, her father had been in his prime; now he was a wraith of that self, lost in some secret world of his own.

The soldiers had been very good with the old man. Captain

Weber had shown him the tanks and had discussed their field of fire, the way they commanded the roads and surrounding terrain, interlocking with the guns behind the Schellhammerhof across the ridge. And there had been several minutes when the General had become quite lucid, discussing the disposition of the guns with, said Weber, wisdom and authority.

But this morning the General was back in that lost place of his, displaying neither recognition nor curiosity, accepting Josef's presence passively—if he was aware of it at all. As usual he ate almost nothing, but he fed himself with neatness and precision.

Suddenly a bell rang. Christa tensed. "The back door. Josef—"

But he was already up, heading for concealment in the pantry. She gave him time to lock himself in before she answered the insistent ringing. Captain Weber was there, sad-terrier face grave.

"Frau Condon. We have a radio message. A lot of Russian planes are shooting their way up the line through the Wienerwald, coming in this direction. We are to retaliate with anti-aircraft fire. That means inevitably we'll draw down their fire on us, and. . . ." Weber was apologetic. "I'm sorry. But you and your father must take cover in your cellar at once." Then he tensed, cocked his head. "The devil! They're already. . . . *Wiederseh'n*, Frau Condon!" He whirled, ran towards the orchard.

Christa heard it, too, a strange thunder from not far away, the harsh rasp of diving aircraft. Now she saw them, high above the Wienerwald, circling. She turned back into the house as there was the slam of cannon fire and the chatter of machine guns from the orchard.

"Josef! Papa! Air raid! *Josef, help me!*" She seized her father, dragged him into the corridor towards the kitchen; they had to get across the courtyard to the deep wine cellars beneath the pressing-house. But as she reached the kitchen, the whole hilltop seemed engulfed in thunder. Plates fell off the wall; glasses jumped from the cabinets, jingling. They were engulfed by sound, vibration, and crumbling plaster. "Josef!" she screamed.

Then he was there, seizing her father by the arms, the old man stood, head raised, listening, staring, as if that familiar roar had triggered associations in his mind. For one wild instant she thought that he was normal; he seemed the man she once had known.

There was no hope of getting across the courtyard. Christa ran to another door. "This way!" She pulled her father by the hand, and Josef pushed him down the steps to the laundry. Now the roar above was muffled. Christa found another key on her ring, fumbled it into another lock. The door swung open, and they went cautiously down the steps of a second, deeper cellar. In total darkness she went sprawling on hands and knees, dragging the General down with her. "Papa! Josef, help me!" They scrambled and finally regained their feet. "Papa! Are you all right?"

"*Ja.*" His voice was toneless.

"Good. Over here." She led them to covered storage bins that would serve as benches and eased her father down on one. There was vibration, a muffled roar from overhead. In the fall, the pistol Weber had given her had slipped from the waistband of her skirt, but for now that did not matter. Josef was beside her then, and she clung to him while the stones of walls and floor jarred in their mortar. Above, something enormous fell, shaking even this deep burrow in the earth. . . .

General Helmer sat in darkness, his back against stone; a dugout, of course. Artillery was firing somewhere close by. But he could not quite grasp the situation. For a moment he felt a certain urgency, knowing he should be out there commanding; then it slipped away. Once more there was the calm in which nothing mattered, people had no faces, words no meanings. The brief flare of thought had been as much as he could sustain. Anyhow, there was the other thing to think about that he had found in the darkness when he fell.

THEY WERE the first human beings Robert had ever killed. He stared at them a moment, not so much in awe as in curiosity. It was not really different from shooting deer or wild boar. The red that stained them was the same.

He rubbed his face. He had never thought to kill two SS men. But he would make it up somehow. Once Christa was safe and he went into combat, he would kill enough Reds to expiate what he had done. But for now . . . the petrol.

He scooped up the dispatch case that contained the list. This must not fall into anybody else's hands. Their small armoured car was parked in the deserted courtyard. Instead of a key it had a standard military switch; and when he flicked it on, the fuel indicator rose to nearly *full*. Robert let out a breath. The vehicle would hold Christa, the General, and himself; and its range would get them out of the Russians' way. Laying the machine pistol on the seat, he slid behind the wheel, started the engine.

He drove the vehicle through the courtyard, out of the high arched gate, and rushed down the hill to the lower town. Half a dozen armed Pioneers were at the main junction in the lower market, but the SS pennant was pass enough without question. He turned west, then took the Ferntal road.

Driven by urgency, he stamped down on the accelerator. Soon he had left Altkreuzburg, was entering the Ferntal. He had not seen Christa in four days. He felt a sudden, overpowering need to hold her, touch her, tell her about his father, have her weep for and with him. Then, without warning, the hills on both sides and the road itself seemed to explode. The scout-car jumped, whirled sideways by concussion. That was his first knowledge of the aeroplanes. Then a Stormovik, diving low, crossed his field of vision. He gunned the engine, shot off the road to the shelter of some trees by the stream. Seizing the machine pistol, he dived from the scout-car, hurtled down the bank, pressed himself against its cold sand, sheltered by its overhang. Panting, he looked up.

The sky was full of planes, red stars on their wings. They swooped and dived across and up and down the valley. From the ridge by the Christinahof, tracers laced up at them from the tank guns. He saw one plane go whirling wing over wing to crash into the Wienerwald not far from old Professor Busch's hut.

Across the valley the Stormoviks came down, flight after flight, bombing, pumping cannon shells. He saw the whole ridgetop explode in white and dirty brown. The spurts of tracer ceased as shells slammed into the tanks. The planes passed over, peeled off, then turned back to the attack.

Now the Christinahof took the full fury. Tiles flew, the yellow walls seemed to lift themselves from their foundations, poise, then

434

split asunder, falling. Furiously Robert pounded on the dirt with both hands. Then he lay there, face buried in his arms. There was nothing he could do.

The roaring overhead receded; such a miracle that at first he did not dare believe it. Not until a silence, total and profound, had settled over the valley did he scrabble up the creek bank and halt, staring up at the Christinahof.

Three of its walls still stood, though its roofs had fallen in and the subsidiary floors collapsed. Robert licked his lips. Surely she had hidden in its cellars; she must have had ample warning. His hands shook as he started the car up again. He drove it across the cratered, pitted road and up the coiling way to the Christinahof.

In low gear, the little car crawled with maddening slowness. Finally he reached the gate, which was hanging awry on the one stone pillar not blown away. The air was pungent, chalky, with plaster, brick dust, explosives. Robert got out. Holding the Schmeisser, he ran around the house to the courtyard. The pressing-house was a mass of rubble, too, its cellar doors totally sealed off. Oh, God, if she were down in there, then she was trapped. Alone he could not move that vast pile of masonry. "Christa!" he screamed. "*Christa!*"

There was no answer. God, was he doomed to lose everything today? He held his breath, but there was only the clack of bits of rubble dropping like water from the eaves after a storm had passed. "Christa," he called again, voice quavering. Then, trying to think, he walked back around the shattered corner of the house.

He knew now; for him, nothing really counted except her. All he had done, all he had based his life upon, had been inspired by her. She could *not* be dead.

Then he raised his head, whirled, and ran back towards the courtyard, where there was the sound of voices. And there they were, three of them, just emerging from the outside entrance to the house's cellars: Christa, face smeared with dirt, the General, looking blankly around him, and behind her a stranger, tall, his black hair powdered with white dust.

They did not see him. They were staring in horror at what had happened to the Christinahof. Then Christa let out a sob. "Oh,

Josef!" she cried and whirled and buried her face against the chest of the man, and he put his arm around her.

"All right, darling," the man said quietly, touching his lips to her tousled hair.

Josef? Darling? Who was this man? Robert's heart was pounding in his chest. "Christa!" he shouted.

The man still holding her jerked up his head; his arm fell away. Slowly Christa turned and he saw her eyes widen, and there was no joy in her expression, only surprise and horror.

"Who are you?" Robert asked, aiming the gun at the man.

He half raised his hands, face pale. "A refugee. My name is Schmidt. Josef Schmidt, Herr Kreisleiter. I—"

But he had held her in his arms and she had pressed against him and he had kissed her hair and Robert saw the lie on his face and finally now Robert had someone that he could make pay for all that he had lost today, and he was not even aware that he squeezed the trigger. Christa screamed. The man, picked up by the burst of lead, fell flopping on the cobblestones, kicked once, lay still.

Christa was frozen for a moment. Then she shrieked, "Josef!" dropped to her knees beside him, touched his chest, drew back a red-smeared hand, and then twisted to stare at Robert.

"Killed," she said hoarsely. "Killed. Are you satisfied now? Is he happy now, your Führer, your little tin god with the sewer mind, your little pervert with the absurd moustache?" She spat the words at him. "And are you happy, too, you great hero, you great stupid bloody-minded idiot?"

"Christa," he whispered. "Darling—"

"Darling? *Darling?* You make me want to vomit. Do you know who that was? That was Josef Steiner. Josef Steiner, the Jew. The *Jew*, you understand? I've been hiding him here, in the house, in the attic. And every night that you were gone, he made love to me. . . ."

She stood there, dust-spattered, blood-stained, her face contorted.

"I don't believe it," Robert whispered.

"Well, it's true!" she shrieked. "And what are you going to do about it? Kill something else? Kill me or Papa? If you want to kill something, why don't you kill yourself?"

He said nothing, only looked at her. The gun came up and he aimed it at her belly.

The first bullet knocked Schellhammer around, and the second hit him in the chest, and he fell like a well-struck roebuck, the machine pistol clattering on the pavement.

"So," the General said, still holding outstretched the gun that he had found upon the cellar floor. It was all clear, everything, for one blinding instant: Christina gone, and now the house; and Robert had meant to— He tried to cling to that clarity, hold it in his mind; but it was no use. Like a live eel, rationality slipped through his grasp. He returned the pistol to his waistband and saw that Christina —Christa?—was sitting in the rubble crying; something pulled him to her, and he touched her shoulder. But then it had all gone away, like his wife, like the house which had somehow vanished; and he dropped the hand and stood there blankly, calm, with nothing real and nothing mattering.

13

At mid-afternoon of the second day, the point tanks of the Russian task force battered down the last feeble roadblock—a squad of Hitler Youth armed with a machine gun and a few grenades. Then the armour topped a ridge, spread out, and Altkreuzburg lay before them, the Danube grey beyond. "Hah!" grunted the colonel beside Lan in the command car. He pointed, grinning, showing front teeth capped with stainless steel. *"Donau? Donau!"*

"Yes," Lan said. "The Danube." As Colonel Kudrya got out, he followed suit. He stared at the sprawling monastery, the coiling river, the huddled town, the hills beyond; and it had not changed. Nothing had changed.

It took two hours to verify that the town was clear, and for Lan Condon every minute was an eternity. Russian planes had come over the previous day. It was said the Christinahof was destroyed. As the townspeople came from their holes he talked to everyone, seeking word not only of Christa but also of Robert Schellhammer.

And then the Bürgermeister told him that Schellhammer had disappeared. Maybe gone off to fight. Maybe he had run. But two

SS men had been found shot to death. Believed to be the work of the resistance. He could make no sense of it.

The tanks formed up. Five of them would thrust up the Ferntal, infantry riding on them. Air cover had been called in, too, and Colonel Kudrya, with a generosity that Lan had not expected, offered him a jeep. But he refused it, his decision already made. He would ride on the lead tank of the patrol. Kudrya shrugged; it was a risk not required of him, but one appreciated, since he knew the country. It would be helpful to the commander of the point.

Westward, behind the hills, the sun slipped lower, filling the hollows with purple shadows. Lan took his place behind the turret. The sergeant commanding the T-34 spoke into his microphone, gave a hand signal. Loaded with clinging infantry, the tank growled and thundered into forward motion. The four behind it followed, the patrol lumbering through the narrow streets.

From the height of the tank's rear deck Lan could see into the courtyards. He saw the stacks of firewood, the spaded gardens, the lilacs putting out their first greenery, the meticulously clipped and winter-mulched roses. Then they were out of the town itself and had entered the Ferntal road, and the tanks speeded up. Behind them, the monastery bells suddenly clanged out with full-throated brazenness, whether in joy, requiem, or simple hypocrisy he could not guess.

And now they were well into the Ferntal, and his heart pounded. The chestnuts along the Fernbach were fuzzed with green. The hills towered up, green and lovely. Then he saw, high up on the ridge crest, the ruins against the sky. As the tank rolled on, he stared, disbelieving, despite all the destruction he had seen so far. It had been blown to bits, and probably she was dead. His throat closed. To come so far, endure so much, and now, after all that, to find. . . .

The tank commander knew the significance of that high ground all too well, and this was his life at stake. Lan screamed at him, disregarded, as the turret slowly turned. Then, with Lan howling, the long gun belched first one round and then another.

The first went over, the second fell a bit short in the orchard; and as Lan froze, the third went home. He saw the ruins lift and tremble, one of the three walls fall in. Then another round and a second wall came down. "You bastard," Lan moaned in English, but the commander ignored him. Now he swung the tank and, followed by another, it ground up the hill.

Slowly it climbed, Lan erect on its deck. Presently the whole Ferntal lay below them. Then they were in beech forest, out again, then next in spruce. After that they were in the open once again, and Lan was already thinking of what the rest of his life would be like without her. What did you do when you had no dream left?

The tank rolled on through the ruined gate, halted. Infantry piled off, spreading out, guns up. Condon leaped down, staring at the bleakness of the ruins. Plaster dust clogged his nostrils. He clambered through the ruins. "Christa!" he yelled, but there was no answer. He waited a moment, yelled her name again. Then he saw the bodies.

He realized that he was looking into the upturned face of what had been Robert Schellhammer, torso half buried under fresh-fallen masonry. It was swollen, dark, but there was no mistaking it, and Lan's last hope died. It had been up to Robert. It was Robert he had counted on.

He walked to the other body, free of rubble but equally distorted with the puffiness of death. Lan frowned. He knew that face, knew it from somewhere. It had changed since last he'd seen it, but—

Raucous shouting and a thick hammering sound made him turn. The Russian infantry had found a door, obviously the entrance to a cellar. Lan searched his mind. With everything blown up and fallen, it was hard to orientate himself. Then he thought, the laundry. The Red soldiers picked up a fallen timber, battered with it. Lan hurried forward just as the lock broke and the door gave inward; and he jumped down the steps, pushed the Russians back, and entered.

WHEN FINALLY she had regained her wits, she had dragged her father back down here, the only shelter left. The laundry was still intact, and so was the cellar underneath. She had found matches on Josef's body, and she knew where the oil lamps were in the lower cellar. She knew, too, that she should have buried Josef and Robert, but where, how? She left them where they lay. The cellar was enough for now.

440

She took the pistol from her father and kept it; there were bullets in it still. Maybe later they would use them. The General sat passively in a corner. Mostly she kept the lamp turned out; they sat in darkness.

She tried to pass the time by talking to her father. "Papa," she said, "how did all this happen? I can remember how happy we all were. You must have been happy too and so was Mama. . . ."

But he only sat there. Still she kept it up; it made the hours go more swiftly and relieved her of the need for action. "Papa, how do you believe in anything? Or do you? Why don't you answer?"

Sometimes, stretched out on the cold stone floor, she slept. She knew that sooner or later she must leave this place. "Papa, do you miss her as much as I miss Lan? Are you the one who found the answer?"

After a full day had passed, her head was clearer, mind sharpened by hunger. They could not stay here. A few more hours and they'd venture out.

"Papa," she said much later, "maybe we had better think about leaving here. Do you understand . . . ?" Then the whole laundry room jarred and she heard the dull, muted thunder of falling rubble. With strange calm, she thought, Now this is the end of it; the Russians have come. Her hand groped across the table and found the gun she'd put there when she took it from her father.

The rumbling subsided overhead. Then, vaguely, she was aware of shouting, and suddenly the courtyard door shook and bulged. Whatever had slammed against it slammed again. Christa gripped the pistol more tightly and lit the lamp. That had to be the Russians.

The door burst open. "Christa!" a man's voice yelled above the alien Russian babble. Surely she was dreaming? She saw the silhouette against the lighted doorway. Then the voice shouted in English, "Christa, are you there? Christa, is that you?"

She rose. Of course it was not true, but— Then a torch played on her face, blinding her; she could not see the man behind it.

"Are you Christa?" said the voice.

She stood there, squinting into the glare. "I'm Christa, Lan," she said. "If you're Lan, I'm Christa." And, hand shaking uncontrollably, she let the gun fall to the table.

Lan stared at the woman in the lamplight. Her hair was tangled, dirty; her face was smudged; she did not smile. Only her voice was recognizable.

He did not run to her, walked slowly, said nothing, found no words. But it was Christa. Then his paralysis broke and he ran. He seized her and she fell against him and he held her. Her flesh had a special feel beneath his hands. "It's all right," he said.

"But there are Russians."

"It's all right," he repeated.

"Papa's here. But he's . . . he needs someone to help him."

"Someone will help him. Christa—" He pulled away from her, led her up the steps. Outside in the courtyard they looked at each other.

She was not what he had dreamed of, not what he had expected. He saw, too, the puzzlement in her eyes. Much of the dream had vanished, but there was still enough to build on. There had to be. They stared at each other, mute with things it might take them years to find the words to say.

"Oh, God," he said, "I thought you were dead."

"No," she heard herself answer. "I'm not dead yet. I've made it somehow."

Lan put his arm around her gently, almost as if he were holding a stranger. He turned, swinging her around. Only the single wall of the Christinahof still left standing stood between them and the sky.

Ben Haas

A native of North Carolina, Ben Haas is a prolific writer who is best known for his novels of the American South. *The House of Christina* grew out of an experience that began in 1964 when the author and his family decided to spend a year living in Europe. With his wife and three sons Mr. Haas moved into the small town of Kritzendorf, not far from Vienna, the first American family to live in that district. "We wanted to be near Vienna," the author says, "because it was a rather remote and very glamorous spot to be in the 60's. And we wanted to be off the beaten path, not living the lives of ordinary tourists."

Kritzendorf had been occupied by the Russians after the war, and Mr. Haas soon became aware of the haunting, fascinating history of the area. The family returned to the U.S. after a year, but in 1972 they were back in Kritzendorf, and the idea for a novel was growing. When Mr. Haas placed an advertisement in a Vienna newspaper for a bilingual researcher, the result was a deluge of people who wanted to tell him their stories of the war years. Thus began the research and writing which filled the following three years.

The Haas family now lives in Raleigh, North Carolina, with the exception of one son who is pursuing a musical career— in Vienna.

THE MELODEON

a condensation of the book by

Glendon Swarthout

Illustrated by Brinton Turkle
Published by Secker & Warburg

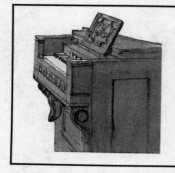

melodeon (m ə-lōdi-ən),
n. a small keyboard organ
in which the tones are
produced by drawing
air through metal reeds
by means of a bellows
operated by pedals....

Webster's New World Dictionary

The melodeon of this story was bought as a present by Ephraim Chubb for his wife Sarah on the occasion in 1863 when he rode off to fight for the North in the American Civil War. Ephraim intended the melodeon to keep Sarah company until the day of his homecoming.

How, mysteriously, he came home many, many years later than he supposed is here recalled by his great-grandson, James Chubb, in a tale that is as remarkable as it is charming, warm and entertaining. It all took place when James was just a boy on a cold and snow-driven Christmas Eve in the depressed 1930's, the night his grandparents chose to donate the melodeon to the local church. What happened then beneath the Christmas stars was for him and his family nothing short of a miracle.

ONE

I write these lines in the fifty-fourth year of my life. They begin a tale I might long ago have told, but an intuition stayed my pen. And so I waited. The years passed. Now, this autumn, as the days wither and the stars recede and another Christmas nears, I am old enough at last to tell it truly, and young enough at last to know what it means.

When I was thirteen years of age I was literally farmed out by my parents—put on a train in Philadelphia and sent west to Michigan to live with my grandparents on their farm a few miles south of Howell. It was the 1930s, the decade of the Depression. My father had lost his job, for months had walked the streets seeking another, and his relief checks of ten dollars a week did not suffice to pay rent and raise a growing youngster. I was fortunate to have a farm to go to, for farmers, everyone said, were luckier than most. No matter how hard the times, they always had enough to eat.

Will and Ella Chubb were my mother's parents. Their farm was homesteaded and cleared by Will's grandfather, a man named Major Chubb. Descended from a long line of Yorkshire farmers, he came west in a covered wagon in 1836. The land had been kind to the Major and his son Ephraim, and Ephraim's son Will. There were twenty-acre fields now, and woods and pastures for the sheep and a huckleberry marsh and a lake, deep and blue and troubled with pickerel. There was a barn, with haymow above and sheep-shed and horse stalls and cowshed underneath. A large granary stored the harvests and a treasury of machinery—thresher, tractor, hay rake, mowing machine, plows, reaper, cultivator, and several wagons. The house itself was white frame, with a bathroom, a screened porch, a parlor with a pump organ, and a feather-tick bed in my very own room upstairs. If one had to be an orphan, I soon decided, this was a good place to be one.

I wore overalls. I walked three miles to the one-room schoolhouse next to the church at Chubb's Corners, where another boy and I constituted the seventh grade. After school I helped Will, my grandfather. I learned to hitch and unhitch the team, to pick Northern Spies and Baldwins in the apple orchard and assist at the cider press. I tried milking but simply couldn't get the grip of it. I was thirteen, all arms and legs and thumbs, and a city boy, and much less a menace to the cows when I did domestic chores for Ella, my grandmother. I dried the dishes. I split kindling and fetched wood for the cookstove in the kitchen. And I separated.

In the woodshed, behind the kitchen, stood a cylinder of steel with two spouts and a wooden handle. You poured pails of fresh milk into the open top, placed a milk can under one spout and a cream bucket under the other, bent your back, braced your feet, laid both hands on the handle, and began to crank. I had no idea what went on inside the separator but there was considerable activity, signaled by a growl which, as you revolved the handle faster and faster, increased in pitch and volume to a howl, then to a scream. Milk streamed from one spout, cream from the other, and a deafening music, appropriate to any number of swashbuckling scenes, assailed the ears. You could crank and crank and close your eyes and be at sea in a typhoon, masts toppling as you fought the wheel to keep your schooner's bow into the wind. My favorite fantasy, though, while cranking and puffing, was that I was spinning the prop of my silver monoplane, *Spirit of St. Louis*, taking off from Long Island, then clutching the controls as the engine droned over the dark Atlantic until we landed, the eyes of the world upon us, at Le Bourget.

And always, always, there were eggs. Ella kept two hundred chickens. Good layers, she called them—a characteristically rural

understatement. Those Leghorns were veritable volcanoes of eggs.
Evidently they never left the nest long enough to cackle, scratch,
or cluck, for I gathered, washed, and crated hen fruit till I couldn't
face it boiled, fried, or scrambled on my breakfast plate. Ella sent
two crates to a grocer in Howell each week. They brought eight to
twelve cents a dozen, and her egg money she divided evenly—half
for staples and half to be hoarded for an automobile.

It was a source of shame and bitterness to her that the Chubbs
were the only family thereabouts without one. The Cadwells, down
the road, trucked their crates to town in a Model A, the Stackables
had a Nash, even Joe and Abby Henshaw strutted a Model T. While
drying dishes I learned from Ella that three years previously, when
she had her husband almost at the point of investing in a car, a
smooth-talking salesman had persuaded him instead to trade in his
old tractor for an expensive new Rumely OilPull. That was the
beginning of payments and the end of the automobile. When it
came to the farm, Will was pitifully "soft on machinery", she
confided. This tragic flaw had kept them poor throughout their
married life, and though she had put her foot down about indoor
plumbing, they still made do with a gas lighting system, the only
one in a neighbourhood elegant with electricity.

And so she saved her money for a Studebaker. When I asked
what was wrong with a Ford, she said nothing. However, an
advertised feature of the Studebaker was "Free Wheeling", and
she believed it implied that you could get up speed, turn off the
ignition, and coast for miles. But when I argued that you could
buy a heck of a lot of gas for the difference in price between a
Ford and a Studie, Ella pursed her lips and dismissed the matter.
She would not admit to inconsistency. She was a woman.

That was my problem. She was not supposed to be. She was
supposed to be a grandmother. I didn't know Will and Ella well
when I arrived at the farm, for I had visited them only twice before.
It took me till Christmas to comprehend that they were
human beings and to love them deeply as such. Grandparents,
meanwhile, was an easier category to handle. A boy could easily
separate "grandparents" from "people". Grandparents were a

little unreal. They might have been young once, have loved and hated and grieved, might have known fear and passion, rage and wonder, but these feelings they had long ago forgotten.

Yes, I was convinced at the start that grandparents were gray and kind and frail and soon to die, and that was all.

It was an eventful autumn. The church at Chubb's Corners burned down in October. Electricity had just been installed, and faulty wiring was probably responsible. The men of the congregation, farmers every one, set to work on Sundays and in rainy weather and by the first of December a new church was built. Money for materials was hard to come by, and while the structure was unpainted on the outside and unfinished on the in, and lacked lighting, it had a pulpit and a woodstove and benches and pews. The Lord, the Reverend Leon Ledwidge assured his small flock at the first service, would be pleased.

The second event was Will's coming from the barn on Thanksgiving eve and informing us that one of his old ewes was pregnant. "I don't believe it," he said, "but she is. Four months along, I calculate."

"What's so impossible?" I inquired.

"Sheep," he said, "never lamb in winter. I know. I've kept sheep forty years. Lambs are dropped in April, May, or June."

"If I was a ewe," said I with urban impudence, "I'd drop a lamb any old time I wanted to."

He looked at me and tugged an end of his drooping mustache. Will called it his tea strainer, because when he drank green tea from a saucer he could strain the leaves through it. "No," said he, "if you were a ewe you'd get around to lovering when you and the ram were ready. Would you like me to explain?"

My grandmother hopped over that indelicate puddle quickly. "Maybe we'll have a lamb born for Christmas—wouldn't that be nice?" she said, putting the morning oatmeal on the stove so as not to waste the overnight heat. "Now that I think of it, Will, I've seen pictures on calendars, of the Christ child in the manger, with Mary and Joseph, and there's usually a lamb nearby, and that was

450

Christmas. So lambs must have been born in the winter back then."

"Those pictures were painted by painters," stated her husband. "Painters do not keep sheep."

The third event was something which didn't happen. It didn't snow. The days were gray, November had turned cold, skim ice appeared on the lake, and Will put a barrel of cider in the backyard, but there was no snow. The neighbors mentioned it at every meeting and over the party line. The winter wheat would suffer.

But it was winter now, unmistakably, and Christmas neared. A time or two, walking home from school, I shed a tear. I wrote my father and mother every other day rather than every week. The barrel of cider froze over. Will chunked out the ice and let it refreeze again and again. When there were but a few inches of clear liquid at the bottom, he clasped the barrel fondly to his chest and carried it into the basement. Meanwhile he studied the old ewe from every angle, but she was irrefutably pregnant.

Then, on the day before Christmas, we woke to a world of snow. A real blinder of a blizzard whirled down upon us from Canada. I gathered the eggs in the afternoon, but the day was so dark and the flakes so thick that, stumbling knee-deep in snow already, I located the house only by its lights. I wore a corduroy cap, with the flaps down over my ears, yet the wind almost tore it off. Will declared he had never seen such a storm.

At supper, Ella said her customary grace. "Dear Lord, bless this food to our use and us to Thy service," she murmured, then added a postscript: "And let the storm pass so that we may worship Thee tomorrow. Amen." The next day, Christmas, fell on Sunday that year, and my grandmother never missed church. For dessert that evening she had made a shortcake filled with black raspberries she had picked in August and canned. The Lord may have blessed the food to our use, but I am sure He envied us that shortcake.

Will went to the barn again after supper to see to his expectant ewe. Usually I dried the dishes and Ella washed, but tonight I volunteered to do them all while she prepared a hen for tomorrow's dinner, scalding the bird and plucking and drawing it, then setting it to cool overnight in the woodshed. In the morning she would

451

stuff and truss it, and put it on to roast while we were at church.

"As long as I live," said my grandmother out of a clear blue sky, "I'll never understand your grandfather."

I accepted that. If you had been married to a man forty-six years and still didn't understand him, you probably never would.

"I told you," she went on, "he's soft on machinery."

"Yes." I paid her only partial attention. Using the pump beside the sink, I had filled a dishpan and teakettle and put them on the stove, and both were boiling now.

"He can't even bring himself to kill a hen."

"He can't?"

"I have to do it myself, always have. And he's certainly soft on the neighbors."

"How come?" I lugged the dishpan to the sink and set to work, dispirited by a tower of baking pans.

"Why, everyone around here owes him for the summer threshing —and last summer's, too," she said. "That's how he justified buying a new tractor. 'I'll do the threshing for the whole township,' he told me, 'so much a bushel, and that way we'll pay off the tractor and you can have a car to boot.' And I let him. And what happened? They didn't pay a penny last summer or this and they don't intend to." She plucked fiercely.

"Why not?" I asked.

"Because wheat's down to twenty-eight cents a bushel, so they're all storing it in hopes of a better price. If he'd only ask them to pay something, I know they could. But he won't. 'Times are hard,' he'll say, 'and they're my friends.' That's what I mean—soft."

"Oh," I said.

"But he can be as stubborn, too. When that ewe drops her lamb, you watch. He'll insist it isn't a lamb at all, because it's the wrong time of year." She put heart, gizzard, and liver away in a bowl for eventual gravy. "I'll give you another example. Did you know that when he was six years old he could play the organ beautifully?"

"He could?"

"But then when he heard his father was dead he never played another note?"

That stopped me. "He didn't? Why not?"

"Stubborn," she replied. "His mother begged him, she told me so, but he never would. That's what I mean—hard and soft at the same time. I'll never understand him if I live to be a hundred."

I rinsed from the teakettle and stood there drying. Some of the family history my mother had told me. Ephraim Chubb went away to war with the 10th Michigan Cavalry from this very farm in 1863. His young wife, my great-grandmother Sarah, received a letter in 1864 saying that he was missing in action. Sarah waited, as did her small son, Willy, who had never seen his father. Five years later, in 1869, she got a second letter from the War Department. Ephraim's remains had been plowed up near Strawberry Plains, Tennessee. He had been killed on a raid and interred hastily by his comrades. He was shipped home to Sarah, who buried him in the Putnam Township ground near the church at Chubb's Corners.

"Maybe that's why Will never played the organ again," I speculated. "I mean, after he found out his father was dead. Maybe his heart was broken."

"Fiddlesticks," she said. It was her only expletive.

In a few minutes we heard Will enter the woodshed and stomp the snow from his boots. I finished the dishes, Ella the hen. Will came into the kitchen and warmed himself at the stove and said he'd never seen such a storm and the ewe was about due. Then Ella said there would be just time to have the tree before my telephone call. That was to be my Christmas present from my parents. They had given up their telephone but would go to a friend's house and call me at eight o'clock, and we could talk precisely three minutes. So Will and Ella and I went into the living room.

The tree was a tall one that Will and I had cut in the huckleberry marsh, and while it lacked the number of ornaments I was accustomed to at home, Ella and I had strung about a mile of popcorn. And when she lighted the tiny candles, the tree was lovely. There were only two presents, both for me. My grandfather's was a walnut-handled pocketknife, my grandmother's a scarf she had knitted, long enough to wind round and round.

"Gee, thanks a lot," I said. "They're really swell. I don't have anything for you, though. I don't know how to make anything and I didn't have any money."

"Why, you're our gift, James," said Ella, and kissed me.

Will put a hand on my shoulder. "We haven't had a pup around here for a dog's age."

We wished each other Merry Christmas, then pinched the candles out and returned to the kitchen, for it was nearly eight o'clock. They sat at the table and I stood by the wall phone. After five minutes I decided someone must be on the line, so I lifted the receiver. Universal sin absolves individuals, and since everyone did it, listening in on a party line was not considered sinful. But the receiver hummed and I hung it up.

Wood hissed in the stove. Over the table the clock ticked. Wind boxed the house. Under us the joists creaked with cold.

"Just imagine," said Ella, crocheting a potholder and making conversation, "a body speaking to someone in Michigan all the way from Philadelphia. Whatever will they think of next?"

"A night like this, maybe the lines are down," Will suggested. His wife frowned at him.

"Now when they call," he said to me, making amends, "don't fritter your time away having us talk to them. We can write. It's your present and you use every blamed second of it."

"Thank you," I said. I was developing a lump in my throat.

When the phone finally did ring, and we held our breath counting three long and one short, I seized the receiver and could scarcely say hello. The lump in my throat was as big as an egg with a double yolk. Then the sound of my mother's voice broke the egg and me with it. She warned me that she was watching the clock and three minutes was all they could manage, and that rendered me even more inarticulate. I determined that she and my father were well. She ascertained from me that I was well and so were Will and Ella. The weather in Philadelphia was clear. We were having a blizzard. My father, to whom I next talked, had not yet found a job. One of Will's sheep was about to have a lamb. I had a dandy new jackknife and scarf. There was an excruciating pause, after which we were wishing each other Merry Christmas and they

454

were saying good-by and I heard a click and hung the receiver and couldn't turn around because my eyes were swimming.

"I have an idea," said my grandmother briskly. "Why don't we go into the parlor and I'll play the melodeon and we'll sing carols."

I swallowed hard, still facing the phone. "I didn't know you could play."

"I can't very well anymore," she confessed. "My fingers, the arthritis, you know. That's why I never do. But I used to. Sarah taught me, Will's mother. Anyway, I'm game if you are."

She nodded at her husband and I tagged after them through the living room, where they opened the sliding doors, and on into the parlor. Will turned up the gas, struck a match, and we had light. I looked at the melodeon as though for the first time.

It was a handsome instrument of cherry wood, thirty-three inches high, forty inches wide, and twenty-one inches deep. The hinged top folded up and back and became a music rack, revealing a five-octave keyboard and above it, in gilt lettering on the fall board, the name of the manufacturer: MASON & HAMLIN. At the base were two ten-inch-wide pedals, which were pumped to fill the bellows, and they were covered with frayed needlepoint in a floral design. At the left of the pedals a small wooden treadle protruded. It was called a swell, or a loud and soft damper. To adjust the volume, one depressed it with the left foot while double-pedaling with the right. There was a bench, covered with needlepoint too. Ella told me later that the coverings had been done by Sarah, my great-grandmother, in 1911, the year of her death.

Ella folded back the top, sat down, and played several carols, singing along with Will and me. We sang "Silent Night", and "We Three Kings of Orient Are". She hit a few black keys when she should have white, and when I glanced at her fingers I saw that they were gnarled by arthritis. She pumped with vigor, though, and we sang with zeal. The tones of the melodeon sounded true and faintly elegaic. The union of their two old voices with my soprano, which would not change to tenor for another year, was not unharmonious. But something gave me gooseflesh. Other presences seemed to join us in the parlor on that Christmas Eve.

Other voices, quavery and distant, seemed to swell our choir. It had never occurred to me that ghosts could sing.

We started "It Came upon the Midnight Clear". Suddenly my grandmother stopped. "Oh, Will!" she whispered. "I've just had the most wonderful notion!" We waited, mouths open. "The melodeon—let's give it to the church for Christmas!" She rose from the bench. Behind her spectacles her eyes were wide. "They haven't even a piano—it would help the singing so much. I never play it—and you won't. Why don't we give it to the church?"

Will tugged his mustache. "No harm in it, I expect."

"Tomorrow's Sunday and Christmas both—we'll surprise them —when they come in, there it will be!"

"Tomorrow?"

"What better time, Christmas morning?"

He shook his head. "Ella, you forget. This blizzard. I couldn't haul it there tonight."

"Can't you take the team? With a wagon?"

"The roads will be drifted deep in an hour. No team could—"

"Fiddlesticks!"

"Girl," he said, "I hate to disappoint you, but there won't even be a service tomorrow."

She turned away and lowered the top of the melodeon over the keyboard. "If only we had an automobile," she muttered.

That angered him. "No damned automobile would get there either! Not even a damned Studebaker!"

"How would you know, Will Chubb?" she demanded. "You've never owned one!"

I held my tongue. I was embarrassed and incredulous. In my four months on the farm I had never heard them say a cross word to each other. Old men were not supposed to call old ladies "girl". Even more shocking, grandparents were not supposed to quarrel, ever, and especially on Christmas Eve.

Will glared at his wife's intractable back, then glared at me, then nodded at the doors. I accompanied him to the kitchen.

"I'm going to the barn," he said gruffly. "Have you ever seen anything born?"

"No. No, I haven't."

"Do you want to?"

"Gee, I don't know."

"Make up your mind. I don't know what in Hades that old ewe will have—fish or fowl or a two-headed Hottentot from Timbuktu—but she can't have a lamb. Not this time of year. Well?"

"I guess so," I said. "O.K."

"Then get a move on."

I took my new scarf and we stepped into the woodshed and pulled on our galoshes, and stuffed pant legs inside, and put on heavy jackets and caps. We lighted two kerosene lanterns and got them burning clean and each of us carried one.

"Females." He scowled.

Since I did not know whether he referred to wives or ewes, I let my silence concur.

We went out into the storm.

TWO

I wound my scarf round and round my head, binding my face to the eyes, but even then a net of wind-thrown snow tangled my eyelashes. Without the scarf over my nose I doubted if I could draw breath. Without his lantern to guide on, I could never have followed my grandfather to the barn. We slid the door open wide enough to pass through, entered, and slapped snow off each other with our mittens. At the far end of the barn we went halfway down a flight of steps and sat down to overlook the sheepshed. Below us a hundred sheep, wearing heavy winter gray, lounged about on yellow straw and considered us calmly.

"Which one?" I asked, unwinding my scarf.

"There." Will pointed at a ewe who lay near the steps. She got up, then lay down again. She was restless.

"How'll we know when she's going to have it?"

"We'll know."

"Well, what do we do now?"

"Meditate."

We raised the earflaps of our caps. It was warmer in the shed than outside, but our breathing still made little fogs before our faces. I peered until I found the horns of Calvin, the ram. They had a beautiful curl, and he knew it. He was a registered Rambouillet and had a long, complicated name on his papers, but for short Will called him Calvin in honor of Mr. Coolidge. Neither the ram nor the former president spoke very often, he explained, but when they did, they were worth heeding.

"I wonder what sheep think about," I said.

"Females," Will answered. "The contrariness of the critters. Isn't it just like a female to drop a lamb on a winter night when a man might better be in bed? And isn't it just like a female to expect a man to haul a pump organ three miles through a snowstorm? Any automobile ever invented would founder in those drifts."

I held my face with my hands. After a time Will said, "I intended to buy one in twenty-eight, but traded for the OilPull instead. Then I intended to buy one in twenty-nine, with the threshing money, and you know what happened in twenty-nine."

The old ewe stood up, then lay down again.

Will said, "She hasn't played that organ in three years."

I concentrated on Calvin. He was chewing and being very nonchalant about the drama which was to unfold, a theatrical for which he bore in large part the responsibility of authorship.

"You can't get blood out of a turnip," my grandfather said. "You can't ask friends and neighbors for money when they don't have it."

"I'm sorry you had an argument," I said. "It was my fault, I guess. If I hadn't been here, she wouldn't have played the melodeon, and if she hadn't played, she might not have got the idea."

"Oh, we fight," he said.

"You do?"

"Don't your ma and pa go at it now and again?"

"Well, sure, but they're younger. I didn't think . . ."

"Old folks fight? Well, they do, sonny. Scratch and bite as much as ever, and love as much as ever. You have to take the vinegar with the honey. That's marriage for you."

458

The old ewe stood up and lay down again. She was making me restless. "Guess I'll go give the team some extra hay," I said. "It's Christmas Eve."

As the delivery drew nigh, I grew less and less inclined to witness it. I hadn't a glimmering what to expect, but I was convinced I was too young and pure to be exposed to the barn-based facts of life.

Taking a lantern, I went upstairs and took a look at Tom and Dolly in their stalls below. Both were standing sound asleep. I pitched three forkfuls of hay down the chute for each of them, which woke them up, and I could hear them munching gratefully. I wished them both a Merry Christmas and went back to the sheep-shed. "My gosh," I said, "hasn't she had it yet?"

"She will when she's a mind to," my grandfather replied.

I took my post on the steps again. The old ewe moved restlessly. I had to think about something else, so I asked Will where the melodeon had come from, and I got another helping of family history.

One day in April, in the year 1863, my great-grandmother Sarah was standing at her kitchen window watching her husband, Ephraim, plowing in a nearby field. Suddenly he stopped, dropped the reins, left the team, and walked toward the house. He had never done that before—once he started a furrow he finished it—and although she was a very young wife, married only two years, Sarah knew what her husband was going to tell her. But she didn't cry or faint, she merely held on hard to a pot in which she was soaking beans when he entered the kitchen.

They were forming a cavalry regiment around Howell, he said without preliminary, and if she were willing, he wanted to enlist. It would tear him in two to leave her, he said, but he wouldn't be gone long, the Johnnies would soon be whipped, he would get her a hired man to work the place, and if she could manage the separation, he would manage the war. It had been on his conscience, he told her. He loved her, but he loved the Union, too, and he revered Mr. Lincoln. He was young and ablebodied and he believed it was his duty to get in a lick for his country while he could.

"What did she say?" I asked.

"She said yes. Of course he ought to go. A man should do what he believed in. It was what she didn't say that cost her."

"What was that?"

"That she was carrying me."

"You?"

"She was two months along with me. If she'd told him that, he'd never have left her. But she didn't tell, and let him go, and that must have cost her plenty. She was a brave woman."

Outside, the storm cried like an animal seeking shelter.

"But what about the melodeon?" I asked.

"Oh. Yes," he said. "Well, he joined up in the cavalry. A week later they brought that organ down from the store in Howell in a wagon. He'd bought it on his way to the war. It was his thank-you to her for letting him go. Not knowing about me, I expect he thought it would keep her company. Sarah could play the piano, so she picked up the organ in no time."

"And later she taught you how," I added.

"Yes. I wanted to play for him when he came home."

"But he never did. I know that part of it. How come, after you found out he was dead, you never played it again?"

He looked at me with such intensity that I wished I hadn't pried. "Because my pa would never hear me," he said. "Nor would he ever see me, nor I him. Reason enough?"

"Sure," I said, turning away from his look. I had not realized that loss could be so long-lived. I tried to imagine how I would feel if I had never seen my father. But I couldn't think about it. So I concentrated on the ewe and did not want to do that either. Suddenly she let out a bleat of distress.

"Holy Toledo!" I jumped to my feet. "What's the matter now?"

"She's due."

I grabbed my lantern. "Guess I'll check the chickens."

"Afraid they'll lay snowballs tomorrow?"

"Just call me Chicken Inspector!" was my retort. I walked across the sheepshed and into the chicken house next door. It was quite a sight to see two hundred hens and several roosters perched on poles, dead to the world. Facing me row upon row, they resembled an impolite audience, and it seemed appropriate to shake them up. I put down the lantern and struck an elocutionary pose.

"Ahem," I began. "Ladies and gentlemen, it gives me great pleasure to address you tonight. But since the hour is late, I will be brief." I drew a deep breath. "Lay off!" I roared.

Not an eye opened, not a feather turned.

"Slow down," I advised. "Rome wasn't built in a day. A Studebaker isn't bought in a week. Cut your output. Enjoy life. And let's try to be artists, not machines. Take a crack at some Easter eggs, nicely decorated. Because I warn you." I gave them a voice of doom. "No matter how hard you strain, someday for your reward my grandmother will take you to the chopping block and *powww!*"

I paused for effect, but nary a rooster squawked, nary a hen went pale. These were really dumb chickens.

"That concludes my remarks, ladies and gents," I said. "I wish you a Merry Christmas and I now depart." I bowed low and took up the lantern.

But before I reached the sheepshed I heard the old ewe over the storm. There was no mistaking it. She was in serious trouble.

WILL knelt beside her in the straw. She was lying on her side with her hind legs stretched out, and bawling her head off. Every animal in the flock, even Calvin, was standing now.

"What's wrong?" I asked.

"I don't know. She's trying, but she can't." He laid hands on her sides, pressing, examining. "Maybe there's a leg tucked up. Or maybe it's a breech."

"What's that?"

"Lamb the wrong way to. The hind end first. Should be head first." My grandfather sat back. "I wish I could tell."

He bit on a knuckle. I had never seen him so upset. Cold as it was, there were beads of sweat on his forehead. Finally he removed his jacket and rolled up his right shirt sleeve and the underwear beneath it to the elbow.

"What're you going to do?"

"Reach into her."

I went weak. "Oh jeepers no," I blurted.

"Have to. Or we'll lose her and the lamb both."

"Oh my gosh," I said. "But what can you do?"

"If it's a leg, untuck it. If it's a breech, turn the lamb around. I've done it before."

I gritted my teeth. "Any way I can help?"

"Yes. Comfort her. Sit down and take her head in your lap. She's in bad pain."

"O.K.," I said. "If I have to."

I had never wanted to do anything less. I was sorry for her, but I didn't know what she might do in her suffering—bite me or kick me or what. Cautiously I sat down close to the ewe and put an arm around her neck and pulled her head into my lap.

"Now old girl," my grandfather said. He came to his knees between her hind legs. "Now let's see."

The scene made me think of a picture on a calendar—the halos of the lanterns, the beaten gold of the straw, the flock standing silent, an old man kneeling by one of the animals as though in prayer. Then I thought of the predicament we were in, and it was too much for me. I squinched my eyes shut. Suddenly the ewe bawled louder than ever, and reared her head, and I had to throw both arms around her neck and hug her against my face to hold her.

"Please, old girl, hold still," I begged, my nose full of the waxen smell of her fleece. "There, old girl, we can do it."

An hour passed, or a minute. Then, just as suddenly she relaxed, and I was sure she must be dead.

"There, by Jehu," I heard my grandfather say.

I could not open my eyes. "What happened?" I choked.

"She had a lamb, that's what."

"Is it all right?"

"Fine and dandy."

I peeked. He was cutting the cord with a loop of binder'twine and swabbing red off something small with a fistful of straw. I squinched shut again.

"A Christmas lamb," Will said. "I will be damned. You can let go of her now," he said. "She wants her kidlet."

I released her head and stood up and opened my eyes. Will laid the lamb on the straw by its mother, and she stretched her neck and commenced at once to lick it. I took one look and wobbled to the stairs and sat down. With a forearm I wiped the sweat from my forehead. I had a grasp of the theory of birth, but I had been vague about the reality. Now I knew how a lamb was born, and therefore how Ephraim, Sarah, Will, Ella, my father, my mother, and even I were born. We had come into the world in agony and struggle and bright blood, and something else, something akin to exaltation. For when I looked at my grandfather he was grinning ear to ear. I stood up and grinned back and felt enormously mature and alive.

Without warning, Will cracked a palm with a fist. "The OilPull!" He yanked on his jacket, clapped on his cap, and faced me with eyes blazing. "James, my boy, do you think we could get it started?"

"The tractor? Why?"

"To haul the organ to the church!"

"Oh," I said. "Oh! Why not?"

"Because I've never seen or heard of one being run in the winter, that's why. But if we could start it, boy—drifts be damned! We could haul anything in Christendom anywhere!"

"Sure we can!" I cried, catching his excitement. "We can do anything!"

"Hold your horses," he cautioned. "It's three long miles and a fearful night. Think we're up to it?"

"Sure we are," I asserted.

"I'm no spring chicken anymore."

"I'll help you."

"That's a mighty valuable piece of wood, that organ."

"We'll be careful."

"It tells in the manual how to start the OilPull in cold weather. But reading's a damn sight different from doing."

"We'll learn as we go along."

"And then there's Ella. It's got to be a surprise or it isn't worth a pinch of dried owl dung."

"We won't tell her."

464

"But she's a light sleeper. And you can hear that tractor from here to D*ee*—troit."

I had no way around that.

"We'd better sit a spell and meditate," he said.

We sat down on the steps. I chewed on a straw. Will tugged his mustache. The question was, could an old man and his thirteen-year-old grandson start a tractor on a below zero Christmas Eve and then, unbeknown to wife and grandmother, transport a melodeon three miles through a blizzard to a church in time for Sunday morning service?

"She may not play it, but she loves that pumper," Will reflected. "It'll cost her to give it away."

This question involved another. I knew Will had the grit, but did he have the stamina? He must be in his late sixties, I reckoned, and men that age had at least one foot in the grave. What if something terrible overtook him en route? What could I do?

"She's a brave woman, though," he said. "Just like my ma."

And he had already told her there wouldn't be a service tomorrow anyway. So what was the use of getting the organ there by then?

"This blow might last all night," my grandfather said to himself. "And then again, it might not. You never know."

"First Christmas I haven't given her anything," Will mused. "This would be a corker, though."

What if Ella heard the tractor and that spoiled the surprise? What if we bogged down and both of us froze to death?

Will touched my arm. He was grinning again, and his eyes snapped with schoolboy delight. "Can't you see her face in the morning when she sashays into that church, and there it is?"

"Can I ever." I grinned.

He beamed, then put out a hand. "Well, partner, shall we give it a try?"

"You bet!"

We stood up, shook on it, and immediately began planning and plotting. Gradually, as the idea evolved, it took on elements of gallantry and heroism which warmed our backsides, plus bonuses of danger and rascality which shivered us to our boots. And the longer we conspired, the bigger the adventure became.

"All right," Will said, dropping his earflaps. He nodded at the ewe and her lamb. "If that old lady can have a baby on Christmas Eve, the age of miracles isn't past by a long shot."

"Absolootle, positivle," I agreed, treating him to a little of the latest Philadelphia lingo.

He snorted. "Let's get a move on."

We plodded toward the house. If our minds conceded that what our hearts had bade us do was beyond our powers, we kept mum. In the woodshed we unbuttoned and unbuckled. Will took a lantern down into the basement and I entered the kitchen.

"Well, have we a lamb?" my grandmother asked.

"Not yet," I lied. "We might have to be up half the night with that darn ewe."

"You poor dears. Where's Will?"

"Oh, in the basement. He'll be right up."

She was putting the soapstones on the stove, a winter ritual. Progress, so-called, had already invented the hot-water bottle and would eventually bestow upon us the electric blanket, but I am not persuaded that these gadgets have been as salubrious as soap-stones used to be. They were smooth-edged rectangles some sixteen inches long and three inches through and weighed approximately ten pounds. You put them on the stove in the evening to absorb heat. At bedtime you wrapped one in a length of worn flannel, toted it upstairs, and shoved it between the sheets. You got into an arctic bed and slowly, with your bare feet, eased it to the bottom. If you were weak, and drew up your legs to bunch into a ball, you lost the good of it. If you were incautious, you could practically fracture a toe or fricassee a knee. But if you were strong, and disciplined yourself to lie full length and wed your body's warmth to that of the soapstone, your reward was as virtuous as it was blissful.

Will came into the kitchen carrying two tin cups. "Thought we ought to try the cider," he said.

"Won't it be hard by now?" asked his wife.

"Shouldn't be. Not with the cold weather we've had. Takes a warm day or two to turn it."

She pursed her lips. My grandmother abhorred alcohol in any form. I never knew her to accept so much as a glass of wine. But rather than pursue the subject, she went to a drawer, took out a large ball of string and a tangle of loose lengths, sat down at the table, and began to unravel the separate bits and pieces. This provided Will with the diversion he required. Getting three small glasses from the cupboard, he poured the contents of one tin cup into two of them and emptied the other cup into the third glass. He winked at me, then offered the third glass to Ella and one of the others to me.

"A toast," he said. "Here's to an end of the blamed storm, and a Merry Christmas tomorrow."

"Peace on earth, goodwill toward men," added his spouse.

Will and I drank our sweet cider. She sipped.

"You're right, Will," she granted. "It isn't hard yet. It's quite tasty." She smiled. He smiled. I smiled.

We seated ourselves with Ella while she balled string. She would tie a loose piece onto the ball, roll it up, tie on another, and so on. "Idle hands do the devil's work," she would say in defense of her industry, but another reason why her hands were never idle, I now understood, was the arthritis. Crocheting and balling string kept her fingers as supple as she could hope.

She had more "cider". Then she said to me, "Let me tell you a little story, James. It has to do with pride." She glanced at her husband and continued. "I've been thinking. Perhaps it was pride that made me want to give the melodeon to the church on Christmas morning and make a spectacle of myself. I don't know. But the story is about your mother and what pride can do."

We watched her intently.

"When your mother was young, sixteen or so, she was invited to a grand party in Howell, at the banker's house. Oranges were a great treat in those days. If you had one a year, you were lucky, and one in your Christmas stocking made the day."

She sipped a little more "cider". "My, that's good." She tried to knot two bits of string together and couldn't seem to. She brought

467

the string close to her glasses. "Gaslight," she sniffed. "If only we had electric. Well, as I was saying, your mother was invited to the party, and we knew that sometime in the evening a bowl of oranges would be passed. So I told her to be a lady of taste and refinement. Not to take an orange when the bowl came around. Be proud, I told her, as though you have an orange every day at home. Let everyone else snatch and grab. Then when the bowl is passed again, hesitate, and finally take one. That's being ladylike. Fiddlesticks."

She was trying in vain to tie another knot. Will winked at me. She sipped again, then began to ball the string without tying it.

What she was imbibing of course was not sweet cider but applejack, a tonic Will had turned out by freezing and refreezing the barrel in the backyard, thus distilling the juice of the apple down to its essence. Taken in moderation, he had informed me in the sheepshed, applejack was "as fine as the fuzz on a butterfly's behind". Taken in excess, it had the "strike of a massasauga rattlesnake". He intended only to get her a little "tiddly", just enough to induce a sleep so sound we could fire a cannon without waking her.

"Where was I?" she asked.

"The party," I reminded her.

"Oh, yes, the party." Her speech was slurred. "Well, sure enough, the oranges were passed, and your mother refused. Everyone was impressed." Ella put down her glass. The ball of string dropped from her lap and rolled across the floor.

"The party," I said.

"What party?"

"Mother refused the oranges."

"Oh, yes. She wanted one so much, but she said no, thank you. The perfect lady." She stared down at the ball of string.

"What happened after she refused the orange?" I asked.

"Oh. The orange. Well, the bowl wasn't passed a second time—I declare . . ."

"Declare what?" Will asked.

His wife rose, putting a hand on the table to steady herself. "I declare. I'm dizzy. I don't know what's come over me. Will, I'm so sleepy."

He was on his feet in a flash. "Let me help you to bed, dear."

He put an arm around her waist and assisted her to their bedroom off the kitchen. While he was putting her to bed, I wrapped a soapstone in flannel and gave it to him through the door. I returned the ball of string to the drawer. Next I sampled the applejack left in her glass. It descended equably enough, but when it hit bottom it went off in the manner of a firecracker under a tin can, with a bang and a clang. I had to sit down.

Ella sang several bars of "We Three Kings of Orient Are" rather loudly. Then she giggled, which was another thing grandparents were not supposed to do.

Will came out and sat at the table with me. We looked at the clock. It was almost ten. We waited. It wasn't long. In a minute or two we heard a soft, reassuring snore. Whispering, he told me to go upstairs and put on a second set of long johns and another pair of socks.

I did so. After I rejoined him, we turned the gaslight low, bundled up in the woodshed, lighted the lanterns, stared into each other's faces for a moment, searching, making sure of each other, then opened the door and stepped again into the storm.

THREE

We went directly to the granary. It was open-ended, fortunately at the south, for the wind raved from the north. First we filled the lanterns. They must not fail us. Then, while I held them, Will filled a ten-gallon can from the kerosene tank, and as I lighted his way through a hodgepodge of implements, he went back and forth to the tractor, fueling it to capacity.

I wish to describe the tractor in as much detail as I have the Mason & Hamlin melodeon, for if one is the end of my story, the other is the means. Let the reader erase from his mind any image of the modern tractor—a pampered darling packed with horsepower and with every luxury from self-starter to headlights to radio. What I present in its stead is a 1928 Rumely OilPull, Model

20-40, a monstrosity which has not been seen on American acreage for forty years or more.

The front end was surmounted by a four-sided smokestack the size of a ship's, which, according to the engine's mood, emitted stinks of black smoke. On its side was lettered OILPULL ADVANCE-RUMELY THRESHER CO. LaPORTE, INDIANA. The engine was an 8 x 10, horizontal, two-cylinder, kerosene-burning, and oil-cooled, with magneto ignition and a spur-gear transmission with two speeds forward and one reverse. Low speed was 2 mph, and shifting into high would hurtle you down the road at 3.2 mph. This engine pulled 20 horsepower on the drawbar and 40 on the belt wheel, turning it at 450 rpm. The wheels were spoked cast iron, and the rear wheels were almost 6 feet high. Over the drive wheels and transmission was an open cab with a four-post corrugated roof covering an iron driver's seat, steering wheel, and the controls. The Model 20-40 was 16 feet long and 10 feet high, counting the cab, and the whole awesome shebang weighed almost $6\frac{1}{2}$ tons. Given some armor plate, and a gun or two, and a rotation rig for the cab, it might have competed on fairly equal combat terms with any tank in the First World War. There was certainly nothing like it elsewhere in Putnam Township.

To my grandmother the OilPull was an abomination of great price—the price being many times that of the automobile she coveted. To my grandfather the OilPull was the symbol of power and glory. It must have been, however, a love-hate relationship between farmer and tractor. Love it he assuredly did, for the Rumely had powered the threshing of every bushel of wheat in the neighborhood for several summers. But hate it he must have, too, for though he had had no pay for the harvest, and in those cruel years lacked the cruelty to demand it, Advance-Rumely demanded its pound of flesh every month. To me, at this hour, on this weather-wild Christmas Eve, the OilPull was but a mighty contraption we had to command in order to move a small pump organ to a church, a process rather like firing up a mountain to move a mouse.

The catch, of course, was starting it. The engine was cold clear through. Will first filled the two priming cups with gasoline.

470

"But I thought it runs on kerosene," I said.

"Well, it does. But gas burns hotter. So we'll start 'er on gas and run 'er on gas till the block gets hot enough to gasify the kerosene. Then she'll purr on that."

He stepped to the flywheel, took off his mittens, extended the handle, which retracted automatically, bent to it, and turned the wheel once, twice, three times, but nothing happened. He spat on his palms and whirled the flywheel perhaps a dozen times, but nothing happened.

"Thunderation," he said.

Motioning me to provide light, he rummaged in a corner of the granary and located a blowtorch. Filling it with gas, he pumped up the pressure, lighted the flame with a match, trimmed it down to a blue cone, returned to the Rumely, and handing over the torch, told me to heat the glowplug. This object extended from the cylinder head. Its function was to transfer heat from outside the engine to the inside, and to concentrate it, thereby vaporizing the gas inside a cylinder so that it would fire more easily. I directed the flame until I got a good glow, whereupon Will seized the handle and whirled the very dickens out of the flywheel, completely in vain.

Breathing hard, he stopped and stood for a moment in thought. "I'm not going to cuss on Christmas Eve," he resolved. "That might put the kibosh on the whole damned thing. But we have one more string to our fiddle. Come around here."

He led me to the other side of the tractor and told me to heat the manifold, which would heat the air taken into the cylinders and thereby vaporize the gas more thoroughly. So I used the torch on the manifold until he grabbed the handle again and rotated the flywheel so fast and so long that if the engine had been a separator he'd have had whipped cream.

When my grandfather let go, I could hear him wheeze even over the keening of the wind outside the granary. I had heard him before, whenever he did anything strenuous. He had what was known as hay lung, a respiratory ailment common among farmers. Years of cutting and raking and mowing hay lined the lungs with its dust, it was then believed, leading to shortness of breath and susceptibility to infection. Medicine now knows that the cause is not dust but rather the inhalation of microscopic spores from a mold which breeds in warm, moist hay. There was no cure for hay lung then, nor is there now, except to quit farming.

"We're whipsawed," he declared. "Heat the manifold and the plug cools. Heat the plug and the manifold cools." He stood for another moment, thinking and wheezing.

"We're not giving up, are we?" I demanded.

He scowled. "What would you recommend?"

"Want me to try it?"

"Help yourself."

Full of optimism, I strode to the wheel, removed my mittens, and took hold.

By dint of spunk, determination, two grunts and a groan, I gave it one grudging half-turn.

I was flabbergasted. It was incredible that a grandfather should be strong enough to spin that wheel like a top when a clean-living young man of my muscle could barely budge it.

"Thank you," he said.

"For what?" I was prepared to be offended.

"You gave me another idea. Your arm won't do, but maybe we can use your legs. Here now."

He placed a lantern on each side of the tractor, midway. "Now you heat the plug," he directed, "and when she's red hot, skedaddle around to the other side and heat up the manifold, and when it's toasty, skedaddle back here and go at the plug again, and meanwhile I'll turn away slow and maybe, just maybe, if you run fast enough and keep 'em both hot enough, maybe we'll do it."

It was worth a try, and for perhaps three minutes try we did— Will rotating the flywheel slowly while I heated and ran, heated and ran, but all we got for our efforts was exhaustion.

We surrendered. He sat down on a front wheel, and I leaned against the smokestack. We were both wringing wet. His faith in the machine had been shaken. My faith in him had been taken down a peg. And then, in the depths of that iron beast upon which we rested, we heard a sound. It was not a sigh of apology, but a protest of discomfort from its very guts. Will put a finger to his lips, tiptoed to the flywheel, took hold, and gave it one tender, almost seductive, turn.

Huff! Combustion! *Huff! Huff!*

Huff-huff-huff-huff! Huff-huff-huff-huff! The OilPull shook, shimmied, and belched black smoke. We had won!

Hands on hips, we grinned at each other like idiots, exulting in sound and smell and achievement. He had to shout in my ear, because the uproar of the tractor was reverberating from the roof. "We'll leave 'er here to warm up! Let's get a move on!"

He had evidently mapped out tactics earlier. Communicating with gestures, we first wheeled the cultivator from the granary. That made way for the stoneboat, a crude sledlike vehicle used originally to clear the field of stone. About eight feet long, it had two small logs for runners, across which rough boards were nailed into a solid floor. Attached to each log up front was one end of a rusty chain. We pulled the stoneboat outdoors, too, then piled onto it two four-foot lengths of two-by-four, two moldy horse blankets, a coil of rope, and a lantern. We started for the house.

We put heads down and closed our eyes and tugged at the stoneboat chain. By the time we reached the house we were snowmen. We pulled alongside the steps of the screened porch, ran the rope twice under the stoneboat's flooring, endwise, left the ends loose, set the lantern aside, and laid the two lengths of two-by-four to serve as skids from the porch down to the stoneboat.

We stomped across the porch and entered the living room. Sliding the doors like burglars, we edged into the parlor. With each of us at one end, we rolled the melodeon through the living room and onto the porch on its casters. So far, so fancy.

We draped the instrument with the horse blankets. Then, together, we hoisted one end onto the skids and let it roll down far enough to raise the other end and place it. I held on to the high end for dear life while Will went to the low and inched the organ slowly down the skids. Then he braked it until I joined him and we warped the thing off the skids and onto the floor of the stoneboat.

We passed the two ends of rope over it and tied it down. I brought out the bench, and set it under a skirt of blanket. Then we swung the skids and lantern aboard and set out for the granary.

Had there not been a slight grade in our favor, I doubt we could have done it. The stoneboat sank under the organ's weight of two hundred and fifty pounds, and we labored knee-deep in the snow. Will wheezed. I panted. The tow chain hurt our hands, even through mittens, and eventually we harnessed it around our waists and leaned into it like a team of horses. It required ten minutes to cover the hundred yards to the granary.

We rested there. The 20-40 huffed away, running on kerosene and readying itself. I could have kissed any part of that cast-iron monster. When we had caught our breath, Will got the bench from under the blanket, mounted the step, stowed the bench beside him in the cab, backed the tractor out and up to the stoneboat. "You ride the boat and steady that pumper!" he yelled at me. "Sit on 'er if you have to!"

I looped the tow chain over the tractor's tow bar, gave Will a lantern, set the other on top of the blankets. He pushed the hand-throttle forward, the two cylinders quickened tempo, he shifted into low gear, the drive wheels dug in, and we were off.

It was a false start. He stopped within ten feet and jumped from the cab with his lantern. "Can't see your hand before your face!"

He disappeared into the granary, emerging presently with two S hooks he'd made by bending pieces of fence wire. Taking both lanterns into the cab, he hung the hooks from the cross struts under the cab roof, then hung the lanterns from the hooks, one on each side, to serve as headlights.

He throttled up, shifted into low, the great wheels revolved, and we were off again, hurtling down the road at 2 mph. The worst was over. We had only three miles to go now, and an OilPull and gumption and Divine Providence to take us.

Huff-huff-huff-huff! Huff-huff-huff-huff! The black breathing of the tractor was borne back to me upon the gale. The OilPull loomed above me like a tramp steamer towing a dinghy. I had glimpses of the lanterns swaying in the wind like masthead lights and of my grandfather seated at the helm, hunched forward, squinting into an ocean of white. The next moment, vessel, lights, and captain were swallowed up, for the spume of snow blinded me.

I did not need to see in any case. My duty was to keep the melodeon in place, protected by blankets and tied down by ropes. It was no easy assignment. The stoneboat rolled and pitched on the drifted township road. Remember, too, that the instrument stood on casters, giving it an agility which belied its bulk. The only way I could be fairly sure of it was to stand behind, plant my boots solidly, bend my knees, and embrace the melodeon with both arms. The position was awkward. My arms turned numb, my teeth chattered, the two sets of damp long johns iced my skin.

The OilPull battered into a drift deeper than most. It slowed. When it crunched ahead again it took up slack in the tow chain, and the stoneboat shuddered. The melodeon trembled in my arms. I hugged it to me as I had the old ewe's head. Only then, there, staying the melodeon in night and storm, did revelation of how precious it was, how beloved it had been, come to me. We were removing it from the only home it had ever known. It had been freighted seventy years ago from the factory in Rochester, New York, to the village of Howell, and from there had been transported by wagon seven miles to a young wife alone on a farm, her soldier-husband gone, on a day in April 1863. She had played it and taught her small son. It was the only tangible link between a boy who had never seen his father, and a father who had never seen his son. The son had grown to manhood, and married, and his widowed mother taught his wife in turn to play it. My own mother's childish fingers must have strayed the keyboard, her tiny feet must once have tried the pedals. Surely, as a young woman, she became aware of the instrument's human and historic value. Ephraim and Sarah, Will and Ella, my mother, and now me—the melodeon had been counterpoint to the lives of four generations. And now my grandmother, with my grandfather's aid and acquiescence, was offering it to her Maker.

I cannot recall whether at age thirteen I believed or not. At that late hour, on that uncharitable eve of Christmas, it did not matter.

475

I prayed that we might get the melodeon safely to the church. And I tacked on a warning: if He were really real, He had better appreciate a gift like this.

No deity, however, takes kindly to an admonition. We came to the one hill between us and the county road—and couldn't climb it. The OilPull did its level best, but the grade was steep and the drift across it four feet deep. The engine did not stall, the drive wheels turned, the V lugs bit into gravel. Sparks struck from iron and clods of dirt and a hail of stones were hurled at the organ and me. Will set the hand brake and got down from the cab.

"I can do it if I get a start! Let's pull this rig to one side and give us room!"

We unhitched the chain and pushed the stoneboat downhill perhaps ten feet. Then we hauled it to one side of the road. He mounted the cab and put the tractor into reverse, then backed to the foot of the hill and thirty yards or so beyond. He shifted into second, throttled up as high as he could and let 'er rip. The 20-40 went up the hill like a locomotive, roaring and scratching. They hit the drift with a terrible thud. They hesitated. Sparks flashed and dirt flew. Then they broke through to the crest, and I cheered.

He backed down and set the hand brake, and we harnessed ourselves with the chain and panting and wheezing pulled the stoneboat into the track and made it fast to the tow bar. This time we made the hill as easy as pie and plowed down the far side.

Through a chink in the dark I saw a light wink on at the right of the road. That would be from a window at the Henshaw place, and of course we could be heard coming. A sound as implausible as a Rumely's, at night and at this time of year, would have Joe and Abby out of bed as fast as the jingle of sleigh bells on their roof.

We ground to a halt in front of the house and Will descended.

"We better warm up! They're awake now, so they won't mind!"

I made no objection. I was as cold as he. We left the tractor puffing away in the road and trudged to the house. But no sooner were we on the porch than the light went out in the window. Will knocked, but the door did not open. He took my arm and led me off the porch where we could speak freely.

I was outraged. "What's the matter with 'em?"

"Ashamed! Because they haven't paid me for the threshing!"

"You haven't asked!"

"Makes no difference! Old Joe believes in paying his debts, and when he can't, it binds him."

"Let us freeze out here?"

"Poor as church mice. Reckon they're the hardest hit folks around."

I knew that. Everyone was sorry for the Henshaws. They had no assets, excepting one emaciated cow and eighty acres of the poorest land in the area. It was remarkable they found money enough to buy gasoline to drive their Model T to church every Sunday.

"I don't care! You have to let people in on Christmas Eve!"

"Hurts them more than it does us. We can't let 'em do it. They'd never forgive themselves!" He took my arm. "Come along."

We returned to the porch and Will knocked on the door again, and after the fourth knock the light went on and the door opened. Joe Henshaw admitted us, apologizing he hadn't known who we were—a barefaced tergiversation if I had ever heard one.

It was practically as cold inside the house as out. The fire in the potbellied stove was low and though Will said we had just stopped by to thaw, neither of our hosts made a move to poke it up, much less add wood. We were seated in the kitchen, on the only two chairs. Three things damped my own heat at the Henshaws: they were even older than Will and Ella, they were small and wrinkled as prunes, and they had no Christmas tree, which proved they were really scraping bottom. Joe wore long johns, evidently his sleeping attire, and Abby had put on over her nightgown a mangy muskrat coat, which must have been as ancient as the melodeon. While my grandfather explained what we were doing out on a night like this with the tractor, husband and wife stared as though we must be crazier than bedbugs.

"I didn't give Ella anything this year," Will added lamely. "So James here and I thought this would be our surprise in the morning."

He realized at once he had put his foot in his mouth, that the

Henshaws had been unable to give each other anything either, and said no more. The four of us stood or sat shivering and twiddled our thumbs till the shortage of conversation became, despite the wind outside, almost audible.

Abby Henshaw broke the ice. "When I was a girl," she said, "my mother would tell me how she used to trade for berries with the Indians hereabouts."

Will pretended he hadn't heard. "Joe," he said, "there's something I want to say to you. We've been good neighbors thirty years. Nobody's paid me a nickel for the threshing, and I don't expect 'em to, not now."

"Money makes the mare go," replied Joe.

"Well, mine'll go awhile yet. I want you to forget about it till times are better."

"I'm a man pays what I owe."

"I know that."

"When I was a girl," said Abby, "we used to pop popcorn over the fire in a skillet. We had all the popcorn we could eat."

"Everybody's hard up," Will said.

"If you're in a pinch, Mr. Henshaw," I piped up helpfully, "why don't you ask the county for relief?"

The Henshaws were horrified. "Relief!"

"Sure," I said. "My father's on relief and we're not ashamed."

Joe bared his three front teeth at me. "We'll starve before we slop at the public trough."

"When I was a girl," said Abby, "I had a dress of taffeta and lace." Her eyes watered. "Mercy, but it was beautiful."

"But there's nothing wrong with relief," I contended.

"Ahem." My grandfather cleared his throat and rose. "We'd best be going," he said to me. "We've got a long row to hoe tonight." He smiled at the Henshaws. "Much obliged for taking us travelers in. See you at service. And a Merry Christmas to you."

"I was married in that dress," said Abby.

We took our leave. When we reached the Rumely, I hollered at Will. "What's wrong with her? Bats in her belfry?"

"Folks get that way sometimes!"

478

"I'm as cold as ever!"

"Wood costs. I offered him a cord this fall, but he wouldn't take it. Pride!"

I thought of Ella's story about my mother. "Oranges!"

He shook his head and climbed into the cab, I posted myself on the stoneboat at the rear end of the melodeon, and we were off again. It was snowing and blowing more relentlessly than it had been when we stopped.

FOUR

We had clear sailing to the county road now, barring an invulnerable drift, and we chugged away at a good hickory, Will steering, lanterns waving, stoneboat slewing, organ secure in my embrace. After a quarter of a mile, lights blinked on like beacons to the right of the road, three of them, upstairs and down. That would be the Stackable place, and our phenomenal passage in the night would rouse Clyde and Kate as surely as it had the Henshaws.

To my surprise, the OilPull stopped. I went forward at once. My grandfather stepped down from the cab very slowly.

"What's the matter now?"

"I'm tuckered, boy!" He wrapped his arms around himself. "We'd better meditate a spell! They're all up anyway!"

I was impatient. Dillydally along the way and we'd never get there. And I especially didn't care to drop in on the Stackables, for four reasons soon to be apparent. I wasn't tired and did not see why he should be. But then, as we headed for the house through knee-deep snow, he staggered, and I had to put my arm through his. He was exhausted.

This time we were welcomed. In bathrobe and hairnet, Kate Stackable opened the door and bustled us in, insisting we take the davenport in the living room, plugging in their Christmas tree, and putting water on to boil for my grandfather's green tea.

"Sorry to get you out of bed," said Will, removing his cap and mittens. "Where's Clyde?"

"Down with the grippe, poor man. Chills and fever and a chest cough. I'm keeping mustard plasters on him when he'll let me— you should hear him yell when I take one off—but I expect he'll be laid up a few days. A pity, over Christmas."

"A pity," Will agreed. "You keep him in bed and well-plastered and let him yell." Politely he acknowledged the row of tousle-haired girls in nightgowns seated on the stairs. "Good evening, young ladies. You know my grandson, James here, don't you?"

They giggled. I warmed up immediately. They were the four reasons why I hadn't cared to drop in on the Stackables. Clyde and Kate had been unfortunate enough to beget girls rather than boys, and four of them—Agnes, Frances, Delores, and Gertrude, or "Toody", ages fourteen, eleven, nine, and six in that order, and arrayed down the stairsteps in that order. I went to school with them. I had no alternative. If I evinced little or no regard for her daughters, who were as pestiferous as most girls their ages, I liked Mrs. Stackable very much. She reminded me of a stove. She was short and stout and reddened up quickly and radiated a hospitable warmth. She put hands where her hips were supposed to be and addressed my grandfather.

"Now tell me. What in heaven's name are you doing out on a night like this with that tractor?"

He told her.

Her cheeks flamed with pleasure. "Will Chubb, that's one of the nicest things I ever heard of in my life! Giving an organ to a church! On Christmas Eve! I can just see Ella's face tomorrow morning! Girls, isn't that wonderful?"

Agnes, Frances, Delores, and Toody nodded like metronomes.

"Oh, I think that's the nicest, sweetest, most loving thing," their mother carried on. "Will, I'll make you green tea till it comes out of your ears!"

She slippered into the kitchen, which left us alone with the girls. I decided to let Will carry the burden of dialogue, and began assiduously to study my knuckles, the Christmas tree, the pattern in the carpet, and the ceiling, conscious that they were simultaneously studying me. It wasn't that I was a snob, or a connoisseur for that matter, but when I contrasted Philadelphia girls with the Stackable progeny, the former, as I recalled them, were paragons of beauty, charm, fashion, intellect, and every classifiable virtue. The fact was, Agnes, Frances, Delores, and Toody were hicks. Moreover, they were mean. They had once persuaded me that dragonflies, which they called darning needles, would sew up male lips if opened, so for a full two weeks that autumn I walked to and from school with lips sealed.

"Here's that tea, Will." Mrs. Stackable came in with cup and saucer. "Will?"

We looked at him. My grandfather had fallen fast asleep on the davenport. His head was back, his mouth open, his breathing so labored that the hairs of his mustache oscillated like reeds.

Kate Stackable put a finger to her lips and motioned us to follow her into the kitchen. When we had, she closed the door. "Here, James, you have his tea. We mustn't wake him."

She gave me the cup and offered me a chair at the kitchen table. Green tea was vile, in my opinion, but no more distasteful than Agnes, Frances, Delores, and Toody, who sat down around me, put elbows on the table, chins in hands, and observed me imbibe as though they'd never seen anyone take tea without saucering it.

For warmth, Mrs. Stackable turned on the oven in her electric stove and opened the oven door. Then she stood at the counter watching me, too. I sipped tea. Occasionally I could hear Mr. Stackable hack and cough in the bedroom, and over the wind the panting of the OilPull out in front.

"Your granddad's worn to a frazzle," Mrs. Stackable said at length. "He ought to get his sleep out."

"Yes, ma'am."

She frowned. "It's dangerous for a man his age to be out on such a night. What you're up to is the sweetest, kindest thing I ever heard of—but his health is more important. James, do something for me?"

"Ma'am?"

"Let him sleep, and when he wakes up, talk him into going home and bringing the organ to service in the morning."

"Oh, no," I said. "Gosh, no."

"Why not?"

"Because that's half of it, the surprise," I protested. "You don't realize how much trouble we've gone to getting this far."

"I see. If Clyde was well, he'd go with you. And I can't leave him. Do you know how to drive that tractor?"

"I never have," I admitted, "but I've watched Will a lot."

"Then let me do this. Let me phone the Dunnings—they're just half a mile past Chubb's Corners. I'll ask Otis to meet you at the church—he'll be glad to—and you let your granddad sleep and go on and meet Otis. Is that all right?"

She had me over a barrel. I couldn't chance anything happening to Will, but on the other hand it would be a prodigal waste of elbow grease to forsake the mission now, when we were so close to success. He had his stubborn heart set on having that melodeon in church tomorrow morning, and so did I, and so had Ella, really.

Still I hesitated. I couldn't handle the organ alone. Otis Dunning wasn't Will Chubb, but in the end it didn't matter who did the job as long as it was done. "I guess so," I said.

She beamed. "Thank you, James. I'll go call."

She went to use the phone in the dining room. I set the green tea aside.

"Don't like it, do you," said Frances.

"Sure I do."

"Liar-liar-big-fat-tire," said Delores.

"It's not polite to stare at people while they're eating or drinking," I instructed.

"It's not polite to go visiting on Christmas Eve and keep Santy Claus away," Toody instructed.

"Banana oil," I rejoined.

"There isn't any Santa Claus," said Frances.

"You shut up," Delores told her. "You know Toody's not old enough to—"

Kate Stackable returned. "Oh, dear, oh, dear. I can't even get the operator. The lines must be down." She confronted me. "Now what're we going to do?"

I was about to say, Mrs. Stackable, it's not what we're going to do, it's what I'm going to do, and I'm going on. To say it with more authority, I stood up and squared my shoulders.

"Mrs. Stackable—" I began.

"I'm going with him," Agnes announced.

I might as well have been flattened by Jack Dempsey in the first round.

"Oh, no, you're not," said her mother.

"Oh, no, you're not," said I.

"He can't lift that organ by himself," said Agnes. "He's too puny."

"I'm going, too!" cried Frances.

"Me, too!" cried Delores.

"I wanna go!" cried Toody.

"Now hold on here!" I cried, springing from my corner like the Manassa mauler. "I can do this by myself! I'm not taking any doggone bunch of—"

"James." It was Kate Stackable. She had slipped off her hairnet, revealing the sausage curls she had set with an electric curler. She had also changed her mind. "James, maybe it's not such a bad idea after all. The girls are strong, and you're really not big enough yet for that organ. It's only a mile or so to the church from here." She looked at the clock. "It's twenty past eleven. I can bundle them up and you can be back here by midnight and take your grandfather home."

"We're going," smiled Agnes, recognizing the signs.

"We're going! We're going!" squealed her sisters, jumping up and down.

I experienced a sinking sensation, that lassitude familiar not only to Samson but to men in all times when hornswoggled by the weaker sex. "But . . . but Mrs. Stackable," I stammered.

"Sssh—don't wake Mr. Chubb," she warned her daughters. "James, if it wasn't such a wonderful thing you're doing, I'd never consider it. But I love your grandma, and if this is what she wants, why, you should let us do our part, shouldn't you?"

"I guess so," I groaned.

483

She sent her four upstairs to dress, and then went to a crockery jar and gave me a handful of sugar cookies. "I'll bet you're starved. I shoo the girls away from these, I don't want them as heavy as I am. But you could use some pick on your bones." She seated herself across from me. "Helping out will put some starch in their spines. Just tell them what to do and see they do it."

Her cookies were excellent, but the taste on my tongue was that of despair.

"I'll bet you miss your folks something fierce, being it's Christmas. Don't you?"

My mouth was full. I nodded.

"That was real nice you could talk to them tonight, though."

My mouth was still full. I stared.

She smiled. "Oh, don't worry, we didn't listen in. But everybody knew they were calling you. Long distance from Philadelphia is news around here."

She tilted her head to check on the girls thumping and clumping upstairs. "James, sometime soon, when you get a chance, you tell your granddad we feel awful about not paying him for the threshing. Clyde stews about it. But we just don't have anything to spare right now. Will you?"

I finished the cookies. "Yes, ma'am."

"That's another reason I decided to send the girls. Money may be tight, but being neighborly doesn't need to be."

"Thank you," I said.

The girls pushed in, swaddled in overalls and sweaters. "All right," approved their mother. "Now go get your presents from under the tree and bring them here and be quick about it."

"Our presents? How could Santy get here already?" a skeptical Toody wanted to know.

Kate Stackable glanced at her older daughters. "Why, he must have come earlier, while we were asleep."

Toody's doubts were not easily dispelled. "I wasn't asleep, and I didn't hear anything."

"Don't fret about it. Get your presents—and sssh."

Agnes, Frances, Delores, and Toody tiptoed into the living

room and returned, their expressions something less than antici-
patory, holding four identical packages wrapped in white paper
decorated with green leaves and red holly berries.

"Well, open them," ordered their mother.

They did. Each girl's gift was a new pair of rubber galoshes.

"Well, well, old Santa really knew what you needed this year,"
said Mrs. Stackable. "Your old ones are just about gone."

"Galoshes," said Agnes.

"Galoshes," said Frances.

"Goody-goody," said Delores.

"I asked for a doll," pouted Toody.

Their mother frowned. "You be glad for them. Millions of kids
won't have anything at all under the tree this Christmas—I expect
times are just as hard for Santa as they are for everybody. Now
into the woodshed and put them on and your coats and caps and
hurry. It's getting late and James is anxious."

"You're a dandy, James," she said to me. "I wish we'd had a boy.
I love my girls, but they need a big brother sometimes, to set an
example."

Her brood entered, new galoshes buckled up, stocking caps
pulled down over their ears, and scarves up to their eyes. She
inspected her troops. "Got your mittens?"

They bobbed heads.

"James is in charge. You do what he tells you or I'll tan your
hides—d'you hear?"

They bobbed heads.

"And you listen. Maybe tonight will teach you something about
the meaning of Christmas. Christmas isn't just getting, whether
it's galoshes or dolls or what. Christmas is giving. That's the joy of
it. So for once in your young lives you behave, and help, and
give—d'you understand?"

They bobbed heads vigorously. She stooped, swooped arms
around them, bumped their heads together, then stood back biting
a lip. "Off you go. Don't wake Mr. Chubb. I won't tell your father
what I've done till you're back safe and sound—I wouldn't dare.
Take care of them, James."

"I will," I said, meaning one way or another.

She cat-footed us through the living room. My grandfather was snoring. I'd have given my new pocketknife to wake him and explain my predicament and beg forgiveness for this treachery.

Mrs. Stackable opened the front door. She took both my arms in her hands and gripped them tightly. "Oh, James," she said into my ear. "May the Lord be your shepherd."

"Yes, ma'am," I said.

FIVE

Taken huff for huff, pound for pound, splash lubrication for magneto ignition, the Rumely OilPull 20-40, I believed that Christmas Eve and do to this day, was the most steadfast, dauntless, radiant tractor then in existence and since invented. What it was asked to do it did, asking in return only a pittance of kerosene and a tithe of faith. An ignoramus could have driven it. I set the throttle up, shoved the shift lever into low. The drive wheels turned and it was on its way once more, smoking and grinding through the malevolent night.

In the rear, riding the stoneboat and hugging the melodeon, were Frances, Delores, and Toody. I had ordered Agnes there as well, but she refused, which got us off to a good, insubordinate start. Instead, she climbed up into the cab and sat on the organ bench beside me. If she had been a boy, I'd have beaten her into pulpy submission, but she was a girl, and taller and huskier than I, and in the eighth grade, too. So I let her get away with it, consoling myself I did so out of pity. That she was obnoxious by nature she couldn't help. That she had warts on her hands was not her fault. And that she had to carry a name like Agnes Stackable to the grave —she would certainly never marry—rendered her automatically an object of compassion. Most pitiful, perhaps, was the evidence that she had developed a crush on me. It was a hopeless cause, of course. I intended to leave a litter of broken hearts behind me for a long, long time.

486

We reached the county road. We turned right and the stoneboat followed our lead obediently. Any troubles from now on would be bubbles. The county road was wide, there were no hills, the drifts were less formidable, and we had just over a mile to go.

The two cylinders settled into a soporific beat. I must have dozed. It seemed to me I was astride a great black horse cantering down a road in Tennessee, saber clanking at a thigh, Colt revolver snug against the other hip. We were on our way to Strawberry Plains. I wore blue. I was young and strong and knightly. The Union must be saved, the slaves freed, and my comrades and I would do these things for Mr. Lincoln and our loved ones. And so I dozed and dreamed. Of Sarah, my sweet wife. Of the letters from her underneath my tunic. Of her silent courage when she let me go, and of the boy she'd given birth to. His name was William, she had written, and we would call him Willy. Of the melodeon she played, and would teach our newborn how to play. I longed to see her, and my son, and hear the music he would make for me. I could not know a sniper's bullet waited for my breast this very day. And so I rode my great black steed, and soon it seemed to me that someone's arms had taken me, and someone's voice was bugling in my ear: "Dummy! You're going off the road, you dummy!"

I woke with such velocity I almost hit the roof of the cab. Agnes Stackable's amorous arms enfolded me, the tractor was tilting to the right—we were indeed rumbling off the shoulder!

I spun the wheel. We lurched left and regained the level. I breathed again, free of Agnes's clutch, but another peril impended. I couldn't see. It was snowing harder than ever. I pulled the throttle back, let the Rumely come to a halt, and set the hand brake.

"Whatcha waiting for?" Agnes caterwauled. "A streetcar?"

I unhooked the lanterns and handed them to her. "Get down!" I yelled through my scarf. "You and Frances take these and walk in front so I can see where the road is!"

"And have you run over us? Not on your life!"

"Remember what your mother told you!"

"Ma's not here!"

"What about the meaning of Christmas?"

"Banana oil!"

I grew desperate. Appeals to law and sentiment were unavailing, as would be resort to brute force. That left guile. "Agnes! You like me, and I like you! But I'd like you a lot more if you'd cooperate!"

"How much more?"

I knew then that Adam had not tried the forbidden fruit to indulge his appetite. It was to save his sanity. "Lots!" I proclaimed. "Pecks! Bushels! Loads!"

To my masculine gratification, she jumped down and slogged back to the stoneboat. In a moment Agnes and Frances, each carrying a lantern, spaced themselves ahead of the tractor, and began to serve as living headlights. I released the brake, throttled up, shouted "Hang on!" to Delores and Toody, and put the OilPull into motion.

That was how we traversed the last half mile. The youngest

Stackables guarded our cargo, I crouched in the cab, while a few yards out front the eldest Stackables guided me down that howling, inconstant path. If it was one degree below zero, it was ten, and much as I disliked to, I had to give credit where it was due. Permitted little or no movement on the stoneboat, Delores and Toody must have been frozen stiff as boards. Now and then the drifts were so deep that Agnes and Frances struggled, slowed, and stopped, and I had to halt the Rumely until they could trample through and wave me onward with the yellow beacons of their lanterns. Kate Stackable would have been proud of her girls. In cold and dark and travail, at a top speed of 2 mph, they were learning the true meaning of Christmas.

It was a road we walked every school day, and we knew when we reached Chubb's Corners. Behind the new church was the

Putnam Township cemetery, and beyond that, the one-room schoolhouse. Following the lanterns, spinning the wheel, I turned the OilPull off the road and transcribed a wide half circle, aiming between two large maple trees and the church in order to come up alongside the stoop. We hit it on the nose. I swung about in the seat and, shifting in and out of low, nudging forward, brought the stoneboat within a foot of the steps.

I bowed my head for a moment. It was done. Hallelujah. I set the hand brake, left the engine running, cramped down from the cab, took the bench, and placed it under the stoop roof.

I turned to the stoneboat. Delores and Toody unhugged the organ and got off as Agnes and Frances came back with the lanterns. Telling them to stand clear, I untied the ropes and dropped them. Then I pulled the ends of the two-by-fours off the floor of the stoneboat onto the floor of the stoop and spaced them, by guess and by gosh, wide enough to accommodate the casters. I shouted to the girls to come close and listen.

"Nice going, you guys! Now here's what we've got to do! This thing rolls on casters! So we've got to lift one end up on these skids and push it up, then raise the other end onto the skids, then push the whole thing up the skids onto the stoop!"

"I'm sleepy!" This was Delores.

"I'm frozen!" This was Frances.

"We can't do it!" This was Agnes.

"I wanna go home!" This was Toody.

"You can in a minute!" I stepped to the instrument, its protective blankets mounded with snow. "Come on now, everybody take hold and lift till the casters are on the skids!"

I bent, got mittens under one corner, and waited till they assembled at the other corner.

"Now! Lift!"

I heaved. The organ swayed. Then I felt their answering pressure. I pulled and heaved and they must have, too, for with a thud, casters settled onto skids.

I straightened up. "Now we've got to pull the other end around straight! Toody, you watch and see the casters don't roll off the skids. You other guys get hold of our end and roll it around!"

Agnes, Frances, and Delores joined me, and after I pushed snow off the flooring with a galosh, we had no difficulty rolling the melodeon around to line up with the skids.

"Now—help me push till we get it up the skids! Push!"

We strained. We rolled the instrument up the skids till the rear casters stubbed the lower ends of the two-by-fours.

"Now—lift!"

We heaved. "Lift!"

We couldn't do it. The angle of incline from stoneboat floor to stoop floor was steep, so that we had both to lift and push two hundred and fifty pounds at the same time.

I got down on my knees. "Lift!"

We couldn't do it. I tried to rise. But the enormity of our failure kept me on my knees. My grandfather and I and Kate Stackable's daughters had brought the melodeon three miles through thick and thin. The bulk of it rested on skids not six feet from the door of the temple to which it was to be my grandmother's offering. Lift the low end two inches and the merest fraction and the deed would be wholly, magnificently done. And three stout girls and I simply could not do it.

I was sweating again, and my back hurt, and kneeling in snow and cold I lost control. Tears came. I felt them hot upon my cheeks. And that made me mad enough to bite nails. I reared up and threw my weight against that of the organ. "Girls!" I raged. "Damn girls! If I had another man here we'd do it, but all I've got is damn weakling rattlebrained good-for-nothing girls!"

Agnes Stackable began to cry, which set Frances to crying, and after her Delores, and after her Toody. There we were, children of the storm, on that handmade, hard-times Christmas Eve, weeping with such abandon that at least a minute elapsed before we woke up to what had happened.

It had ceased, suddenly, to snow.

The wind had ceased, suddenly, to blow.

We stood there on a midnight clear, in lantern light, except for the respiration of the OilPull, at the crystal center of a silence.

We ceased, suddenly, to cry. For in the wake of the wind we heard them, far away at first and muffled in snow, coming up the road from the south. They were not the slow clip-clop which precedes a wagon or sleigh. They had the rhythm of a canter.

They were the hoofbeats of a horseman.

IN THE DARK he was upon us suddenly. He rode a black horse. He was hidden by a greatcoat, and on his head was a pillbox cap. He dismounted at one of the maple trees, looped reins over a limb, and laid his coat on the saddle. He strode to the tractor and pulled the kill-switch. The engine gasped and died. Then with the squeaking of boots in snow, he marched in our direction.

He entered the yellow light, a tall young man with a brown spade beard which gave him an ancestral expression. His frayed uniform was blue, with a stripe down the cavalry breeches. Hanging from his belt on the left side was a saber, while on the right a revolver was snug against the hip.

He towered over the five of us. The Stackable sisters stared up at him, eyes over their scarves as big as buttons.

He touched the visor of his cap. "Good evening, misses."

He inspected me in an almost military manner, and I squirmed. "Well, well," he said.

I did not know whether I passed muster or not, but I had to set a bold example for my staff. "You shouldn't have turned off the tractor," I said. "I might not be able to start it again."

"We'll see about that, sonny." He rubbed his hands. "Now let's leave off cussing the ladies and get this old pumper inside. You stand guard up there and keep a sharp eye on those casters."

It was an order. I moved to the skids, elbowing Toody away.

The cavalryman bent to the low end of the melodeon, hoisted, set the casters on the skids as slick as a whistle, put a shoulder to the instrument, and with one powerful lunge shoved it up and over the skids and onto the stoop. "Open the door," he directed me. "And you, misses, fetch the lanterns."

I opened the door. Agnes, Frances, Delores, and Toody had turned to stone. I got the lanterns and waited by the door.

He lifted the organ over the doorsill, then rolled it into the church and down the aisle between the benches. I lighted his way.

"Whereabouts?" he asked.

"There, I guess." I indicated a place near the pulpit.

I went outside, picked up the organ bench, and hissed at the girls. "You get in there and help!"

But all they could do was shiver and hold on to each other.

"Oooooh!" moaned Toody.

"Ohhhh!" groaned Delores.

"Eeeee!" squealed Frances.

"A ghost!" quavered Agnes.

"He is not," I snapped.

"Then who is he?"

"Never you mind! Come on, shake a leg!"

Finally they crept into the church. I closed the door and herded them down the aisle. But they would not go near the stranger, huddling down on a bench as close together as they could squeeze.

He had removed the horse blankets from the melodeon. I brought the organ bench and placed it.

"There," he said. "There." He stepped back and feasted eyes on the instrument. "Good as new, big as life, and twice as natural. Ain't it a beauty, though, boy?"

"Yes, sir," I said.

"Hmmm," he mused. "You don't reckon my note's still there? Let's have a look."

He folded back the keyboard top, raised a lantern, and bending, peered inside the cabinet. "I'll be dogged. It is."

"What note?" I asked.

"Why, the one I stuck inside for her to find. Lookee here."

I went to him, and while he held the lantern, squinted into the cabinet. Sure enough, at one side, pasted to the wood, was a slip of yellowed paper with a faded brown inscription: "For my Sarah, to keep her company."

"Don't know if she ever found it," he said. "D'you?"

"No, sir."

He set his lantern down and seated himself on the needlepoint bench, taking care to put his sabre aside. "Oh, I recollect that day. Traded a cow and two hogs for it, and what cash money I had, and would've given my right arm if need be," he said. "I won't so much as touch it, but I'd enjoy to sit a spell and meditate."

We were quiet, the girls and I. The cavalryman sat motionless at the melodeon, his long back to us. The lanterns uncovered a rude mural of raw walls, bare floor, rows of unbacked benches, a white-pine pulpit, and beside that, the gift of my grandparents. In the lantern's glow the cherry cabinet was enriched, and the scrollwork of the music rack possessed the symmetry of art. What we had come to was a small, poor place, as houses of worship go, but I understood then what the Mason & Hamlin would mean. It would do much more than keep the hymns on key and accompany the passing of the plate. The love and loss and resurrection of which it was a symbol would consecrate the little church.

"Have you got a real beard?" Toody's voice gave us a start.

The man on the bench turned round. "I have. Why don't you sit on my knee and give it a pull?"

Toody was reluctant. "Are you Santy Claus?"

"I might be."

Toody was dubious. "Santy Claus rides in a sleigh with reindeers and wears a red suit."

"Sometimes."

"And he's fat and jolly and you're not."

"That's so. But then, I expect Santa comes in many a shape and suit and disposition."

"Anyway," said Toody, getting down to brass tacks, "I wanted a doll, and you gave me darn old galoshes."

"I see. I'm sorry. But let me tell you, missy, I know a regiment would trade their boots for yours and be glad of it."

Toody was unappeased. "Well, I have to have a new doll next Christmas. A Bye-Lo Baby that opens and shuts her eyes."

"Will you be a good girl?"

"I'm always good."

"Then I'll think on it," he promised.

Turning back to the instrument, he lowered the folding top

494

and covered the keyboard. "How I wish I'd been there, to hear my Sarah play," he sighed. "And little Willy, too."

He sat for a moment more, then sprang up with a jangle of his saber chain and smote a palm violently with a fist. "Criminy, I've got an idee!"

He reached and grasped my chin in his hand. "James, tomorrow morning, when you come to meeting, you get Willy to play. The song he was a-going to when I came home. So's I can hear him!"

My chin might as well have been in a vise. "He won't," I managed between my teeth.

He released me. "Won't? Why not?"

"He never would. Not after you didn't come home."

"I know that, boy. But why?"

It was difficult to express. I tried to recall Will's words earlier that night in the sheepshed. "I asked him why, and he said, 'Because my pa would never hear me. Or see me, nor I him.'"

The cavalryman's eyes clouded with pain. Only now I noted how ashen was his color, how drawn and weary was his face.

"Oh," he said. "He couldn't know, but I would have heard him. And if he will play tomorrow morning, I can hear. You've got to get him to, James."

He was asking the impossible. "I don't know how. He's too stubborn. Can I just tell him you said to?"

"Oh, no." He shook his head. He swept the girls and me with a glower. "That's the one thing you mustn't do, none of you—tell a soul I was here. They won't believe you anyhow, because they're grown up and past believing. No, you mustn't tell."

"I can if I want to," said Toody.

He looked pins and needles at her, then at her sisters, then at me. He drew himself to full parade-ground height. "You let out one peep," he said evenly, "and I'll be around someday when you're not looking and fetch you a swat on the behind with the flat of my saber 'll make your teeth rattle and your ears fall off."

We knew he meant it, and even Toody did not dare sass him again. But when he saw that his threat had sunk in, his face softened. "Time you rascals were in bed. James," he said wistfully, "you'll mind now about tomorrow? I lend you a hand tonight, you give me a song in the morning—turnabout's fair play."

"I'll try," I said. "I really will."

"Good lad. Oh, you're a Chubb, I'll vouch for that. Time to go, young ones. Bring the lanterns."

I took one and handed Agnes the other and we went down the aisle before him and outdoors onto the stoop. He closed the door behind us.

The night was still as before. No wind gusted, not a single snowflake fell. Over by the maple tree the horse nickered.

The cavalryman dropped to one knee. "Come near now, all of you." He spread his long arms and drew us into a circle. "It don't take a soldier to be brave. You've done a fine thing tonight, as brave as ever I saw. And I thank you every one."

"You're welcome," said Toody.

Since he was leaving, I thought I'd better ask while I had the opportunity.

"The war," I said. "Was it as awful as they say?"

He nodded. "It was."

"Well, was it worth it?"

"Worth it? What do you say, boy?" he demanded proudly. "Good times or bad, ain't it a grand and glorious Union?"

"Yes, sir," I said.

"And don't you forget it," he advised. Then he smiled at us. "And now good night, young misses, good night, James. And a Merry Christmas to you."

Before we could wish him one, too, he rose and marched to the OilPull. Seizing the handle, he gave the flyweel a mighty whirl, and instantly the engine banged into smoky life.

The cavalryman tipped his cap to us, strode jangling and squeaking through the snow to his black horse, hauled on his greatcoat, unlooped the reins, mounted, gigged the animal about, and rode off beyond the trees, heading south.

Agnes, Frances, Delores, Toody, and I stood where we were until the sound of his hoofbeats became the canter of the tractor cylinders and were gone.

496

SIX

We were homeward bound, and through the commotion of the 20-40 the odious Agnes shrieked in my ear. "Who was that?"

I shook my head.

"He knew your name! You knew him!"

I pretended not to hear.

"I'll tell my pa!"

I heard that. "Agnes, you better not! Remember what he said about a swat of his saber!"

"Banana oil!"

"He said don't tell a soul!" I roared. "You tell anybody and I'll hate you!"

That sewed up her lips as effectively as a darning needle, so I could steer the OilPull in peace, and down the country road we rumbled, lanterns swinging as we turned onto the township road. It was easy going, following the tracks we had previously cut through the drifts, the stoneboat dragging submissively after us. The four girls perched on the fenders over the drive wheels, Agnes and Frances on one side, Delores and Toody on the other, facing me, while I maintained a captain's composure on the bridge and allowed them to admire my seamanship.

Lights blazed from practically every window at the Stackable place, and when we halted, and the girls hopped off the fenders, Kate Stackable and Will were standing by the road. Kate hugged her darlings as though she had never expected to see them again.

"Bless you, James! See you in the morning!" she called. "Merry Christmas!"

I waved a modest mitten.

Will climbed into the cab, but I sat where I was, in the driver's seat, throttled up, shoved the lever into high, and took off with such a jerk that he had to grab an upright. He seated himself on a fender, and the rest of the way home superintended me with a mixture of amusement and apprehension.

It was a straight run. I thought about my grandmother and what she would say and do when she walked into church in the morning. I thought about the cavalryman, and how the Sam Hill I could ever persuade his son, my grandfather, to try the melodeon in public when he hadn't touched it in private for sixty years or more. I thought about my father and mother for the first time since they had telephoned me, and preened myself on how proud I would be when they heard what I had accomplished tonight. Then I remembered the moral of Ella's fable and made up my mind to decline pride and settle instead for a big, fat orange of contentment.

When we reached the granary I piloted the Rumely into its berth. Will descended, pulled the kill-switch, and the engine breathed its triumphant last. We unhitched the stoneboat and dragged it where it belonged. We put away the ropes and horse blankets. Everything had to seem undisturbed to Ella in the morning. Then we stood for a minute outside the granary and listened to the tinking of iron and steel as the OilPull cooled to rest again till spring.

"Storm's over," said my grandfather.

"Yup."

"I'll wager it's ten below."

"At least."

I glanced up at the stars. They twinkled in the cold and black, but they were remote.

"I'm sorry I went to sleep," he apologized. "I was just tuckered out."

"That's O.K.," I said affably.

"You made it to the church all right then?"

"In a breeze."

"And you and those girls got that organ inside by yourselves?"

"Sure."

"How?"

I had to be careful. "Same way you and I got it out of the house onto the stoneboat. On the skids."

"Bosh. That's too damned big a load for kids to heft."

"Oh, those girls are strong."

"Boy, I don't believe you."

"You wait. You'll see in the morning."

498

He was looking at me, but I was looking at the distant, secret stars of Christmas.

"Well, if you did," he said, "I'll be eternally grateful."

"My pleasure, Gramp," I assured him with an adult insouciance.

We started for the house.

"Hey," I said. "Hadn't we better take a look at the lamb?"

"All right, if you've a mind to."

We took the lanterns to the barn and walked halfway down the steps to the sheepshed. Most of the flock were lying asleep. Calvin, the ram, was awake, however, and so was the old ewe. She was standing. Her lamb knelt at her side having a midnight supper, its tail alive with delight.

My grandfather tugged at his mustache, I noticed how much, if he had worn a spade beard, he'd have resembled someone else.

"I still don't believe it," he harped. "Unless you had help."

"You didn't believe that lamb either," I said.

We headed for the house again, plodding through snow. We were sleepy and numb and our soapstones would be cold by now, but we didn't give a whoop.

I WAS wakened early by a hullabaloo in the backyard. Then I realized it was Christmas morning and we'd be on our way to church soon and somehow I had to figure out PDQ how to get Will to play the melodeon.

I dressed, shivering, in my best bib and tucker and went downstairs. It was a dashing winter day, colder than a dogcatcher's heart but bright and sunny. I washed and combed my hair and searched my upper lip as usual for omens and stepped into the kitchen. Ella was simultaneously getting breakfast and plucking another chicken.

"Merry Christmas," I said.

"He did it," she said.

"Did what?"

"Your grandfather killed a hen—the first time ever. I'll never understand him as long as I live."

"Where is he?"

"Doing the chores."

"How did you sleep?" I inquired.

"Like a log. I declare, I don't know what came over me last night. Oh, Merry Christmas, James."

Will entered and said he thought we could get to service after all, provided the Cadwells put on chains, because it appeared to him—with a wink at me—that the county equipment had been down our road during the night and broken the drifts.

The next two hours were busy ones, which was ideal, for Ella had neither opportunity nor excuse to stray into the parlor and discover anything missing. We breakfasted on eggs, about which I wasn't particularly thrilled, and on johnnycake, about which I was. Then I did the dishes while Ella stuffed our chicken and put it in the oven to roast while we were gone and dressed the second hen, Will's victim, and packed it in a basket.

By the time Mr. and Mrs. Cadwell came by for us in their Model A sedan we were ready and waiting—Will in suit and shirt, although he eschewed a necktie, and Ella gussied up in a cloth coat and crepe dress and little green hat stuck modishly to the side of her gray hair with a pin. We climbed aboard, me in back with the ladies, and Will up front with the basket, and found the heavy snow no obstacle to our progress, thanks to chains and the indefatigability of the Ford. There was much talk about the storm and speculation as to whether or not the minister could get down to us from Howell for the service.

At Will's request Reuel Cadwell stopped at the Henshaw place. Joe and Abby had already gone to church, and Will deposited the basket on the front porch. No one made any comment. Charity in those days, unlike that of the present, was for the most part individual and spontaneous rather than impersonal and systematic.

We passed the Stackable place and soon turned on to the county road. I had only minutes now to come to a decision. The cavalryman had me over a barrel. Oh, I could tell myself he hadn't really ridden to our rescue last night, that the girls and I had wrestled the melodeon from stoneboat to church stoop by ourselves—a lie is often the nearest exit from an adolescent dilemma. But the truth is a better way to maturity, and the truth was: what was to happen in a few minutes was owed almost entirely to the man on the black horse. He had asked for a song from his son, the son he had never seen, the song the boy had planned to play for him on his return from war, and I had said "I'll try." Try I must, then, and chance the anger and embarrassment and laughter.

We were late arriving at church, and it was apparent from the number of cars that there would be a full house. Reuel Cadwell parked the Ford, and we got out and tramped through the snow. Will delayed the three of us and let the Cadwells go in first. It was a ruse, I knew, to be certain his wife would have the full, undistracted impact of our surprise.

"What else did you put in the basket for the Henshaws?" he inquired of her.

"Peach preserves, some hickory nutmeats, a mince pie—for goodness sake, why would you ask now?"

"I just wondered."

"Fiddlesticks." And she adjusted her hat and preceded us to the door with a spry, impatient step. She opened it and entered, Will and I behind her.

I will not attempt to describe the look on my grandmother's face as exactly as I have described the Mason & Hamlin melodeon and the Rumely OilPull. She must have seen the rows of benches crowded with friends and neighbors, their every eye upon her. She must have seen the iron woodstove in a corner, roaring with religious ardor. She must have seen the Reverend Leon Ledwidge, white haired and benign, standing by his pulpit smiling at her. She saw them, but perceived them not. The organ transfixed her. She looked at it, then at Will, then at me, then at the organ again. And the long-awaited look on her face was—language is too often imprecise, but I shall do my best—beatific. Her face itself, for a moment, was young as that of the girl she once had been. And after that moment, Will took one elbow, I the other, and together we escorted her to a bench.

A little overwhelmed, we heard Reverend Ledwidge say he wished, before beginning service, to acknowledge the generous

gift of Mr. and Mrs. Will Chubb to the church—a melodeon which, so he understood, had belonged to the family since 1863. Such a gift, he said, would be appreciated by the members, he was sure, to the same degree it had been cherished by its donors. He understood also that special thanks were due Will Chubb and his grandson, since it was only through their efforts that the instrument had been delivered, by tractor and stoneboat and despite last night's storm, to the church in time for Christmas devotions.

"Reverend?" It was my grandfather.

"Yes, Mr. Chubb?"

"I'm afraid I can't take much credit," said Will. "We got as far as the Stackables', and I couldn't go on. We had a miserable time trying to start that tractor, and then, earlier, we'd had a lamb born. And so I—"

502

"A lamb?" Charley Greeve was startled into asking.

"This time of year?" scoffed Emmett Roach.

"Yes, siree, we did," Will maintained. "And so I was plumb tuckered out. And I think folks should know Kate Stackable sent her girls on with James here, and the youngsters did the rest."

Everyone smiled at Agnes, Frances, Delores and Toody, who wiggled on their bench and produced demure blushes.

"Then we thank them, too," said the minister. "And now, I think it would be fitting if Mrs. Chubb did us the honor of playing the first selection on the organ."

"I'm sorry, Reverend." This was my grandmother from her seat. "I simply can't. I wish I could, but I'm troubled with arthritis in my fingers, and I'd be ashamed of my mistakes. So I hope you'll forgive me if I ask to be excused."

There were murmurs of sympathy.

"Of course, Mrs. Chubb," said the parson. "Then I'm afraid we must—"

"My grandfather can play." I was on my feet. "Ephraim wants Will to play the song he planned to when he came home from the war."

Except for the ebullience of the stove, the silence was absolute. But I could not turn tail now. I had already decided to tell the truth. It was the only way to close the mortal circle, to restore a father to his son, and to assure that son his father had not forgotten him even in death. And it was also time I grew up and ceased to treat two people near and dear to me as grandparents rather than the human beings they so stubbornly, inconsistently, and passionately were. So speak I must, and trust in Christmas.

Reverend Ledwidge frowned. "Who is Ephraim?"

"My great-grandfather, sir. Ephraim Chubb. He was a cavalryman in the Civil War, and he gave Sarah the melodeon when he went away."

"Sarah?"

"My great-grandmother. And she taught Will to play when he was a little boy. But when Ephraim, his father, was killed, he never did again. His father wants him to, this morning."

"How do you know this, James?"

"Because he told me."

"When?"

"Last night, sir. Right here."

"Here?"

I fixed upon the eyes of the minister. If I had caught even a glimpse of Will's or Ella's face, I might have collapsed.

"Yes sir. The truth is, the girls and I couldn't get the organ up the skids onto the stoop—it was too heavy. Then the cavalryman came along and helped us. And afterwards he asked me to get Will to play the song he learned for when his father came home. And I said I'd try. He told us not to tell anybody he'd been here, because they wouldn't believe us. But I don't know any other way to get my grandfather to play. I'm sorry."

To this day I wonder that I got it all out. But I stood stiff as a

504

ramrod and tried to make sense, because I had a bone-deep conviction that someone else besides those present was watching.

"Maybe you don't believe me," I said. "But the girls will tell you. He was here last night, wasn't he, Agnes?" I appealed.

Perfidious creature—she pretended I didn't exist.

"Wasn't he, Frances?" I implored. "Wasn't he, Delores?"

The loobies sat like bumps on a log.

"Toody!" I cried. "You've got to tell!"

The youngest Stackable stood up on cue. "Yup, Santy Claus was here," she said. "I think," she said. "He had a beard all right, but he wore a blue suit, not a red one, and he rode a horse, not a sleigh, and he had a sword, not a bag of presents, and he wasn't fat and jolly, he was sad and skinny. That's all I'm telling. Oh, and he promised to bring me a doll next Christmas because all I got last night was darn old galoshes."

She remained standing and might have taken a bow had Kate Stackable not pulled her down. She had not helped. The disbelief could have been cut with a knife. I grew desperate.

"I can prove it!" I cried, and my voice cracked in a new and interesting way. I entreated the minister. "Sir, if you'll just fold up the top of the organ and look inside, you'll see the note Ephraim pasted in there for Sarah to find—he showed me last night. It says 'For my Sarah, to keep her company.' Honest it does."

Reverend Ledwidge stared at me, then stepped cautiously to the melodeon, folded back the top, peered, adjusted his spectacles, and peered again.

He straightened. He pinched the bridge of his nose. "There is a note," he announced. "And those are the words—'For my Sarah, to keep her company.'" He cleared his throat. "Mrs. Chubb, were you aware of this note?"

Everyone strained to hear. "No," she said, almost whispering. "Sarah wasn't either. None of us were." She shook her head. "I don't understand it."

Nor did anyone else. Men studied their hands. Women looked in other women's faces for confirmation or dissent. Children scuffed their shoes. The yarn I had spun about a cavalryman on a black horse could be safely discounted. I was a boy, and it was a fact that boys were prone to whistle in the dark. And the jabber of a six-year-old like Toody could be attributed to candy, excitement, and an upset stomach. But the note was also a fact, and two hundred and fifty pounds deadweight was a fact, and it was clear to practical farmers and their wives that one feckless boy and four girls could not, unaided, have transferred these facts from stoneboat to stoop.

I could stand no longer. I sat down.

"Friends," Reverend Ledwidge said finally. "It may be that we have been witness to a miracle. Children have eyes to see things we cannot. It is a miracle, is it not, that in these times, and on the ashes of the old church, we have built a new? Is it not miraculous that we have an organ today, and brought to us by children? Last night was Christmas Eve, which has always been a time of mystery and magic. A child was born long ago upon that holy night, a child our Lord and Saviour. Which of us then, shall doubt the mystery and magic of this morning?"

He paused. "Let us pray. O Lord, we thank Thee for the courage of these children, who have brought to Thy sanctuary the gift of music. Bless this good woman, Ella Chubb, and her husband, Will, for the generosity and love they have manifested to Thee. And finally we ask of Thee another miracle. We ask that one of us be generous of his spirit, that he play the song his father never heard, and give him peace. We ask it in Christ's name. Amen."

The old man raised his head and looked at the three of us. "Will?" he asked.

My grandmother took my hand in hers, tightly.

Slowly Will rose, moved down the aisle. He stood before the melodeon, then slowly seated himself. He put his feet on the pedals. He pumped. He lifted hands above the keyboard, hands trained to plow and sow, hands which had the night before brought forth a lamb. He closed his eyes.

We held our breath. Time seemed to tick backward. And as we waited, the man at the melodeon, withered now upon the tree of life, seemed to alter, to sit erect, to ripen into prime, then green

506

into a boy, fatherless and lost. Would memory fail him? Could fingers do the bidding of his brain?

He touched the keys, filling the church with music haunting and lovely, a song familiar only to the elders in the congregation. One by one they rose, those like him whose wounds had never healed, those who had not forgotten sacrifices made, loved ones lost. Their voices were quavery but brave:

> *"We're tenting tonight*
> *On the old camp ground,*
> *Give us a song to cheer*
> *Our weary hearts,*
> *A song of home*
> *And friends we love so dear.*
>
> *Many are the hearts*
> *That are weary tonight,*
> *Wishing for the war to cease;*
> *Many are the hearts*
> *That are looking for the right,*
> *To see the dawn of peace.*
>
> *Tenting tonight,*
> *Tenting tonight,*
> *Tenting on the old camp ground."*

SEVEN

I stayed at my grandparent's farm till the next summer. My father found employment then and the means to bring me home.

Two years after my sojourn on the farm the land which had been the family's for a century was sold. I never saw it again. I do not know if the barn and granary still stand, or the church at Chubb's Corners. I do not know what became of the Stackable girls, if Toody got her doll, for example, if Agnes ever lost her warts or found a husband. I hope they did.

It has been forty-one years. I have not encountered the cavalry-man a second time. For many years I disbelieved in his appearance on that Christmas Eve, but I am young enough at last to know better, to accept the minister's assertion that children have eyes to see things we cannot. I trust that in the meantime my forebear has forgiven me for telling on him and that I may never feel, on my mature backside, the flat of his terrible swift sword. Now and then in cold and dark of night I hear the *huff-huff* of the OilPull on its invincible way, just as I sometimes hear, on a winter morning, the antique strains of a pump organ.

I will never forget the gifts of that Christmas. If my grand-father gave the melodeon to his wife, in one sense, together they gave it to their God. I received a jackknife, which remains in my possession, and a hand-knit scarf, and better yet, the beginning of awareness that no matter what its failings, ours is indeed a grand and glorious Union. Best of all, however, storm and Christmas and selflessness and a horseman out of the past gave me two beloved human beings, not grandparents but a man and woman I could esteem and learn from and remember.

Will Chubb died the last week of that April. He was afflicted with hay lung, the reader will recall, and caught a cold while plowing. The cold developed into pneumonia. The doctor drove down from Howell several times—Will was too ill to be moved to the hospital. He worsened rapidly.

It happened in midmorning. Clyde and Kate Stackable and Joe Henshaw and Mrs. Cadwell had come by with a cake and a pie and a loaf of new-baked bread, expressed their sorrow, and departed. Ella emerged from the bedroom off the kitchen and said that Will had regained consciousness and asked for me. I went in, to stand tentatively by the bed. I was frightened. I did not know Death then, that he is no more to be feared than the man on the black horse. He can be kind, time teaches us. In the end he prevails, but triumphs not, so long as we remember. And so, thirteen and afraid, I knelt beside my grandfather. His color was gray, the eyes sunken, and his mustache drooped, bereft of luster. His lips moved.

"Go for a walk," he whispered. I shook my head.

"Go find the flock. Find our lamb."

"No. I won't."

"Go!" The word came out of him like a command. I had hopped to that kind of authority before, outside the church on Christmas Eve. Startled, I raised my head to look at him. His eyes reminded me of my great-grandfather's. They were soldierly.

I stumbled through the kitchen and out the door, marched between barn and granary and down the road, more lorn than I had ever been in my life. I hiked through the huckleberry marsh, then climbed a fence into a pasture, and there, at the far end, was the flock. I walked toward them. I knew now that Will had ordered me away so that I would be somewhere else, doing something, when he died. I knew that when I returned to the house Ella would be waiting for me and that she would say, "He's gone, James."

It was a lucent morning. The sun was warm, the grass rich, a few clouds like puffs of tractor smoke floated under a blue sky, and the air was sweet with birdsong and fertilizer and innocence.

I approached the grazing flock. They were white now, having just been sheared of their winter gray. Some of the ewes were fat and would be lambing soon. Calvin, the ram, scratched his hind-quarters against the fence and cast, occasionally, a benevolent glance in their direction. I tried but could not identify our lamb. And the reason was, I couldn't see the animals clearly, and when I addressed them, it was with considerable difficulty.

"You stop!" I shouted. "You stop eating and standing around acting like nothing's happening!" They were impervious. I began to sob. "You damn sheep! Don't you know what's happening to the man who's fed you and dipped you and sheared you and helped bring your babies into the world? Well, you better know! He's dying!" I bawled between sobs. "Will Chubb is dying right now! He's going away and never coming back! Do you hear? Or don't you care?"

It was evident they did not, and I turned from them and began to run. I ran across the pasture and over the fence and down the road and between the barn and granary and slowed down and wiped away the tears with a sleeve, because my grandmother stood in front of the house, waiting for me. I walked toward her endlessly, just as Ephraim had left the team and walked endlessly over the field toward his wife in another April.

I came to her, and she put her arms around me, and I put mine around her. I thought of Sarah, and of Strawberry Plains.

"Oh, James, he's gone," she said.

Services for my grandfather were held in the church. Ella played a hymn on the melodeon because she thought Will would want her to:

> *"Abide with me!*
> *Fast falls the eventide,*
> *The darkness deepens—*
> *Lord, with me abide!*
>
> *When other helpers fail,*
> *And comforts flee,*
> *Help of the helpless,*
> *Oh, abide with me!"*

She never got her automobile. She herself passed away two years later, of loneliness I have surmised, but she is no longer alone. She was laid to rest beside Will and his parents in the township ground.

So my Christmas story ends in springtime. They have long been reunited now, Ephraim and Will, father and son, and their dear wives, Sarah and Ella, gathered unto each other beneath the oak trees near the church. May the music of the melodeon attend their dreams forever.

Glendon Swarthout

Above Mr. Swarthout's desk is a Colt revolver, a family heirloom he was given when he became twenty-one. The pistol once belonged to his great-grandfather, a cavalryman who left his ploughshare to go off to war, and was of course, an inspiration for his latest book.

There is much else in *The Melodeon* that is real: the names of the people, the midwestern farm setting, the OilPull tractor, and the melodeon itself. In fact, the author explains, the novel is "a sort of memorial to my grandparents and great-grandparents, a labour of love as you might say." And although it was conceived over many years, it was written in haste, so that three or four of Mr. Swarthout's closest relatives, now in their eighties, would live to see the book in print.

Mr. Swarthout, who graduated from Michigan University in 1939, began a career as a teacher, writing fiction in his spare time. The Second World War, when he served as an infantryman, temporarily interrupted this routine. Then, in 1958, the success of his novel *They Came to Cordura* enabled him to become a full-time writer. Since then he has published a number of successful books, most recently *The Shootist*, which was adapted for the cinema by Mr. Swarthout's son, Miles, a screenwriter.

Although he grew up in Michigan, as did four generations before him, Mr. Swarthout now lives at the edge of the Arizona desert. The nearest he comes to the halls of academe nowadays is to present the annual creative-writing prizes he and his wife have set up at Arizona State University, his way of "giving a little back".

"Probably there are only two singular things about me," he has said. "One, I feed and exult in a flock of practically pet Gambel quail, which are indigenous to these deserts. Two, I have a Ph.D. in English literature yet have the gall to make a good living at writing fiction. My anecdotes, most of which are unprintable, I'm saving, as does every prudent writer, for my memoirs."

MM95